Sometimes, love is the most dangerous business to deal.

Illicit Affair

The Illicit Series

RAGHAVI

AF080606

BLUEROSE PUBLISHERS
India | U.K.

Copyright © Raghavi 2025

All rights reserved by author. No part of this publication may be reproduced, stored in a retrieval system or transmitted in any form or by any means, electronic, mechanical, photocopying, recording or otherwise, without the prior permission of the author. Although every precaution has been taken to verify the accuracy of the information contained herein, the publisher assumes no responsibility for any errors or omissions. No liability is assumed for damages that may result from the use of information contained within.

BlueRose Publishers takes no responsibility for any damages, losses, or liabilities that may arise from the use or misuse of the information, products, or services provided in this publication.

For permissions requests or inquiries regarding this publication,
please contact:

BLUEROSE PUBLISHERS
www.BlueRoseONE.com
info@bluerosepublishers.com
+91 8882 898 898
+4407342408967

ISBN: 978-93-7018-131-1

Typesetting: Pooja Sharma

First Edition: May 2025

To those who hide because they broke you—
You are not a coward.

Playlist

You're Gonna Go Far —Noah Kahan
Gorgeous (Taylor's Version) —Taylor Swift
Guilty as Sin? —Taylor Swift
Shivers —Ed Sheeran
Paris —The Chainsmokers
ILYSB (STRIPPED) —LANY
Inside Out —The Chainsmokers, Charlee
All We Know —The Chainsmokers, Phoebe Ryan
Arcade —Duncan Laurence
Down Bad —Taylor Swift
Happier —Ed Sheeran
imgonnagetyouback —Taylor Swift
Stargazing —Myles Smith
Mirrorball —Taylor Swift
Thinking out Loud —Ed Sheeran

Author's Note

This is a work of fiction. Any references to real-life figures, events, or media are purely for narrative purposes and should not be taken as fact. The story, its characters, and all original content exist solely within these pages.

Now, let the journey begin.

Contents

Chapter 1: Mia 3
Chapter 2: Mia 7
Chapter 3: Miles 12
Chapter 4: Mia 16
Chapter 5: Miles 19
Chapter 6: Miles 23
Chapter 7: Mia 28
Chapter 8: Mia 34
Chapter 9: Mia 41
Chapter 10: Miles 48
Chapter 11: Miles 55
Chapter 12: Mia 60
Chapter 13: Mia 67
Chapter 14: Miles 75
Chapter 15: Mia 78
Chapter 16: Mia 83
Chapter 17: Miles 93
Chapter 18: Mia 111
Chapter 19: Miles 114
Chapter 20: Mia 117
Chapter 21: Miles 121
Chapter 22: Miles 131
Chapter 23: Miles 145
Chapter 24: Miles 157
Chapter 25: Miles 166

Chapter 26: Mia	181
Chapter 27: Mia	204
Chapter 28: Miles	211
Chapter 29: Chloe	234
Chapter 30: Mia	238
Chapter 31: Miles	251
Chapter 32: Mia	265
Chapter 33: Mia	275
Chapter 34: Miles	280
Chapter 35: Miles	291
Chapter 36: Mia	297
Chapter 37: Miles	300
Chapter 38: Miles	316
Chapter 39: Mia	325
Chapter 40: Miles	347
Epilogue: Miles	352
Acknowledgement	355

Prologue

Mia

The last time I stepped into a hospital, it was to say goodbye to my grandmother. Her frail body, barely holding on, finally gave up. I didn't cry then. My heart had been numb, refusing to break. But now...

Now, my dad is gone. And my mom is fighting for her life in the emergency room. I sit frozen in the sterile, cold blue waiting area as the fluorescent lights hum above me, mocking the silence of despair. Tears burn my eyes, but they don't fall.

The surgeons are battling against the odds, trying to pluck shards of glass from her brain like extracting tiny, cruel daggers. They've told me the truth no one wants to hear—her survival is less than 1%. A cruel, insignificant 1%.

And yet, I cling. Desperately. To the thinnest, most fragile thread of hope.

Hope that she'll defy those impossible odds.

Hope that she'll breathe, smile, and hold me again.

Hope that I won't have to burn both my parents in one brutal, unforgiving flame of ritual.

My chest tightens as grief claws its way into me, daring me to break, but I can't. I won't. Not yet. Instead, I pray to a God I'm not even sure I believe in anymore. Because what else is there to do?

What else is left... but hope?

3 Years Later…

CHAPTER 1
Mia

Open it.

"Open it bitch!" my best friend Nidhi urges, practically bouncing in excitement.

I hesitate, staring at the two emails in my inbox. "What if I didn't get into either of them?"

"You won't know unless you open them." Her voice is sharp but laced with nervous energy. I can tell she's just as anxious as I am.

Months ago, I applied to two universities—Berklee College of Music and Columbia University's Young Writers Program. Both offered scholarships, my only shot at attending. Now, their decisions sit before me, poised to shape my future.

Music has been my life since I was six, and Nidhi practically forced me to apply to Berklee. But Columbia was different—my mom's dream school, one she never got to attend. A piece of connection. A sign from above.

But without a full scholarship, none of it matters. Since my parents' death three years ago, my relatives have taken care of me, but money is tight. No scholarship means no escape. And I *need* to escape.

Nidhi huffs, then grabs my hand and clicks the email from Berklee herself. My heart pounds as she reads aloud:

"*Dear Ms. Malhotra,*

We are delighted to inform you that you have been accepted to Berklee College of Music..."

We scream, our voices echoing off the walls.

Without hesitation, she clicks the email from Columbia next.

"*Dear Ms. Malhotra,*

On behalf of the Committee of Admissions, I want to congratulate you on your acceptance into the Young Writers Program..."

We scream again, even louder. The whole neighbourhood must've heard us, but I don't care. I expected rejection, yet here I am—accepted into both. But the choice is easy. Columbia offers a full scholarship. Berklee doesn't. Columbia wins.

"Why don't you guys scream a little louder? Maybe wake up the whole town while you're at it." Nidhi's younger sister, Niya, deadpans from the doorway, her puppy-eye mask pushed onto her forehead as she glares at us.

"Go to bed, Niya." Nidhi huffs.

"I would—if a bunch of dummies weren't screaming next door!" she snaps.

With exasperation, Nidhi gets up, shuts the door right in her face and sighs, "Sisters." Then, climbing back onto the bed, she looks at me expectantly. "So, have you decided?"

I take a deep breath and nod. "Yes. Columbia."

Her face lights up as she pulls me into a tight hug. "I knew it! And Happy Birthday. It's about time you got some good news on your birthday."

Her words hit me like a gut punch. Three years ago today, I was backstage at my school's annual dance function, scanning the audience for my parents. I wanted to make sure they didn't miss my performance. But instead of them, my class teacher found me. The look on her face told me something was wrong.

I still remember her words as clear as daylight.

"I wish I didn't have to tell you this." she said gently, sadness creeping into her eyes. "Your parents were in a car accident. They've been taken to the hospital."

She drove me there herself. My sixteenth birthday—the day that should have been filled with joy—became the worst day of my life. After all this time, today is finally a day I can smile about.

And I'm going to embrace it.

We went shopping, packed, and after what feels like forever, the three of us collapse onto the couch, completely drained. The only sounds in the room are the hum of the ceiling fan and our heavy breathing.

"I'm leaving tomorrow. Isn't that crazy?" I say, breaking the silence.

No response. Uncle Rohan—my mom's younger brother, the only family member who cares about me—is already asleep, and Nidhi looks like she's about to cry. I quickly pull her into a hug.

"Hey, don't cry. It's just two years. I'll be back before you know it."

But the moment a single tear escapes, the floodgates open. She sobs into my shoulder, her tough exterior crumbling. I don't stop her. Sometimes, you just need to let it out.

Nidhi has always been soft-hearted, no matter how much of a badass she pretends to be. Me? I don't cry unless it's absolutely necessary. The last time I really broke down was after my parents' funeral. I hid in my cupboard so no one would see me—until Uncle Rohan found me.

After a few minutes, Nidhi wipes her eyes and looks up. "I'm going to miss you."

"I'll miss you too." I say softly.

"I'll call you all the time. I'll text so much you'll get annoyed."

"You could never annoy me."

She gives me a serious look, holding out her pinky. "Promise you won't replace me with someone American."

I laugh. "How could I replace you? You're my only best friend, and you always will be, Ni."

"Still, pinky promise!"

I hook my pinky with hers. "Pinky promise."

She pauses, then mutters in a low, threatening voice, "Tell anyone about this, and consider your existence erased."

"Got it." I smirk—then, without warning, tickle her.

She yelps before bursting into laughter, and I can't help but join in. I half expect my uncle to wake up, but instead, he lets out a loud snore.

"He could sleep through an earthquake." my mom used to say.

I smile at the memory.

Grabbing a pillow and blanket, I gently tuck him in. Then, Nidhi and I head to bed, exhausted but ready for tomorrow.

As I drift into a tired sleep, a chill runs down my spine. I'll be flying toward the unknown. Toward a new chapter in my life. It's terrifying and exhilarating all at once.

I don't know what awaits me on the other side, but I'm ready to embrace it—every challenge, every discovery, every new experience.

My heart jumps—whether from excitement or fear, I can't tell. Probably both.

This is where one chapter of my life ends, and a new one begins.

Good luck, me!

CHAPTER 2

Mia

The view from my dorm room window is breathtaking. Below me, the campus stretches out in a sea of trees, their leaves swaying gently in the breeze. For a moment, I just stand there, soaking it in—the quiet, the newness, the sense of possibility.

My dorm is on the third floor. Thankfully, I have my own room, though I share a common area and bathroom with a roommate. She hasn't arrived yet—at least, I haven't seen any signs of her—but I'm relieved we each have our own space.

"What do you think?" Molly, my campus guide, asks from behind me.

"I love it." I respond honestly.

Molly's been surprisingly nice. I expected my guide to be rude, but she's friendly and helpful—and, thankfully, hasn't treated me differently for being Indian. Some girls gave me weird looks earlier, the kind that make you feel dirt under their shoes, but Molly's been nothing but welcoming.

"I'm glad," she says with a grin. "Because even if you didn't, you'd still have to stay here."

I smile.

As we head toward a food cart, she runs me through some campus rules. Then, her tone shifts slightly. "By the way," she says, more serious now, "there's something you should know."

I raise an eyebrow. "What is it?"

"It's not a big deal," she adds quickly. "But just a heads-up—the dorms for the Young Writers Program were full. Instead of sticking you and a few others somewhere far from your classes, they put you in a different dorm building, one shared by psychology and fashion students."

I blink. "Psychology and Fashion."

She nods. "So, depending on how you see it, you either got lucky or really unlucky. But...I mean you could end up friends with a future therapist or fashion designer. That's good."

I nod slowly, letting it sink in. I don't have a problem with that. I just hope my roommate isn't like the girls who gave me those weird looks.

When we reach the food cart, Molly helps me enroll in a meal plan, her cheerful energy a small comfort amid the overwhelming newness. Before she leaves, we exchange numbers. She waves goodbye, her warm smile lingering. And just like that, I'm alone again.

I start my trek back to the dorm, the unfamiliar campus sprawling around me like a labyrinth.

Three weeks.

That's the time I have to figure out this new world. Three Weeks before classes begin. Three weeks to find my footing, to carve out my place. Three weeks to meet people who don't just accept me but truly *see* me.

Three weeks to embrace the adventure I promised myself.

But as I look up at the vast, open sky, a rare feeling of peace washes over me. For the first time in a long time, I feel their presence—my parents, smiling down at me, proud and unwavering.

I'm finally here.

Finally living my mom's dream.

And for now, that's enough.

I woke up to the sound of my stomach growling.

I hadn't eaten anything last night—wasn't hungry then—but now I'm desperate. After a quick shower, I head straight for the campus food cart that Molly showed me yesterday.

Normally, a walk across the university campus I dreamed of attending would feel exciting. I'd take it all in, appreciate every step. But right now, hunger makes my feet move fast, eager to just get there.

After about ten minutes, I reach the food cart. It's nestled between two residential buildings, its bright colours standing out against the plain white facades. The menu for today is scribbled on a chalkboard, the handwriting bold and a little uneven. There's a small canopy fluttering above, offering just enough shade to make the place feel cozy. Underneath the canopy, tables and chairs are arranged to sit. I order a sandwich and coffee and take a seat.

My food arrives quickly. The cart isn't busy, so I enjoy my breakfast in peace, watching a few students pass by. Once I'm done, I take a stroll around campus, letting my feet lead the way.

When I reach my dorm and pull out my key, the door swings open before the key even touches the lock. My roommate must've arrived.

Curiosity tugs at me, but I don't want to barge in or knock on her door just yet. I'm not ready for a potentially awkward introduction. Instead, I head for my room—until a sharp yelp makes me freeze.

Without thinking, I rush in.

My roommate is sitting on the floor, clutching her foot. She looks up at me, her expression tight with pain.

"Are you okay?" I kneel beside her.

"Yeah. Just a little shock of pain." she says, her tone clipped.

"Are you sure?" I ask, concerned.

She gives a slight nod before extending her hand. "I'm Samantha Winchester, but everyone calls me Sam."

I shake her hand. "Mia Malhotra."

Her grip is firm but friendly, her smile genuine despite the pain. There's something about her energy that instantly puts me at ease—fun but not over the top.

Samantha Winchester seems like the kind of girl who lights up every room she walks into. With her straight warm brown hair, kissed with subtle highlights, falling just to her shoulders, and her striking pale blue eyes gleaming with curiosity, she exudes an infectious energy. She seems like the life of every party—always ready with a quick laugh or a wild idea that pulls everyone into the moment.

She tilts her head. "Wait... Mia? You're from India, right?"

"Yeah." I nod, amused. "Total cliché—my parents met at a newly opened American restaurant called Mia's Diner in the city. Love at first sight, and then they named me after the place that started it all."

Her face lights up. "That's adorable. They must be a fun bunch to hang out with."

I pause, my tone dips, smile faltering as I brace for the inevitable. "Um...yeah. They were. Now they...they're dead."

Her smile vanishes. "Oh! I didn't know—I'm really sorry."

"It's okay." I offer a small smile, though the familiar awkwardness creeps in. I've been through this enough times to know what comes next—the uncomfortable silence, the unsure expressions. I don't like putting people in that position, so I shift the conversation before it lingers.

"So... how'd you hurt yourself?" I ask, glancing at her foot.

She gestures toward a paperweight lying a few feet away. "That thing. Tripped over it."

I pick it up and place it on her desk before helping her to her feet. She winces slightly, so I guide her over to the chair by her desk.

"What would I have done without you?" she teases, grinning.

"Probably screamed until someone heard you." I smirk.

She grins, and I find myself smiling too. I like her already—her energy, her warmth. She reminds me of Nidhi.

This might actually work out.

We might be good friends.

CHAPTER 3
Miles

The soft morning sunlight filters through the sheer curtains, casting a white glow over the dining table. My mom—Seraphina—sits at the very end of it, the picture of elegance even in her casual attire, sipping green tea from her favorite cup.

"Good morning, baby." She smiles warmly as I take a seat adjacent to her.

"Morning, Mom."

Eve, our cook, brings over a cup of coffee, placing it in front of me. "Thank you, Eve." I say with a small smile.

"Is Audrey awake yet?" Mom asks.

"No, she's still asleep."

"That girl." Mom mutters with a shake of her head. "I guess I'll have to wake her up myself."

I down the rest of my coffee in one go and set the cup aside. "I should get going. I'll see you later, Mom—"

"No." She grabs my arm, stopping me mid-motion. "You're not leaving without breakfast."

"Mom, I need to get to the office early. Dad's not there today." I protest.

"That's why there are employees. They'll manage without you for an hour." She shakes her head, her voice firm but gentle. "Miles, you just graduated, and you're already running so fast. Slow down."

Eve returns with a plate of scrambled eggs and bacon, placing it in front of me. I sigh but pick up my fork. "A small price to pay for ownership." I mutter between bites.

The second I graduated, I stepped into my role as COO at Baudelaire Global Enterprises. A sleek office, an assistant, and a simple deal with Dad: work hard now, and in two years, I'll be CEO. It's a fair trade. I still go out, just not as much. Cutting back on parties and late nights with my friends is a little sacrifice for the top seat.

"You'll make CEO sooner or later." Mom's voice is softer now. "That doesn't mean you should stop enjoying life."

I glance at her as she continues. "Doesn't Alex have a party tonight? I think you should go."

"I would, but I have to attend the Dawson's party."

"Oh, right." She nods slowly, finishing her apple.

I take another bite, noticing she hasn't moved. "Weren't you about to wake Audrey?"

"Yes, but I'm not leaving until you finish your breakfast." She sips her tea, unfazed.

I shake my head with a small laugh. "Alright, alright."

The Baudelaire building gleams in the sunlight, its glass panels reflecting the city skyline. It gleams in the morning sun like a diamond. I pull into the underground parking, and head inside.

The lobby is quiet, except for the faint hum of conversations and the clack of heels on the marble floor. I nod at the receptionist and step into the elevator, swiping my badge. As the doors close, I glance at my watch. It's going to be a busy day.

When the elevator dings open on my floor, Melanie, my assistant, is already waiting. She looks slightly flustered, holding a stack of papers.

"Good morning, Mr. Baudelaire." she says, walking quickly to match my stride.

"Morning, Melanie. What's on the agenda?"

"A lot. You have a packed day." she says, flipping through her papers. "You've got the operations update at ten, a call with the marketing team at noon, the party at Dawson's at eight pm, and," She pauses.

"And what?" I ask, glancing at her.

"There's a meeting with Mr. Wexley in five minutes." she blurts out.

I stop in my tracks. "Wexley?"

"Yes, sir. Your Dad was supposed to handle it, but since he's out of town, it's on you." She looks apologetic.

I glance at my watch. "Five minutes? Why wasn't I told earlier?"

"I just found out myself." she says quickly. "I've already prepped the file and sent you the key points."

I let out a breath and start walking again. "Alright. Bring the file to the conference room. Anything else I should know?"

"He's... intense and opinionated. Very opinionated."

"Great." I mutter under my breath.

I step into my office, and grab my laptop. The glass walls give me a perfect view of the city, but there's no time to admire it. If Dad thinks I can handle Wexley, then I'll prove him right.

"Let's go." I say to Melanie as I head toward the conference room immediately greeted by Wexley.

The meeting with him really is intense. He's every bit as sharp and intimidating as the rumours suggested, but I keep my cool. I present my ideas, listen to his input, and make sure to show my authority without backing down. By the end of it, he seems satisfied. His icy expression softens, just a little.

"You did well, Miles." His voice is calm, but there's an underlying approval. I shake his hand. "Thank you, Mr. Wexley. I'll follow up with the next steps."

As he leaves, I let out a slow breath, rolling my shoulders to ease the tension. I stay in the conference room for a moment, gathering my thoughts.

One meeting down, a dozen more to go.

CHAPTER 4

Mia

I slip into my jeans and zip up my lilac crop top. Instead of tying my hair back like usual, I let it fall loose around my shoulders, brushing it one more time. A swipe of my favorite clear lip gloss finishes the look, and I toss it into my small purse along with my phone.

With one last glance in the mirror to make sure everything's in place, I step out of my room.

Sam's door clicks shut just as mine does, and she turns with a grin. "Ready, M?"

"Aww. I already have a nickname." I mutter.

"You were bound to. It was either M&M or M." she jests.

"Wow, single M. I'm flattered."

"Yeah, single M." she smirks. "Kinda poetic, don't you think? Matches your dating status."

I scoff, shooting her a glare, but she just laughs as we make our way downstairs.

Outside, a sleek black Benz is parked just a few feet away. I'm guessing that's our ride. Leaning against the trunk is a girl with honey-blonde hair, who waves excitedly at Sam the second she spots us.

"That's Audrey." Sam says, picking up the pace. "Come on, she's been dying to meet you."

As we approach, Audrey's hazel eyes land on me with excitement. "You must be Mia! Oh my god, finally!"

She clasps her hands together like she's holding back the urge to squeal. I blink, slightly taken aback by the enthusiasm.

"Hi... yeah, Mia," I say, offering a small smile. I'm still adjusting to how expressive people are here compared to back home.

Audrey's eyes sparkle. "You're so pretty!"

"And you," I say, glancing at her flawless skin and effortless style, "look like you just stepped off a Vogue cover."

She grins, brushing her honey-blonde waves over her shoulder.

Audrey Baudelaire—half American and French—has that sun-kissed, outdoorsy glow, a sprinkle of freckles across her nose, and hazel eyes that shift between amber and green. Her casual deep green tank top and perfectly fitted jeans scream *effortless beauty*.

Before I can dwell too long on her perfect aura, Sam interrupts, turning to me. "Audrey is moving into her dorm next week."

Audrey nods excitedly. "We're going to have so much fun!"

I let on a quiet smile before Sam narrows her eyes suspiciously at the car. "Audrey... this isn't your car, is it?"

Audrey laughs. "No, this is Miles's. My car bailed on me. I may have... *guilt-tripped* him to give us a lift." She leans in, lowering her voice. "He's a little grumpy though. I interrupted his plans. So Sam, do not get on his nerves today."

Sam shakes her head in disappointment. "Noted"

A car door slams shut.

"Let's go." a low, commanding voice cuts through the air. "Audrey, I'm running late. You've got one minute, or I'm leaving— with you or without."

Audrey's playful demeanor vanishes, replaced by steely determination. Sam smirks, clearly enjoying the impending sibling showdown.

But I'm not focused on their banter. I'm focused on *him*.

Miles walks closer to Audrey, and my breath catches.

Tall. Raven-black hair falling in carefully controlled waves around his pale face. Sharp, aristocratic features lending him a striking maturity. But it's his eyes that stand out the most—sapphire blue, intense and calculating, locking onto Audrey with an air of quiet authority.

Dressed in all black, a sleek turtleneck beneath a dark blue blazer, he looks like a modern-day prince.

Everything about him—his presence, his gaze—demands attention. He's composed yet impatient, radiating confidence. It's intimidating. And... kind of hot.

Audrey huffs. "Would you just *chill* for a minute?"

Miles, ignoring her, warns. "You've got forty-five seconds." already heading back to the driver's seat.

The engine roars to life, and we scramble into the car—Audrey sliding into the front seat while Sam and I squeeze into the back.

Everybody stays silent as we pull away.

For the entire ride to the theatre—for a movie Sam forcefully dragged me to—the only sound is the hum of the engine... and the racing of my own thoughts.

CHAPTER 5

Miles

I'm finally at the party hosted by Mr. and Mrs. Dawson—my best friend Nate's parents, at their billion dollar penthouse in Manhattan. The penthouse's interior matches its extravagant exterior well with its futuristic modern designs. Upon entering, an enormous sparkling chandelier hangs from the ceiling, and at first sight, it looks like it's made entirely of diamonds.

My dad was invited to this event, but he had to fly to Los Angeles for an urgent meeting, so I'm here in his place. I was dreading it—these parties are dull, predictable, and filled with people pretending to care more than they actually do. But I have to get used to them. One day, I'll be stepping into my father's shoes, and these rooms, these conversations, will be my world.

Still, I'm here with a purpose.

I spot Mr. Kline making his way toward the bar. That's my cue. I weave through the room, ready to take my shot. My father has been trying to sign a deal with the Kline's for months, but they've been difficult to pin down. This might be my chance to change that. I'm confident—I managed to impress Mr. Wexley today, and I'm still riding that high.

As I pass through the elegantly dressed crowd, I catch sight of Mr. and Mrs. Dawson near the window, engaged in conversation with a small group. Mrs. Dawson notices me first, her face lighting up as she waves me over.

"Miles, darling! It's been too long." She pulls me into a warm hug.

"Good to see you, Mrs. Dawson." I smile politely.

Mr. Dawson turns toward me with an approving nod. "Ah, Miles! Filling in for your father tonight, I see?"

"Yes." I nod. "He had to fly out for a last-minute meeting."

"Well, we're glad to have you here. You're doing great things already—I hear your name more and more these days." Mr. Dawson winks.

Mrs. Dawson chimes in, "Yes, we're so proud of you, Miles. It's wonderful to see the next generation stepping up. Your father always speaks so highly of you."

A flicker of pride stirs in my chest, but I keep my expression composed. "I'm just trying to keep up with him."

"You're doing more than that." Mr. Dawson claps me on the back. "Keep it up. I have no doubt you'll be running the show soon enough."

I offer a polite smile. "Thanks, I appreciate that."

After a few more pleasantries, I excuse myself and head toward the bar, refocusing on Mr. Kline.

For the next hour, I engage him in conversation, carefully steering the discussion toward business. I can tell by his shifting expressions that he's more interested than he was before, but before I can solidify anything, his wife calls him away. He excuses himself, leaving me alone at the bar.

I take a sip of my whiskey, letting the smoky burn settle as my thoughts drift elsewhere—to someone I saw just two hours ago.

When Audrey mentioned an Indian girl was joining them for movie night, I didn't expect her to unsettle something in me—like a quiet pull, a shift in the air, a feeling I couldn't quite place but suddenly needed to understand.

When I stepped out of the car earlier, the evening air clung to the last warmth of the day, laced with the faint scent of lilies from the nearby bushes. And then, there she was—Mia.

She stood with Audrey and Sam, the setting sun casting a golden hue across the land, highlighting the smooth fairness of her skin and the wavy black hair cascading just past her shoulders.

She stood out—not in a loud or attention-seeking way, but in a way that was impossible to ignore. Unlike Sam and Audrey, who buzzed with excitement, Mia was quieter, more reserved. But something about her pulled me in.

Her brown eyes, mysterious yet soft and calm like the rich soil of fall, darted nervously around, taking in everything. They lingered on me briefly before shifting away, as if she didn't want to be noticed. But it wasn't easy to ignore her.

I wanted to steal another glance, to study her a little longer, but I held back. I didn't want to make her more nervous than she already seemed.

A firm pat on my back pulls me from my thoughts.

"Miles! Haven't seen you in ages, man."

Devon Dawson—Nate's older brother—grins as he slides onto the barstool beside me.

"Devon." I shake his hand. "How's it going?"

"Pretty good. What about you?" He runs a hand through his golden hair. "How's the position of COO treating you?"

"Like driving a brand-new car." My tone is light, but the weight of the title lingers in my words.

Devon raises an eyebrow. "Not bad, huh?"

"I remember my first time as COO." He shakes his head. "Worse than being CEO." He smirks, swirling the drink in his glass. "So, what's next, prince? The king?"

"I hope so." My voice is steady, unwavering.

Devon grins, lifting his glass in a mock toast. "Well, here's to that. And when you take over, let's make sure the parties are better than this snooze fest."

"So we both agree this party is boring."

He nods. "Don't tell my mom."

I chuckle, then hesitate before a thought strikes me. "Hey, Devon, is that apartment in Brooklyn still on the market?"

He tilts his head, considering. "The one you nearly swooned over? Yeah, I think so. Want me to check?"

"I didn't swoon," I huff. "But yeah, that'd be great. I need to get out of my parents' mansion. It's stifling."

Devon chuckles. "Ah, the joys of living under the parental roof."

We talk for a while, catching up and exchanging stories, but when I check my watch, I realize it's time to pick up the girls from the theatre. "I've gotta run." I stand, shaking his hand again. "Let me know about that apartment."

"Will do."

Grabbing my coat, I weave through the glittering penthouse toward the exit. And as I step into the night, my thoughts tangle back to Mia—the way the evening sunlight touched her skin, the way she looked at me for just a second too long before turning away.

Her quiet beauty lingers in my mind like a melody I can't shake.

A timeless picture.

Something to praise.

CHAPTER 6
Miles

I stopped at a decent restaurant called Nick's Grills—a bit of a detour from Columbia. But after eleven, most hotels on the way to campus turn into pubs, and the girls—well, Audrey specifically—were hungry. Apparently, dozen buckets of popcorn weren't enough.

The restaurant is packed as usual, even at this late hour. Warm yellow lights glow through the large glass windows, illuminating the bustling space inside. Outside, the parking lot is a tight squeeze. I pull up in front of the entrance, letting the girls out before manoeuvring into a narrow spot wedged between a sleek Range Rover and a worn-down Ford. The night air is crisp as I step out, the lingering scent of gasoline mixing with the faint aroma of grilled meat drifting from the restaurant.

As I turn toward the entrance, my steps falter.

There, just outside the doorway, stands Mia.

The silver gleam of the moon softens her silhouette, painting her in ethereal light. The strands of her dark hair shimmer with hints of silver as if the night itself had woven them into something almost unreal—elegant in its simplicity.

She has a phone pressed to her ear, her voice low and warm. As I get closer, her final words drift through the cool air.

"Bye, Nidhi."

She hangs up, exhaling softly before slipping the phone into her pocket.

Something in me hesitates. My body halts, like an invisible force had reached out and gripped my chest. I stare down at my shoes for a beat, inhaling deeply, trying to shake off whatever had momentarily settled over me. By the time I look up, she has already turned to walk inside. I follow, keeping just a few steps behind.

The scent of sizzling steaks and freshly baked bread welcome me as I step through the doors. The place is buzzed with life—couples engaged in quiet conversations, families laughing over late-night meals, and groups of students animatedly discussing their weekend plans. The soft hum of jazz floats from hidden speakers, but it barely cuts through the low murmur of voices and the rhythmic clinking of cutlery against porcelain.

Sam and Audrey have somehow managed to snag a table tucked into a cozy corner, shielded slightly from the crowd. I spot Audrey waving Mia over as she weaves through the maze of tables. She slides into the seat beside Sam just as I reach them, claiming the only available chair—next to Audrey, directly across from Mia.

"Have you ordered yet?" I ask, resting my forearm on the table.

Audrey shakes her head. "No, we were waiting for you."

I signal the waiter, and as he approaches, Audrey orders first, followed by Sam. "I'll have the grilled steak with potatoes." Sam then turns to Mia. "What about you?"

"I'll have the same." Mia replies, folding her hands on the table, her fingers lightly tracing an invisible pattern against the wood.

The waiter's gaze shifts to me. "And for you, sir?"

"Chicken Alfredo and a glass of white wine." I hand him the menu, and he nods before disappearing into the kitchen.

The low murmur of conversation continues around us as Audrey suddenly speaks up. "You both haven't officially met." Her gaze flickers between Mia and me.

There's a pause. Mia tucks a strand of hair behind her ear, the movement fluid, almost absentminded. There's something fascinating about the way she moves—like each gesture is careful, but not forced. Natural, yet guarded.

Audrey continues, "Mia, this is my brother, Miles. And Miles, this is Mia."

I extend a hand across the table, a slow smile curling at the edges of my lips. "Enchanté. Welcome to America." I greet, my voice dipping into a smooth French accent.

Mia hesitates, her fingers stilling in their tracing. Her gaze meets mine, something unreadable flickering in the depths of her sweet brown eyes—uncertainty? Amusement? It is hard to tell.

Then, with quiet confidence, she tilts her head slightly and responds, *"Namaste.* Nice to meet you."

I smirk. Not obviously—just enough.

As she shakes my hand, her fingers brushing lightly against mine, the touch featherlight, fleeting. But for a fraction of a second, she lingers longer than expected before pulling away.

Beside her, Sam snorts. "Okay, that was unnecessarily fancy."

Audrey smirks, turning to Mia. "He does that sometimes. Greeting people in French."

Mia glances between them, then back at me, as if deciding whether or not to respond. Instead, she just presses her lips together in a small smile.

The moment passes as the conversation shifts, laughter bubbling between Audrey and Sam, but my eyes keeps landing back to Mia.

She doesn't demand attention. Yet she has it anyway.

And I have a feeling she doesn't even realize it.

As the food arrives, something shifts. Her fingers clutch the fork a little too tightly, her knuckles pale. The air around her changes, the light in her eyes dimming into something different. There's a flicker of unease in her features, so quick it could've been mistaken for nothing at all.

My stomach tenses. What changed? Is it the food? No, that can't be it. Then what?

But why am I even thinking about this? I was thinking about her at the party. Then again while driving to pick them up. And now, sitting across from her, I can't stop wondering what's going on in her mind.

I need to stop.

But how?

Mia

It's a dark freeway in middle of nowhere.
The sky is the colour of ash, starless and heavy.
Two cars crash into each other.
The first car belongs to my parents and the second one to a drunk driver.

I keep getting woken up by the same dream.

It's not just a dream. Not exactly. It happened three years ago. My parents. A crash. A drunk driver. I didn't witness it—thank god I didn't. That would have haunted me even more than it already does.

And this dream isn't new. Every time I hear about another life lost to liquor or because of it, something in my brain clicks, like a trigger pulled without warning. And at night, the dream returns, keeping me awake feeling cold, my palms sweaty and tears staining the edges of my eyes. Not a good feeling.

Earlier tonight, at the restaurant, when our orders arrived, I noticed Miles had ordered wine with his meal. And it scared me. I know he's an adult. I know it was just one glass. In America, wine isn't even considered strong alcohol. But none of that mattered. The thought of him driving afterward terrified me. That's why, when Sam and Audrey dozed off in the car, I couldn't.

I'm not sure if Miles noticed that I was the only one awake.

But it's fine. Tomorrow, I'll wake up and feel fine. The weight of tonight will fade, vanish into the background, and I won't think about it again until something else sets it off.

Sometimes, I remind myself that it's not as bad as it was two years ago. Because there will always be that unfillable gap left by my parents, and I'll always try to cover it with the good memories I have of them.

Two years ago, I couldn't even bear to think about them or talk about them with my friends or with anyone, especially when they'd share stories about their parents. Just hearing their conversations would send me into a tailspin, a grief I couldn't control. But now, I've grown. I've learned to manage it. I've found a way to live with the pain without completely snapping or breaking down like a storm without warning.

Now, I can even talk about my mom, how she used to make tea in the mornings with her warm smile. I can even laugh about how my dad would attempt to prepare a traditional cuisine but end up frying the fryer.

I call that progress.

CHAPTER 7
Mia

The cafeteria radiates a woodsy vibe with its warm brown wallpapers and lower half walls panelled with woodboards. A chandelier hangs from the ceiling, illuminating the hall. The hall is spacious, with all the tables arranged at the centre, and the air filled with gossip and laughter.

We're already seated, our trays laden with food after a much-needed break from helping Audrey move into her dorm. The rhythmic clatter of cutlery and the hum of conversation surround us as we fall into easy conversation—laughing at Sam's sarcastic quips, exchanging fashion tips with Audrey, and me, sharing stories about India. There's a comfort in it, a warmth that settles in my chest. These girls—Sam and Audrey—are funny, kind, and effortlessly welcoming. It's in moments like this that I realize just how lucky I am to have found friends like them.

I'm mid-bite when two figures pull out the chairs beside us. One sits next to me, the other beside Audrey. Their presence is familiar before I even lift my gaze.

Alex Prescott—the one sitting next to me, has a confident posture that draws attention wherever he goes. His tousled dirty-blonde hair is perfectly styled and his blue eyes carry an ever-present glint of mischief and warmth, with a hint of boyish charm that makes him approachable.

Sam says that he has a crush on me because he flirts with me. I think that's ridiculous, because he flirts with everyone, half of the girls on campus must have been flirted by him. That's a part of his personality.

Then there's Nate Dawson, the complete contrast. Where Alex thrives on attention, Nate is quietly self-assured, his athletic build making it obvious that sports are second nature to him. Dark hair falls effortlessly over his forehead, complementing the warmth in his hazel eyes—eyes that remind me of sunlight filtering through autumn leaves.

Alex flashes me a grin, the kind that's equal parts charming and dangerous. "How are you doing, Mia?"

And so, the flirting begins.

I swallow a spoonful of mac and cheese, making sure to chew slower than necessary, as if prolonging my response will somehow prevent more conversation. "Good, Alex. I'm doing well."

His smirk deepens, but before he can say anything else, Sam groans dramatically.

"Oh, for the love of God." She stabs her fork into her salad with exaggerated disgust. "Get a room, guys."

Confused, I follow her gaze and—oh.

Nate and Audrey are in their own little world, sharing a brief but sweet kiss.

Audrey gives Sam a playful side-eye, but Sam just scoffs, rolling her eyes.

"We're actually here for a reason." Alex announces suddenly, his voice cutting through the easy conversation. He leans forward, his energy shifting from lighthearted to something...different. Something almost ominous.

The table falls quiet. Even Sam pauses mid-bite, her fork frozen in the air.

Alex gestures dramatically toward Nate. "Our homeboy here, in his infinite wisdom, pissed off the captain of Colombia's football team while drunk and—wait for it—challenged him to a match."

Silence.

Then, slowly, I turn to Nate, who exhales sharply, rubbing his temple like just hearing it out loud makes it worse.

"The match is next Saturday," Alex continues, now fully in storyteller mode, leaning forward like he's narrating a tragic tale. "At Adler's High football court. And *guess what*—we're lucky this idiot still has our old high school football team willing to back him up."

He pauses dramatically, letting the weight of his words sink in, while Sam and I take another bite of our food like we're watching a particularly gripping movie.

Alex huffs, throwing his hands up. "Audrey, this is big news. Why are you not saying anything? He's going to lose. They're going to lose, and he's still not calling it off."

Audrey, ever composed, simply sighs. "Alex, I already knew." She folds her arms, casting a knowing glance toward Nate. "And it's going to be fine. I'm sure they'll win."

Alex looks personally offended. "You're too confident about this."

"I am," she says, her voice steady. "Because Nate is good at football. In case you've forgotten." Then, with a sly smile, she adds, "And this is his chance to show the Colombian Tigers that they should've let him try out for their team when he first came here."

Nate's lips curve into a slow smile, his hazel eyes gleaming with something unreadable as he presses a quick kiss to Audrey's cheek. "Thank you, Aud."

Sam snorts. "You know, I *could* feel bad for you, but you had this coming."

Nate raises an eyebrow. "Had what coming?"

She shrugs. "I don't really know. I just wanted to say it."

Nate shakes his head, amused. "Sam, I'm actually happy about this match so don't feel bad. And you know, for a psychology student, you're not really giving off the best impression."

Sam leans back, completely unbothered. "Hey, I know how to separate my academic and personal life. You, my dear friend, fall into the personal category—the roast-the-friend one, to be specific."

Alex suddenly straightens up, like a light bulb just went off in his head. "Let's take a vote."

"On what?" Audrey asks.

"If Nate and his team—"

"It's called Brooklyn Panthers." Nate interrupts.

"Right. If the Brooklyn Panthers are going to win or not."

"That's so unnecessary." Audrey mutters, but before she can shut it down, Sam jumps in.

"Brooklyn Panthers are going to humiliate themselves." Sam says without any hesitation.

"Seriously, Sam." Nate glares. "You are terrible at this."

Sam just smirks. "Personal life, Nate."

Audrey, confidence unwavering, says, "I obviously believe they'll win."

"I stand with Sam." Alex declares, stealing Sam's soda and sipping it with an unnecessary amount of intensity.

Nate turns to me. "What about you, Mia?"

I blink, caught off guard. "Oh, you want *my* vote?"

"Well, yeah," he says, like it's the most obvious thing in the world. "You're our friend."

Something about the way he says *our friend* makes me feel...good. Like I belong. Like this isn't just a passing phase, but something real.

I clear my throat. "Okay. I have faith."

Nate grins. "Thank you."

Alex groans. "Fine, that's a tie. I *guess* we'll just have to cheer for you at the game."

"That's all I need, Alex. Thank you." Nate says.

"So you didn't want my concern." Alex starts again.

"This is gonna be a long lunch." Sam mutters.

"Alex, pick a new distraction. Please." Nate pleads.

Alex, swinging his arm over the back of his chair, shifts to face me. He looks at me with intent, like he's deep in thought, and it's honestly more concerning than uncomfortable. Then, after what feels like eternity, he finally speaks.

"Mia, would you like to go on a date with me?"

I freeze.

Somewhere around me, I *physically* hear Nate slap a hand over his face while I just stare. From the corner of my eye, I see Audrey regret her existence. And Sam? Well, she is clearly entertained.

A date?

The thought is completely foreign, something I never even considered. I replay it in my mind, trying to decide whether I'm more confused or flattered.

And I can't tell if Alex is joking or actually serious. But it's Alex Prescott—he's never really joking, and he's never completely serious either. He's just... Alex. He just exists in this weird in-between space where sincerity and playfulness blurs into one.

I shake my head, snapping back to reality. "Alex, *no*. Switch your distraction."

He smirks, unfazed. "Come on, I'm a solid choice. Good-looking, charming, exceptional conversationalist, and organised." He gestures to himself like a salesman.

"You sound desperate." Sam deadpans.

"Well, I am desperate." He winks. "Desperate for Mia."

Collectively, we all make disgusted faces.

"No. Alex, *no*." I say, shaking my head.

Audrey tilts her head, amusement flickering in her eyes. "Oh, Mia, take it easy on him. Captain Flirt isn't used to rejection." Alex dramatically shifts to the other side of his chair, slouching and crossing his arms with a faux-wounded expression.

Laughter ripples across the table, and as I take it all in—the teasing, the ridiculous banter, the absurdity of a football challenge looming over us—the sound ringing through my wonderment, I realize something.

These are my friends.

And for a moment, everything is weightless. Just friends, food, and a little bit of chaos that somehow makes perfect sense.

CHAPTER 8
Mia

They lost.

Brooklyn Panthers lost.

The evening sunlight drapes the football field in a golden glow, stretching long shadows across the bleachers. A soft breeze carries the scent of fresh-cut grass and the distant hum of chatter from students dispersing after the game. Sam, Audrey, Alex, and *also* Miles rise from their seats, making their way toward the sweaty yet well-played Brooklyn Panthers—toward Nate.

I get up too, stepping down one bleacher, but I don't move further. Instead, I linger, my gaze fixed on the team that fought with everything they had yet still fell short.

And they're smiling.

There's no anger, no frustration—just a raw, untamed kind of joy. They played well, gave it their all, and lost to the Colombian Tigers in a game that was as brutal as it was beautiful. And somehow, that's enough.

The trees in the distance sway gently; their rustling leaves blending with the soft chirping of birds, as if the world itself is offering quiet applause. I watch as the captain of the Colombian Tigers steps forward, offering a handshake to Brooklyn Panthers. He says something—words too quiet for me to hear—but whatever it is, it makes them smile.

And just as I am about to look away, Miles glances up toward the bleachers. His eyes scan the empty rows, until—somehow—they land on mine.

For a heartbeat, everything else fades. His eyes locked on mine, and for a second, I feel like we are the only two people on the ground. He doesn't smile, I don't smile. There is just this strange current between us which I cannot figure out.

Then, just as quickly, he turns back to his friends, his face lighting up as they celebrate the victorious... loss. But that fleeting moment lingers, curling around my thoughts like an unfinished sentence.

Before I can dwell on it, Alex steps up beside me on the bleacher, shoving his hands into his pockets. "So they lost."

"I know," I murmur, still watching the field. "They don't really look sad, though."

"No, they don't." He follows my gaze.

I glance at him, raising a brow. "I bet you already told Nate *I told you so.*"

"Hey, I'm not a monster." he says, feigning innocence.

I roll my eyes. "Stop lying, Alex."

He exhales dramatically. "Fine. I'm going to do it tomorrow. Right now the timing is wrong." A pause. "Not because they just lost, but because they're too damn happy. It won't hurt."

I chuckle. "Oh, Alex."

He hums, shifting his weight onto one foot before tilting his head toward me. "On that note, where are we on the date part?"

I turn to him, my lips twitching. "Alex, I'd rather watch paint dry."

Alex lets out an exaggerated sigh, clutching his chest. "Rejection. My new friend. We meet again."

I laugh, shaking my head as I lightly slap his shoulder. "Stop being so dramatic."

The air feels magical, and as I look back at the field—at my friends, at the way the evening wraps around us like an old song—I think, just for a second, that moments like these are what makes life worth it. No matter how chaotic.

##

The sun hangs low on the horizon, streaking the sky with shades of soft orange and fading blue. Long shadows stretch across the field, the air still warm from the day but carrying the first hints of coolness.

"The captain of the Colombian Tigers just asked me to actually try-out for their team next year." Nate announces, his voice brimming with pride.

"What?" Audrey gasps before breaking into a wide smile. "I'm so happy for you!" She throws her arms around him, hugging him tight before pulling him into a kiss.

I immediately avert my gaze, staring up at the sky, focusing on the distant chatter of the crowd as people slowly trickle out of the field. Anything to avoid looking at my best friend and my sister making out.

That's when Alex and Mia approach, their footsteps light against the turf.

"Nate got asked to try-out for the Colombian Tigers next year." Sam fills them in.

"That's amazing," Mia says, her voice warm. I glance at her—just for a second—but then my gaze lingers a little too long.

She's standing close to Alex, her dark hair catching the glow from the setting sun, her brown eyes reflecting calmness. The way she absentmindedly shifts her weight on one leg, the small, almost knowing smile on her lips—it does something to me. I quickly glance away.

She mutters something to Alex. "Now you can't say I told you so."

Alex frowns but steps forward to clap Nate on the shoulder. "Congrats, man."

"Even though you lost, at least we have something to celebrate," I quickly mutter.

"Yeah. We all should go for dinner somewhere," Audrey suggests. "You know, the whole Panthers team and us."

"Yeah. I'll go tell the guys." Nate nods before jogging off, his excitement radiating off him.

The moment everyone's distracted, I seize the opportunity, turning to Alex, my voice deliberately casual. "I heard you like Mia."

Alex barely hesitates. "Yeah."

A strange, unwelcome sensation creeps up my spine. "I also heard you asked her out." I say, not entirely sure why I'm bringing this up.

"Yeah. But she declined." His voice holds no bitterness, just a shrug-like acceptance. Then he adds, "Twice."

My stomach tightens. "You asked her again?" My voice jumps slightly, betraying me.

Alex shrugs again. "Yeah, a few minutes ago." His tone is light, casual—completely unaware of the turmoil churning inside me.

Before I can stop myself, I blurt out a little too loud, "Maybe you should stop asking her out."

What the hell, Miles?

Alex tilts his head, brows furrowing. "Why? You want to?"

"No." The denial comes too fast, too sharp. My pulse stutters when Alex's expression shifts—his mouth parting slightly as realization dawns.

"Oh." His eyes narrow slightly. Then he smirks. "Oh." He lowers his voice, his words barely above a whisper. "You were jealous."

The accusation slams into me like a freight train.

Jealous? No. That's—no. I don't know what the hell I'm feeling. I don't know anything anymore.

My chest tightens, an unsettling mess of emotions tangling inside me, making my head feel light, my pulse unsteady. I don't respond. I can't. Instead, I turn sharply on my heel and start walking toward Audrey, leaving Alex frozen in place, still piecing it all together.

Damn it.

I lean against my desk, pondering out the office window at the city sprawled beneath the morning light. The skyline is painted in hues of fresh blues and pure whites, the distant drone of life below a quiet reminder that the world never stops moving. A cup of coffee rests in my hands—well, it had coffee in it a few seconds ago. Now, it's just a cup.

I'm waiting.

Waiting for Melanin to bring me the documents she needs me to sign.

The door slides open, but I know it's not her. Melanin's heels always clank loudly against the floor. Then again, every woman's heels echo in this office. There's not much here to absorb the sound—just a desk, a chair, a cupboard, and a single oversized vase filled with flowers I didn't choose.

I turn.

It's my dad.

"I heard Nate's team lost the match," he says, his tone unreadable. He isn't interested in the game—he's just initiating conversation, setting up for whatever point he's about to make.

Still, I listen.

"And you all celebrated with a dinner party. Interesting." He pauses, then nods slightly. "It's a good thing. Celebrating loss is as important as celebrating victory."

I hold his gaze and nod. "I agree."

And, for once, I actually mean it.

But then his expression hardens. "Although, celebrating failure is only dignified when you've given everything and still lost. Otherwise, it's just pathetic, and the person is worthless."

I nod. When I think there will be silence between him and I now, my dad speaks, "Miles, are you dating someone? Seriously dating someone? Not flinging around."

"No."

His gaze sharpens. "Do you remember Chloe Harrington?"

I raise an eyebrow. "Yes."

"Good." He nods, satisfied. "I want you to ask her out."

And that's my dad—Lucien Baudelaire.

The owner of Baudelaire Global Enterprises. A man who built an empire from the ground up in France—*dust to dominance*, as he likes to say—before expanding it worldwide. He came to the U.S., married my mother, the then-heiress and now-owner of the Browning's Empire, and now, here we are.

He continues over my silence, "I was going to ask you to marry her, but you kids these days like to go on dates first."

"If you think you made a good joke, you didn't." I say, my voice flat, caught somewhere between disbelief and irritation.

And he laughs. "Dad jokes."

Clearly he doesn't know what dad jokes are.

"But why?" I find myself asking.

"You know our business affairs," he says smoothly. "The Harringtons have an impeccable influence in the Asian market. We say we're global, but we're not as strong there. We need that expansion."

He exhales, and then continues, "But the Harringtons are selective about who they partner with—and I respect that. I believe you and Chloe could be the key to earning their trust. And, let's be honest, it would be beneficial for you, too. She's a brilliant young woman, raised in the same world as you. A perfect match." He pauses. "And you're not dating anyone, so."

Before I can argue—which would be pointless anyway—he stands, already heading for the door. "*Essaie. Invite-la à sortir.*" (Give it a try. Ask her out.)

Lucien Baudelaire may be in his late forties, but he still controls everything—his business, his reputation, his family. And when those control slips, even for a moment, his temper ignites like wildfire.

So yeah, I have to give it a try. I have to ask Chloe Harrington out. And while I'm at it, I'll be praying every bone in my body that she's already involved with someone.

I sink into my chair, wondering why the hell I'm not fighting back for at least my romantic life. It's not like we're living in the olden times when marriages were just fragile financial agreements.

Although... Chloe and I have met at events before. She's intelligent. Pretty. Strong. We'd probably get along. Maybe I'd even like her.

But then, a memory from a few days ago burns itself into my mind.

Adler High's football field. The Brooklyn Panthers had just accepted their loss. I wasn't just casually looking around—I was looking for her. I didn't expect her to look back. But when our eyes met, it was like the air between us sparked with electricity. It wasn't just eye contact; it was something more. A connection.

Alex is my best friend. I've never had an issue with his dating life. He can date whoever he wants.

But when he asked Mia out?

That hit differently—like something inside me shifted.

Alex was damn right!

I was jealous.

CHAPTER 9

Mia

I am sitting at my desk, typing away on my assignment. It is only the first week of university, so there isn't any rush to finish it. I am just enjoying the quiet and focusing on my work, which feels nice.

Suddenly, the door bangs.

I jump a little, startled by the loud noise. What is that? I stand up and walk to my door to find out. I open it a little to see what's going on.

To my surprise, there's Sam. She's with a guy I don't know. They are frantically kissing each other as they stumble inside Sam's room. I blink, feeling a mix of surprise and curiosity. I was kind of expecting this as Sam is an out-going kinda girl. Since my time here, this boy, whoever he is, is the third guy I've seen her with, but it's the first time she has bought somebody in our dorm.

I stand there for a moment, trying to process what I've just seen. I have a feeling that things might escalate between Sam and *the guy*. I don't want to hear anything through the thin walls.

I look back at my desk and think about my assignment. I can work on it later. I decide that a walk will be better.

I grab my phone and keys and slip out of my room and leave the dorm. The cool night air hits me, and I feel better just being outside. It's nice to have a little break and get some fresh air.

The evening air bites at my skin as I walk close to the campus building, enjoying the crisp breeze—until it gets *too* cold. A shiver racks through me, and I realize, with an annoyed sigh, that I forgot my coat. I rub my palms together, hoping the friction will bring some warmth, but it does little against the chill creeping up my spine.

I consider turning back, my arms wrapping around myself in a poor attempt to shield against the cold. The wind whistles, cutting through the near-empty pathway.

Then, out of nowhere, warmth envelops me.

A blazer—heavy, expensive, *nice*—settles over my shoulders, and an unmistakable presence appears beside me.

My breath catches as I glance over.

Miles.

A surge of heat rushes through me, sending a shiver down my spine that has nothing to do with the cold. My heart does an irrational little stutter, and for a moment, I just stare, my brain short-circuiting.

Why him, God? *Of all the people on this planet, why him?*

His scent lingers in the fabric—sandalwood and something subtly sweet, like coffee. It's intoxicating, and suddenly, the blazer feels almost unnecessary. The warmth spreading inside me isn't from the fabric but from him. Just being near him ignites a slow, quiet burn, a mixture of nervous energy and something I refuse to name.

I stop walking and turn to face him, my lips parting as if to speak. But nothing comes out.

Under the dim streetlights, he looks unfairly good. Shadows stretch and flicker across his face, highlighting the sharp cut of his jaw, the shape of his cheekbones. His white t-shirt clings to his frame, the sleeves rolled up just enough to reveal his forearms—because apparently, the universe *wants* me to suffer.

"Hi, Mia." he says, his voice smooth, deep.

It's a simple greeting, but it skates down my spine like a whisper of something dangerous.

"Hi!" I manage, and then, in a desperate attempt to fill the charged silence, I add, "Um... thank you!"

"You're welcome." He smiles.

My heart skips. Literally *skips*.

I start walking again, *because if I stand still, I might actually die* from the sheer awareness of his proximity.

Miles effortlessly keeps pace beside me, his hands slipping into his pockets. "So, any reason why you're out here in the cold without a coat?"

I hesitate. I could make something up, but there's no real point in lying. "Sam brought a guy to the dorm, and, well… I didn't really want to stick around to hear things escalate."

He exhales a quiet laugh, looking up at the sky. "Oh."

For a while, we just walk. No words, just the quiet sound of our footsteps against the pavement.

But my mind is loud.

Miles graduated last year—that much, I know. So why is he here? *Does he have a girlfriend on campus?* The thought comes out of nowhere, and I hate that it latches onto me with claws, refusing to let go. I barely *know* him, so why does the idea of him being here for someone else feel like an itch I can't scratch?

I chew on my lip before curiosity gets the best of me.

"So, how come you're here this late? At a university you don't go to?" I ask, stealing a glance at him.

A soft chuckle escapes him, low and warm. "I just… I wanted to see someone."

I freeze for half a second before blurting the question that's already formed in my head. "Is that someone your girlfriend?"

The second the words leave my mouth, I regret *everything*.

His gaze flicks to mine, unreadable under the dim lighting. "No." Then, after a beat, his lips curl into a smirk. "Not yet."

My stomach flips.

I look away, ignoring the way my heart betrays me by racing at his words. "Did you… see them, then?" I ask, because hey, at this point, talking is better than silently combusting.

"Yeah." His voice is quieter now, but there's an unmistakable intensity in his gaze as he looks at me.

Something soft, something magnetic.

I nod slightly, pretending that my heart isn't currently playing hopscotch in my chest.

A moment passes. Then another.

"Well... I think I should go now." I force my voice to sound casual as I turn toward the building. "Bye, Miles."

"Bye, Mia." His voice is softer this time, almost reluctant.

I take a few steps, then glance back.

He's still standing there, hands in his pockets, watching me leave. There's something in his expression—something I can't quite place—that makes my stomach do another flip.

I quickly turn away and head inside.

It isn't until I reach my dorm and slide the key into the lock that I realize something—I'm still wearing his blazer. I should feel guilty for not returning it, but instead a hush falls over my senses, and my heart flutters wildly, and I can't help but smile, just a little.

I step inside my room, closing the door behind me, and do the weirdest thing I've ever done: hold the blazer up to my nose. It still smells like sandalwood and coffee. It smells like him.

I'm startled out of my haze by a voice.

"Enjoying yourself over there?"

I nearly jump out of my skin, spinning around to see Sam lounging on my bed, a wicked grin stretched across her face.

"Sam!" I squeak, clutching the blazer like I just got caught doing something illegal. "How long have you been sitting there?"

She raises an eyebrow. "Long enough to see you getting all dreamy over a blazer."

I sputter. "I was not—"

"Who's it from?"

"No one." My voice is *way* too high. "And thanks for informing me that you were bringing a *boy* in our dorm." I add.

"Oh, actually nothing happened." Sam replies.

"Oh, okay." I say, sitting down beside her on the bed. "So is he… uh…"

"Jake." she supplies.

I nod. "Is he still in your room?"

"No, he left a few minutes before you came back."

We sit in silence for a beat before Sam's eyes zero in on the blazer again. Suddenly, she squeals with surprise. "That's Miles's blazer!"

I look at her, shocked. "How do you know?" She grins wickedly. "It's embroidered on the inside. Small font, but it's there."

I flip the blazer over, and sure enough, there it is. Embroidered at the bottom in tiny letters. *Miles Baudelaire*.

"How do you have his blazer?"

"Um… I ran into him… or he ran into me. I don't know, but I was cold, so he gave me his blazer. That's it." I manage to answer Sam's question with a straight face.

"That's it!" Sam repeats sarcastically. "There's something going on between you two."

"No, there isn't. I barely know him. There's nothing going on. I swear." I say firmly.

"Whatever you say." Sam says, glaring at me for a minute before saying, "I have to go now."

"Wait, where are you going?"

"So there's this guy across campus who wants to talk to me about his problems. I am kinda his therapist." She explains.

"You just started first term. You don't even know the T of therapist yet." I state.

"Well I gotta start somewhere." She grins.

"wow." I mutter as she leaves.

The room is quiet now, and I'm trying to make some sense of my swirling feelings causing a hurricane in my brain. But Miles's face flashes in my mind—our brief eye contact at the stadium, him lending his blazer. His Sapphire eyes. His jaw, perfectly sculptured as if God personally took his time to design it.

Sam's right. There *is* something going on between us, but it's not physical or anything—it's undeniable, like the way the rain feels on your skin in the middle of a long, quiet drive.

I mean, maybe I have a crush on him. But I get crushes all the time, but they never feel like *this*. This is different. It's not just the usual butterflies; it's like my whole body is tuned into him. Maybe I'm reading too much into this, but that doesn't change the fact that whenever he is around, the air thickens, my heart beat escalates and I feel this invisible pull that I can't shake off.

I pick up my dear guitar and strum random chords, trying to make sense of the storm Miles Baudelaire just left inside me.

Miles

I watch Mia's silhouette disappear into the building. I stand still, my hands shoved deep into my pockets, feeling the crisp night air settling around me, but it barely registers. My mind is still caught in the conversation we'd just had—the way Mia looked up at me with those brown, curious eyes, and the embrace of her small frame under my blazer, the way she said my name, so delicately, with those lips.

I slowly exhale, running a hand through my messy hair, but my mind is too tangled up in her, and the way she asked me if I was here to see my girlfriend.

Is that someone your girlfriend?

I smirk at the memory, but it is laced with an unexpected frustration. The answer had been simple. *No.* But *not yet* slipped from my mouth without me acknowledging it. I wish she knew that *the someone* was her only.

The truth is, I came here to relax with Nate and Alex. We were just hanging out near the fountain, like toddlers on a playdate—but it was nice. I didn't come here hoping to see Mia, not exactly. But maybe a part of me did. And I did. It's the best way I could've ended the day.

The best way to store a new picture of her in my mind.

"Hey! Miles. Hello!" Sam's voice ring's out, breaking through my reverie. She is standing in front of me, waving her hand.

I blink, meeting her gaze.

"You good, or are you planning to stare at the building all night?" An amused smirk hangs on her lips.

"Hi! Sam."

"You know she's not going to just pop out of our dorm just because you're standing out here doing *absolutely* nothing." She ribs with a wide grin plastered on her face.

I frown. "Do you ever say things that actually make sense?"

Sam tilts her head, pretending to think. "No, I think I do," she counters, her pale blue eyes dancing with mischief. Then, as if suddenly remembering something important, she gestures at me. "And wipe that frown off your face. You look like a kicked puppy."

I roll my eyes, but before I can respond, she turns on her heel to leave.

"Off to collect another boy already, Sam?" I tease, crossing my arms.

"Oh, yes. Wanna join?" She throws a smirk over her shoulder, sarcasm dripping from her words.

I huff out a small chuckle as she walks away, her presence like a wild, untamed breeze—brief but unforgettable.

Nothing ever fazes Sam. Nothing ever weighs her down.

And maybe that's what I like about her the most.

CHAPTER 10

Audrey's hand sways over the surface of the wooden picnic table placed under a wise old tree. She absently folds it into a loose fist and says, "So, what did Chloe say?"

"Yes." I respond.

"So you're going on a date with her." Audrey repeats, as if confirming it for herself.

I nod.

"It'll be fine." she assures me, offering an encouraging smile.

Before I can reply, a voice drifts toward us from a short distance away. "I'll meet you at six."

I glance up just as Sam walks into view, her phone slipping into the pocket of her jeans. She plops down beside Audrey with a sigh.

Audrey watches her curiously. "Who were you talking to?"

"A boy from my lecture. It's for an assignment."

Audrey nods, casually humming, but then Sam's sharp gaze swings to me. "So, Miles, how's the date planning going?"

I narrow my eyes at Audrey. "You told her?"

"She overheard our call." Audrey admits, looking apologetic. "Sorry."

I exhale, rubbing the back of my neck, but Sam just waves a dismissive hand. "Serious question, though." She leans forward, propping her elbow on the table, her eyes assessing me. "Are you actually looking forward to this date, or are you just doing it because you *have* to?"

The wind stills.

The distant chatter of students, the occasional burst of laughter, the rhythmic rustling of leaves—all of it fades.

I part my lips to answer.

But then, I feel it.

A shift in the air, subtle yet undeniable.

I glance over my shoulder just as Mia approaches, a neatly wrapped sandwich in her hands. The breeze tugs at the loose strands of her dark hair, sunlight catching on the strands like spun silk.

She hesitates, scanning the table. The only empty seat left is the one beside me. Her eyes flick to mine, and for a fleeting moment, uncertainty passes through them.

I shift slightly to the side, making more room. It's barely anything, but after a beat, she finally sits down.

My pulse stutters.

I turn back to Sam, ready to answer. I was going to say I'm willing to give it a shot. That the date with Chloe makes sense, that it's a step forward.

But now?

With Mia sitting so close that I can feel the warmth of her presence, her scent—a faint trace of coffee and something soft—drifting into the air between us?

I don't know anymore.

So instead, I just say, "I don't know."

Sam, completely oblivious to the sudden tightness in my chest, just shrugs. "Okay."

The crinkle of sandwich paper starts a new gab. Audrey turns to Mia. "Do you have another sandwich by any chance?"

Mia shakes her head. "No, but I can break this in half."

And she does. They eat in easy companionship while the air around me feels anything but easy.

Sam suddenly turns back to me. "What are you still doing here on a Tuesday, anyway?"

I force a casual shrug. "No reason. I just needed a break."

Sam eyes me skeptically. "So you decided to take a break at an educational center?" She scoffs, shaking her head. "I guess, if you're not going to tell the truth, I will."

"What truth?" Audrey asks, her gaze darting between us.

I frown. "Yeah, what truth?"

Sam smirks, leaning in like she's about to spill some grand secret. "Your brother is double-dating. He must be here to see his campus girlfriend."

"What?" I say, baffled. "I don't have a campus girlfriend. And I'm not double-dating."

Audrey folds her arms. "Where did you hear that, Sam?"

"Okay, in my defence, she's a psychology student. She gets things out of people." a voice says rapidly.

Mia.

I glance at her, but she doesn't look at me.

"It's not her fault," Sam says smugly. "I *am* very good at breaking people. *Although*, I confess, I twisted the girlfriend part. I honestly think Miles might just be sleeping with her."

"What—" I nearly choke. "Everything you're saying is false."

Audrey looks to Mia, her expression puzzled. "Wait—why would you say something like that?"

Mia lifts her chin, her voice quick and defensive. "I didn't. He said it himself." She points at me.

"When did I—" I start, then suddenly stop.

Memories surge forward.

That night.

The night I saw Mia wandering through the cold.

The night she asked me why I was here, and I told her, *I'm here to see someone.*

God, if only she knew it was her.

The only reason I came here this early in the morning was because I *wanted* to see her. Because the break I needed wasn't from work, or life, or responsibility.

It was from the confusion she made me feel.

And the only way I felt I could understand it—was to see her again.

And now that I have, it feels like a crime.

I clearly have feelings for her.

But I can't confess them.

Not because I asked Chloe out.

Not because it's too late.

But because it's too *wrong.*

A rustling sound pulls me from my thoughts. I glance to my side. Mia shifts in her seat, her fingers toying with the edge of the sandwich wrapper. Her eyes remain fixed on the table, but there's a slight tension in the way she holds herself—like she can feel the weight of my gaze.

I drag a hand down my face and force myself to focus, only for Sam to stomp on my foot under the table.

I flinch. "What the hell?"

"You spaced out," she says, entirely unapologetic. "And I *hate* when people do that mid-conversation. So rude."

I scowl. "I didn't—"

"You did." Audrey grins, casually taking out her phone.

Mia doesn't say anything. But the corner of her mouth twitches. Almost like she's amused. Almost like she wants to smile.

It's enough to completely wreck me.

A slow ache blooms beneath my ribs, something warm curling in my stomach. I should look away. Instead, I commit it to memory. That almost-smile. That fleeting softness.

I barely register the conversation around me until Audrey suddenly gasps.

"What happened?" Mia asks.

She holds up her screen, eyes wide. "Listen to this."

The voice of a news reporter crackles through the tiny speaker:

"Breaking news—one of the world's most wanted criminals, the Blackout Master, has been spotted in New York City just after nine this morning. Authorities have initiated a city-wide patrol as they search for the suspect..."

A beat of silence follows.

Then—

"Wow," Sam exhales, her brows shooting up. "It's been, what, three years since we've heard from the Blackout Master?"

"Why are you saying it like he's an old friend of yours?" Mia intones.

"I'm not. It's just... interesting. I mean, the guy can shut down an entire city to break into a place. That takes insane power," Sam says. "It's almost like that thing Dumbledore gave Ron—the illum..."

We all wait, holding our breaths.

"Ah! The Deluminator."

She's not wrong.

The Blackout Master is more than just a thief—he's a force of nature. Cities, towns, have been plunged into darkness at his hands, his crimes executed with such precision that even the highest-level security systems are useless against him. And yet, despite his ability to take anything he wants, he never does.

He'll break into a high-security vault, a luxury store, a heavily guarded museum—only to walk away with one or two things. Never more. Never less.

It's as if his motive is something else entirely. Something beyond just stealing.

"I mean, it is interesting," Audrey admits. "But it's still wrong."

A strange hush settles over the table.

Then, softly—

"Wait."

Mia's voice is barely above a whisper, but it makes all of us turn toward her.

"He was spotted here," she says, her fingers tightening around her sandwich wrapper. "In New York."

"New York is his next target." Audrey states.

Sam throws her arms around herself. "We're going to die."

"We're not going to die." I say firmly. "He doesn't target civilians."

"But he did kill one in his last attack." Mia recounts.

The memory of the headlines flashes through my mind—*first confirmed civilian death linked to the Blackout Master.*

I meet Mia's gaze, unwavering. "The civilian got in his way. That's what the cops said."

She studies me for a moment. Then, quietly, "But a kill is still a kill."

The weight of her words lingers while Sam, seemingly lost in thought, murmurs, "Maybe that's why he went on hiatus for so long."

Audrey gapes. "So now you pity him?"

"No. That's not what I mean." Sam shakes her head. "He's been stealing for years, but he's never killed anyone before. And then that time... he had to. That might've messed with him."

I blink.

And despite myself, I realize—she might not be so wrong.

For all his infamy, for all the power he holds in the shadows, at the end of the day, the Blackout Master is still human. And if there's anything common about humans, it's that we all have breaking points.

"Maybe choosing Psychology as your major wasn't such a bad idea." I say, glancing at Sam.

Her face lights up. "Did Miles Baudelaire just compliment me?"

I roll my eyes, but before I can retort, a quiet shift in movement catches the corner of my eye.

Mia is smiling. Just slightly, just enough that if I blinked, I might miss it.

But I don't blink.

And it makes me feel great.

CHAPTER 11

Miles

The slow hum of a violin drifts through the restaurant, blending seamlessly with the faint melody of a piano. The atmosphere is rich—exclusive. Dim, golden chandeliers hang from the ceiling, casting a soft glow over the dark red walls, their color reminiscent of aged wine. The scent of expensive leather and freshly uncorked champagne lingers in the air, mingling with the delicate aroma of gourmet cuisine.

Waiters in crisp white uniforms move with practiced elegance, their black bowties neatly in place, their every step measured and precise. Conversations are hushed, spoken in refined tones, as if the very air of this place demands sophistication.

I barely notice any of it.

This dinner—it's nothing more than an arrangement. A conversation forced into existence by people who believe tradition holds more weight than desire.

Across from me, Chloe sits upright, her posture elegant and composed, just as she always is, but her emotions are veiled—like a suavely painted mask.

She's beautiful—blonde waves falling perfectly over her shoulders, green eyes steady as they meet mine. But as I stare at her, I don't feel the spark that should be there. There's no excitement, no pull in my chest that urges me forward. Instead, there's only an unshakable weight pressing against my ribs as if the universe itself is holding its breath, waiting for something that'll never come.

The candle on our table flickers between me and Chloe, its small flame dancing as though mocking the silence stretching between us. I lean back in my chair, exhaling slowly before speaking.

"Chloe, we can't get along with each other if we are forced." My voice is calm, controlled. "We can't build a relationship based on our parents' wishes. The whole night has been fun, but it simply seems... weird."

She doesn't react immediately. Instead, she swirls the deep red liquid in her glass, watching the way it moves before finally meeting my gaze.

"We don't really have a choice, Miles."

A choice.

A humorless chuckle threatens to escape me. "Yes, we do. We are not living in the eighteenth century." I try again, hoping to get through to her.

She exhales softly, her gaze dropping to the napkin she's twisting between her fingers. "I can't disappoint my parents." Her voice is quieter now, laced with something I can't quite decipher. Resignation, maybe. Or hope. "And maybe we'll grow to like each other. Give it some time."

Her lips curl into a small, reassuring smile, but I don't return it.

I should consider what she's saying. Maybe she's right. Maybe, with time, I'll grow to feel something more for her. Maybe the expectations placed upon us won't feel like shackles but rather something... inevitable.

But then, like a ghost haunting my thoughts, I see her.

Hair as black as ebony, cascading over her shoulders like a midnight waterfall. Eyes, deep and golden, swirling like aged whiskey under the dim glow of the morning sun. The slight furrow of her brows, the softness of her lips when she brightens up.

Mia shouldn't be here, not in my mind, not when I'm sitting across from the girl I'm supposed to be considering a future with. But she is. She always is. And suddenly, all the possibilities of liking

Chloe vanish into thin air, burned away by the fire Mia has set inside me.

I don't understand how a girl as innocent as Mia has consumed my mind like an illicit drug—illegal but addictive.

"Miles. Miles!"

Chloe's voice cuts through my thoughts, dragging me back to reality. My surroundings sharpen—the soft glow of the candle on our table, the waiter standing beside me, holding out a receipt.

"Mr. Baudelaire, the bill."

I nod, reaching for my wallet. The numbers on the receipt blur together, my mind elsewhere, but I hand over my card and sign without hesitation.

As the waiter leaves, I glance at Chloe and gesture for her to follow me out.

The evening air is crisp as we step outside, the city lights casting a golden glow on the pavement.

"Where did you get lost?" she asks, her voice light, almost teasing.

I keep my expression neutral. "Nowhere."

And as I open the car door, I realize something.

I might be standing here with Chloe.

But my heart?

It's already somewhere else.

"Pass me the T.V. remote." Nate tells Alex, his eyes glued to the screen.

"That's the AC remote." Nate adds, seeing Alex grab the wrong one.

"Oh! Here." Alex says, handing the right one, and the soft hum of the screen flickers to life, the dim glow illuminating the room as the crinkle of an In-N-Out bag fills my living room.

"How was the date with Chloe?" Nate asks, putting on a random movie. The bright, flickering images on the screen contrast the casual atmosphere in the room.

"It was fine." I say stoically. "We're going on a second date," I add.

"Why'd you say it so blandly? Like it's a bad thing." Nate says, teasing.

"It's not a bad thing," I reply, shrugging. "I mean, she's pretty, and ambitious, but I just... I don't like her like that. It feels forced."

"Yeah, cause you've got your eyes glued on Mia." Alex says, taking a bite of his burger, his voice light but knowing.

"What!" Nate exclaims, looking between us.

"That's not true, Alex." I say sharply, but there's something in my chest that pinches.

"Then why were you jealous at the game?" Alex presses, raising an eyebrow.

"I wasn't." I argue, but it sounds weak even to me.

Alex raises his eyebrow, his gaze piercing.

"It was momentary." I insist, more to myself than anyone.

"And you better keep it that way." Nate interjects gravely.

"Mia is not someone Lucien will approve of." he adds, concern in his voice.

"I know." I say, trying to hide my disappointment. The T.V. flickers with random scenes, but it feels like everything around me has faded.

I know my dad won't approve of Mia. That's why I'm trying to bury my feelings for her, but it's hard—close to impossible.

"Forget about that," Alex says, switching gears as the movie dims in the background, "and tell me what you guys are wearing to my party?"

"We're not kids to play dress-up, Alex." Nate barks.

"Did you not read the invite? It clearly states to dress up. It's a Halloween party, not an orgy. People are supposed to play dress-up." Alex retorts, his voice upbeat despite the argument.

"Then I haven't decided." Nate shrugs, eyes flicking between the screen and the conversation.

"What about you, Miles?" Alex asks, leaning forward, a mischievous grin on his face.

I shake my head, not caring much about costumes.

"Neither have I." Alex says, sipping his milkshake, the glass clinking lightly.

"Dude!" Nate and I say together, laughing at his attitude.

CHAPTER 12

Mia

Every house we pass is decked out with Halloween decorations—ghosts, skeletons and eerie lights casting shadows over the lawns. One house even has a witch hanging from the roof. But the best setup by far is at the house we're approaching: there's a figure of Max from *Stranger Things* floating in mid-air without any visible support. Whoever created that effect is an absolute genius.

"Here we are." Sam says as she pulls into a posh neighborhood in Bushwick in NYC where the Prescott abode is.

I stare, wide-eyed, as we step out of the car. "Whoa!!"

A few kids in costumes rush past us, running up to the house next door with their trick-or-treat bags. Watching them makes me smile, and for a second, my nerves settle.

This is my first party, and inside, I'm an absolute wreck. My heart pounds against my ribs, my fingers twitch at my sides, and every instinct is screaming at me to turn around and leave. But I don't. I can't.

Audrey picked this outfit for me—tight, short, and completely out of my comfort zone. The hem brushes against my thighs, leaving me feeling exposed, vulnerable. But it's fine. I'll be fine. I'M GOING TO HAVE FUN.

"Let's go." Audrey says, nudging me forward with a grin.

I can feel the low thud of music from inside as we walk up the path, people in all kinds of costumes milling around the front yard.

The house is practically glowing with the mix of orange and purple lights, casting everything in a spooky but magical glow. I take a deep breath, still feeling nervous, but a little thrill of excitement starts to mix in.

Inside, the party is even louder. Music pumps through the speakers, and people dance, laugh, and shout over each other. Halloween decorations cover every inch of the house—fake cobwebs, ominous candlelight, and creepy dolls set up in various corners.

I stick close to Audrey and Sam as we weave through the sea of costumes. A guy dressed as a zombie grins at me, his face covered in expertly smeared fake blood. I muster a polite, awkward smile before looking away.

We finally make it to the kitchen, where Nate stands by the counter, his easygoing smile lighting up as soon as he spots us.

"Hi!" Audrey greets him, pressing a quick kiss to his lips.

"Looking gorgeous," he murmurs, his eyes warm as they take her in.

Then his gaze flickers to me, amusement dancing in his eyes. His lips curve into a smirk. "You look fantastic..." he jokes, "...clown."

I narrow my eyes at him. "Yeah, totally. Big red nose, rainbow-colored hair. I even arrived in a tiny car with twenty other clowns. You got me."

Nate chuckles, clearly entertained, while Audrey rolls her eyes and nudges him. He raises his hands in mock surrender before holding out a red plastic cup toward me.

"Truce?" he offers. "It's just a drink."

I eye the cup warily. "No thanks. I don't drink."

Nate tilts his head. "Yeah, that's what every foreigner says when they first get here. But they always end up wasted."

"Well, trust me, I'm not one of them." I gently push the cup back toward him and swiftly change the subject. "So, what are you supposed to be?"

"Romeo," he replies easily.

Audrey raises a brow. "How'd you come up with that?"

"I didn't," Nate admits with a shrug. "I just put these clothes on, and people started calling me Romeo, so I'm rolling with it."

"Romeo." I repeat, nodding. Then something clicks, and I blink in realization. "Wait... this is kinda crazy, but... Audrey's *Fearless* Taylor, and you're Romeo. Like in *Love Story*—the Taylor Swift song. You know? Never mind." I trail off, suddenly feeling ridiculous.

"Oh my God!" Audrey exclaims, catching on. "Fearless *is* the album with *Love Story* on it! The song's literally about Romeo and Juliet." She turns to Nate, laughing. "What a coincidence!"

"So... you're a Swiftie." Nate grins at me.

I nod, grinning. "Guilty."

He chuckles, just as his gaze sweeps over the crowd. "Where's Sam?"

"She was right here a second ago." Audrey says, frowning as she looks around.

"There she is." I say, spotting Sam lounging by the couch in the living room, deep in conversation with some guy I don't recognize.

Audrey follows my gaze, raising an eyebrow. "Well, looks like she found someone to keep her busy."

Nate takes a sip from his drink. "She'll be off my back tonight. Thank God."

Before I can reply, I hear approaching footsteps, and suddenly, Alex and Miles appear beside us. But they're not alone.

There's a girl with them.

A girl whose arm is wrapped around *Miles's* arm.

A flicker of something sharp and unwelcome twists in my stomach. My gaze snaps to the girl, her face half-hidden behind a delicate mask, her posture effortlessly close to him.

My throat goes dry.

Who is she?

Why is she holding onto *his* arm like that?

Is she *the someone?*

The thought is unsettling in a way I don't want to examine too closely.

Miles

I've just arrived at Alex's party, scanning the room for him when I spot Nate, my sister, and... Mia, gathered in the kitchen.

She's wearing a ringmaster's costume—the deep red jacket, fitted at the waist, accentuating her figure in a way that makes it impossible to look away. Gold buttons glint under the dim party lights, adding just the right amount of flair. She's paired it with black shorts that show off her lower thighs and high, lace-up boots that only elevate the entire look. It's stunning. Confident. Undeniably sexy. And the subtle touch of eyeliner and red lipstick? It draws my gaze straight to her lips.

My thoughts begin to drift somewhere they shouldn't, so I rein them in, forcing my eyes away.

"It wasn't momentary, was it?"

Alex's voice jolts me back to reality. I blink at him, feigning ignorance. "What?"

He gives me a look, one eyebrow raised. "I'm not an idiot, Miles."

I shift uncomfortably, shrugging it off. "I don't know what you're talking about."

"Come on, man." His tone is laced with impatience. "You're not fooling anyone. The way you look at her says it all."

I don't respond. Because maybe he's right—maybe I've been fooling myself more than anyone else.

"Ask her out." Alex says casually.

I frown. "As if it's that easy. I'm already going out with Chloe."

"Forget about her." he shoots back.

I argue. "You know what my dad will think."

Alex shrugs. "Who cares what your dad thinks? If you like her, you like her. And if you feel like it's worth a shot then maybe it is.

It's as simple as that." He pauses before smirking. "Honestly, I'm surprised a smart guy like you hasn't figured this out yet."

He's not entirely wrong.

Navigating feelings is like stumbling through the dark with my eyes closed, but this much is clear—I feel nothing for Chloe. She's great, but nothing about her keeps me up at night. Nothing about her pulls me in. But Mia? She's magical. My heart has whispered her name since the first time I saw her. That has to mean something. That calls for action—maybe asking her out.

Though a part of me wonders if she'd reject me like she rejected Alex. But everyone knows Alex's reputation—no serious relationships. Maybe that's why she turned him down. Maybe she's looking for something real.

"I guess I can't ask her on dates anymore, can I?" Alex teases, catching my lingering gaze.

"No." I say flatly, my eyes still locked on her.

"I'm happy for you. But I'm damn sure she would've said yes to me today if I asked." He winks.

I smirk. "Not in that Slappy's costume. No one's going to wanna go out with you."

Alex sighs, all mock drama. "Says the buzzkill in a plain black shirt."

Before I can fire back, arms suddenly wrap around me.

"Miles!" a girl squeals, squeezing me. "I've been looking for you everywhere."

I break the hug, blinking in confusion. "Uh—sorry, who are you?"

She laughs, pulling off her mask.

"Oh! It's me."

It's Chloe.

I shouldn't be surprised—Alex invited her since we are technically dating now. I force a smile, masking my discomfort.

"Hi, Alex!" Chloe chirps, her voice carrying a slight slur. She slides her mask back on, swaying just a little as she scans the room.

The moment she spots someone, her face lights up. "Oh! I see your sister! Let's go say hi."

Before I can protest, she grabs my arm, dragging me along. I glance back at Alex, shooting him a desperate *help me* look. He only smirks, following us.

As we reach the group, Chloe waves enthusiastically. "Hi, Audrey! I'm Chloe."

"Hi." Audrey says, smiling politely.

"It's nice to finally meet you!" Chloe adds.

"Yeah." Audrey replies, a little awkwardly as she glances at Nate.

I tune out their pleasantries, my focus shifting elsewhere. Mia stands quietly, observing everything. She isn't forcing a smile or jumping into the conversation—just taking it all in. I wonder what's going through her mind.

Nate clears his throat. "Has anyone guessed what you're supposed to be? I mean you're so dressed up." He's looking at me now, his lips twitching.

And now he's laughing.

"Yeah, yeah. Make fun of my plain shirt. You should be honoured I even showed up." I reply dryly.

"We *are* honoured. Soo honoured." Alex smirks.

"You guys are cute!" Chloe chirps, cutting back in.

I'd almost forgotten she was still here.

Before I can say anything, she turns to me with a determined look. "And I hate to interrupt, but I'm going to steal Miles for a minute."

She doesn't wait for a response before dragging me away *again*.

This time, I feel an actual flicker of annoyance. I didn't want to leave. I wanted to stay close to Mia.

"Where are we going?" I ask, irritation creeping into my voice.

"To meet my girlfriends." she says cheerfully.

She pulls me into the piano room, where her friends are lounging on the couches, chatting and sipping drinks.

"Hey, ladies! This is Miles." She introduces me with a proud smile.

"Hi, Miles!" they greet in unison.

"Hello, everyone." I reply, keeping it polite.

One of them, dressed as Marilyn Monroe, stands up and extends a hand, flashing a confident smile. "Hi! I'm Zoe—Zoe Williams. And I just have to say, you're even more handsome in person."

I open my mouth to respond, but before I can, Chloe cuts in. "I *know*, right?" she gushes, looping her arm through mine.

The others start chiming in too—saying something, asking something—but I stop listening. I paste on a smile to make it seem like I am.

Seven minutes pass. Then, Nate appears at the doorway, looking like my personal saviour.

"Hello, ladies! If you don't mind, I'm stealing Miles." He grins.

"Sure." Zoe replies, flashing a playful smile.

As we step out, I sigh in relief. "I'm not a toy for you all to *steal*, you know."

Nate laughs, patting my back. "But I saved you, didn't I?"

I groan but follow him as we weave back toward the living room. Near the edge of the crowd, we both lean against the window.

Across the room, Audrey, Sam, and Mia have started dancing to the music with a few other partygoers.

But my focus is only on *her*.

Mia moves effortlessly, her body swaying to the music. No hesitation, no nervous glances—just the rhythm carrying her. I watch, utterly captivated—until I force myself to look away.

CHAPTER 13

Mia

"I'm gonna get a glass of water." I tell Sam.

Honestly, I'd be lying if I said I'm not having fun. At first, I had no idea what people even do at parties, but once Audrey, Sam and I hit the dance floor, I forgot about everything that had me so tense.

"Could you refill this? Please!" Sam asks, holding an empty red liquor cup.

"No. You've had enough to drink." I scold. "I'm gonna bring you water."

I reach the kitchen, but it's crowded—like, crowded-crowded. All the guys are clustered around the counter, refilling their cups at a beer pitcher. Unfortunately, that's exactly where I'd get water, too. I look around, trying to find another option, but then Alex steps in to help.

"Need something?" he asks.

"Yeah, just a glass of water." I reply.

"I'll get it. Wait here." he says, moving toward the most crowded part of the kitchen.

Five minutes later, he's back with a glass of water.

"That was quick." I say, smiling.

"I'm the host so." he replies, handing me the glass.

I raise an eyebrow. "You don't look drunk—which is rare around here. Everyone else is freakishly wasted."

"That's why I'm keeping my alcohol intake in check." he says with a grin.

"Smart. Good host move." I say appreciatively.

"Thanks!" he replies, flashing a smile.

"A while back, I was kind of afraid you'd ask me on a date again." I joke.

He chuckles. "I was considering it, but you're kinda off-limits now."

I frown, confused. "I'm off-limits? What?"

But he glances past me, his smile slipping. "I see someone I need to talk to. See you later." he says quickly before vanishing into the sea of partiers, leaving me in mild confusion.

What was that about?

I bring the glass to my lips and gulp it down in one go but the second the liquid hits my mouth I know something's wrong. There's a sharp, unfamiliar taste—not the clean, neutral taste of water. It's bitter, and the burn is instant, catching me off guard as it slides down my throat, leaving a trail of heat that makes me cough. I lower the glass, feeling the warmth spread fast, radiating from my stomach like fire moving through me.

What the—? My throat is stinging, and I feel my pulse start to pound. I glance down at the glass in shock, my mind racing as I try to make sense of it.

This is definitely not water.

What did Alex give me?

Did he pull a prank on me?

Before I can get angry at Alex for this stupid prank, my mind starts to go foggy, and the room begins to spin, and the music—it gets loud, louder than it was before, making my head ache. I close my eyes to stop the room from spinning and open a few minutes later. It works but the music is still loud, it feels like my eardrums are going to explode.

I glance around, desperate for an escape from the cacophony. My eyes land on a staircase in the corner of the room. I push myself away from the kitchen island, using it for support as I begin to make my way toward the staircase. My legs feel a bit unsteady, and I stumble slightly, catching myself just in time to maintain my balance.

With each step, I concentrate on putting one foot in front of the other as the alcohol makes me slightly dizzy from motion I try to ignore the thumping in my chest and the blaring music that seems to vibrate through my bones. I can do this. I just need to get to a quieter place.

Finally, I reach the stairs and start climbing slowly and carefully, gripping the railing as a support so I don't trip. I reach the second floor and spot a couch. I make my way over to it and sit down. I close my eyes for a few seconds, trying to calm myself. The music is still audible but muffled, and this floor is much quieter than downstairs, which helps. When I open my eyes, I feel a little more relaxed; there are no flashing lights here, just a plain yellow glow softly lighting the room.

Just when I think I'm back in control, a wave of heat rushes through my body, and I feel the need to cool down. I get up to look for a bathroom, hoping that washing my face with cold water will help.

I enter a hallway and open the door to my right, but it turns out to be a storage closet, so I open the door to my left hoping it to be the bathroom.

But as I push it open, my heart skips. There, in the bright yellow light, is Miles and the girl he came with. She had introduced herself earlier; I just don't remember it, maybe because of the alcohol in my system.

Her hand is on his chest, and the sight makes my breath hitch. A sudden heat rises in me, and before I can stop myself, I blurt out, "Oops! Sorry to interrupt."

"I opened the wrong door. Continue, I'm just… gonna go." I mumble, slurring slightly as I shut the door behind me.

Did I just say continue? What the fuck?

The alcohol is taking control, I need to get out of here before I do or say something that'll embarrass the shit out of me. I need to get out of this house.

I hurry down the stairs, this time faster, threading through the crowd in the living room before slipping out the front door into the calm night air.

Miles

I push open the doors to Alex's room. He asked me to bring his phone, so that's what I'm doing.

I instinctively move toward his nightstand, but it's not there—just a family picture of Alex and his mom. I scan the room and spot the phone on top of his dresser. I grab it, but just as I do, Chloe steps into the room and closes the door behind her.

"What are you doing here?" I ask.

"I was looking for you." she says, stepping toward me.

"I was kinda hoping to spend the evening with you, but your friends pulled you away." she murmurs drunkenly, placing a hand on my chest.

Before I can pull away, the door swings open. I freeze.

Mia stands there.

Her expression shifts as she takes in the scene, and my stomach drops—she must think the worst of this.

She hesitates, then blurts, "Oops! Sorry to interrupt."

"I opened the wrong door. Continue, I'm just… gonna go." she mumbles, her words slightly slurred as she steps back and closes the door.

She sounds drunk—really drunk. A while ago, on the dance floor, she didn't seem wasted or even holding a drink like everyone else. So how did she get drunk so quickly?

Anxiety tightens in my chest. I remove Chloe's hand from me and push past her without another word.

"What the fuck? MILES?" she calls after me, but I don't stop.

When I step into the hallway, Mia is nowhere to be seen. She must've headed downstairs. I push through the crowded rooms, scanning for her. Then I finally spot her slipping out the front door.

I weave through the crowd and step outside. She's standing a few feet away on the lawn, her eyes shut tight, lost in thought.

I don't even know why I ran after her. Was I escaping Chloe or chasing Mia? Why do I feel like I owe her an explanation? But I also can't ignore the fact that I like her. And I've finally made peace with it.

"Oh, hi!" Mia says suddenly, snapping me from my thoughts.

"You guys are done fast." She slaps a hand over her mouth as soon as the words slip out. "Oops. Sorry."

"It's not what you think it is." I say, a note of panic slipping into my tone.

"I don't want the gory details." Her expression hardens.

"I just went to grab Alex's phone, and Chloe walked in, and—"

She cuts me off.

"You don't owe me any explanation." She looks away, then mutters under her breath, "her name is chloe, hmm."

"What are you doing out here?" I ask, shifting the conversation to safer ground.

"It was too loud in there. Too much light, it was hurting my head." She rubs her temple.

"What did you drink exactly?" I question.

"I don't know." She lets out a frustrated sigh.

Then suddenly, she blurts out, "Your best friend... Alex—pulled a prank on me by handing me a cup of alcohol instead of water." Her voice is sharp with anger.

That doesn't sound like Alex. It must've been someone else. The urge to storm back inside and find the asshole responsible flares in me, but I can't leave Mia alone like this.

Her mood is shifting rapidly; whatever she was given was strong.

"That son of a bitch is gonna get punched tomorrow. Right in the face." she mutters, making a fist.

It's the first time I've ever heard her curse.

"As much as I'd love to see that, Mia, I don't think it was Alex." I say, trying to calm her.

"OH, sure, it wasn't him. Maybe it was the Halloween spirit handing out drinks, right?" she says, sarcasm and anger mixing in her voice. "It *was* him. I'm not blind. He handed me the cup." She barks, her face two centimetres away from mine.

If she says Alex handed her the drink, then he must have been out of his mind. But I can handle that later. Right now, I need to get her home.

"Let's get you home."

"I can't. I can't drive, and I don't even have a car to drive. I don't know the subway system either because your sister, she spoiled me by taking me everywhere in her car." Her words come out in a rush, her tone slightly calmer but still frazzled.

"Well, you're not driving or taking the train because you're wasted." I say.

She sighs dramatically, her shoulders slumping. "I know. And I hate it." She kicks at a pebble, sending it skittering across the driveway, and almost losing her balance, but I catch her elbow before she stumbles, steadying her.

"Let's go." I say, my hand gently sliding to her waist for support.

"What?" she exclaims, pulling back a little. "But... you're also drunk." she accuses, squinting her eyes at me suspiciously.

"I had one drink." I tell her, already moving to open the front passenger door.

"NO!!" She declares, shaking her head firmly and planting her feet on the ground like a stubborn child.

I blink at her. "You'll have to sit inside."

She blinks.

Then lets out a dramatic sigh.

"I'll sit in the back then." She mutters firmly after a struggling pause.

With a sigh of my own, I open the back door, and she slides in, settling herself with a satisfied look with her arms folded and her legs crossed.

I can't help but smile at her adorable whimsy as I close the door behind her.

"Why did you want to sit in the back?" I ask, curious as I pull out of Alex's driveway.

She hesitates, then says quietly, "Because... if my parents had been sitting in the back, they'd still be alive."

I catch a hint of the look in her eyes as the light from the streetlamps passes by—pain.

I grip the steering wheel tighter, her words hitting me like a slap. I didn't know that. I knew her parents were gone, but I didn't know the reason. For a second I don't know what to say.

"I'm sorry." I finally manage to speak, though a *sorry* doesn't cover enough.

She shrugs, her voice flat, "Yeah, everyone's always sorry."

The car falls silent except for the sound of the tires on the road. I don't push her to say more, and she doesn't offer anything else. I just drive. I take her to my place because it's closer than Colombia.

As I pull up in my driveway twenty minutes later, I sneak a look at her in the rearview mirror, expecting her to be asleep. But she's awake—still a little drowsy, but awake.

"Where are we?" She asks as I get out the car.

"My place." I answer, opening her door.

"Why?" She retorts, not moving from her place.

"Because my place was closer." She still doesn't move. "And Audrey or Sam wouldn't be at Colombia to look after you if you do something stupid."

"They're also drunk." She points, eyebrows raised.

She stays put, arms crossed, staring me down like a stubborn kid refusing to eat their vegetables. It's clear she's not getting out on her own. I take a deep breath, steeling myself, "So this is how it's gonna be." I say.

I scoop her up before she can argue, cradling her against my chest.

"Noo!!!" She yelps, squirming like a cat. "I'll walk. I'll walk. Put me down." She shouts.

"Fine." I say, setting her down gently.

She straightens her outfit with exaggerated dignity, lifting her chin like she didn't just fight me like her life depended on it. Her cheeks are flushed, a mix of frustration and embarrassment.

With determined steps, she marches forward, head held high—well, wobbly forward.

"You're going the wrong way." I say, barely suppressing a chuckle.

She freezes mid-step. Her back stiffens, and for a second, I swear she considers just owning the mistake and walking straight into the abyss. But then, with a dramatic huff, she spins around, narrowing her eyes at me.

"Then lead the way mister."

I smirk, motioning for her to follow me. And as she does, a thought crosses my mind—

Drunk Mia is something else.

CHAPTER 14

Miles

I walk into the café, the warm scent of coffee and fresh pastries greeting me. The low hum of conversation and the soft clink of dishes create a cozy, familiar atmosphere. My eyes scan the tables, finally locking onto Chloe, who's seated near the window, bathed in the soft afternoon sunlight filtering through the glass.

I make my way over, pulling out the chair opposite her and sitting down.

"Hello, Miles!" she says, setting her phone down with a soft smile, the light dancing in her emerald green eyes.

Before I can greet her back, the waiter arrives with a glass of water, setting it down on the table with a quiet *clink*. He stands there, waiting expectantly.

"Sir, anything for you?" he asks politely, his voice smooth and routine.

I glance at the menu for a moment before replying, "No, I'm fine."

The waiter nods and leaves. Chloe's expression shifts slightly, her gaze sharpening with a hint of seriousness.

"I'm going to get straight to the point." she says, her tone soft but firm.

"Do you like her?" she asks, her voice almost a whisper as she locks eyes with me, her eyes searching, waiting for the truth.

I knew she would ask me something like this when she texted me to meet up. The way I went after Mia the other night at the party had made it obvious, even if I wasn't ready to admit it yet.

I stay quiet, running a hand through my hair, fingers brushing the strands nervously. My thoughts race, and I contemplate what to say, the weight of the question pressing on me.

Chloe lets out a small, soft laugh—somewhere between a chuckle and a smirk. The sound is bittersweet. "Remember during our date when you said, *we can't get along with each other if we are forced*. Well, for me, it's not business anymore. I actually like you. But if you don't feel the same, just tell me so I can move on. I don't wanna chase an invisible hope, Miles. I don't want to be stuck in a one-sided love story; I'll get out of the way for the betterment of both of us. Just be honest."

The sound of the coffee machine whirring in the background almost drowns out her words, but I catch every syllable. The world feels suddenly distant, like everything is happening around me but not to me.

"Do you like her?" Chloe repeats after a pause, her voice steady but laced with an underlying vulnerability.

She already knows the answer. She just needs to hear it from me.

I take a deep breath, my chest tightening as I quietly respond, "Yes."

Chloe's face doesn't change immediately, but the way she gulps down her water—the glass clinking against the table—says more than words could. Her eyes flicker with a mix of hurt and resignation as she stands to leave.

"I'm sorry." I say, the words tasting bitter in my mouth as I watch her gather herself, putting on a brave smile.

"It's okay, Miles. You made it quite clear from the start, so I kinda knew what to expect. I'll move on soon enough." she says softly, her voice calm but tinged with sadness. "Bye."

And then she leaves, the door chimes softly as it closes behind her, leaving me in the quiet aftermath.

I sit there for a moment, staring at the wall in front of me. The room around me feels distant now, the buzz of conversation muted, the clatter of dishes fading into the background. I don't feel empty, but I don't feel entirely whole either. Instead, there's a strange sense of clarity settling in, like a fog lifting from my mind.

I feel remorse for hurting Chloe. She didn't deserve this. But somehow, having this conversation with her, even though it was painful, makes me feel free in a way I didn't expect—free from chains I didn't even know I was tied to. I feel a jarring clarity about what to do now, like a truth I couldn't pinpoint before.

I have feelings for Mia. I most certainly do. And no one can stop me from feeling that. Not even my dad.

CHAPTER 15

Mia

It's a dark freeway in middle of nowhere.
The sky is the colour of ash, starless and heavy.
Two cars crash into each other.
The first car belongs to my parents and...

I'm the one driving the second car.

...

I'm...

I'm... I am the drunk driver.

I jolt awake, breathing heavily, my chest heaving as my heart pounds like a drum, the remnants of the nightmare still clinging to me like a second skin. Wrapping the blanket tightly around myself, I struggle to process what I'd just dreamed.

I've had this dream plenty of times but I've always been the bystander, watching the scene unfold like a horror movie—don't want to watch it but can't escape it. But this time, it was different. This time, I was the one behind the wheel. I was the one steering the truck which slammed into my parent's car like it was made of paper.

A teardrop escapes, sliding down my cheek as I cry silently, careful not to wake Sam.

The campus around me is silent, but the windows of the dorms glow with fragments of life. Shadows flicker behind the glass—people laughing, studying, existing. But out here, in the dim-lit hush of the night, the weight of my own reality presses down on me.

I walk along the pavement, my arms wrapped tightly around myself—not for warmth, but for something to hold onto. Something to keep me from not breaking. My chest feels too tight, like I've been breathing wrong all night.

I have done something bad.

The ghost of liquor lingers on my tongue, burning at the back of my throat, a cruel reminder of my mistake. I can still feel the warmth of it slithering down, blurring the lines between right and wrong. That night, it hadn't mattered. It had numbed me, loosened my limbs, and softened the jagged edges of my thoughts. But now? Now it clings to me, venom seeping into my mind, poisoning me with guilt.

And then there was the dream.

A cold shiver crawls up my spine. No. I don't want to think about it. I don't want to remember gripping that wheel, the reflection of my own panicked eyes in the rearview mirror. I wasn't the driver. I wasn't. I can't be.

The pavement crunches under my boots as I walk faster, trying to outrun the thoughts reaching for me. But then, a shadow falls into step beside me.

I stiffen.

It takes me a second to recognize him, but when I do, my stomach twists. Alex.

I pick up my pace.

Alex sighs, but he doesn't fall behind. He matches my speed effortlessly. "Mia, can we—"

"Go away." I say, my voice hollow.

"Mia, come on."

I don't stop. I don't want to speak to him. I don't want to see him. I don't want to hear whatever he has to say.

"Mia, just—wait."

His hand brushes my shoulder.

I react instantly.

I spin around so fast that my heel scrapes against the pavement, my breath ragged, anger curling in my chest like a storm. "What?!" I snap, my voice slicing through the still night air.

Alex immediately leans back, hands half-raised, as if bracing for impact. His posture flickers with something I can't quite name—uncertainty, regret. But that isn't what catches me off guard.

It's the hockey helmet on his head.

I blink, thrown. "Why the hell are you wearing that?"

He hesitates before shrugging, his lips twitching like he's trying not to smile. "So you wouldn't punch me."

For a split second, I almost laugh. Not because it's funny, but because it's so stupid. But instead, I turn away, shaking my head.

"Please, wait." Alex steps in front of me, blocking my path. His voice is different this time. A little more serious. "Just hear me out."

I inhale sharply and fold my arms, locking my emotions behind a wall. Alex takes it as permission to speak. "Sam told me what happened."

My stomach turns. "And what is that exactly?" I bite out.

"She told me why you don't drink." His voice is quieter now, heavy. "And then I felt—guilty. I—I didn't know, Mia. I thought I was giving you water. But I had two cups with me. So I handed you the vodka one. It was a mistake. I didn't mean to—"

My eyes widen. "You gave me vodka."

He swallows. "Yeah. I—" He exhales sharply, lifts a hand to run it through his hair, then stops when his fingers hit the helmet. A flicker of irritation crosses his face, but then he lets his arm drop. "I thought you'd be fine, but then Sam told me today, and I—" His voice drops. "I felt like I should die."

I stare at him, my body rigid. He looks sorry. I think. The dim lighting makes it hard to tell. And the stupid helmet isn't helping. But my fury doesn't care if he's sorry. My voice turns sharp. "Maybe you should die."

The words slip out before I can stop them. The second they do, regret jams my heart.

Alex's breath catches. "If I die," he says, voice quiet, "will you forgive me?"

"No." The word rushes out of me. "I didn't mean it. Don't die."

His shoulders relax slightly. "Thank God." Then, more confidently, he says, "Then, this is what I'll do. I'll stop drinking alcohol. Forever."

"Forever?" I blink.

"Okay, three months," he amends, offering me an awkward, cautious smile. "Am I forgiven?"

Two students pass by, glancing at Alex's helmet with raised eyebrows but I barely notice them.

I think about it.

Alex made a mistake. It wasn't a prank. It wasn't intentional. It was just a mistake. Humans make mistakes. And it's Alex we're talking about. He's obviously going to make more mistakes.

But is he forgiven? Because he brushed against a part of me that was raw and vulnerable. Because he made me feel guilty for something I wasn't responsible for.

"Okay, you know what?" Alex says suddenly, his voice quieter, rougher. He looks almost... ashamed. "You can punch me. If that's what it takes."

I scrunch up my face. "What?"

He slowly takes off his helmet and lets it drop onto the pavement. The soft thud echoes in the quiet night. He rubs his hands over his face, then tilts his head back to look at the sky, exhaling. "Goodbye, pretty face."

Then he looks at me. "I'm ready." And closes his eyes shut.

I stare at him.

There he is, standing in front of me, giving me permission to wreck him. To destroy his face if it'll make *me* feel better.

But the only thing I want to do... is hug him.

I step forward and wrap my arms around him. Not in a romantic way. Just as a friend. Because I've heard so many times that a hug fixes everything. I want to see if it's true.

I feel Alex tense, his body going rigid with shock. But after a second, he relaxes and his arms come around me. His hold is warm. Solid. "I like this punishment." he murmurs against my hair.

I let out a soft, tired laugh, pressing my face against his shoulder.

Maybe a hug doesn't fix everything.

But right now, it's enough.

So I forgive him.

CHAPTER 16

Mia

"Submit the assignment by next Wednesday." Professor Kessler announces, dismissing the class.

I exhale, stretching my fingers before sliding my notes into my bag. As I reach for the zipper, a voice speaks up behind me.

"You look like you've got this whole diligent student thing down."

I glance over my shoulder and find a boy with short, tousled brown hair and warm brown eyes, his expression lined with amusement.

"Maverick Parker." he introduces himself, extending a hand.

I hesitate for half a second before shaking it. "Mia Malhotra."

"Indian-American?" he asks, tilting his head curiously.

"Nope. Born and raised in India." I let go of his hand and sling my bag over my shoulder.

"Interesting." He falls into step beside me as I walk toward the door. "So, how's America treating you?"

I shrug. "It's... fine." The words come out more indifferent than I mean them to.

"Fine?" Maverick clutches his chest like I've mortally wounded him. "Wow. Way to humble an entire country."

His exaggerated reaction catches me off guard, and a small laugh escapes before I can stop it.

Maverick grins. "There we go! Progress. Stick with me, Mia—I'll make sure your American experience upgrades from fine to amazing."

I roll my eyes but can't help the small smile that tugs at my lips.

As we step outside, he slows his pace. "Well, it was nice meeting you. See you around?"

"Yeah, see you around." I reply.

Maverick flashes one last smirk before peeling off to join a group of people, leaving me to continue toward the food truck. The cobbled path crunches beneath my feet, a light breeze rustling the leaves of nearby trees, their branches casting dappled shadows on the ground.

But then, a familiar scent of sandalwood and coffee, with a hint of lavender, drifts toward me. I glance to my side, and there he is—Miles, walking beside me.

"Hello, Miles." I address, my tone light.

"*Bonjour!*" He replies, his mood relaxed.

"Are you attending Colombia again?" I ask mockingly.

"No." he simply replies.

"Then what are you doing here? Don't you have a company to run?" I prod, my tone still teasing.

"I have people for that." He replies, unfazed by my mocking questions. "You seem pretty affected by me being here." he adds, a hint of polite mockery in his tone.

"I'm not affected." I shoot back, though my defence is weak. "Just curious why you keep showing up here for no reason."

"I'm here to see that girl." he says, digging his hands in his hoodie's pockets.

"Oooh, Miles Baudelaire is love struck." I tease, nudging him lightly.

"He actually is." he responds softly, his sincerity catching me off guard.

"Lucky girl... whoever she is." I say, my playful mocking replaced by a genuine tone.

"Yeah, lucky Mia." He says, stopping me in my tracks.

Did he just utter my name? No, it can't be. There are plenty of girls named Mia out there. It doesn't have to be *me*.

But despite my attempts at logic, my heart betrays me, pounding rapidly, threatening to explode.

I turn to Miles, my expressions a mix of shock and disbelief, while he stares back at me with a cool, calm, collected look—as if he just hadn't upended my entire world.

"Did you slip and hit your head somewhere this morning?" I ask, my tone a little too loud, but not that loud to draw any attention.

"No, I'm perfectly fine." He replies, his tone annoyingly steady.

"No, you're not because you don't know what you are talking about." I say, turning on my heels and heading towards the food truck cause now I really need that coffee—maybe even a double espresso.

He continues to follow me, saying, "Would you go on a date with me?"

I skid to a stop, feeling the telltale heat creep up my face.

"You already have a girlfriend—Chloe." I remind him after a shocking pause, but he responds right away with a subtle shake of his head. "She was never my girlfriend."

He stares at me, his Sapphire eyes sparkling like the ocean under the late morning sunlight as a small smile tugs at his lips, waiting for a response.

"I'm going to give you the same answer I gave Alex. NO!" I reply, holding my tone steady, ensuring my words carry weight.

"Now don't follow me." I warn, not letting him respond as I promptly walk away towards the food truck so I don't give in by looking at his smug smile and that gorgeous face.

I have this impulsive thought to glance back and look at him but I control it, instead I straightaway call Nidhi when I am at a distance from him.

"Ni, you have no idea what just happened." I gush out.

"Talk fast. I have a class in five minutes." She mentions. "And it better not be anything related to your studies." She warns over the phone.

"Wait, isn't it night time there? What class do you have?" I ask, glancing at the Indian clock on my phone.

"It's an art thing. Now spill." she replies, brushing off my question.

"Okay, so Miles just asked me on a date." I blurt out, my heart racing as I replay the moment which happened moments ago in my head.

"What!! The blazer boy." She exclaims.

"Mmhm!" I reconfirm.

I reach the food truck which is packed with students. The ordering counter has a queue formed. I stand last in the line as Nidhi speaks through the phone. "Did you say yes? Please say you said yes."

"I said no." I reply, taking my phone away from my ear as Nidhi screams, "Miaa...!"

"Have you lost it?" She scolds. Maybe calling her was a wrong idea. "You rejected that... that French charm."

"You also rejected that other dude TWICE." She continues.

Why do I tell her things? *Because she's my best friend and at the end of the day she's helped me pick up my mess.*

"Ok, Alex is a flirtious guy. He would've left me stranded for some prettier girl. Might I add in middle of the date. Have you looked into his dating history. Oh wait, there is no dating history cause he doesn't stick around." I shoot back in defence.

"Ok, that point taken." She replies.

"You should go to your lecture, five minutes are up." I remind her.

"I'll go in late, tell me one thing, did you wanna say yes... to Miles?" She probes, her tone a little soft now.

I hesitate before replying in regret, "Yesss!"

"Then why'd you say no?" she drawls.

"I was caught by surprise." I answer. I reach the end of the line and order a double espresso as Nidhi speaks into my ear, "Can't you go back and tell him your actually answer?"

"Then that's humiliating." I reply. A scene of Miles embarrassing me in front of the campus as the students laugh flashes my mind. I quickly shake it off.

The vendor hands me my coffee as I say to Nidhi, "Go join your class now. You don't wanna be too late."

"Okay, bye stupid." She says, hanging up the call.

I take a seat at an empty table, set under a large tree, offering amble shade as the cool, dappled light filters through the leaves. I fixate on the empty land where Miles asked me out a while ago, and I can't help but replay the moment in my mind as I take a sip of my steaming hot coffee.

I think about all the reasons why saying "No" felt like the right choice. I'm not here to date—I'm here to learn, to stand on my own two feet. If I had agreed, if the date had gone well, it would've most definitely led to a kiss, and maybe more. And I know myself well enough: I would've backed out before anything happened, just like always, and people would've called me pathetic. I don't want that.

But... what if I'd liked the kiss? What if I'd enjoyed the things that came after? What if I could've found the kind of love my mom and dad had for each other? Wouldn't that have been nice? To have someone by my side in this big, lonely world?

This is what I do—I tear down opportunities, destroy the good things life sends my way. I answer quickly, without thinking it through, driven by my insecurities, my fears, and my past experiences. And I do it over and over again.

"Professor Maybell gave a ton of homework today." Sam complains, as we climb the stairs to our dorm after a long day.

"Same here." I reply, exhausted.

Reaching our dorm door, I fumble through my bag for the key while Sam pauses, noticing something. She bends down and picks up a bright yellow gift bag left on the doorstep.

"Did you order something?" I ask, still digging through my bag.

"Nope." she answers, looking at the bag with curiosity.

I finally unlock the door, pushing it open, and we step inside. I drop my bag and plop down on the couch, while Sam starts to open the gift bag and takes out a delicate bouquet of white lilies, their soft fragrance already filling the air.

"There's a note." Sam says, holding it up. I lean forward as she reads aloud:

"Think it over and then text me on this number."

"Think what over? There's not even a sender's name." she says.

I take the lilies from her hand and inhale their scent, a soft smile forming on my lips. I know exactly who these are from—and to whom. Sam notices my smile and, with a knowing smirk, asks, "Mia, what are you not telling me?"

My smile widens, my cheeks tinge with colour as my heart flutters. This is something every girl dreams of—receiving flowers from a boy just to make her smile. I might be getting ahead of myself, but Miles leaving flowers for me, even after I turned him down and teased him, albeit playfully, is a gesture I never imagined I'd receive from him, or from any boy.

I don't know what happened to Miles that made him wake up this morning and decide to ask me out, and maybe I don't even want to know. But in this moment, I know exactly what I'm going to do. I pull my phone from my back pocket and text the number on the note: "*Yes.*"

I throw my phone across the couch and close my eyes, my pulse thumping. This is definitely way out of my comfort zone.

Sam picks up my phone, noticing I haven't responded to her question. She sees the message and asks, "What yes?"

"I said yes to a date." I reply in almost a whisper, opening my eyes.

"To Alex?"

I shake my head. "To Miles."

She gasps, slapping her hand on her mouth. "I knew there was something going on between you two. Holy shit!"

"There was nothing going on between us before. He asked me out today." I say truthfully.

"Same thing." she says, flopping down on the couch beside me. "I wonder what you said to him when you were drunk that made him ask you out." She teases, a mischievous grin on her face.

But then a tear slips from my eye, and Sam notices. "Wait, are you crying?"

"I'm not crying, I'm just scared." I reply, wiping the tear away.

"Scared of going on a date?" she asks, teasing me gently.

I nod. "I don't know what to wear, what to do, what to say. I'm a mess."

"Aww! Don't worry. These are just first date jitters." she says, comforting me.

"I'm having a lot of firsts since I've come here."

"Yeah, and soon you'll have your first kiss, and then soon you'll lose—"

"Sam, don't say it." I warn, playfully hitting her with a pillow.

Just then, our dorm door bursts open as Audrey barges in, practically out of breath.

"Okay, what's with the dramatics?" Sam asks.

Audrey ignores her. "Let's go eat. I'm starving."

I frown. "That's what you were running in here for?"

"Yes. Food is the priority." she says as if it's obvious.

We head to the cafeteria and grab our dinner. Nate and Alex join us, abandoning their friends, but I barely register their presence when my phone pings. I pull it out, curious, and see a message from Miles:

Miles: *I'll pick you up at seven, this Saturday :)*

A big smile forms on my lips unexpectedly.

"What are you so cherry about?" Audrey asks, narrowing her eyes suspiciously as Sam peeks at my phone.

"Oh…" I start, but Sam jumps in, cutting me off. "Miles asked her on a date."

"*WHAT?!*" Audrey shrieks, slamming her hand on the table. "I cannot believe it."

I glance over at Alex and Nate, whose faces are suddenly locked in some kind of silent, intense telepathic conversation. Their eyebrows are practically doing a dance routine.

Sam catches on immediately. "Anything you two want to share with the rest of the class?" she asks, her tone sharp as she points her fork at them.

"Uh, actually…" Nate says, his voice a bit too loud, "we, uh, just remembered—we've got somewhere to be. Like, right now." He nudges Alex, who nods rapidly, already halfway out of his seat.

"Bye, Aud!" Nate says, planting a quick kiss on Audrey's cheek before bolting, dragging Alex with him.

Audrey watches them go, her mouth hanging open. "That was… weird."

"When were they not weird?" Sam says, stabbing the fork she pointed at them into her salad.

As we continue eating, I chew over my decision. Now that I've had time to think about it, I'm not so sure about saying yes to Miles. What if it's some kind of prank? I've seen this in movies—guys play Truth or Dare, Spin the Bottle, or something, and they get dared to ask a girl out, take her on a date, and then tell her it was all a joke. What if this time, that girl is me?

But… Miles wouldn't do something like that. I don't know him well, but he just doesn't *seem* like that kind of guy. But still…?

"Hey, come back." Audrey says, waving her hand in front of my face.

"Mmmh!" I snap out of it.

"You spaced out." she says. "What happened?"

"I'm kinda second-guessing saying yes." I admit.

"Why? Because it feels weird? Trust me, it's not weird. That's how first dates work." Audrey says.

"But what if it's a prank?"

"My brother wouldn't do something like that." she reassures me. "That's Sam's department."

"Hey!" Sam exclaims.

"I'm still nervous." I say.

"Well, duh. It's your first date. It would be weird if you *weren't* nervous." Sam points out.

That makes me feel a little better.

Miles

"Hey, Nate." I greet, putting my phone on speaker as I continue working on my laptop from the couch in my living room. "Dude, have you *lost* it?!" Nate's voice explodes through the speaker.

Right to the point.

"Nate, I'm missing the context," I reply, frowning.

"You asked Mia out?"

"So what?" I set my laptop aside, already bracing for the argument.

"So *what?!* You *know* Lucien will kill you—and *her*—if he finds out."

His words hang in the air like a warning.

"Nate, stop overreacting." I sigh, folding my legs on the couch.

"I'm *not* overreacting. And you can't date Chloe and Mia at the same time. That's *cheating*."

"I'm *not* dating Chloe anymore." I say, realizing they have no idea about the conversation I had with her. "We called it off."

"What?! And you didn't think to *tell* us?" Nate exclaims.

"It just happened, like... two days ago," I explain. "We met at a café and ended things for good. Not that we were ever *officially* together."

"Really?!" Alex's voice chimes in, excitement lacing his tone. I didn't even know he was with Nate.

"But why Mia?" Nate presses. "I mean, I hold nothing against her—she's smart, kind, and pretty—but she's far from Lucien's standards."

"Nate! I don't care about his stupid standards anymore. And he doesn't have to know—not yet." My tone is firm, but I hope it's reassuring.

Silence lingers for a moment. Then, in a quieter voice, almost like I'm admitting it to myself, I say, "I *like* her, Nate."

"But—" Nate starts, only for Alex to cut in. "Dude, think about it. Has Miles ever—and I *really* mean *ever*—asked a girl out willingly? It's always been a one-night stand." Alex's voice is filled with amusement. "He's *in love*."

"Whoa, let's not go *that* far." I interject, though I can't help but smile.

"Fine." Nate warns, "But, Miles, this does come with risks. Big risks."

"I know. And I'm ready to take them."

And the risks begin *this Saturday*.

The date is this Saturday. I still can't believe she said *yes*. I knew the lilies would work, but I wish I'd been there to see her face when she received them. To see her lips curve into that soft, hesitant smile she does when she's happy or nervous.

Chloe made it clear to my father that she wasn't interested in me. That alone was enough to set him off. He was furious—but at least now, he's off my back. *For now.*

And he doesn't have to know about Mia. Not yet.

I want to see where this goes. I want to know *what she feels about me*. Then, and only then, will I decide how to deal with *him*.

CHAPTER 17

Miles

I stand in front of Mia's dorm, clad in a blazer—black, sharp and perfectly fitted—the top two buttons of my crisp white shirt loosened to add a leaner and easing touch to my otherwise polished look. In my hand is a bouquet of lilies, their soft redolence enchanting the air around me. I glance at my watch, its silver face catching the hint of the dim hallway lights, and knock on the door as soon as the needle strikes seven.

Sam swings the door half-open, leaning casually against the doorframe with her signature smirk-ish expression. "Hello, Miles!" She says in a sing-song tone.

"Hi, Sam!" I greet back, keeping my expression deliberately bored.

"You know, it's still surprising—*you*, Miles Baudelaire, asking a girl out on a date. It's fascinating, really." she teases, crossing her arms as though she's the gatekeeper of Mia's approval.

"*Soo* fascinating." I deadpan, running a hand through my hair. My patience wearing thin in the await of seeing the girl who has consumed my thoughts like the seductive fragrance of Stargazer lilies—calm and electric.

"This must be noted in the Guinness Book of Records." She snarks.

"Are you done, Sam?" Mia's soft voice filters from behind the door.

Sam grins and steps aside, opening the door wider, which brings Mia into view. Seeing her in a black top and a mini plaid skirt, with her wavy black hairs falling smoothly on her shoulders, gives her a charming yet understated elegance that takes my breath away as time slows down like a movie. Her minimal makeup highlights her natural beauty, and her warm brown eyes meet mine with a mix of excitement and nervousness.

"You look... gorgeous." I say, my voice softer than I intended.

Mia's cheeks tint pink as she brushes a strand of hair behind her ear. "Thank you. You look... very dashing yourself." Her words are shy but sincere, and they make me feel like the luckiest man alive.

"Alright, Miles." Sam cuts in, handing Mia a black coat from the hanger. "My girl better be back by ten, safe and sound, or I'll hunt you down."

Mia groans, grabbing the coat. "Sam!"

I chuckle. "Noted. Safe and sound."

Mia slips on the coat, adjusting her bag which slungs casually over one shoulder. That's when I remember the bouquet of lilies.

I gently offer them to Mia. "Shall we?"

She takes them with a smile, hesitating before saying, "We shall."

As Mia begins to step out of the dorm, Sam gently takes the lilies from Mia's hand. "I'll put them in a vase." she says with a wink.

Mia nods, closing the door behind her. The air is blessed with a mix of anticipation and excitement. As we walk, her arm brushes lightly against mine, and I fight the urge to glance at her every few seconds.

As we descend the stairs in silence, I notice Mia is tense. I'll need to make her feel comfortable—keep things easy and within her comfort zone. Like not kissing her on the first date, which, as much as I want to, isn't the right move right now.

When we step outside, the cool night air brushing past us, we walk together toward my Benz. Just as I unlock the car, Mia hesitates before turning to me, her voice soft and unsure. "I know this is a date, but... can I sit in the back?"

I pause, though not out of confusion, but because I recall the night outside at the Halloween party.

"*I'll sit in the back then.*" She had said.

"*Why did you want to sit in the back?*" I had asked.

"*Because... if my parents had been sitting in the back, they'd still be alive.*" She had answered.

Even now, the weight of her words from that night settles on my heart.

"Off course." I say, meeting her gaze as I open the back seat door instead of the front like a gentleman. "Whatever makes you comfortable."

Her lips twitch into a faint smile, one that doesn't quite reach her eyes as she deliberately slides into the back seat. I gently shut the door, walking around to the driver's side. I start the ignition and turn on the radio, filing the car with soft music

The drive starts out silent, save for the occasional shifts of Mia in the back seat. I change the current channel to a different one, and that's when I find the perfect station. The moment the drum beats of *Shake It Off* by Taylor Swift starts to play, I catch Mia's face light up.

"Turn it up." Mia says, her voice suddenly brighter as she softly sings along.

That's what people say, mm-mm
But I keep cruising

"Seriously? You're not gonna sing along?" Mia says.

"I don't know the words." I reply, glancing at her in the rearview mirror.

"Are you kidding me?" she says, sounding genuinely surprised. She leans forward, her voice playful. "Actually, it doesn't surprise me, you look like the kind of guy who listens to whale sounds." She teases.

I laugh, shaking my head. "Whale sounds? Really?"

"No whales, okay. What about piano music?" she quips, mimicking an imaginary piano with her fingers, her movements exaggerated.

"You are way off." I chuckle, unable to stop smiling. I desperately want to look back at her, but I can't. I have to keep my eyes on the road. The occasional glance in the rearview mirror is the only way I can steal a look at her until we reach the restaurant.

She leans forward even more, as if trying to read me better. I feel her gaze on me, the intensity of her stare reaching me even from the corner of my eye. I finally break the silence. "What are you doing?"

"I'm trying to guess your music taste." she replies, her tone light as she rests her elbow on the corner of the passenger seat.

As she moves closer, the soft scent of her perfume fills the car—citrus and lilies. I can't help but smile, remembering how I sent her lilies. They remind me of her—innocent, pure, calm, yet undeniably charming and beautiful.

"What about Arctic Ocean?" she asks, after a long pause.

I shake my head.

"The Neighbourhood?"

"No, but I've heard of them." I reply.

"I'm kind of getting the hint that you don't listen to music." she says, giving up with a playful sigh.

"I do, very rarely, but I do." I answer. "I listen to Ed Sheeran. It's always in my background."

"Shut up. You listen to Ed Sheeran?" Mia exclaims, her face breaking into a cute, shocked expression. "Never would've thought that."

I laugh, warmth spreading through me as I notice her posture relax. She leans back against the seat, her smile lingering as she gazes out the window, the soft smudge of trees passing by as we exit New York City.

The song ends, and the radio commentator speaks briefly before the familiar opening notes of *Bad Habits* by Ed Sheeran plays.

Mia bursts into laughter, and I can't help but join her. "What a coincidence." she says through her giggles.

Her voice lifts in a playful challenge. "Now you can join too."

My bad habits lead to late nights endin' alone
Conversations with a stranger I barely know...

Her enthusiasm is infectious, and for the first time, I hum along softly, keeping my voice low to avoid completely butchering the tune.

I pull into the restaurants parking lot as the song comes to an end. "We are here." I let her know softly. Leaving the driver's seat, I move toward Mia's back seat door to open it for her, but before I can, she's already out, brushing a strand of hair behind her ear as she glances at me with a small smile.

I extend my hand. She hesitates for a moment, but then takes it. Mia's fingers brush mine, warm and delicate, as I lead her out of the parking lot and toward the restaurant.

As we approach the counter, Mia murmurs, "cute.", glancing around and admiring the interior. The restaurant—Browning's Tranquil Cove, nestled on the outskirts of New York City, still carries the charm of the fifties, with vintage booths and retro lighting, but it's been updated with some modern touches—sleek tables, and polished elegance—keeping the essence of its past intact. Despite its roots in the fifties, it remains one of the finest dining spots in the United States, having recently celebrated its 70th anniversary.

The manager greets us with a polite smile, "Welcome back, Sir and Ma'am. Your boat is ready if you'd follow me."

"Ma'am. Boat." I hear Mia whisper under her breath, her curiosity evident as we follow the manager outside.

When we reach the treasure of this place, I pause, letting Mia take in the view. The restaurant, standing proudly on the edge of a vast, shimmering lake, with its crystal-clear waters stretching across 55 acres, has a timeless charm to its magnificent beauty. Celebrities, tourists, and locals alike are drawn to this place, not just for the impeccable cuisine but for its unique location.

Anchored near the dock is a long boat reminiscent of the ones used in olden days but built with thoughtful modern enhancements for stability and comfort. It isn't like a big-white yacht or a cruise ship, it's a traditional vessel, and a stunning piece of craftsmanship that seems like a memory brought to life. Its sturdy wooden frame gleams under the soft light of hanging lanterns, exuding an aura of warmth and nostalgia. The motor is discreetly installed at one end while at the opposite end, an open kitchen for the chef to cook. In the middle, a single dining table sits elegantly, set with fine silverware and a delicate floral centrepiece of white lilies.

"We'll be having dinner on the boat. It's one of the unique experiences this place offers." I explain, a hint of pride in my voice as I guide Mia toward the dock.

"So, you're saying we're going to eat on *this* boat?" Mia's voice is a mix of awe and surprise, her eyes scanning the vessel as if trying to absorb its beauty.

"Mmhm." I nod, a smile tugging at the corner of my lips.

"Huh, okay." She lets out a small breath.

"We can eat inside if you'd prefer." I add quickly, suddenly aware of her hesitation.

"No... no. It's just... unbelievable and serene." Mia says, her smile returning, this time reaching her eyes and making them sparkle in the soft light.

Noticing her hesitation, I step onto the boat first. Then, I turn back, extending my hand. "Here, let me help you."

Mia looks at me for a moment, then places her hand in mine. Her fingers tighten around mine briefly, as if seeking reassurance, before she steps onto the boat, her movements cautious but graceful.

"This is... beautiful." she murmurs, her eyes scanning the setup with quiet reverence, as if afraid to disturb its perfection.

The chef, standing at his small cooking station at the far end, smiles and approaches us. "Good evening, and welcome aboard *Epiphany*. I'll be preparing your meal tonight. May I take your order?"

Mia glances at me, a hint of uncertainty in her expression. "What's good here?" she whispers.

"The salmon is excellent." I suggest with a smile.

She nods. "Okay, I'll have that. Maybe with roasted vegetables?"

The chef notes her choice with a nod and turns to me. "I'll have the steak, medium rare, with garlic mashed potatoes." I say.

"Very well. I'll get started right away." the chef says before returning to his station.

As the gentle hum of the motor and the soft lapping of the lake's waters fill the air, I turn to Mia. "So, what do you think?"

Her gaze drifts over the water, her expression thoughtful. "It feels... magical. Like something out of a story." she says softly, her lips curving into a small smile as the trees surrounding the lake sway from the breeze making a peaceful rustling sound.

I watch her, in awe of the scenic panorama. Then, I turn her attention back to the table and pull out a chair, saying, "After you."

She chuckles softly, her smile growing as she sits down. "Okay."

"My grandma brought me here for the first time," I say, initiating a conversation while the chef prepares our dinner. "This is where she met my grandpa. She was eighteen, having lunch with her family. He was in his mid-twenties, overseeing things—he'd just invested a big chunk of his savings into the place. They met, fell in love, and the rest, as they say, is history."

"Grandparents, as in... Theodore and Grace Browning?" Mia's voice holds genuine curiosity, her words soft and thoughtful. I can hear the spark of interest in her tone.

I nod. "Yeah. Actually, that boat over there is named after her. My grandpa proposed to her on it." I gesture toward the other dock, where a weathered boat is anchored. "It's not in use anymore, though. It's old—barely standing, just held up by supports for now. But we're keeping it as a memory."

Mia tilts her head slightly, a soft expression crossing her face. "That's so sweet."

Her gaze lingers on the boat a little longer, admiration flickering in her eyes, as if she's picturing them there—lost in a memory that isn't hers but one she can almost feel.

Her gaze shifts back to me. "Where are your grandparents now?" she asks gently.

"Retired." I reply. "Living peacefully in Utah."

"Good for them." Mia says smiling. "So, is the business in your mom's hand now?"

"Yeah, but it mostly merged with Baudelaire Enterprises after she married my Dad." I explain.

"And you are going to inherit it someday?" Mia asks, her tone light but genuinely curious.

"Yeah... probably next year." I reply with a slight shrug.

"Good for you." She tilts her head slightly, her lips curling into a playful smile. "Okay, so this is a date, aren't you going to ask me where I'm from? You know, all that first-date stuff?"

I raise an eyebrow, lowering my head with a guilty smile because, well, I already know. I know where she's from, who her parents were, and even where she went to school. My curiosity got the better of me when I first saw her, and I'd asked Audrey a few questions here and there.

"You already know, don't you?" Mia says, her eyes narrowing with mock accusation. "Stalker."

I smile sheepishly. "I don't know everything about you, though. I don't know what your dreams are or what keeps you up at night. I don't know what you love or hate. That's not something you can find out from anywhere."

I lean forward slightly, resting my arms on the table. "So tell me, Mia—what are your plans after Columbia?"

Her expression shifts, her gaze flickering with uncertainty. "I might apply for a job at creative writing sectors." she says tentatively, then pauses. "Or... maybe walk into a studio one day and demand to record a song. Although, let's be real—I'd be way too scared to actually do that."

"Wait, a song?" I ask, surprised. "You sing?"

She smirks, her confidence returning. "I bet your stalking skills didn't tell you I was also accepted to Berkeley."

I lean back slightly, processing her words. "Berkeley? As in the music school?"

She nods, a hint of pride in her expression. "Yeah. I applied to both Columbia and Berkeley."

"So why'd you choose Columbia?" I ask, a cold realization hitting me. If Mia had chosen Berkeley, I might never have met her—never seen her soft smile when she's nervous, the way her cheeks flush when she's flustered, or the fire in her eyes when she's stubbornly drunk. I push the thought away as she answers, her tone soft.

"Well, my mom always wanted to go here but never got the chance. I thought I'd fill in for her. Plus, I figured I'd already learned a lot about music on my own. Columbia seemed like a better place to grow as a writer."

"So... writing was not what you wanted?" I ask, curious.

She shakes her head slightly. "No, I love writing—stories, songs. It's something I take after my mom. She was always creative. Although, my dad, on the other hand, was sporty and loved numbers. In the morning, he'd be the ready with perfect pitches, and by night, he'd be in a jersey, cheering wildly for his favourite team."

A wistful smile crosses her face, but her voice falters as she adds, "He would've loved meeting you. You probably would've talked more with him than with me."

Her words hang in the air, heavy with a tinge of sadness. "Sorry." she says quickly, her tone apologetic. "I didn't mean to be such a downer."

The soft sound of water lapping against the boat fills the quiet. I watch her for a moment, taking in the way her shoulders stay firm even as her voice falters. She's sad, but there's a strength in her, one that makes me want to know her even more.

"You're not a downer, Mia." I say gently. "Talking about them keeps them close, doesn't it?"

She looks up at me, and for a second, it feels like she's letting her guard down. A small, fragile smile appears on her lips. "Yeah, it does. Sometimes I just feel like I'm holding on too tightly, like if I let go, I'll lose them completely."

"That's not a bad thing," I say, leaning forward. "It just shows how much they meant to you. And honestly, from what you've told me, I think they'd be really proud of you."

Her eyes soften, and I can see that my words hit home. "Thanks, Miles." she says, her voice quiet but sincere.

As the moment stretches and the chef brings out our dinner, I find myself marvelling over how Mia is opening up to me. This isn't the reserved, cautious girl who hesitated to accept a date with me. This Mia, seated in front of me, is warmer, softer, letting me in piece by piece. It's like watching the first rays of sunrays breaking through the cloudy sky.

I can't help but think back to when I first met her—how she was quiet, as though she was always guarding herself. And now, here she is, telling me about her family, her dreams. It's a privilege to witness this side of her, and it evokes something deeper in me.

The breeze picks up, and I notice the way strands of her hair sways subtly. She tucks a loose strand behind her ear, and the gesture is so simple, yet it leaves me utterly mesmerized.

"So." Mia says suddenly, her tone teasing, "Were you born here or in France?"

"Here." I reply.

"Do you have grandparents in France?"

"No. Dead." I answer bluntly, taking a bite of my steak, noticing her pause mid-bite.

"Don't worry—I wasn't close to them."

"Okay." she says, smiling awkwardly.

"Is this rapid-fire now?" I ask with a raised eyebrow.

"I'm sorry, but I don't have expert hackers to dig up information on someone." Mia teases.

"I wasn't digging—I was curious so I just casually asked my sister."

"Oh, so I'm that unimportant to you that you just *casually* asked?" she sets her face in an impassive mask but it crumbles within seconds.

I grin. "I'm going to stay quiet now."

Her laughter bursts free, filling the air with a lightness I didn't know I needed. Watching her, I feel grateful to be here, to be the one making her laugh like this.

Mia continues her rapid-fire questions, asking, "What's the weirdest thing you believed as a kid?"

I chuckle, rubbing the back of my neck. "Okay, don't laugh too hard, but I genuinely believed that if you swallowed a watermelon seed, a watermelon would grow in your stomach." I pause, my grin widening. "I remember one summer, my sister convinced me I'd accidentally eaten one, and for weeks, I was terrified I'd wake up with a watermelon belly. I even made my mom take me to the doctor for a scan."

Mia bursts out laughing, her eyes crinkling with amusement. "No way! How long did you believe that?"

"Too long." I admit. "What about you?"

Mia sighs, swallowing her food before answering, "Don't judge me, but when I was little, I thought countries were actually different planets."

"Oh no." I exclaim.

"It gets worse. Our neighbours came back from a month-long vacation from Italy, and you know how schools teach that there's no gravity on other planets, so you float? Well, I asked them if they enjoyed floating. It was stupid."

I burst into laughter.

"Okay, serious question now." Mia says, trying to hold back giggles.

"Have you…" She continues, struggling to control her laughter, which makes me smile like an idiot. "Have you ever killed someone?"

"What?!" I ask, shocked. "Have you?"

"No, I'm too delicate and clumsy for that shit." She replies, still giggling. "If someone sees us like this, they'd think we were high on laughing gas."

"I won't mind."

Mia is the kind of girl who comes off as quiet and extremely closed off at first, but once she warms up to you, it's a whole new territory—one I'm more than ready to explore, every inch of it.

After dinner, the boat docks gently against the pier. I hop off first, the boat slightly swaying from the loss of my weight. Turning, I extend a hand to help Mia. Her fingers slip into mine, velvety and comforting, as she steps down with carefully.

"Thanks." she says, her lips curving into a small smile.

"Anytime." I reply, gently releasing her hand.

We decide to linger by the dock, the lake stretching out before us like a sheet of liquid silver under the moonlight. Our coats keep us warm from the chilly winds as the water calmly laps against boats in the water.

The moment lingers between us, but after a while, the quiet settles in. This moment, standing here with her, feels… different. Heavier. Like she has something on her mind.

After a while, Mia breaks the silence, her voice quiet, almost hesitant. "Um… you didn't ask me anything when I insisted on sitting in the back seat."

I glance at her, the soft moonlight casting a glow on her face. "You said the same when you were drunk." I say after a pause.

"Oh."

"When I asked you why," I continue, keeping my tone gentle, "you said your parents might still be alive if they'd been sitting in the back."

There's a minute of silence as if the world has stopped breathing, and when I think Mia will change the subject, she speaks again. "They were driving back from Mumbai—Mumbai's like the New York of India. They were with a friend, and he got tired of driving, so my dad decided to take the wheel. My mom sat in the front to keep him company. And then…" She pauses.

"You don't have to." I say, carefully.

"Its fine." she says, though her voice wavers. "A truck came from the front on the highway, full speed, the driver drunk, and hit them. The friend, sitting in the back, was injured but alive." She stares at the lake, takes a deep shaky breath and speaks, "I mean, I'm glad he survived, but I can't help thinking… what if."

Her voice cracks on the last two words, and she looks down, her hair falling like a curtain over her face.

I take a step closer, unsure if she wants comfort or space, but unable to let her carry this alone. "Mia…"

"I used to cry every time I thought about it." she says, her tone steadier now, though her eyes glisten. "Now, I just… I don't cry anymore. I just get sad. And then kinda move on."

Her honesty cuts through the air, as unguarded as a secret spoken to the stars. I don't say anything because there's nothing that could make this better. Instead, I stay by her side, as the lake's gentle ripples continue their endless rhythm.

"Did I say anything else stupid when I was drunk?" Mia asks, her tone light, trying to lighten the mood.

"I think it's better left unknown." I say, recalling her walking in Alex's room during the Halloween party when Chloe was there, and getting the wrong idea of the situation.

Mia lets out a small laugh. "Oh no." she says, her voice filled with mock horror. "What did I do?"

I shrug, keeping my face straight. "It wasn't you, it was me."

"What." Mia says, smirking. "Now I wanna know."

"Forget about it. Let's go." I say, grinning, already turning to exit the restaurant.

"Oh no, Miles. You have to tell me." Mia says, smiling, catching up with my pace.

"Maybe sometime later." I say with a wink.

"I'm gonna hold on to that." Mia replies. "Wait…what about the bill?" She suddenly asks.

"My mom owns this place." I remind her.

"Oh, right. I forgot you're kinda like the boss of this place." She teases.

"You could say that."

Exiting the restaurant, the manager says to Mia, "Hope you had a great time, Ma'am." She replies with that same soft smile, saying, "I did. Thank you."

The laughter from dinner still lingers in the air, but as she climbs into the car, something shifts. The moment stretches, thicker than before. And when she settles into the back seat, I can't help but that someday, maybe soon, she'll be able to sit shotgun without any fear in her mind. With that thought in my mind, I start the engine and pull out of the parking lot and hit the road. Mia might think the date is over, but it's not. Not yet. I have something planned.

As we enter the city, I park my Benz in a lot near the subway entrance. Turning to Mia, I smile. "Let's go."

"Where?" she asks, her curiosity piqued.

"You'll see." I reply, stepping out and circling the car to meet her as she follows.

The streets are bustling, the chaos of the city in full swing even though it's almost eleven pm. Feeling the crowd press in, Mia instinctively reaches for my arm. It's a small gesture, but it means more than I care to admit. I warmly hold her hand, guiding her through the sea of people as we make our way toward the entrance to the subway.

As we glide down the stairs, I explain, "There's this thing you mentioned when you were drunk; that you don't know how to use the subway system. So I'll show you. It's not that complicated."

"Nice." She mutters.

As we reach the bottom of the stairs, the roar of the subway fills the air. I turn to Mia, giving her a reassuring smile.

"Okay, so here's how it works." I say, stepping up to the ticket booth and buying our MetroCards. I hand one to her. "This is your key to everything." I point to the turnstile, swiping our cards and entering.

"We're taking the train uptown." I explain, leading her down to the platform. "It's the red line on the map." I say, pointing to the map on the wall above us. Mia looks up at it, squinting at the maze of lines and numbers.

"Okay, so this red line will take us straight to Columbia?" she asks, trying to wrap her head around the map.

"Yep." I confirm. "We'll get off at 116th Street and walk from there. It's only a few minutes away."

She gives me a small smile. "This doesn't seem so bad."

"You'll get the hang of it." I gesture to the platform, where the train approaches.

The train screeches to a stop in front of us. I step aside, letting Mia board first, and I follow suit. Late night have its perks because we easily find seats, settling in as the train begins to move.

"This wasn't complicated at all." she says softly.

"I told you." I reply with a small grin. "And don't stress about missing a train. Subways to Columbia run every half hour. Worst case, just ask at the help counter."

Mia nods, absorbing the information, she asks, "How do you know all this? Weren't you raised to travel in luxurious vehicles with drivers that called you *sir*?"

"Most of my childhood—yes." I admit. "But when I started college, I sometimes used to take the train. I found it chaotically calm."

She nods, her gaze slowly turning towards a child sitting across from us. The child smiles at her and she smiles back, warmly and softly, her eyes twinkling from the act. She turns back to me, her tone playful, "Okay, spill it."

"Spill what?" I ask.

"What did you do when I was drunk?" She says, her tone teasing yet insistent.

"I said I'd tell you later." I reply, stalling. The memory of her walking into Alex's room flashes in my mind. Definitely not first-date material.

"This is later." She insists. "Oh, come on. It's on top of my mind now. I won't stop thinking about it."

"Please." She smiles big and I give in.

I sigh, relenting. "Fine. But let me finish before you react."

"Deal." she says, crossing her arms but leaning in slightly.

I steel myself and begin. "I went to Alex's room to get his phone during the party. Chloe then happened to enter." I glance at her briefly, looking for a reaction, but her face remains neutral. "She put her... uh, hand on my chest, and... that's when you walked in and got the wrong idea."

Mia's expression doesn't change at first, then she lets out a soft laugh. "Oh. Honestly, I'm glad I don't remember that."

"Why didn't you want to tell me this?" she asks. "It's not like you did anything wrong."

"First of all, this is a date." I reply. "Second, I didn't want you to get the wrong idea again."

She shakes her head, her lips curving into a smirk. "Why would I? I mean, we can laugh about it now."

When I say Mia's not like other girls, it's not a cliché—it's fact. Most girls' mascara would be running, tears streaming as they called their friends to dissect every detail. Mia? She just says, *"We can laugh about it now."*

"It wasn't funny then." I point out.

"It is now." she counters, her smile widening.

The train comes to a screeching halt at 116th Street, the doors sliding open. I stand, offering a hand to Mia as we both make our way out of the train, stepping onto the platform. The sky above is dotted with stars, and the cool breeze brushes against my face as we emerge onto the street. Columbia University's grand buildings are visible from here, bathed in the soft glow of streetlights.

Mia glances at me, concern evident in her tone. "How are you getting home?"

"I'll take a different train back." I reply casually, shrugging off her concern.

"You should go now, or you'll miss the next train." she insists. "I can walk back myself."

I shake my head lightly, a small smile tugging at my lips. "Don't worry. Trains heading back to the city run frequently this late. I'll make it back just fine."

She hesitates but nods. "Okay, if you're sure."

Without really thinking, I reach for her hand, lacing my fingers through hers. The movement catches her off guard, and her eyes widen for a split second before she relaxes, a subtle smile playing on her lips as she walks beside me.

The night is quiet, the streets emptying out as we approach the gates. The glow of the campus lights feels warm, almost welcoming. Neither of us says much, but the silence feels comfortable, not awkward.

As we approach her dorm, Mia pulls out her keys, sliding it into the lock. The door clicks open with a soft creak, and she steps inside, turning to face me. I lean against the doorframe, tinge of a smile on my lips.

"Hope you had fun tonight." I say, my voice low.

She nods, her gaze flickering to mine. "Yeah, I did."

Her words stir something deep within me. I should say goodnight and leave—it's only the first date—but the way the glow from the hallway light catches her face makes me pause. My heart tightens, and for a split second, the thought of kissing her floods my mind. But I push it down. It's too soon.

"So," I say, clearing my throat, "do you think there's a chance for a second date? Or am I going to have to fill this entire dorm with lilies to change your mind?" My smirk is teasing, but my chest feels tight, like the air between us is charged with something unspoken.

Mia laughs, her voice light. "Hmm, I'll have to think about it."

"Flowers it is." I say without missing a beat, my smirk widening, though the tightening in my chest doesn't ease.

"Goodnight, Miles." she says softly, starting to close the door.

"Goodnight, Mia." I echo, stepping back into the hallway. But as the door begins to close and I take another step away, I feel an ache—a magnetic pull I can't ignore.

Don't. It's the first date. Walk away. The rational part of me is screaming to stop, but every other part of me is on fire. I hesitate, halfway down the hall, my breath shallow. And then I think, *Fuck it.*

I push the door open, stepping back into the room with a firm yet hesitant resolve. Mia looks up, startled, her wide eyes meeting mine. Her lips part slightly as if to say something, but I don't give her the chance.

In one swift motion, I close the distance between us, my hand finding her waist, pulling her closer as my lips meet hers. It's soft and fleeting—not deep, not rushed, just enough to feel the warmth of her breath and the sweetness of her lips.

Her body tenses for a heartbeat, hesitant before she relaxes against me, her lips responding ever so slightly. My hand lingers on her waist, steadying us both as my heart pounds in my chest, louder than I'd like to admit.

Then, as quickly as it began, I step back, my gaze flickering to hers. Her cheeks are flushed, her lips still parted in surprise, her eyes surprised and still, and for a second, neither of us speaks.

"Goodnight, Mia." I murmur, my voice quieter now, carrying all the weight of what I just did. She blinks, her surprised eyes still locked on mine, then whispers, "Goodnight."

I step back into the hallway, the air between us charged, the ghost of the kiss lingering like a spark I can't shake, like a secret I'll carry until the next time I see her.

CHAPTER 18
Mia

I can't believe that just happened. I had my first kiss. And it was flawless. My stomach churns as I step into my room and plop down on my bed. Did that really happen? Or was I imagining things? Before I can make sense of it, Sam bursts through the door with a big smile, not able to contain her excitement.

"Did you guys just kiss… on the first date?"

"I think so. Is that bad?" I say, the moment still quite fresh in my mind, both thrilling and nerve-wracking.

"No!" she exclaims, flopping down beside me. "So, did he propose?"

"Shut up." I squeal, giggling like a nerdy teenager when the hottest guy in school notices her with a nod of his head. "Why are you still up?" I ask.

"I was asleep, but I heard the door open, so I was kinda eavesdropping." she explains, shameless as always.

"I'm surprised you woke up because of the slightest click of the door." I say.

"You and me both girl." She grins. "Now tell me everything that happened on the date!"

"No, right now I'm tired. I'll tell you in the morning. Now go to sleep." I nudge her toward the door.

"Fine." She pouts dramatically, yawning as she leaves my room and shuts the door behind her.

The quiet settles in again, but my mind refuses to follow suit. I lay on my bed, staring at the ceiling, my heart racing as the night replays like a highlight reel in my head. The laughter, the way he looked at me, the softness of his voice—it all feels surreal, like a scene out of a book.

Was it too soon? Did it mean as much to him as it did to me?

My hands tremble slightly as I sit up. There's too much to feel, too much to process, and my thoughts are spiralling into chaos. I swing my legs over the edge of the bed and glance toward the corner of my room, where my guitar rests against the wall.

Music has always been my anchor, the only way I know how to make sense of emotions this big. Without thinking twice, I grab the guitar and settle back on the bed, its familiar weight comforting in my lap. My fingers find the strings instinctively, strumming soft, tentative chords that match the rhythm of my racing heart.

The melody comes first, something quiet and wistful. The lyrics tumble out, new and imperfect, but they feel right. Each line helps me unravel the whirlwind of emotions, turning confusion into clarity, fear into hope.

When I finally stop playing, the silence is deafening, but it's not uncomfortable. It's the kind of silence that feels like an answer. I set the guitar down gently, letting the last note linger in the air. The chaos in my mind has settled, at least for now. I know I won't be able to sleep yet, but for the first time tonight, I don't mind it. Instead, I lie back down, a small smile tugging at my lips.

My phone pings, the display lighting up, I reach for it and see a text from Sam: *That was a good song. Send it to Miles.*

I chuckle under my breath, texting her back: *Go to Sleep.*

Almost immediately, three dots appear on the screen, followed by her reply: *I mean it! It'll knock his socks off.*

I roll my eyes, fighting a laugh. *I'm not sending it. Besides, he'd probably think it's cheesy.*

She shoots back: *The guy kissed you on the first date. Pretty sure he likes cheese.*

I laugh out loud this time, clutching my phone as warmth spreads through me. Trust Sam to turn my vulnerable moment into something so hilariously endearing through a text.

I type quickly: *Night Sam.*

Her response is immediate: *Good night.*

I set my phone down on the nightstand, shaking my head at her antics. As I settle back against the pillows, the weight of the day finally begins to fade. My mind drifts to Miles—his smile, the way he pulled me close to him by the waist while kissing, and the overwhelming sense that something between us has shifted.

We're not strangers anymore nor are we just friends, and I don't what to label us yet because everything just happened, but after this kiss, I know one thing for sure—we can't go back to those old labels.

There's no undoing the way his lips lingered against mine, no erasing the way my heart raced when he whispered goodnight. It's like I've stepped into uncharted territory, and while it's thrilling, it's also terrifying. But guess what? I'm here for it.

I close my eyes, letting the memory wash over me like a song I don't want to end.

CHAPTER 19

Miles

I saunter into the living room to find my grandma sitting on the couch, flipping through this year's tycoon magazine.

"How'd you get in?" I ask, keeping my tone calm.

"Your mother gave me the key." she replies, setting the magazine down on the coffee table.

Grace Browning, my grandmother, is in her eighties but still as bright as ever. The wrinkles on her face have deepened since the last time I saw her, yet she radiates a vibrance that makes her seem years younger.

She mentioned she was planning to visit New York for a change, but I didn't expect her to show up at my apartment this early in the morning.

"Did Grandpa come with you?" I ask as I head to the open kitchen and start the coffee machine.

"Oh no, dear. He didn't want to miss his weekend golf with his buddies." she delicately shrugs, following me into the kitchen.

"Coffee?" I offer.

"No."

"Eggs?"

"No, thanks. I already ate at your mother's. Do give me a glass of water." She replies.

I hand her a glass of water.

She slowly drinks the water as I pour myself a cup of coffee.

Just when I'm about to take a sip, Grandma speaks again.

"I heard from Audrey last night that my little smiles went on a date and didn't even tell me."

I freeze mid-sip, setting the cup down carefully. "I was going to tell you. You know I never keep things from you." I say, trying to sound casual, but I can already feel my cheeks warming.

"I know, my little smiles." She grins, her voice taking on a teasing lilt. "I just love teasing you." She's been calling me that for as long as I can remember—*little smiles*—and while I'm not exactly fond of it, I've learned to roll with it.

"So, do you love her?" she muses, her eyes narrowing slightly as she watches me.

"I like her." I correct her quickly, not ready to admit anything more than that.

"Oh, stop it." She waves me off with a dismissive flick of her wrist. "I've been around long enough to recognize when my grandson is smitten." She tilts her head, studying me as if I'm an open book. "Do you have a photo of her?"

I wince, realizing that I actually *don't* have a photo of Mia. "No."

"You're telling me you don't have a single photo of the girl you like?" she asks, her disbelief obvious.

"There was never an opportunity." I explain.

Grandma hums, clearly not satisfied with that answer. "You didn't take any photos on the date?"

"No." I reply, running a hand through my hair. "We were too busy in getting to know each other."

"I suppose that's nice." she says with a soft, knowing smile. There's something about her tone, like she understands more than I realize.

I lean against the counter, sipping my coffee, trying to process the whirlwind of emotions from last night. "It was nice." I admit. "It felt real."

"Sometimes," she begins after a long pause, "the things that feel real are the ones worth holding onto the most." She smiles softly, her eyes twinkling with wisdom. "Don't let go of that feeling too quickly, Miles."

I nod, feeling the weight of her words settle in. Grandma might tease, but she knows me better than anyone else, and when she speaks like this, I know she's speaking from experience.

"I won't." I assure her, finishing my coffee.

Her expressions shift to something lighter as she asks, "Are you meeting her today?"

"Yeah…actually." I reply.

"When?" she presses.

"In an hour or so." I reply.

She claps her hands together, her enthusiasm infectious. "Then what are you waiting for? Go get ready!"

I chuckle, standing up and stretching. "Alright, alright. I'm going."

As I start heading toward my room, her voice stops me mid-step. "Oh, and Miles?"

"Yeah?" I turn, one eyebrow raised.

"Drop me at the *Ladies-Talk* studio on your way, will you? Hope it's not a detour." she says, casually inspecting her nails.

"It's not."

"Good. I have to gather new tea from the insides, and I don't want to be late." she says, already rising from the couch with the energy of someone half her age.

I shake my head, amused. "I'll be ready in thirty."

"Make it twenty!" she calls after me, her laughter trailing behind as I head into my room.

CHAPTER 20

Mia

I step out of the lecture hall with Maverick at my side, our conversation drifts back to the assignment due next month. Even though it's the weekend, our professor called an emergency lecture because he's taking two weeks off. To make up for it, he left us a daunting pile of practice work.

"So, are you going to try something experimental with your piece, or stick to what you're good at?" Maverick asks, his tone half-curious, half-challenging.

"I'm not sure yet." I reply, stifling a yawn. Sleep deprivation is catching up to me—last night's date, followed by a late-night songwriting spree, left me running on fumes. The unexpected morning announcement of the lecture didn't help either. "I'm tempted to play it safe, but I also feel like I need to step outside my comfort zone. I mean, that's why we're here, right?"

"Exactly. Risk or bust." he says with a grin, holding the door open as we step into the bright sunlight outside the building.

As I climb down the few steps of the building, my eyes catch a familiar figure in the distance. Miles. He stands near a bench, his hands shoved in his pockets, looking effortlessly casual as he leans slightly against the backrest. My heart does that ridiculous thing where it skips, then races to catch up.

What is he doing here?

Panic flutters in my chest. The memory of our kiss from last night floods my mind, bringing with it a kaleidoscope of emotions—excitement, nervousness, and something I can't quite name yet. But as much as I want to see him, talk to him, the idea of facing him so soon leaves me feeling completely unprepared.

I freeze for a moment, praying he hadn't noticed me yet. Miles seems preoccupied, looking at his phone. Relief washes over me.

"Hey, I just remembered something I left inside." I blurt out to Maverick, cutting our conversation short. "I'll catch up with you later, okay?"

Maverick raises an eyebrow but shrugs. "Okay."

I spin around and hurry back inside the building. My footsteps echo as I make a beeline for the nearest bathroom, pushing the door open and leaning against the cool tiled wall. I press a hand to my chest, trying to calm my erratic breathing.

That was close.

I squeeze my eyes shut. *Why am I like this?* It isn't like he's done anything wrong. In fact, everything about last night had been perfect. But seeing him now feels like being caught red-handed even though we didn't do anything wrong.

And just like that, what happened last night feels wrong. The jitters of having my first kiss fades replaced by the creeping horror of crossing some unspoken line. If I ever share this with Uncle Rohan, he'll exile me from his respectable people's list faster than I can say *Romance*. My name will be engraved, in bold, in his long-running catalogue of mannerless individuals.

You don't relate? Fine, here's this: I'll be on Santa's naughty list for eternity.

I groan, running a hand through my hair, feeling like my brain is staging a civil war. *Maybe it's not that big of a deal. My parents had a love marriage—they most definitely kissed before eloping. But they weren't nineteen.*

And just like that, my overthinking side charges onto the battlefield.

But I'll be twenty next month, I counter.

Yeah, but your parents were twenty-five when they got married. You're still very young.

But this is America. In fact, Teens do more than kissing here like it's no big deal.

But you're Indian.

I let out another groan and lean my head back against the tiled wall. My inner monologue is exhausting me. It's as though the cultural expectations and my very American reality are in a relentless tug-of-war, and I'm the fraying rope in the middle.

I take a deep breath, grounding myself, and step out of the restroom hoping that Miles has gone by now. But as I walk into the corridor, I hear his voice. It's sharp, a question directed at someone.

"Have you seen an Indian girl? Black hair, kinda tall?"

I freeze. *Oh no, he's still here.*

The girl he's talking to shakes her head, saying, "No.", her eyes dreamily lingering on Miles with obvious interest. "No. But I could be your..."

"No." Miles, whose back is to me, cuts her off before she even finishes, and my heart does that weird thing where it flutters, like a confused butterfly.

I see the scene unfold before my eyes from a distance, and I can't help but want to stay to see the girl's reaction to Miles's reply but instead, I turn around and make a beeline for the nearest empty lecture hall.

I walk in and freeze.

Of course. Of course, there are two couples, fully in makeout mode, at the back of the room. They look at me like I've just walked in on a scene from *The Bachelor*.

"What's up?" I say, reluctantly informal, as if I haven't just intruded on their PDA party. "I'm just going to sit in that corner seat. You won't even notice me."

I move to the farthest corner, like I'm trying to hide from an entire army of angry mobs. I flop down into the seat, crossing my arms and laying my head down on the desk. It's like one of those middle school days when the teacher would tell us to *head down* so she could finish some work, and we'd all pretend to nap so she won't give us extra homework. Yeah, that's the vibe I'm going for right now. Except, I'm definitely not napping.

As I rest my head on my arms, I can't help but imagine myself as the protagonist in some *Wattpad* rom-com, where the girl storms up to her man and kisses him boldly, just to make the other *girl* jealous.

I should've done that.

And then I try to stifle a laugh at the thought.

Me? Pulling off a jealousy kiss? Yeah, that's about as likely as Voldemort giving out hugs. My introverted side would faint before my lips even got closer.

I shrug at myself.

With my head already resting on my arms, the quiet hum of the room lulls me. My eyelids grow heavy as my last nights unfinished sleep catches up to me, and before I realize it, I drift off to sleep.

CHAPTER 21

Miles

I lean against the bench outside the lecture hall, my hands stuffed into my pockets as my phone buzzes with updates. The bright sunlight does little to calm the flurry of thoughts spinning in my head. Last night's kiss with Mia wasn't just a kiss—it was a game changer. Every time I close my eyes, I feel her soft lips against mine, the faint scent of her perfume, the warmth of her breath mingling with mine. It's the kind of memory that grabs hold of you and doesn't let go.

But where's her head at? That's the real question.

I glance at my phone, shooting off a quick text to my grandma, confirming when I'll pick her up.

Shoving my phone back into my pocket, I glance toward the building, my pulse quickening. Any moment now, Mia should be stepping out. I picture her walking down those steps, her hair catching the sunlight, her eyes meeting mine. Will she smile that soft smile? Or will she pretend nothing happened?

Then I see her—or at least, I think I do. She lingers near the entrance for a moment before abruptly turning back, disappearing into the building. And she's in a hurry. My brows pull together. What's that about?

Pulling my phone out again, I type:

Miles: *Hey, where are you?*

I hit send and wait, scanning the entrance of the building. No reply. With a sigh, I push off the bench and head inside.

The warm air inside the building contrasts sharply with the cool breeze outside, and my footsteps echo in the quiet corridor. I check the nearest lecture hall, pushing the door open slightly, only to find it empty. Same with the next lecture hall.

No Mia.

I fire off another text: *Saw you go back inside. Everything okay?*

Still nothing. My stomach twists as the minutes stretch longer. Is she avoiding me?

A girl appears at the end of the hallway, and I quicken my steps toward her. "Hey." I say, my tone casual but purposeful. "Have you seen an Indian girl? Black hair, kinda tall?"

She tilts her head, her lips curling into a flirtatious smile. "No." she says, dragging out the word. "But I could be your…"

"No." My voice comes out sharper than I intended to, and her expression falters. Guilt flickers for a second, but I push it aside. My focus is Mia, not whatever this girl was about to suggest.

I glance past her, down the hallway. Still no sign of Mia. Where could she have gone?

"Sorry to bother you." I add, already turning to walk away.

The girl's voice is faintly indignant as she mutters something under her breath, but I don't stick around to hear it. My mind is racing.

I check my phone again. No new messages. My gut tells me she's somewhere close, but why is she hiding?

I take a deep breath and lean against the wall, trying to think. The Miles from a year ago would've shrugged this off and left. But this is different. She's different. She matters.

Tucking my phone into my pocket, I start walking again, determined to find her. Wherever she is, I need to know where her head—and heart—are at after last night. There's one more lecture hall around the corner of this corridor.

I stride toward it, my pulse quickening with every step. Reaching the door, I push it open slowly, and there she is.

She's sitting at a desk in the far corner, her head resting on her arms. Her eyelids are shut, soft and still. Her face has a serene quality, completely opposite to the mess of emotions I've been dealing with all day.

But then I catch movement at the other end of the hall—a couple locked in a full-blown makeout session. They freeze, turning to glare at me like I've interrupted some grand romantic moment.

"Seriously?" the guy mutters under his breath, his expression a mix of annoyance and embarrassment.

The girl rolls her eyes, grabbing her bag. "Let's go somewhere else." she huffs.

I watch them shuffle out, the door clicking shut behind them. The silence that follows feels heavy, yet somehow comforting.

I take a step closer to Mia, pausing for a moment. She's sound asleep, completely unaware of everything around her. Quietly, I sit down beside her, not wanting to wake her.

I never got why guys in movies would sit and stare at the girl they liked while she slept. It always seemed a little weird to me. But now, sitting here, I think I finally understand.

Mia looks so relaxed, as if completely untouched by the mayhem of the world outside. Her face is peaceful, her breathing steady, and for the first time since last night, I feel like I can breathe too. I wonder what she's dreaming about. Something light and happy, I hope.

Just then, she shifts slightly in her seat, her face scrunching up in discomfort. Her head is still resting on her arm, but her hand has gone pale where the weight is cutting off circulation. She stirs again, her brow furrowing as if her body's trying to find a more comfortable position without waking her.

I hesitate for a moment, unsure if I should do anything. But watching her like this—so clearly disturbed—feels wrong. Slowly, carefully, I reach out and gently lift her head, sliding my arm under her shoulders and letting her rest against me instead.

Her head leans against my shoulder, fitting there as if it was meant to. I hold still, barely breathing, waiting to see if she wakes up. But she doesn't. Her face relaxes again, the tension melting away as she settles against me.

I let out a quiet breath. Her warmth seeps through my shirt, and I can feel the faint rhythm of her breathing, steady and calm. It's oddly comforting, and I find myself rejuvenating too.

But a feeling settles heavily in my chest—Mia was trying to avoid me. She didn't reply to my texts, and I saw her go back inside the building, only to end up here, sleeping in some random lecture hall instead of the comfort of her bed.

The thought gnaws at me. Is she second-guessing last night? Or is this just her way of processing things? Either way, it leaves me feeling restless.

I turn on my phone and shoot off a text.

Miles: *I know it's the weekend, and I'm sorry. But can you inform Shaby's Blooms to deliver the lilies to the recipient's address?*

Miles: *ASAP.*

Five minutes later, my phone pings.

Melanin: *Consider it done.*

I put my phone away, my gaze drifting back to Mia. She's still nestled against my shoulder, her breathing soft and even. I can't help but wonder what's going on in her head.

I want to know everything. The songs she'll hum when she steps into a recording studio for the first time. I want to be there for her first job interview—to watch her straighten the sleeves of her blazer and smooth down nerves she can't quite hide. To see the way she practices her smile in the reflection of a car window, whispering answers she's memorized like prayers. Every piece of her story, every thought she's too afraid to say out loud.

I want to be there for it all. For her.

Even if it takes a room full of lilies to make her understand that.

Just then, the extra whiteboard attached to the main one on the wall clicks open, sliding down with a loud bang. Mia jolts awake, startled. Her breathing quickens, and her hands grab onto my thighs without her even realizing it.

Her eyes dart around the room, looking for the source of the noise, before landing on me. When it clicks where she is—and who's she with—her face turns bright red. She quickly pulls her hands back like she's touched something hot.

"Sorry." she mumbles, looking flustered.

I smirk, unable to resist. "I didn't mind it."

Her eyes go wide, and she stammers before finally blurting, "Ha ha!" in the most unconvincing way possible.

I laugh softly. "Relax, Mia. I'm just kidding."

"How long have you been here?" she sighs, sliding an inch away from me.

"Barely ten minutes." I pause, then add, "Though I did notice you ignoring me earlier."

She looks at me, her brow furrowing. "Why would you… you think that?"

I raise an eyebrow. "Let's see—A, you didn't reply to my texts, and B, you're napping in a random lecture hall instead of your dorm."

She shifts awkwardly. "Well, this might surprise you, but some people actually like napping in lecture halls. It's very… refreshing. It's like all the knowledge just flows into your brain, very powerful—" She pauses with a sigh. "I'm not really convincing, am I?"

I shake my head.

She sighs again.

I release the playful demur, my tone softening. "I shouldn't have sprung that kiss on you last night."

"No. It's just…" she exhales. "It's not you, it's me."

I stay quiet, giving her space to explain.

"I grew up in a small town filled with criticizing people, and even though I was raised by open-minded parents, that nature somehow has affected me. Those are my roots." She pauses, her voice soft. "So whatever happened last night, it was magical, and I liked it, but it's hard for me to digest it."

I nod, listening.

"Mia," I say after a moment, my voice steady. "I won't push you. If you need time, I'll wait. One step at a time."

She studies me.

Then, finally, she says, "So you're ready to wait seventy years for a kiss?"

"However long it takes." I reply without hesitation.

She narrows her eyes. "I'm gonna say it. What's wrong with you?"

"What do you mean?"

"You're different. Sam and Alex always say you've never been in an actual relationship. You don't even *flirt*. It's always... one-night stands. And now, all of a sudden, you're chasing *me*?"

I tilt my head. "What's wrong with you?"

She blinks, caught off guard. "I don't know, *I freaked out over a kiss*. You tell me."

"Mia, when you talk, it's like the world shifts—like the cracks and shadows don't seem so harsh anymore. You make the chaos feel poetic, the ordinary seem extraordinary, and that's rare." I hold her gaze. "And who *doesn't* freak out over their first kiss? It's not about the kiss itself—it's about what it means. And let me be clear, Mia. I'm not chasing you. I *like you*."

My words hang between us, steady and unwavering.

She blinks again, her lips twitching like she wants to smile. "Geez. If you put it that way..."

I grin, deciding to lighten the mood. "I wanna be that guy. I wanna kiss your eyes. Drink that soft smile."

She smiles big. "Yeah... you *definitely* hit your head. You've started quoting Ed Sheeran."

"That was the plan."

She stands, slinging her bag over both shoulders before gesturing for me to move. I slide out of the desk, letting her pass.

She faces me, her eyes still holding a mix of determination and lingering sleep. "Yes."

"To what?"

"The second date."

I grin like a kid opening presents on Christmas morning.

She huffs. "Now, I'm going to my dorm for a *much-needed* nap."

She turns to leave but stops midway. Then, before I even process it, she's stepping back—her lips pressing softly against mine. A peck. Barely a kiss. But to me, it's everything.

She pulls away, her face flushed.

"I thought I had to wait seventy years."

"Well, lucky for you, I'm good at digestion." She groans. "And yes, I *know* how cringe that was. Now, don't follow me, don't talk to me—I'm going to go cry in humiliation and sink into my bed."

With that, she turns and walks off, leaving me standing there.

A dumb, ridiculous smile tugs at my lips, lingering exactly where Mia's kiss just was.

Miles's grin lingers in my mind as I step into the usually cold corridor which now feels strangely warm, my cheeks turning hundred shades of pink.

Holy shit.

Who am I?

Exiting the building into the biting November air, I glance back. He's still there, standing at the entrance, a quiet smirk playing on his lips. My heart somersaults, and my cheeks somehow flush even deeper. I turn forward quickly, determined to reach my dorm before I combust.

I can't believe it. I initiated a kiss. And on top of that, I said something cringe. My intrusive thoughts really won this round. But I couldn't help it—the guy listens to Ed Sheeran, *the* most respectable male artist in my opinion, and even quotes his lyrics.

And then there's what he said, about waiting seventy years without hesitation, taking things one step at a time. He had me genuinely wondering if I should go for him because he's such a considerate gentleman—or run away from him *because* he's such a considerate gentleman.

But I guess the kiss was my answer.

The winter breeze nips at my face, but it does nothing to cool my racing thoughts. I want to see him through, just like he does with me. I want to know what makes him laugh, what keeps him up at night, and what hides behind his too-good-to-be-true charm.

And maybe, just maybe, I don't mind if I find myself falling for him along the way.

Climbing the stairs to the third floor, I near my dorm and spot Sam outside the door, her palm rubbing her temple as if she's nursing the world's worst headache. She's still in her pajama set, looking like she just rolled out of bed—probably because she did.

"What are you doing out here?" I ask, but my question answers itself when I glance into our dorm room. Lilies. Everywhere.

So. Many. Lilies.

"They won't stop unless their boss tells them to." Sam says, frowning. "At first, I thought, who on earth is this obsessed with lilies? Then it hit me. Miles."

"Could you just say yes to the second date—or better yet, tell him to stop?" Sam pleads, shooting me a look that's both desperate and hilarious. "I love flowers, but I don't want to live with them."

"I already said yes!" I reply, my voice defensive but a little sheepish.

"Then what's this?" Sam gestures at the stream of people filing in and out of our room, each carrying massive bouquets.

A man with yet another bouquet brushes past us, and Sam groans like she's reached the limit of her patience. I sigh and pull my phone out of my bag. The notification bar is flooded with messages from Miles: *Where are you? Saw you go back inside? Is everything okay?* A pang of guilt tugs at me—I really need to start checking my texts. Nidhi's always scolding me for it, and maybe she has a point.

I tap on Miles' name and call him. He picks up almost immediately.

"Hello!" His voice is soft yet firm, with just a hint of excitement that makes my stomach flip.

"Um, there are people bringing endless bouquets of lilies into our dorm, and they're not stopping." I say, cutting straight to the issue.

"Oh, shit." he mutters on the other end. "I completely forgot I'd ordered those. I wanted it to be a nice gesture—guess I overdid it."

"That's really sweet, Miles, but, you know, one bouquet would've been more than enough." I say, my lips curving into a small smile. Who does this? Nobody. Not in a million years did I think I'd ever experience such grand romantic gestures.

"Yeah, I'll tell them to stop." he says, sounding sheepish now.

"And ask them to take back the ones already in the dorm!" Sam cuts in, speaking loudly into the phone. Her arms are crossed, and she looks ready to throttle someone. "The scent is getting *irritating*."

"Yeah, yeah, I'll fix it." Miles says, his tone amused. "Bye, Mia."

"Bye." I hang up, sliding the phone back into my bag.

"How is the scent irritating you? It's beautiful!" I glance at Sam.

She gives me a murderous glare.

"Someone woke up on the wrong side of the bed." I mutter under my breath.

One of the delivery men's phones rings, cutting through the faint hum of activity. The man holding a bouquet pauses, listens intently, and then nods. He turns to his team, murmuring something, and just like that, the parade of lilies reverses. One by one, they start carrying the flowers back out, leaving behind only the faint, sweet scent of their brief invasion.

Sam lets out a relieved sigh, her shoulders visibly relaxing. "Should we grab some coffee while they clear out our dorm?" she asks, already turning toward the hallway.

"Yeah." I agree, and we head down the corridor to the common kitchen.

CHAPTER 22

Miles

"I heard you and Chloe broke up." Shay says, clicking the ballpoint pen in his hand.

Shay Hawkins isn't just an employee at Baudelaire Global Enterprises; he's also one of my closest friends. As the head of our Marketing sector, he's sharp and resourceful. Of course, we also like to joke that he's the unofficial head of the office gossip community—a title he denies every chance he gets but still somehow embodies every day.

"First of all, we weren't even dating to break up. And secondly, where did you hear that." I glare, leaning back in my chair.

"A true man never reveals his secrets." he says with a grin.

I shake my head, smirking. "Someday I'm gonna find out your sources."

Shay raises an eyebrow. "Wow. A challenge? Okay, good luck with that."

Just then, my phone pings. I pull it out of my pocket and glance at the screen. It's a text from Alex.

Nate just had another panic attack.

A phantom fist grips my lungs with worry. I push my chair back and stand abruptly. "I gotta go." I say to Shay, my tone clipped.

Shay barely looks up from his computer, nodding in acknowledgment as I stride toward the elevator. I quickly text Alex back.

Where is he?

Alex's reply comes almost instantly. *Dorm.*

Me: *I'll be there in twenty.*

I shove my phone back into my pocket as the elevator descends to the ground floor, my mind racing.

Once in the parking lot, I climb into my car, start the ignition, and pull out onto the road. My thoughts churn restlessly; *Is Nate okay?*

Nate's panic attacks started after the appearance of Blackout Master in New York last month. The criminal raided the Dawson's Planetary Museum at night. The infamous thief had stolen the multi-million-dollar working model of the creation of Supernova—a devastating blow to the museum's reputation, and, consequently, to the Dawson family. The pressure from the fallout hit Nate hard and fast, and since then, the panic attacks have become a rare but unwelcome occurrence.

But what could've triggered him today? There hasn't been any news of Blackout Master's sightings or another theft.

My grip tightens on the steering wheel as I speed toward the campus. Whatever's going on, I need to be there for him.

I park my car in front of the entrance to Nate and Alex's dorm building at Columbia. I almost sprint to the second floor and knock on their door. Alex opens it, his expression tense. "He's in his room. And he's refusing to see a doctor. Again."

"I'll talk to him." I tell Alex, moving toward Nate's room.

I slowly open Nate's door, careful not to disturb him. He's sitting on the edge of the bed, his head buried in his hands. I sit beside him, trying to keep my voice calm. "Wanna talk about it? What happened?"

A minute ticks by, another minute passes, until Nate finally looks up, his face red. "There's something going on, and they're not telling me and Devon anything. It's frustrating."

I pause, searching for the right words. "Hey, I'm sure it's nothing. Was there another robbery?" I ask, trying to keep things light.

"No." he replies, shaking his head. "No, there was a note. Devon and I tried to ask Mom and Dad about it, but they just waved it off." He pauses, taking a deep breath. "But they looked worried. Maybe even scared. But they're not telling us anything."

I don't say anything for a moment, thinking through what he's said. "Maybe they're just trying to handle it themselves. Maybe it's nothing that big so they don't want you and Devon to worry. It's fine, Nate. Everything is fine." I assure him, even though I don't fully believe it.

Nate's parents have been more closed off since the Blackout Master incident, but I assumed it was just the stress from losing a valuable project. Now, hearing what Nate is saying, I'm starting to feel concerned. But I can't let him see that. He just had a panic attack, and I need to keep him calm.

He's like a brother to me. I can't let anything get to him.

My eyes scan Nate's tense posture. The room feels thick with unspoken worries. I try to keep my voice steady, not wanting to overwhelm him. "Nate, you should really see a doctor, man. You're not doing yourself any favours by holding this in."

Nate's hand curls into a fist on his lap. He looks away, avoiding my gaze. "I don't need a doctor." he mutters, his voice thick with frustration. "I just... I just need to know what's going on. What they're hiding."

I exhale sharply, rubbing the back of my neck. "I get that. But you're not going to figure it out by locking yourself in here and stressing yourself out. You've had a panic attack before, and you know they don't just go away. A doctor might be able to help."

Nate shakes his head, his fingers running through his hair in agitation. "I don't want to go to a doctor. They'll just say the same thing—'You're stressed.' 'You're overthinking.'" he mimics in a mocking tone. "It's not just that. I can't... I can't keep pretending like everything's fine when it's not."

I sigh, sitting back on the bed. I can see where he's coming from. The pressure of everything—the museum, the family secrets, his own anxiety—it's all building up on him. But he's not making this any easier by pushing away the one thing that might help him.

"Look, I get it. You're frustrated. But you don't have to go through this alone." I say softly, placing a hand on his shoulder. "I'm not going anywhere. Alex isn't going anywhere. But you need to take care of yourself, Nate. You don't have to solve everything right now. Let a doctor help. Please."

Nate's eyes flicker with something like relief, but he quickly pushes it away. "I'm fine for now. Just... give me a little more time, okay? I just need to figure some things out first. I promise I'll see someone soon."

I stare at him for a moment, weighing my options. I can see how much he's holding back—how much pain he's trying to mask. But I know Nate well enough to recognize that pushing him too hard will only make things worse. He needs space, but he also needs support.

"I'll wait," I finally say, my voice quiet but firm. "but if you need me—if you change your mind—you know I'm right here with you, right?"

He nods slowly, and for the first time since I walked in, I see a faint glimmer of gratitude in his eyes. "Yeah, I know. Thanks, Miles."

I glance back at him, lost in thought. I know this isn't over—not by a long shot—but for now, he's made his decision. And I'll respect it. But I won't stop looking out for him.

Nate suddenly looks at me. "You drove all the way from your office to Colombia just to check on me?" He chuckles softly, trying to lighten the mood.

A small smile tugs at my lips despite the tension still hanging in the air. "Yeah, I did." I say, shrugging casually. "I was worried, dude." I pause, looking at him seriously, "I don't want you going through this alone. Not if I can do something about it."

Nate raises an eyebrow. "I didn't know I meant that much to you."

"Well you know now." I reply without hesitation, my tone more sincere than I realize. "I'm not just going to sit back and let you get swallowed by this without at least checking in."

Nate's gaze softens, and for a second, it's like the weight on his shoulders lightens a little. "Thanks, man. I appreciate it." he mutters quietly, a small smile creeping onto his face.

I nod, standing up, patting him gently on the back. "Anytime, Nate. Just... don't be a stranger. We'll figure this out together."

He slowly, knowingly nods. "Um...Miles,"

"Yeah?"

"Don't tell Audrey. Not yet. I don't want her to worry." He says.

I nod and with that I walk out of the room, closing the door behind me. "Give him some time." I tell Alex.

"Okay." Alex says.

With that, I make my way to the stairs, but I can't shake the feeling that there's more going on than Nate's letting on. Still, for now, all I can do is be there for him.

As I make my way towards my car, another thought pops into my mind. I was going to call Mia to confirm our second date, but now that I'm already on campus, I might as well talk to her in person.

I pull out my phone and send her a quick text: *Where are you?*

As I move toward Hamilton Hall—her lecture building, I wait for a response. Almost two minutes pass before her reply comes in: *At the food cart near Hamilton Hall. Why?*

A small smile creeps onto my face as I type back: *I'm coming.*

For a couple of minutes, there's no response, and I picture her trying to figure out why I'd suddenly show up unannounced. Then, her next text arrives: *Okay.*

I chuckle quietly, slipping my phone back into my pocket. Mia definitely didn't expect an encounter with me today.

When I reach the food cart, I spot her instantly. She's standing off to the side, her arms crossed as she waits for her order, her hair catching the late-afternoon sunlight. She hasn't noticed me yet, so I take a second to watch her. She's biting her lip slightly, probably lost in her thoughts, and it's oddly fascinating.

Finally, I approach, calling out humorously, "Fancy meeting you here."

Mia spins around, her eyes widening in mock surprise. "Miles," she says, looking me up and down. "So, what are you doing here?"

"I was already on campus." I say, shrugging. "Thought it'd be better to talk to you about our second date in person."

She raises an eyebrow, clearly trying not to laugh. "You do realize you could've called, right? Or are you just using this as an excuse to cover up the fact that you failed last year and had to repeat your classes—hence why you keep coming back to campus? It's fine. There is nothing to be ashamed of. I understand."

"Umm... I only failed one class." I say, trying to keep a straight face.

"And which is that?" Mia quips, her tone playful.

"On how to stop looking at you." I reply smoothly.

Her head dips, but there's a small smile tugging at her lips, her cheeks already flushed pink. "You're something else, you know that?"

"So I've been told." I say, leaning casually against the food cart. "Anyway, I was thinking next Saturday. We could keep it casual this time—a walk in the park, some coffee after. What do you think?"

Her lips curl into a thoughtful smile as she tilts her head slightly. "That sounds nice. No fancy plans, just us?"

"Just us."

She nods, her eyes meeting mine. "Next Saturday it is, then."

I smile, feeling a small sense of accomplishment. "Great. It's a date."

Mia's order is called, and she grabs her coffee and muffin from the counter. She gestures at me with the cup, her expression teasing. "Since you're here, do you want anything?"

"Nah, I'm good." I say, waving it off. "Just needed to lock this down."

"Well, consider it locked." she says, laughing softly.

As she takes a sip of her coffee, I notice the way her eyes crinkle slightly at the corners, and it hits me how much I enjoy moments like these—simple and unscripted.

I'm about to leave when something nags at the back of my mind, a thought I've been trying to bury for days now.

We're both moving forward.

Before, having feelings for Mia was just a thought. A what-if. But now, after the date and kisses... it's real. Tangible. And that means I have to think about what I'll say to my dad—if I say anything at all.

Maybe I don't have to.

Maybe I should just see how far this goes first.

Maybe I don't have to awaken the volcano before the ground is even steady.

Without thinking, I take a seat at the table and blurt out, "Could this be a secret?"

Mia sets her cup down and gives me a quizzical look. "What?"

"My dad..." I hesitate, struggling to find the right words. I don't know how to explain this to her, and I'm terrified she might pull away before anything between us even has a chance to begin. But I have to be honest, I have to brave through this. "He won't really approve of me dating someone who isn't part of a billion dollar company inheritance. Someone who doesn't fit the family's expectations."

She raises an eyebrow and rubs her temple, trying to process what I've just said. "Where are you going with this?"

"I just..." I take a breath, the words tumbling out before I can second-guess them. "I just want to say I really like you. I really do. But the thing is, my dad... he has certain expectations for me. You remember Chloe, right?"

She nods, and I continue, "Well, he set up that date between me and Chloe. I was never interested in her, but I thought maybe it'd grow into something. Then you came along, and I realized there's no one else but you. But now that we're talking about dating, I need to ask—would it be okay if we kept this between us for now? Until I become CEO. I know it's complicated."

Mia pauses, her expression softening as she processes what I'm saying. "I'm glad you told me that. And I appreciate your honesty," she says slowly. "but I just need some time to think about it."

"That's okay." I reply, swallowing hard. "Take all the time you need."

She stands up, swinging her bag over her shoulder. Her gaze drifts away from me, lost in thought as she walks away, further and further until she disappears behind a large tree.

I've fucked this up. How can I be so afraid of my own father? Of course Mia's not going to want to be part of this secret arrangement. It's not fair to her. She's someone who should soar, not be trapped in some secret trysts.

I sit there, feeling the weight of my own stupidity settle around me.

Mia

I close my laptop, relieved to have finally finished the daunting assignment that's been weighing on me. At least that's one thing off my plate. I step away from my desk, turn off the lights, and crawl under the warmth of my comforter, hoping to quiet the whirlwind of emotions Miles stirred up.

I'm exhausted from all the thinking, typing away on my laptop, but as soon as my head hits the pillow, sleep refuses to come. My mind keeps circling back to him, to the answer I owe him, an answer I don't even have yet.

He wants us to keep our dating—one that hasn't even officially begin—a secret until he becomes CEO. I get it—his father looms over him like a dark cloud, controlling and unyielding. Audrey doesn't talk much about Lucien Baudelaire, but from what I've heard from Alex and Sam, the man is ruthless, the kind who thrives on power and annihilates anything that doesn't fit his plans. "*Cross his mind and get crushed.*" That's how Alex describes his nature. But why wait until Miles is CEO? What difference would that make?

And why the hell am I pining over this?

The second Miles said "Let's keep this between us for now." my instincts screamed, *Call it off. Call it off. Abort. Abort.* But my heart wouldn't let me. Instead, I told him I needed some time to think. Think about what? There's no manual for this. Every step I've taken so far feels wrong.

I was never supposed to get caught up in all of this—the dating, the messed up feelings. Yet here I am. I kissed a boy and I liked it, and not one person back in India knows, not even Nidhi. Deep down, I know why. As much as I've accepted what I've done, I can't shake the weight of it. I've crossed a line I can't uncross, and for what? For feelings I can't control?

I'm trying to hold myself together, but I need someone to pull me out of this spiral.

My brain knows what's right—what's rational. But my heart, full of feelings, emotions, and damn butterflies, refuses to listen. And somehow, it's winning. I even caught myself trying to text Miles that I'm okay with secret dating—twice. That's why my phone's locked away in my drawer right now.

Because I like him. And there's no shutting that off.

When he says he likes me too, I believe him. His eyes give him away every time. And when he says this secrecy is temporary, I believe him. But then I wonder—why am I projecting so far ahead? A future with Miles isn't guaranteed. Nothing about us is guaranteed.

Right now, we're just two people who like each other. That's it. There are no declarations of love, no promises of forever—just the beginning, fragile and untested. And yet, the potential for more is there, tempting me to take the leap, signaling the green light. I want to see where this could go, to demystify the layers of whatever *this* is.

But the secrecy—it's unsettling. It feels like standing too close to a cold, blue flame. Hidden, restrained, yet just as capable of burning everything down.

And for God's sake, I don't even know when he'll become CEO.

But then a thought hits me—aren't we already a secret? Uncle Rohan doesn't know. My first date, my first kiss—all of it is already hidden. And when Miles says 'secret' maybe he doesn't mean from Audrey, Sam, Alex, or Nate. They already know. So what difference does it make? I doubt I'll cross paths with the rest of his family anytime soon—at least not before he becomes CEO.

Maybe, just maybe, I'm overthinking this.

Half an hour passes. I try everything to sleep—I blinked my eyelids very fast, tried deep breathing, and bawled my eyes out staring at a particular spot on the wall—but nothing works. Only one remedy to my dilemma is left, which I had kept as my last resort. I get out of the warmth of my comforter, free my phone from its prison, and call Nidhi, praying she's not in the middle of a lecture.

She picks up in two rings, saying, "I was just thinking about you."

"I missed you too." I say. "You're not in a lecture right now, are you?"

"No," she says. "today we got a holiday because the supervisor of our college died last night."

"Oh, that's so sad." I say, my tone filled with sympathy.

"Don't be sad, he was old and a pain in the ass." she replies with a snort.

"Nidhi, that's a bad thing to say about a dead soul." I scold.

"Oh, forget about that. Why'd you call right now?" she asks, her tone shifting to curiosity.

"Because I miss you." I say, avoiding the real reason—how I called to rant about Miles, the kiss, and the loaded "secret us" proposal he dropped on me. And how I'm starting to feel like I'm slipping away from the values I once held so close to my existence as a good human being.

"We usually talk on weekends or just text. So, you need to vent, something's bothering you, and now you can't sleep because of it. Am I right?" she presses, a knowing edge in her voice.

"You know me so well." I admit with a sigh.

"How do you think I've managed to stay besties with your annoying ass for this long?" she teases.

I smile, already picturing her smirking on the other end of the line.

"Wait," she says suddenly. "I'm switching this to a video call."

I turn on my bedside lamp as her face appears on the screen. She's sitting cross-legged in her room, her hair a messy ponytail, holding a plate of *Poha*.

"Okay, spill." she says, raising an eyebrow.

I hesitate before blurting out, "So, I might've left out a teeny-tiny detail about the first date."

Her eyes narrow, and I launch into the story—how the date ended with Miles kissing me, and then how I kissed him the next time we met. As I speak, her jaw drops lower, her spoonful of Poha frozen mid-air. It's 10 a.m. in India, and I know she's probably just woken up, as usual for her on a no-school day just like Sam, and I'm bombing her with all this information.

When I finish, Nidhi stares at me like I've grown a second head. "What. The. Hell?" she finally says, her voice incredulous.

"I know! That's what I've been screaming at myself. What. The. Hell. Have. I. Done?" The words tumble out faster than I expect, my frustration spilling over. "I'm a bad person. A bad daughter, a bad niece, a bad best friend. I've lost my way. Since coming here—and since Miles—I've been acting like a spoiled, ungrateful brat. I don't know how to stop or control these feelings."

"Whoa, slow down. I just woke up." Nidhi says, cutting me off with a grin. "I meant *what the hell* as in, since when did you start having more fun than me on your own?"

Her playful tone lightens the weight in my chest, and I can't help but crack a small smile. Her grin stretches wider, teasing, like a horse that just kicked its wicked owner in the gut.

I dip my head down for a second before continuing, "When he came to propose the secret thing this afternoon, before things went south... I so desperately wanted him to kiss me," I confess, my voice faltering. "I needed it. I genuinely, willingly wanted him to kiss me. And now... now, I'm stuck in this tight spot."

The words spill out in a rush. "Part of me thinks—let's take the chance. Let's go with the secret dating. But then all the doubts start creeping in. How I'm disappointing Uncle Rohan, how I'm probably setting myself up for heartbreak. It's all stopping me and confusing me. And the fear of getting hurt again—falling into the endless pit of pain and judgment—is not helping either. If I do this, I'll lose the respect from Uncle Rohan and God knows how many others back home. But not going for what I want feels like I'm stopping myself from discovering a new me." I groan in frustration.

Nidhi leans forward, her gaze sharp and unyielding. "M, look where you're at."

"In my dorm." I reply hesitantly.

"No. I mean, yeah, technically, but—you're in *America*." she says, her voice laced with emphasis. "Far away from India, far away from all the pain, the loss. You're somewhat free now. So fly little bird. Let go. Nobody's gonna judge you anymore—not your family, not me—and not even *you* should judge yourself."

I stare at her through the screen, the truth in her words making my heart clench.

"I'm not going to tell you what to do about the secret dating thing with Miles," she continues, her tone softer but resolute. "But I'll tell you this: go with your heart. I know its cliché but stop overthinking every tiny step. Stop worrying about crossing lines because, quite frankly, M, you've already crossed an *ocean*–literally."

Her words linger, filling the space between us.

"You've worked so hard to get there. You've earned the right to live your life without constantly looking over your shoulder or second-guessing every move. Dating someone isn't going to take that away from you—not unless you let it. So have fun. Go wild. Live a little."

"What if it all ends in a breakup?" I whisper, my doubts rearing their ugly heads again. "What if it just ends up hurting me?"

"Well," she says with a wry smile, "aren't you already accustomed to pain bigger than a silly little breakup?"

I slowly nod, letting Nidhi's words sink in the pit of my stomach. There's a lot to think about. And I have time. I think.

But then again, I say, "But it feels weird—dating, kissing—that's not something I imagined myself falling into. And it feels so out of place for me."

"Well, then, if it makes you feel any better, the teens from Mumbai aren't any different from the teens there. The times have changed." she says.

"In the city, not in our small town." I interject.

"Who cares?" She shrugs, her carefree demeanor like a gust of wind blowing through my storm of thoughts. Then she starts singing Let It Go from Frozen with a little spin of her own, her untrained, free, very off-pitch vocals carrying through the line. "*Let it go, let it go, don't let it hold you back anymore. Turn away and open the door. Just don't care 'bout what they're going to say. Let the storm rage on. The pain never bothered you anyway...*"

I can't help but crack a smile as her voice fills my small, dimly lit room. The warmth of the comforter wraps around me, but it's her off-key rendition that truly eases the weight in my chest.

I take a deep breath. "I think I'm gonna hang up on you now."

She smirks. "Seriously, you have to stop overthinking. In fact, don't think at all."

"You know I can't do that—the not-thinking-at-all part." I say, though there's a small laugh in my voice now.

"I know." she mutters, almost to herself. Her face softens, and for a moment, her teasing smile turns into something warmer, more supportive.

"Goodnight, Mia." she says with a grin that reaches her eyes, like she knows she's managed to chip away at my circling thoughts.

"Have a good day, Nidhi." I reply, the tension in my shoulders easing just a little.

And we end the call with a small laugh, the sound lingering in the quiet of my dorm room. I set my phone down, staring at the ceiling as her words echo in my mind: *Fly. Let go. Live a little.*

My heart flutters at the thought, but my rational mind urges me to tread carefully. Then, my phone pings, the display lighting up with a text from Nidhi:

It's worth a shot. Have fun. Go Wild!

A small smile tugs at my lips as I sink back into my bed, deciding to shut off the helix-like thoughts of Miles, if only for tonight. Nidhi's laughter and her hilariously off-key singing linger in my head, lulling me into a restless but strangely lighter sleep.

CHAPTER 23

Miles

The air is cool against my skin, the faint scent of rosemary drifting up from the gardens below. The mansion's balcony stretches wide, overlooking the fountain at the center of the perfectly landscaped grounds. The sun hasn't started setting yet, but the sky is shifting—gold seeping into blue, like a warning that the day is running out.

Audrey stands beside me, her arms folded, her gaze fixed on the view. I don't look at her when I ask, "Did Mia join Sam's place for Thanksgiving?"

Audrey exhales. "No. She's hanging out in the dorm. Alone."

Mia is lonely on Thanksgiving.

Your fault, Miles.

My grip tightens on the balcony railing, my jaw clenching. Audrey doesn't miss it. She continues, her voice even. "She doesn't really care about Thanksgiving. Makes sense—it's not her holiday." Then, after a pause, she adds, "But she seemed upset. For a whole other reason."

Her words are careful, but firm.

"Sam and I asked what was wrong. She just waved it off. But I think we both know it's because of you."

I don't respond. I don't need to.

Audrey shifts beside me, smoothly folding her arms. When I finally glance at her, she's giving me a look that's far too knowing for my liking. She's pissed. And she's trying *really* hard not to explode on her older brother.

"What did you do, Miles?" Her voice is quiet but it carries a cold egde. "Were you just messing around with her?"

A pause.

"Please say no."

I roll my eyes, but her words land harder than I want to admit. This is me we're talking about—the guy who never stayed past sunrise, who made sure every goodbye came with a distraction. But Mia? She's different. She's everything different. And somehow, I've managed to screw it all up.

"No," I mutter.

"Then what happened?" she presses.

"It's complicated."

"Try me."

I shove my hands into my pockets, staring down at the garden below. "You know how Dad is. He's obsessed with his perfect little image. Everything has to be controlled—including me. And Mia? She's amazing, but she's not the kind of person he'd ever approve of. So, I asked her if we could keep things quiet... until I'm in a position to make my own rules."

Audrey raises an eyebrow. "Secret dating? That's bold." But then she sighs. "But, you had to do what you had to do."

I shake my head. "It's not bold. It's stupid." The words leave me like a confession. "I told her I wouldn't make her uncomfortable, that I wanted this to be different. Better. And then I go and pull this crap—make her feel like she's something I'm ashamed of."

Audrey studies me for a second. "Did she say that?"

"No." I exhale sharply. "But she didn't have to. You should've seen her face. She looked—stunned. Like I'd just betrayed her."

Audrey frowns. "Sounds like she wasn't expecting it."

"Of course she wasn't!" The frustration bubbles up before I can stop it. I drag a hand through my hair, trying to keep myself in check. "Sorry. It's just... I wanted to protect her. And Dad's not just controlling—he's vindictive. If he knew about us, I don't even want to imagine what he'd do."

Audrey leans against the railing, her voice softer now. "I know how Dad is, but did you actually explain that to her? The part where you're trying to protect her?"

I hesitate. "Not exactly. I mean, she needed time, but I told her it was just until I'm CEO."

"Yeah, no." Audrey shakes her head. "That's not how it works, brother. You should've told her right then. To her, it probably feels like *you* care about what people will think."

I groan. "That's what I'm afraid of. I thought I was doing the right thing, but now I'm pretty sure I just made things worse."

Audrey tilts her head, a small smirk forming. "You really like her, don't you?"

I glare at her. "That's not the point."

"It kind of is," she counters. "Because if you're serious about her, you need to figure this out. And if she's serious about you, she'll listen. But you've got to talk to her, Miles. Really talk."

I exhale, staring out at the garden again. "I don't know, Aud. You don't understand how big this is for her. Mia's not like us—where she's from, dating isn't casual. Saying yes to me wasn't just stepping out of her comfort zone—it was a leap. And then the kiss... That was monumental for her. For Mia, every one of these things carries weight. Trusting me, letting me in—it's huge."

Audrey watches me, thoughtful. "Sounds to me like she's already crossed more lines than she ever imagined she would—for you."

I nod, laughing bitterly. "And I went ahead and screwed it all up by asking her to hide. She deserves better than that. Hell, she deserves better than me."

"You're being too hard on yourself," Audrey says. "You're in a tough spot, balancing Dad's expectations and your feelings for her.

But it's not all on you. If she likes you—and I know she does—she'll find a way to meet you halfway."

I shake my head. "I don't know, Aud. She's been through a lot—loss, pain. She doesn't trust easily. Asking her to keep this a secret feels like I'm asking her to doubt me, to doubt what we could have."

Audrey steps closer, her voice lower now. "Then don't make it about doubting or hiding, Miles. Make it about protecting what you two could have. If she knows your reasons—really knows them—maybe it'll make a difference."

I sigh, rubbing the back of my neck. "I just wish it were simpler. I don't want to hurt her, but I'm afraid I already have."

"You don't know that yet. You might still have time."

"I might." I murmur.

I have to explain myself to her.

Because Mia is different.

I know *"she's made me feel different"* is a classic statement, maybe even a cliché, but it's the truth. She's made me feel different. She's made me feel like a piece of music I never knew I could play—one I've always wanted to hear but couldn't, until she came along.

It's the way she smiles, not just with her lips but with her whole being. It's the way her eyes light up when she talks about something she loves, as though the world itself could never contain her joy.

Mia's not just different—she's extraordinary.

And maybe that's what scares me the most. Because I'm not sure I'll ever find another piece of music like her again.

That's why I'm afraid to lose her.

Thanksgiving break is quiet, almost eerily so. The usual hum of chatter in the dorms has faded, replaced by an unsettling stillness. Most students have left for the holiday, eager to escape the pressures of assignments and exams.

But not Maverick.

We are camped out in my dorm room, surrounded by scribbled notes, and two empty coffee cups. Maverick had claimed it was "too much traveling, too many assignments" to go home for Thanksgiving, and I had believed him—until I caught him watching *The Hunger Games* on his laptop an hour ago instead of doing his part of the assignment.

"You're not even *trying* to work." I mutter, nudging his arm with my pen.

He smirks, not even glancing up. "I *was* trying. But then my brain shut down from overuse, and I needed a survival break."

I roll my eyes. "Your brain wasn't even *on* to begin with."

"Ouch." He places a dramatic hand over his heart. "And here I thought we were bonding."

Before I could argue, something thuds in Sam's room.

I purse my lips, turning to Maverick, wide-eyed. "Please, just ignore the human in that room."

Maverick tilts his head. "Oh, there's a human in there?"

I snort, about to respond when—knock, knock.

A sharp rap at the door cuts through the silence.

I glance at Maverick, who is now looking at me with a curious tilt of his head.

"Expecting someone?" he asks.

I shake my head, standing up. "No."

I make my way to the door, brushing loose strands of hair behind my ear before pulling it open.

And my eyes widen.

It's Miles.

He stands there, hands stuffed in the pockets of his jacket, his piercing blue eyes immediately scanning past me.

Straight to Maverick.

His gaze hardens, the air between us shifting in an instant.

Before he can say anything, I quickly step out into the hallway, closing the door behind me.

"What are you doing here?" I ask, keeping my voice steady despite the rapid beating of my heart.

Miles, however, isn't interested in answering that just yet. His eyes flicker toward the closed door behind me, his voice dropping into a sharp whisper.

"Who is that? What is he doing here?"

Something about his tone—possessive, demanding—makes me bristle.

"Firstly, none of your business." I shoot back, my arms crossing defensively. "Secondly, that's Maverick. He's my friend. We were studying. That's a thing students have to do to graduate."

Miles exhales sharply, some of the tension easing from his shoulders. His jaw clenches as if he was trying to bite back another question, another demand. Finally, he murmurs, "Sorry."

I sigh, forcing myself to relax. "What are you doing here anyway? Aren't you supposed to be with your family eating turkey?"

Miles shifts on his feet. "I made an excuse and bailed." His voice is lower now, less sharp, more raw. His eyes lock onto mine. "We need to talk."

A cold, anxious weight settles in my chest.

I wasn't ready for this. I thought I had *time*.

But I had to talk to him eventually.

I swallow hard. "Okay."

Miles runs a hand through his hair, exhaling slowly. When he speaks, his voice carries a weight that tugs at something deep inside me.

"I'm sorry."

I blink. "Oh"

"I'm sorry for making you feel like I was ashamed of you." He takes a hesitant step closer, the hall lights casting soft shadows across his face. "When I asked to keep things secret, it wasn't because of you. It was because of my dad. I just… I wanted to protect us. To protect *you*." He pauses, his throat bobbing. "I really like you, Mia. I don't want to lose you. And I'm sorry—sorry for being so bad at saying what I mean."

My heart lurches, caught in a chaotic storm of confusion, guilt, and something dangerously close to hope. His words echo in my head, each one pulling at the fragile walls I've built around myself. He looks at me now with those piercingly hopeful eyes, the kind that seem to see every corner of my soul, and I freeze, my breath hitching. My mouth parts in shock, the words I want to say tangling in my throat.

I want to respond—to tell him I understand, to demand more answers, or maybe to just say something that will stop this aching pull inside me.

"I'm not expecting an answer right now." Miles begins, his voice steady but low, "You can tell me no, but before you do…"

His words muddle into the background of my thoughts, and I can barely focus on them. My mind is stuck on the conversation from earlier—about protecting me from his dad, about fearing I'd think he was ashamed of us. The questions rise in my chest, pushing to the surface.

"Why do you feel the need to protect me from your dad?" I interrupt, my eyes meet his, challenging him to give me the truth.

Miles doesn't hesitate, his gaze unwavering. "He expects me to marry someone who's the heir to billions, someone who brings more power and status to the family—not someone I actually care about. If he finds out about us, the aftermath won't just be bad—it'll be devastating. Secrets are the only way to keep you safe."

His words are direct, almost matter-of-fact, but I can see the tension in his jaw and the rigid set of his shoulders. He's not just explaining; he's bracing himself for my reaction.

"You care about me." I murmur, almost to myself.

"Didn't I make that obvious from day one?" Miles steps closer, his voice softening as he speaks. There's something susceptible in his expression, a quiet plea for me to believe him.

"No, actually," I say, a small smile tugging at my lips despite the weight of the conversation. "On the first day, you were kind of grumpy."

Miles chuckles, the sound low and warm. "Fair. I was stressed about Audrey's car and my tight schedule. But normally, I'm very cool and collected."

"Cool, maybe." I tease, crossing my arms. "But collected? Debatable."

The faint grin on his face grows wider, and for a moment, the tension between us dissipates, replaced by something lighter. But the reprieve is brief, and the weight of everything unsaid settles over us again.

"I never thought you were ashamed of me." I admit, my voice quieter now. "I knew you had your reasons for what you said, but the idea of dating in secret threw me off. It felt... different. Like someone was watching me, waiting to judge me for changing. But I want to change. I want to make choices that push me out of my comfort zone. And yet, there's always this invisible person acting as a barrier in the way." I drop my gaze, running a hand through my hair as the words spill out.

Miles steps closer again, his hand moving as if to comfort me, but he pauses, looking at me with an intensity that's both calming and fierce. "The thing about invisible people is that they're never seen. And neither are their opinions or criticism."

His words hit me harder than I expect, and I drop my gaze. "You make it sound easy."

"It's not," he says simply. "But it's worth it." He pauses, his voice growing softer. "You're worth it."

I look up at him, and for a moment, everything feels smaller, quieter, as if it's just the two of us in this vast world.

"But why wait until you're CEO?" I ask, voicing the question that's been gnawing at me. "Why not stand up to him now?"

Miles exhales slowly, his expression darkening. "Because right now, he has all the power." He pauses, his shoulders stiffening as though bracing against an invisible weight. "My dad's an aggressive man—aggressive with words and influence. He can upend anyone's life with the snap of his fingers. But if I'm the CEO, he'll have to do more than just snap. I'll hold the upper hand. I'll have the freedom to choose." His gaze sharpens but his voice softens. "And when that happens, I want you there, beside me."

I feel my breath catch, uncertainty creeping into my voice. "How can you be so sure it's me?"

"Because I know myself." he says simply, his eyes never wavering from mine. "You've changed me into someone even more incredible. I've never felt this much interest, care, or curiosity about anyone else. I know what I want, and it's you. You're my *endgame*."

A startled laugh escapes me. "Did you really just squeeze in a Taylor song title?"

He smirks, a playful light entering his eyes. "I did. But I mean it—no matter what I have to face, even if it's going against my dad *someday*."

The corners of my lips twitch upward, and I can't help the small laugh that escapes. "I could say you shouldn't let your dad dictate your dating life, but then again, I'm letting some invisible, non-existent person control mine. So, I guess we're both at fault here."

Miles grins, leaning slightly toward me. "Then to silence them both, we just have to stick to the plan—if you're willing to join my weird world."

I smile faintly. "We have something in common—weird worlds. Miles, there's one small crack in the plan. I'm only here for two years."

"That's fine," he says, stepping closer again, his voice resolute. "I'm going to be announced CEO in less than two years."

I shake my head, a small laugh escaping me. "That doesn't change anything. I'm only here for two years."

"Well," he says, his gaze locking with mine as he steps just an inch closer, "aren't you planning on settling here?"

"I mean, I haven't thought about it," I admit, biting my lip. "But maybe. I had to make some bold and weird choices since I've come here. And I hate it, but at the same time, I kind of like the change.

So... I might consider it. Living here, I mean." I pause, a grin sneaking onto my face, "I just realised what you did there."

"I didn't do anything." Miles says, his tone feigning innocence.

"You slipped the idea into my head." I mutter, narrowing my eyes. "And I liked it."

"I swear," he replies with a grin, "I didn't do it on purpose."

"Okay, if you say so." I mutter, a chuckle escaping me.

Silence stretches between us, but it's not empty—it's charged. Every unspoken word, every lingering doubt, and every reckless desire hum between us like an unsung melody. I need to give Miles an answer. I need to say what terrifies me most.

The girl I used to be—the one who clung to rules, who feared what she couldn't control—would hate this. She'd warn me that secrets like this only lead to disaster. But every choice comes with risks. And maybe, just maybe, I'm ready to take this one.

I inhale deeply, steadying myself. "I know it's been an eternity since we started planning our second date." My voice is soft, yet firm, like I'm bracing for impact. "Maybe it's time we finally go on it."

Miles blinks, as if he wasn't expecting that. Then, slow and sure, a grin spreads across his face—boyish, dazzling, utterly him.

"What about tomorrow?" The words slip out as easily as breathing, as if he's been waiting to ask. "Just coffee. Nothing fancy."

"It's a date." I reply.

And just like that, the air shifts. The world feels a little lighter, a little brighter, like a storm passing and the sun breaking through.

Miles steps back slightly, his hands stuffed into his pockets, but he's still looking at me like I've just rewritten the stars. "I'll see you tomorrow then." His voice is soft, almost dreamy.

"Yeah."

He turns, ready to leave, but instinct pulls at me. "Wait."

He stops mid-step, turning back.

I hesitate for only a second before saying, "I should probably tell Maverick. I mean he's inside and we're outside." I gesture vaguely between us. "And I trust him."

Miles exhales a quiet chuckle. "Okay."

"And also…" I lower my voice slightly, shooting a glance at the door. "I'm pretty sure Alex has been eavesdropping this entire time."

Miles freezes. "Alex is here?"

"Yeah." I sigh. "He showed up right before you, looking for something Sam stole from him."

As if on cue, the door swings open, revealing Alex with a smirk so smug I want to throw something at him.

"Glad you two finally figured it out." he drawls, strolling past us like he owns the place. "Otherwise, I was gonna suggest just waiting until he's CEO."

And with that, he's gone, disappearing down the hallway, leaving nothing but his usual trail of mischief.

Miles lets out an exasperated scoff, shaking his head. "If he ever actually liked a girl, he wouldn't have said that."

I bite back a laugh. "And what would you have done if *I* had said that?"

Miles turns to me, disbelief in his eyes. "I'm relived you didn't, but I would've decorated all of Colombia in lilies.'"

I gape at him. "You wouldn't."

"I would." He's dead serious.

Narrowing my eyes, I cross my arms. "And how exactly would you explain that to your dad?"

Without missing a beat, he shrugs, smirking. "Easy. I'd blame it on Nate and Audrey."

A new voice cuts through our banter.

"You two," someone says, sounding utterly amused. "Never did I expect that."

I turn to find Maverick standing in the doorway, arms crossed, an eyebrow arched. His expression is one of pure astonishment, like he's just walked into the season finale of his favorite show.

"Maverick, this is Miles." I say, gesturing between them.

Maverick doesn't hesitate. He steps forward, extending his hand. "Hi. Nice to meet you man."

Miles doesn't move.

Not immediately.

A full minute stretches between them, thick with unspoken thoughts. The air feels electrocuted, like Miles is calculating something, debating. Maverick doesn't waver. His smirk remains, but there's a flicker of curiosity behind his eyes now—like he's trying to figure Miles out.

And then, finally, Miles shakes his hand.

Firm. Measured. A little too intentional to be casual.

Maverick tilts his head, amused. "Hesitation there, buddy?"

Miles meets his gaze, unreadable. "Just taking my time."

Silence lingers.

Then Miles' gaze lands on me. His hand grazes mine as he mutters, "I'll see you tomorrow. Bye, Mia."

I watch as he walks away, his steps unhurried, a small smile lingering on his lips. The moment feels fragile, like something I shouldn't hold onto for too long.

"So, you're dating him." Maverick states.

I nod. "You do know that you'll have to keep it quiet."

"Yeah, I got that." He confirms. A beat of silence. Then Maverick claps his hands together. "Great. Now, can we go back to watching the movie—I mean, working on the assignment?"

I roll my eyes, sinking back into my seat. Outside, the hallway is empty again, as if Miles had never been here at all. But the warmth on my skin where his hand touched mine lingers, refusing to fade.

CHAPTER 24

Miles

"Since when did we start bowling on weekends?" Audrey asks, raising an eyebrow.

"Since it's about time we spend more time together as a family." Dad answers, adjusting his jacket with a sigh.

The bowling alley is a blend of retro charm and modern vibes, with polished wooden lanes stretching out under soft, colourful lighting. Neon signs flicker above the lanes, casting a warm glow that makes the entire place feel alive and hyped. A faint hum of background music is playing from hidden speakers, punctuated by the rhythmic crash of bowling pins and the occasional burst of laughter from other players.

Bright digital scoreboards hang above each lane, displaying names and scores in bold colors. The air carries the faint, nostalgic scent of waxed floors and buttery popcorn, mixing with the sound of rolling balls and spinning strikes.

At the far end, a cozy snack bar with retro-styled stools serves everything from nachos to root beer floats, adding to the alley's family-friendly atmosphere. Small clusters of bowlers gather around the seating areas beside the lanes, where cushioned benches and low tables offer a place to relax between turns. It is a lively yet strangely comforting setting—the perfect backdrop for a night of strikes, spares, and maybe a little drama.

For the Baudelaire family, though, with Dad suddenly acting out of character in a place like this, something is definitely off. Drama isn't just a possibility—it's practically guaranteed.

Audrey leans in, her voice dropping to a whisper. "I think he woke up on the wrong side of the bed this morning."

"Tell me about it."

Dad moves towards the corner lane, grabbing a bowling ball and saying, his French accent very clear, "I'm a bit rusty, so I'm going to practice a few throws."

Audrey leans over to Mom, her curiosity piqued. "Psst…Mom."

Mom looks up, a gentle smile on her face. "Yes, honey?"

"What's wrong with him today?" Audrey asks, glancing at Dad, who's still fiddling with the bowling ball.

Mom shrugs, her smile growing. "He's just being young again."

Audrey's eyes widen in surprise. "He was like that when he was young?"

"Kinda." Mom says, nodding.

Audrey chuckles, shaking her head as she heads toward the small computer at the side of the lane to enter our names for scoring. Her fingers tap quickly on the touchscreen as she adds our family members. Then she turns, a teasing glint in her eye.

"Miles, should I add your name as Little Smiles?"

"Don't you dare do that, Aud." I shoot, narrowing my eyes as Mom tries to stifle a laugh.

Audrey smirks. "Just because you resisted, I'm going to do exactly that."

I close the distance between us in two quick strides, leaning over her shoulder to stop her from typing my grandma-given nickname.

"You're impossible." I mutter, trying to wrestle the screen away from her.

Audrey bursts into laughter. "Relax, Little Smiles, I was just kidding—maybe."

Our repartee is interrupted by the sound of footsteps getting closer and closer.

The Harringtons walk in, and Dad's face immediately lights up. He straightens, his ever-composed demeanor softening into a genuine smile as he spots them.

"Lucien! Long time no see!" Mr. Harrington calls out warmly.

Dad steps forward, shaking Mr. Harrington's hand with a firm grip. "It's been a while. I'm glad to finally see you." he says, his tone calm but welcoming.

Mr. Harrington claps Dad on the back. "Very generous of you to invite us to your family bowling night."

I lean toward Mom, whispering, "You didn't tell us the Harringtons were joining."

Mom smiles, her voice low but steady. "Your father thought it should be a surprise."

Before I can press any further, Chloe Harrington and her mom steps forward, there gazes immediately finding Mom.

Chloe smiles politely, "Hello, Mrs. Baudelaire, it's nice to finally meet you."

"You too, dear." Mom replies, returning the smile.

As if on cue, she and Chloe's mom hit it off right away, exchanging pleasantries with a shared laugh. Chloe turns to Audrey, offering a sheepish grin. "Hey, Audrey. It's nice to meet you when I'm not wasted."

Audrey smirks. "Yeah, same here."

"Sorry if I came off rude at the party." Chloe adds, her voice tinged with regret.

"Oh, no, and that was a long time ago." Audrey assures her with a casual wave of her hand.

Finally, Chloe turns to me, extending her hand. "Miles."

I shake her hand, matching her firm grip. "Chloe."

The moment feels oddly formal, considering our last encounter. I glance at Audrey, who scrunches her eyebrows at me, slightly questioning the drift in ambience.

"Ready to bowl?" Chloe asks, her tone light as she steps back to join her family.

I watch her walk away, my chest tightening with a mix of irritation and disbelief. I glance at Dad, who's now deep in conversation with Mr. Harrington, his expression unrevealing but oddly pleased.

I feel so betrayed right now. Dad wasn't trying to spend quality time with his family. This entire evening was just a ploy to patch me up with Chloe. If he thinks he can manipulate me like this again, he's wrong.

And Chloe—what's her game here? She was the one who confronted our issue that we wouldn't work out. Now she's trying to make small talk and play nice? It doesn't make sense, and I'm not about to play along.

"He didn't wake up on the wrong side of the bed," I say bluntly to Audrey. "He just chose to brush his teeth after showering."

Audrey snorts. "Come on, maybe it's just friends catching up—not him trying to play matchmaker. And maybe Chloe's just trying to clear the air. Not everything is a grand conspiracy."

I raise an eyebrow at her. "You don't believe that any more than I do."

Audrey sighs, trying to look reassuring. "Okay, maybe not. But just ignore it. Let's get through tonight and survive."

We exchange a knowing look.

"This is going to be an interesting night." I mutter.

Audrey nods, taking a deep breath. "Yeah, family time officially out the window."

With reluctant determination, we join the game that's about to kick off between the Baudelaires and the Harringtons.

It begins with Dad going first, of course. He takes his time picking a ball, adjusts his stance like he's at a professional tournament, and rolls it straight down the lane. A strike. Naturally.

Audrey claps lightly, leaning over to whisper, "Show-off."

Next up is Mr. Harrington, who knocks down eight pins. "Not bad for an old guy." he jokes, earning a laugh from everyone.

When Chloe's turn comes, she grabs a bright red bowling ball and rolls it with decent effort. Seven pins fall. She smiles, clearly unfazed. "I'll get the rest next time."

Then it's my turn. I step up, grab a ball, and take aim. It feels good the moment it leaves my hand, and when all ten pins fall, I can't help but grin.

"Not bad, Little Smiles." Audrey teases, earning a glare from me.

The game goes on like this—Chloe's awkward throws, dads throwing strikes like it's a competition, moms just playing for fun, and Audrey taking absolutely no effort to even throw the ball properly.

By the third round, Dad clears his throat and speaks up. "Looks like we're running low on snacks. Miles, why don't you and Chloe grab some more from the snack bar?"

I stiffen. "I'm sure someone else can—"

"No objections." Dad interrupts smoothly. "You're already sitting closest to the aisle."

Chloe looks equally reluctant, but she forces a smile. "Sure, Mr. Baudelaire."

Audrey gives me a look that screams *you're doomed,* and I glare back at her before standing. Chloe falls into step beside me as we make our way to the snack bar.

The walk passes in complete silence, the weight of the tension hanging between us. When we reach the counter, I order a couple of bags of popcorn, along with a mix of other snacks and drinks. As they prepare our order, I pay the bill. The items are neatly laid out in front of us, and Chloe picks up the tray with the drinks while I grab the popcorn and snacks.

"I didn't know either." Chloe says suddenly, her tone light with a hint of amusement. "Looks like our dads set us both up."

I glance at her, raising an eyebrow. "You've only seen me as the love struck girl, but that's not me. I'm more like the one behind the brick walls of an office, aiming for the glass-panelled suite with the throne."

She pauses, her words lingering in the air. I can't help but believe her—the conviction in her voice tells me we're both after the same thing. The big prize. The real one. The one that actually matters.

"Seems like it." I respond, my voice steady, and nod.

Chloe's lips curl into a mischievous grin. "You know what, Miles? Let's make this interesting. We'll act like total buddies—fist bumps, high-fives, the whole 'What's up, mate' thing."

I smirk, half-amused. "'What's up, *mate*?'"

She shrugs nonchalantly, raising an eyebrow. "Well, I just flew in from England, so…" Her voice trails off with playful intent.

I chuckle, shaking my head. "Fair enough." I concede with a shrug.

Her expression softens, and her gaze shifts. "So… are you dating Mia?"

My heart skips a beat. I hesitate, wondering if I should say it, but the silence between us is probably already giving it away. And I trust Chloe—she was the one who helped me break free and gave me the push I needed to finally be with Mia by eliminating the idea of us from the board.

"Yeah." I admit. "I am."

Chloe's smile brightens, genuine warmth flooding her green eyes. "I'm happy for you, Miles. Or should I say… mate?" She adds with a playful twinkle.

I smile back, but curiosity tugs at me. "What about you?" I ask, trying to keep the conversation light.

Chloe tucks a strand of hair behind her ear, her gaze thoughtful. "No, I'm not seeing anyone. I've realized that relationships aren't really my thing right now. I've been focusing on helping my dad with the business instead."

I nod, impressed by her dedication. "That's great. Sounds like you've got everything figured out."

She laughs softly, the sound warm and honest. "Not quite. But it's looking promising."

Arriving at our bowling lane, we set the snacks on the table, and I'm halfway to sitting down on the lounge when Dad comes up to me, his voice low. "I need to speak to you."

I stand fully, scanning the room. Audrey's started another round of bowling with Chloe, and Mr. Harrington is deep in conversation with my mom and his wife. I follow my dad, trying to suppress a sigh as he gestures toward the far end of the lane, where a small hallway leads to the bathrooms.

"So, how'd it go with Chloe?" he asks, his expression hopeful. The hopeful look catches me off guard—I've never seen him like this before.

"What?" I ask, though I know where this conversation is going.

"Is she interested in you again?" he asks, his eyes trained on mine.

"Dad, no." I say, holding his gaze. "We're just friends. Why do you think we both want to try again?"

He's quiet for a moment, but his eyes flicker to the side, and then back to me. "I thought you both broke up because of something that happened at Alex's Halloween party."

I clench my jaw. "Dad, Alex's party has nothing to do with it," I say, forcing calm into my tone. "Can we just drop this? Stop interfering in my love life. It's my choice."

He crosses his arms, narrowing his eyes. "You don't even have a *love* life." he snaps. "Sleeping around with random girls might've been fine in college, but it's not anymore. If you're going to take over the Baudelaire Empire, you need a partner, someone stable. Someone with a good reputation. Just like I had your mother. Handling a multi-billion-dollar business alone is reckless. And this... this *Liaison éphémère* approach to relationships? It's damaging to the family's image and mostly yours. We can't have you running the company like this. It's irresponsible."

My frustration flares, but I push it down. "I'll find the partner I want, on my own." I shoot back. "And stop pretending this is about me. It's not. You want control over Asia, and the Harringtons want Europe. So why don't you two work out a corporate deal without dragging Chloe and me into it as pawns? This has nothing to do with my relationships."

For a moment, his expression falters, like he's caught off guard. But he quickly regains his composure, trying to brush it off. "You're still stuck on this idea that everything's a power play, Miles. Harrington and I were talking business, not trying to manipulate you and Chloe. But you have to understand—this is about securing the future of the company. Your future too. You need to think long-term."

I feel my blood pressure rise, my chest tightening as I fight the urge to yell. "You don't get it." I say, trying to keep my voice steady but failing. "This isn't just about the damn empire. This is my life. I don't want to be part of some power-hungry scheme. I don't want my relationships, my future, my happiness to be controlled by some corporate deal. I want to make my own decisions. I don't need you making them for me."

Dad looks at me, his face closed-off. Then he takes a deep breath, like he's trying to calm himself. "You're not seeing the bigger picture." he says, quieter now, his voice almost pleading. "You think I'm trying to control you, but I'm not. I'm trying to protect you, to ensure your future. You're going to be running this empire one day, Miles, and it won't be easy. You need to be prepared for it. You need someone you can trust, someone who will be with you through all of it. A partner who will help you navigate this world."

I swallow hard, the weight of his words hitting me in a way I wasn't expecting. But as much as I understand his concern, I can't ignore the sense that he's manipulating me. The feeling that he doesn't see me, just the legacy he wants me to inherit.

"You think I need someone to *help me navigate this?*" I ask, my voice quieter now, more uncertain. "What about me figuring it out on my own? What if I want to be with someone because I care about them, not because it looks good for business?"

Dad's expression hardens again, his patience wearing thin. "You're not ready for that, Miles," he says firmly. "You're still too young. You need someone who understands the stakes, someone who knows what it takes to run this empire. I'm only looking out for you."

I stare at him, feeling a mix of anger and something else—disappointment, maybe? "You think I can't handle it," I say quietly, the words carrying more weight than I intended. "But I'll figure it out, Dad. And when I do, I'll be doing it on my terms, not yours."

For a moment, he doesn't respond. Then, with a sigh, he turns and walks away, his back stiff, leaving me standing there, feeling more alone than ever.

I had braced myself for a volcanic eruption, expecting him to explode, attracting the workers and people around us, but compared to the usual fiery outbursts, he was oddly calm. The way he controlled himself—so different from his typical temper—makes me wonder if I should've told him about Mia. About how perfect, balanced, sweet, and hilarious she is. The kind of partner I'd be proud to have by my side forever.

But then again, maybe he wasn't calm for my benefit. Maybe it was all an act—his restraint just a front because we were in a public place. The Harringtons were ten lanes away, and he probably didn't want to give them any ammunition. It was about maintaining his reputation, not wanting to lose face.

I warned you there'd be drama.

CHAPTER 25

Miles

"Alright, everyone knows the drill. The moment the door opens, we shout 'Happy Birthday'." I say, scanning the room. I glance at the group: Alex, Nate, Audrey, and Maverick Parker. I'll be honest, I don't like the guy, but he's Mia's friend, so I'll grin and suck it up for her.

All day long, no one—not a single person—has wished Mia a happy birthday. That's part of the plan. And right now, Mia and Sam are on their way back to the dorm, Mia completely oblivious to what's waiting for her.

The room is dark, save for the soft flicker of candles on a cake set in the middle of a coffee table. Gold and white decorations are scattered across the room, balloons hanging overhead, and a banner reading "*Happy Birthday, Mia*" proudly displayed on the wall. The air hums with excitement, and everyone holds their breath, waiting.

I check the door. The anticipation is killing me. I want this to be perfect for her.

Then I hear it—a key turning in the lock. The door swings open, and the moment Mia steps inside, we all shout in unison, "HAPPY BIRTHDAY!"

Mia freezes in the doorway, her eyes wide with surprise. She doesn't move. For a second, she looks completely confused, her gaze darting around the room like a startled cat. The silence is deafening, and I swear we all collectively hold our breath. My mind starts to spin—is this too much for her?

I mean, I could've gone big. I considered organizing a full-blown party, but that's not Mia. She's not the type for strangers spilling into a house just because there's music and free drinks. Mia loves celebrations filled with the people she cares about, with laughter and conversations—not noise and chaos.

The room feels like it's hanging by a thread, the tension thick in the air.

Finally, Mia breaks the silence. She blinks, looks at us, and says, "Sorry, I forgot it was my birthday."

A wave of relief sweeps through the room, and we all let out the collective breath we didn't even realize we were holding.

"I swear she's the first human to ever say that." Alex remarks, his voice dripping with loud disbelief.

The tension shatters into laughter, and Mia's confusion melts into a radiant smile. She steps further into the room, her face softening as she takes it all in—the decorations, the cake, and the people here just for her.

"Guys..." she starts, her voice thick with emotion. "This is amazing. Thank you."

I smile, a slow ember ignites through my chest. "Happy Birthday, Mia." I say quietly.

She looks at me, her eyes shimmering, and in that moment, I know it was all worth it.

Every moment—getting to know her, going on those few coffee dates after Thanksgiving, the hours spent just talking and being together—has led to this. And as I look at her now, I can't help but think that whatever the future holds with her, it's going to be worth it, too.

Audrey steps forward with a bright smile, nudging Mia gently. "Come on, birthday girl. Time to cut the cake." She hands Mia the cake knife, the handle wrapped with a delicate ribbon.

Mia looks at the cake, her eyes taking in the intricate decorations—a swirl of white frosting, golden accents, and her name written beautifully in the center. She hesitates for a moment, glancing around the room as if still trying to absorb it all.

"Alright." Alex says with a grin. "Let's not keep the cake waiting."

Everyone laughs, and Audrey waves her hand, encouraging Mia to move closer. "Go on! We've been waiting for this all day."

Mia finally steps up to the table, gripping the knife carefully. As she leans forward, the group breaks into the good old classic, "Happy Birthday to You."

The room fills with cheerful voices, some on key, others (like Alex) definitely not. But it doesn't matter—it's a symphony of warmth, friendship, and celebration. Mia's face softens with every word, her smile growing wider as the song continues.

When the final *"Happy Birthday to you!"* echoes in the air, Mia presses the knife into the cake, cutting a perfect slice. The room erupts into cheers, Nate pops the confetti canon and everyone claps as she lifts the slice, holding it up like a small victory.

She pauses, her eyes scanning the room before locking with mine. There's a mischievous twinkle in her gaze as she gestures for me to step closer.

I move toward her, my pulse quickening. "Here." she says softly, holding the slice up to my lips.

For a moment, I hesitate. "Mia, it's your birthday! You're supposed to have the first bite." I murmur, my voice low.

"How am I supposed to eat my own cake slice?" she counters, her tone playful. "That doesn't make sense."

I chuckle, leaning in and taking a bite, but the sweetness of the frosting doesn't compare to the warmth of her gesture.

"Your turn." I say, grabbing a fresh slice of cake. Carefully, I break off a piece and hold it up to her.

Mia hesitates, her cheeks turning a soft shade of pink, but then she leans forward, her lips brushing my fingers as she takes the bite.

"Alright, alright." Alex chimes in, clapping his hands dramatically. "Let's go, guys. We're not getting any cake tonight. These two lovebirds are in their own little world."

Everyone laughs, and Mia's blush deepens. "Oh, stop it." she says, her voice a mix of embarrassment and amusement.

"Who's next?" Mia asks, breaking the moment with a grin.

"I'm next." Alex pipes up, stepping forward with mock seriousness. "I think I deserve it for being the best birthday singer in the room."

"Debatable." Nate retorts, rolling his eyes with exaggerated flair, drawing a chorus of laughter.

Mia shakes her head, clearly entertained. She cuts another slice, places it on a plate, and hands it to Alex—but as soon as she does, Alex and Sam mischievously smear cake on her cheeks.

"Noo!" Mia exclaims, her eyes widening in mock horror. She dips her finger into the cake slice she handed Alex and retaliates, smearing it on both Sam and Alex's faces.

"That's what it feels like!" she says triumphantly.

The playful cake fight escalates faster than a corporate merger negotiation. I immediately pull out my handkerchief, offering it to Mia. She takes it, gratefully rubbing the cake from her cheeks.

"Someone hand me a piece before Alex eats the whole cake!" Audrey's voice cuts through the laughter.

Just then, Maverick Parker steps forward, moving toward Mia with a slight nod. "Hey, Happy Birthday," he says, his voice sincere but low.

"Thanks!" Mia replies politely, giving him a soft smile. "Thanks for coming."

He grins. "It was my pleasure. Actually, I got you something."

Mia looks up, curiosity sparking in her eyes. "You didn't have to."

"I insist." he says, reaching into his bag like he's about to pull out a magic trick. He hands her a neatly wrapped gift. "Open it."

Mia raises an eyebrow and starts peeling away the wrapping paper. When she sees what's inside, her eyes widen.

"Wow, how'd you get this?" she exclaims, holding up a vinyl record of The Tortured Poets Department: The Anthology by Taylor Swift.

"I have my ways." he says, a hint of pride in his voice.

"I can't believe you found this!" Mia says, holding the sold-out edition in her hands. "I thought I'd never get my hands on it."

"I wasn't sure if you'd like it." Maverick says, smiling. "I know it's been out for a while, but I thought it was worth a shot."

"I don't care how long it's been. You could've given me her first album's vinyl and I'd still be over the moon." Mia says, practically glowing with excitement.

"It's just a vinyl." I blurt out, my jaw tight.

Mia glances at me, unfazed by my outburst. "A sold-out vinyl." she says, grinning at Maverick Parker.

"Okay." I mutter, my voice tinged with jealousy.

"Thank you, Maverick." Mia says again, smiling at him.

Maverick steps away, joining Nate in a conversation. Mia watches him go, a soft smile spreading across her face. It's the kind of smile that could melt any frustration or jealousy—like it's doing to me right now.

She turns back to me, catching the way my jaw tightens. Her smile morphs into something smug, eyes glinting with amusement. "You were jealous, weren't you?"

I scoff. "Of Maverick Parker? No." The sharpness in my tone betrays me.

Mia arches an eyebrow. "Ah, so *that's* the issue."

I cross my arms, shifting my weight. "I just think it's funny," I say, voice casual, "how he went out of his way to get you that vinyl. Almost like he's trying to impress you."

Mia hums, clearly entertained. "We're just friends, Miles."

I exhale, rubbing a hand over my face. "I know. But *he* doesn't want to be just friends with you."

She tilts her head, considering my words. "Maybe not," she admits, "but he's well aware that all we'll stay is friends."

I look at her, searching her face for any trace of doubt, but there isn't any. Only confidence. Only reassurance.

"I know you're friends," I confess, "but you can't really control feelings, can you? No matter how hard you try."

"No, you can't." Mia agrees. She slips under my arm, resting her head on my shoulder. I instinctively wrap my arm around her, smiling at how comfortable she's become around me. It surprises me, but it shouldn't—because this is Mia, and this is us now.

"If we could control or delete feelings, I wouldn't be dating you." she adds, her voice soft, her eyes shining with something deeper.

"Now, I'm glad we can't." I whisper back, my voice carrying more weight than I expected.

"Me too." she murmurs, offering that smile again, the one that makes my heart flutter.

We both turn our attention back to the party. The cake is being passed around (mostly to Alex), the chatter between our friends picking up again, but I catch her sneaking another glance at me. Her eyes hold a softness I haven't seen before, a quiet gratitude that sends comfort spreading through my chest.

I meet her gaze, and in this moment, I realize that tonight isn't just about celebrating her birthday. It's about celebrating her— everything she's brought into my life. And I know, without a doubt, I'd do it all over again.

I've never been more certain of anything in my life: Mia deserves every moment of happiness, every reason to laugh, and every reason to smile. And I want to be the one who gives her those reasons, again and again.

The party has ended, and everyone has left—by everyone, I mean Maverick Parker. Alex has crashed on the couch, and Nate, Audrey, and I are cleaning up while Sam is doing absolute nothing.

Mia starts to clear the confetti from the table, but Audrey stops her. "Stop, you're the birthday girl. Sit down."

"But I want to help." Mia protests.

"You can help by sitting down." Audrey insists. "You know what, Miles, it's getting late. Don't you have to head back to New York? You should go. Mia, you should accompany him to his car."

"Very subtle, Aud." Mia says, rolling her eyes.

Nate nudges me, grinning. "Bye, dude."

I grab my coat and phone, while Mia slips into hers. We exit the dorm together, climbing down the stairs in silence. The silence could be awkward, but with Mia and me, it's comfortable. It feels like everything.

As we step outside, Mia softly mutters, "Thank you."

I start to say, "It was nothing." But what actually slips out is, "You're welcome."

She glances at me, her expression softening. "I said I forgot it was my birthday because... since my parents died, the only people who ever wished me were my best friend and my uncle. And I didn't get any messages from them yet. Time zones, I guess. So, it just slipped my mind."

Her words settle heavy in my chest, each one a window into the quiet pain she's been carrying. I want to reach out, to hold her hand, but something about her strength stops me—it's as if she's already holding herself together.

I look at her, my voice gentle. "Well, I won't let you forget your birthday from now on."

She gives me a small smile. "I know you won't."

For a moment, she pauses, her eyes focused ahead. "For the first time tonight, I was cutting a cake with purpose. All those other birthdays, when my best friend celebrated with me, I was just slicing a cake—serving it on a plate for people to eat, no real meaning behind it. It was just a cake."

"Just a cake." I echo softly.

"Yeah." she continues, her voice quieter now. "What was the point, right? What was the point of celebrating a birthday when it's followed by the anniversary of my parents' death? What's the point of being happy, then grieving? It didn't make any sense."

I glance at her, my chest tightening. "Are you still grieving?"

She shakes her head. "No. I don't think I am anymore. I think I've healed. I mean I had to, eventually."

She smiles again, and in that moment, I can see it—that quiet strength. It's as if she's finally healed, and maybe when she thinks of her parents now, it's not just the pain of their loss. Instead, she's reminded of the good parts—the laughter, the moments when they'd throw their heads back and laugh together. The good memories, not the dark ones.

"God, it feels like I've actually celebrated my birthday for the first time in four years." she says, her voice light and full of happiness that makes me smile.

I grin at her, teasing, "I didn't realize December fourteenth lands on a leap day."

She laughs softly as we reach my car, the sound of it settling somewhere deep in my chest, like a melody I never want to end.

I pull out a small, neatly wrapped box from my coat pocket. My fingers brush against the box in my pocket, the edges smooth but sharp enough to remind me how much this moment matters. *What if she doesn't like it?* I wonder. *What if she thinks it's too much?* But I force the thoughts aside, trying to focus on her.

"Mia. I have a gift for you." I say, my voice steady despite the nerves bubbling beneath the surface.

Mia looks at the box, then back at me with a teasing smile. "I thought the party was the gift."

"No." I reply, holding it out to her. "The party was just a warm-up. This is the real deal."

Curiosity flickers across her face as she takes the box, the paper crinkling softly under her fingers. "Alright."

"Open it." I urge, shifting slightly, feeling the weight of the moment.

She carefully peels back the wrapping. Inside, she finds a small velvet pouch. Her eyes flicker to mine, a mix of curiosity and something I can't quite place.

She opens the pouch and pulls out a delicate silver bracelet, its charm a tiny treble clef and quill pen encrusted with small, sparkling stones. Her breath catches, and for a moment, she doesn't say anything.

"Two of your favourite things." I explain, scratching the back of my neck awkwardly.

Mia looks at me, her eyes topaz bright under the soft glow of the streetlights. "Miles, this is—" She pauses, her voice thick with emotion. "It's perfect."

I watch as she slips it onto her wrist, the charm catching the light. She turns her hand, admiring it for a moment before looking back at me, her smile radiant. "Thank you."

"You're welcome." I smile back.

A delicate pulse stirs in my chest, like the soft rustling of leaves in an unseen breeze.

Mia steps closer, her arms wrapping around me in a hug. It's soft, but there's a depth to it that makes it feel like more. Like gratitude, comfort, and something I'm still figuring out.

When she pulls back, her cheeks are slightly flushed, and she's grinning. "Okay, you've officially outdone yourself."

"Well, I had to make sure you wouldn't forget this birthday," I say with a smirk. "Leap day or not."

She laughs again, and it's the kind of sound I'd happily bottle up and carry with me everywhere.

I lean in slowly, my breath catching as her eyes lock onto mine. Her smile fades, and in that moment, everything around us seems to dim, leaving just the two of us. The space between us feels like forevermore, but I don't pull back.

Mia leans in too, and when our lips meet, it's different this time. It's not hesitant or unsure. There's no doubt, no insecurity. It's as if every barrier she'd built around herself has disappeared, leaving only the naked vulnerabilities we've both been holding back.

The kiss deepens, soft and slow, and for the first time, Mia feels free to kiss me without holding anything back. No more delicate truths. No more second-guessing. It's just her and me, and nothing else matters.

But just as I feel everything fall into place, Mia's phone rings, cutting through the moment. She pulls back quickly, a little flustered. I look at her, half-smiling, not at all upset by the interruption.

She takes out her phone, seeing the caller ID and her face lighting up. "Sorry," she says, flashing me an apologetic smile. "It's Nidhi. My best friend—she must be calling to wish me."

I grin, happy to see that her best friend hasn't forgotten her birthday. "Go ahead. It's great that she's calling."

Mia answers the video call, her voice soft and full of warmth as she greets Nidhi. "Hey!" I watch her, a smile playing at the corners of my mouth. Despite the interruption, the moment still feels special, and I can't help but feel glad that Mia has people who care about her.

"Happy twentieth birthday, M!" Nidhi practically shouts with excitement.

Mia chuckles. "Thank you, Ni." Her tone is softer now, but there's an unmistakable happiness in her voice.

"Where are you right now?" Nidhi asks, adjusting the camera.

"I'm out." Mia replies. "What about you?"

"You know the art function I was telling you about?" Nidhi starts, her voice brimming with excitement.

Mia nods, a small smile playing on her lips. "Yeah, the one you've been looking forward to for weeks."

"Well, I'm in my hotel room getting ready for it. It starts in like an hour."

Mia tilts her head slightly. "Why aren't you there already?"

"I wanted to be the last one to walk in, you know, make an entrance." Nidhi smirks dramatically.

Mia laughs softly, shaking her head. "Classic Nidhi."

"Yeah, nobody can compete with my sass." Nidhi mutters, then quickly adds, "Hey, I'm sorry I forgot to wish you earlier—well, your morning, my night. Your birthday technically started yesterday for me, so I was going to wish you at the crack of dusk of my Indian time... until I got lost in the whole time zone chaos. I'm still lost."

"That's fine, I understand." Mia reassures her, holding up her hand like a peace offering.

"I knew you would. But you know, it's a lot! I have to juggle Indian time, American time, and now, Aussie time." Nidhi says, practically throwing her hands in the air.

Mia's eyes widen. "Wait, Vinit really went to Australia?"

Oh. Who's this Vinit guy? A small part of me feels the need to pay closer attention.

"Oh yeah. And no, I didn't cry for a whole day or anything," Nidhi says, voice dripping with sarcasm.

Mia frowns. "I'm so sorry, Ni. I didn't know."

Wait, Mia is confronting Nidhi. I exhale quietly. Okay, crisis averted. Vinit's probably her boyfriend. Not Mia's. Definitely not Mia's.

"It's okay." Nidhi says, the sarcasm melting away.

Mia's tone softens. "You could've called me." she says, sounding like she carries the weight of not being there for her best friend.

"Oh, come on, I didn't want to interrupt your love bubble with your boyfriend." Nidhi teases.

Mia freezes, her eyes darting to me like she's a deer caught in headlights.

I can't help but chuckle quietly, thinking I can get away with it. But of course, Nidhi hears me.

"He's there, isn't he?" she asks, grinning like she just found out a juicy secret.

Mia's cheeks instantly flush the shade of spilled wine. "Uh, yeah."

"Well, perfect opportunity for me to meet him, at least virtually, huh? He needs my approval." Nidhi says with seriousness.

"Okay." Mia says, sounding unsure if she's about to sign me up for some sort of weird initiation.

Mia turns to me, mouthing, "Sorry in advance."

I smile, mouthing back, "It's fine."

Mia hands her phone to me, and I can finally see the infamous Nidhi's face. She has almond-shaped eyes, a warm and radiant complexion, and chestnut hair, but it's not just her looks that stand out—it's her boldness and confidence. Maybe that's why Mia and Nidhi are such ride-or-die friends. They balance out everything for each other.

Mia's on the introverted side, and Nidhi balances it with her extroversion. Mia's calm, while Nidhi seems like an unstoppable and undetectable storm.

She appraises me for a second, her eyes sparkling with mischief. "Well, well, look at you." she says, her voice light but dripping with authority. "You definitely pass the 'Nidhi Approval Test'."

I exhale dramatically, relieved. "Phew, that's a relief."

"But," Nidhi continues, her grin turning a shade darker, "you do one thing that'll make her cry like a squirming cat, and I swear I'll put a dagger through that pretty face of yours. And trust me, I'm very skilled with a knife."

Mia's face goes from burgundy to a shade of pink that's never been discovered as she slaps a hand on her forehead. "Yeah, thanks for caring and for insulting me at the same time, Ni."

"Anytime, Mia." Nidhi says with a sarcastic wink.

I can't help but chuckle. "Umm, thanks for the... threat?"

Nidhi shrugs. "It's not a threat. It's a promise."

Mia turns to me, her eyes pleading for mercy, and I raise my hands in surrender. "I'm aware." I say, nodding dramatically like I've just survived a near-death experience.

Nidhi winks at me again. "Good, now that we're clear, I've got to go. Art function to bedazzle. Bye, Mia! I'll catch up with you later! Happy Birthday again."

As the call ends, she does this thing where she points two fingers at her eyes and then swings them toward me, like some exaggerated spy-movie gesture that screams, *I'm watching you.*

I can't help but laugh. "Wow. She's really something."

Mia gives me a look that says she's both mortified and kind of amused by the whole thing. "Yeah, that's Nidhi—the chaos in my life."

"Well," I say with a grin, leaning just slightly toward her, "I'm happy to brave through any chaos in your life for you, I mean I did pass the first test so."

Mia shakes her head, her cheeks still a little pink. "That's so French"

I reply lightly, "Well, I am half-French, so kinda in my genes."

With a half grin, Mia teases, "You know I've heard that French are more rude than romantic."

Feigning mock offense, I clutch my chest. "Wow, harsh. Who told you that? Nidhi? Because I'm starting to think she's sabotaging me."

Mia laughs softly, her eyes sparkling. "No, it was actually Vinit. He has this theory that French charm is just a cover for bad manners."

"Well, *Vinit* clearly hasn't met me." I counter, leaning back with a smug grin. "I'm the perfect blend—half French, full romantic, and one hundred percent polite."

She smirks, folding her arms. "Oh, really? What's the most romantic thing you've ever done, then? Impress me."

I tilt my head, pretending to think deeply. "Hmm. Once, I had hundreds of lilies delivered to the girl I liked. But, unfortunately, she had me take 'em back." I finish with mock hurt, shaking my head like it's a tragic tale.

Mia bursts into laughter, her face lighting up in a way that makes it impossible not to smile. "Umm... did you ever consider that maybe the girl's roommate held her hostage to make her send the lilies back?"

"Oh, right, the scent irritated her." I recall with exaggerated realization.

Before Mia can reply, her phone pings. She glances down, her smile fading slightly as she reads the notification.

"Everything okay?" I ask.

"It's from Nidhi." Mia opens the message, and her brows furrow as she stares at the screen. She turns it toward me—a photo of an Indian guy and a foreign girl in a PDA-heavy pose. Beneath it, Nidhi's text reads: *Just what I needed before my event.*

I frown. "Is that Vinit?"

Mia nods, quickly typing a reply: *You're Nidhi. You don't let a boy distract you from your passion.* She mutters, "That's the best I can do over a text."

"Who exactly is this Vinit?" I ask, curious now.

"Oh, Nidhi's undying, *crushing* crush since second grade." Mia replies, her voice laced with dry humour. "Those are her words."

"I thought he was her boyfriend." I say, confused.

"He is," Mia replies with a shrug, her tone carrying just enough humour to soften the jab, "in her delusional world."

I laugh, shaking my head. "She sounds... obsessed with him."

"She is. But that's Nidhi for you. Chaos personified."

A comfortable silence settles between us, the kind that feels more like understanding than an absence of words. Mia glances down at her wrist, her fingers brushing over the delicate bracelet, a gesture so casual yet full of meaning.

"I should go before my Uncle calls." she says finally, her voice softer now. She looks up at me, and there it is—one of those rare, unfiltered smiles that feels like a gift. "Goodnight, Miles. And thanks for this... and the party."

She gestures to her wrist, where the bracelet sits perfectly, like it was made just for her.

Technically, it was.

"Goodnight, Mia." I reply, my smile lingering—this one reserved just for her.

She turns and walks away, her figure disappearing into the night. I stay for a moment, watching, before sliding into the driver's seat, the scent of lilies seems to linger in the air—imaginary, maybe, but undeniable.

Her smile stays with me as I drive, a quiet flame in the cool night air. Tonight, I feel a little closer to her world—and I'm not ready to leave it just yet. Maybe I never want to.

CHAPTER 26

Mia

5

4

3

2

1

HAPPY NEW YEAR!!

The crowd erupts with cheers, laughter, and the clinking of glasses, their voices blending with the crackle of fireworks bursting across the star-studded sky. The air is charged with excitement, and I take it all in—the hum of celebration, the glittering decoration of fairy lights strung between poles, creating a soft and dreamy glow. Everything is magical.

I glance around me. Audrey and Nate are lost in their own world, their lips locked in a kiss that seems to scream *forever*. Sam is kissing some random guy she probably won't remember tomorrow, and even Alex is leaning into someone with a playful smirk, his hand curling into her hair.

Everywhere I look, couples are kissing, friends are embracing in a tight hug, and people are swept away in the moment, caught in the tide of affection and connection as a new year begins. And for the first time, I feel the pull too.

Why not?

After endless nights of texting, after the small but meaningful gestures that only someone like Miles could pull off, his constant sweet presence in my life, I finally feel ready. Ready to close the gap between us.

I turn to face him. He's standing there, his eyes crinkling with that smile of his which feels like home. His hands are in his pockets, his posture casual and comforting. He leans slightly toward me, about to say something—probably, "Happy New Year." But I don't let him.

Instead, I close the space between us, standing on my toes, and press my lips to his.

For a moment, time halts.

He stills, clearly caught off guard, but then I feel it—the moment he realizes what's happening. His lips respond, soft but deliberate, as if he's been waiting for this. His hand finds my waist, and the brief contact sends a jolt through me, a spark igniting a fire I didn't know I had inside.

As the kiss deepens, his fingers graze the bare edge of my waist, like sunlight slipping through winter's chill, his warmth igniting where the cold lingers. It's innocent yet electrifying, like a spark catching fire, leaving you hungry for the blaze that follows. His other hand slides up my back, pulling me closer until there's no space left between us.

Above us, fireworks burst into radiant cascades, painting the heavenly night sky with shades of pink, gold, and emerald. The light dances in his eyes when I finally pull back to catch my breath, and it feels like the entire universe is celebrating this moment with us.

I don't know how to describe what just happened except to say that it feels... right. It feels like everything. It's fearless. Like the lyrics of a song finally falling into place with the melody. Like every hypothetical word I've ever written about longing and love suddenly comes alive, and starts to makes sense.

"Happy New Year!" I manage to whisper, my voice barely audible over the pounding of my heart.

Miles smiles, his lips curving in way that makes it impossible to look anywhere else. "Happy New Year, Mia!" he says softly, his voice like velvet. Then, with a playful glint in his eyes, he adds, "Truly new for you."

I laugh quietly, still breathless. "Tell me about it." I whisper back.

I start to step away, suddenly overwhelmed by the intensity of the moment, but his hand doesn't let go. Instead, his grip tightens, anchoring me in place. His fingers splay gently over my waist, grounding me, as though silently telling me I don't need to run.

I exhale, leaning back into him. Turning slightly to face forward, I let my back rest against his chest. His heartbeat is steady, like a lullaby, as the second round of fireworks bursts overhead. Brilliant shades of red, violet, and silver light up the sky, their reflections shimmering on the glassy pond below.

"Miles," I whisper, not even sure what I'm about to say, but then we're interrupted.

"Happy New Year, lovers!" Alex's teasing voice breaks the spell.

I turn to see Alex and Sam standing beside us, both grinning like they've won some sort of prize.

Miles glares at Alex, his brows furrowing in mock annoyance. "Do you have to ruin everything?"

To my surprise, he doesn't let go of me. If anything, he pulls me closer, his thumb brushing absentmindedly along my side, as if to remind me I'm right where I'm supposed to be.

Sam giggles, nudging Alex. "Leave them alone. Let them have their moment."

Alex raises his hands in mock surrender. "Oh, sorry! My bad." he says with a cheeky wink.

Just then, Audrey and Nate appear, Audrey waving her phone triumphantly in the air like a prize. "Selfie time!" she announces, her excitement lighting up her face.

We all shuffle closer together, the six of us cramming into the frame. Miles keeps his arm firmly around me, holding me in place as if it's second nature. His warmth seeps into my skin, and I find myself leaning into him without even thinking.

"Alright, everyone! Say 'Happy New Year!'" Nate calls out as Audrey raises the phone.

"Happy New Year!" we all chorus, our voices blending with the fading sounds of celebration. The camera flashes, freezing the moment in time.

As we pull apart slightly, the others chattering and laughing, I can't help but glance around. The fireworks above start to fade, leaving a smoky haze in their wake, but the magic of the night lingers. I take a deep breath, letting the cool air fill my lungs as I smile to myself.

Audrey pulls out her phone, her eyes sparkling with excitement. "Okay, you guys have to see this." she says, motioning for Sam and me to join her.

She scrolls through the photos and videos she's taken throughout the night, her thumb swiping across the screen like a tour guide leading us through our own memories.

"This one's cute." she says, stopping at a selfie of all of us under the twinkling fairy lights. Our faces are lit with laughter.

"And *this*," she says, barely containing her laughter, "is my favourite." She flips to a video of Nate trying—and failing—to pose dramatically in front of the water fountain. The result is a hilarious freeze-frame where his expression looks like a cross between confusion and sneezing. Mostly sneezing.

Sam doubles over laughing, clutching my arm. "Oh my god, he's going to hate us for saving that."

"But I'm still keeping it." Audrey replies with a mischievous grin.

We flip through more photos and videos, giggling at the funny ones and smiling at the sweet ones. It's like reliving the night in miniature, each image bringing back the magic of a moment that already feels unforgettable.

In the middle of our laughter, I glance over at the boys. Miles, Nate, and Alex are huddled together a few steps away. They seem to be talking about something, their expressions ranging from amused to exasperated.

"What are they doing?" I ask, tilting my head to get a better view.

Audrey smirks. "Oh, they're probably trying to convince Alex *not* to do something ridiculous."

I watch as Miles gestures animatedly, his brows furrowing as he says something to Alex. Nate looks equally exasperated, shaking his head and throwing his hands up in mock defeat. Meanwhile, Alex leans back, arms crossed, with a grin that screams *I'm not listening to a single word you're saying.*

Sam nudges me. "I bet he's still on about that car racing tournament."

"Oh, the race, right." I murmur.

Audrey laughs, swiping to another picture. "Honestly, the only thing Alex listens to is his own dramatic monologue."

We dissolve into laughter again, the sound mingling with the distant hum of celebration. For a moment, I forget about everything else—the pressure, the doubts, the uncertainty—and let myself soak in the warmth of the people around me.

It's one of those rare nights where everything feels perfect. Like the kind of memory you tuck away in your heart, knowing you'll pull it out years later and smile.

Before Audrey could swipe through more photos, Nate approaches us, his expression tense. "Alex is doing it."

"Oh, no." I mutter under my breath.

The race Alex is participating in isn't dangerous or illegal—nothing like that—but the stakes are high. If you lose, you lose your car. And for Alex, his car is the one constant in his life. It's his longest-standing relationship. So, if he's betting his car, he must be prepared for the consequences. But if he loses, Nate and Miles will need to prepare for therapy because the aftermath is going to be a nightmare.

Sam raises an eyebrow. "Should we stop him?"

I look over at Miles, who is now rubbing his temples like he already knows the nightmare he's about to endure. "I don't think we can stop him," Miles says, "but we can stand in the stands and hope for the best."

Audrey shakes her head. "And by that, you mean help him find a way to gracefully lose his car without losing his dignity?"

"Exactly."

"Hey, I mean, Alex doesn't always think things through, but I don't think he's unreasonable about this race. Maybe he's trained and prepared to win." I say, trying to stay positive.

They all look at me intently, and I realize I don't know much about Alex's past like they do. I don't even know who his father is or other family members are, except that his mother is the president of our university.

"I guess I'm missing some pages from his history book." I add.

"Not some, a lot." Nate replies, a grin tugging at the corner of his mouth. "But yeah, let's go with the positive attitude—He'll win."

Now I'm curious about Alex's life, but before I can ask more, Miles says, "The race is about to start."

We all rush to the track, which is conveniently close to the party ground. The track itself isn't complicated. In fact, it's about as straightforward as it gets—a long, straight line that seems to stretch for a mile. There are plenty inclined areas on the tract, but nothing too difficult.

In my daze, thinking it looks easy, I say to Miles, "This track is simple. No twists or turns at all."

"That's what someone who hasn't seen the stunt at the far end would say." Miles replies calmly. "See that inclined area? That's the tough part."

"But it's just a hill-type platform." I protest.

"That's what we can see from here," Miles explains. "But it's actually a jump. A car jump. Big one."

"What? Fuck!" The curse slips out before I can stop myself.

Miles grins. "It's cute when you curse."

"Miles, that's a literal jump. What if Alex can't pull it off?" Panic starts to rise in my voice.

"Mia, don't worry. He's done it before. Well, it didn't go exactly as he wanted, but he's familiar with it." Miles reassures me. "Nate and I are more worried about Alex's emotional stability if he loses."

Engines roar to life, shaking the air as the cars line up at the starting line, my concerned gaze glued to the track. Alex's polished black Aston Martin stands out, bold and impossible to miss. The crowd, who had come to celebrate New Year's, is now roaring with excitement, their cheers blending with the thunder of the engines.

My heart races in tandem with the revving cars. I glance at Miles, his face calm but his jaw tight. He's not fooling me—he's just as worried as I am. Beside him, Nate fidgets with his watch, an uncharacteristic sign of nervous energy. Even Sam, usually the voice of casual indifference, has her arms crossed tightly over her chest. Audrey, unlike Nate and Miles, makes no attempt to hide her unease, clasping her hands tightly as if offering a silent prayer.

The announcer's voice booms over the speakers. "Ladies and gentlemen, racers, take your marks! Three... two... one... GO!"

The cars shoot off like lines of bullets, tires screeching and leaving trails of smoke. Alex's car quickly keeps up with the leader, a sleek black Ferrari. The race is a daze of color and noise, with each car fighting to stay ahead as the crowd cheers wildly.

At first, it looks simple. The straight track is all about speed, but as the cars get closer to the incline Miles mentioned, I notice on the big screen how scary it really is. The hill shoots up steeply, and at the top, the track just vanishes. There's nothing but air for about ten feet before it picks up again.

"This shouldn't be legal." I whisper, more to myself than anyone else.

Miles glances at me, his expression grim but steady. "But it is. Barely. It's also the part where a lot of racers chicken out."

"But Alex won't," Nate mutters. "Because he's Alex Prescott."

I squint at the track as Alex's car speeds up the hill, the front wheels lifting a bit. My breath catches in my throat. His car soars through the air, almost like time slows down, and then lands with a loud thud. For a moment, it looks like he's about to lose control—the car swerves close to the edge—but he quickly gets it back on track. The crowd cheers loudly.

"Holy shit!" I breathe, my fingers gripping Miles's arm. He doesn't pull away, though his lips twitch into a small smile despite the tension.

"He nailed it." Miles says, relief softening his voice. "But it's not over yet."

The race continues, the cars jostling for position as the finish line comes into view. Alex's car is still near the front, trading the lead position with the Ferrari in a fierce back-and-forth. Every time it looks like Alex has secured his spot, the Ferrari streams ahead again.

"He's pushing his engine too hard." Nate murmurs under his breath, his eyes narrowing. "If he keeps this up, he could blow it."

I don't know much about cars, but I can see what Nate means. My stomach knots. Why would he risk everything like this? What does this race mean to him?

The finish line is just a few hundred meters away now. Alex and the Ferrari are side by side, their speeds so close it's impossible to tell who's ahead. The crowd is on their feet, screaming and waving their arms.

"Come on, Alex." Sam whispers, her knuckles white as she clutches Nate's arms.

Nate mutters, "God, Sam, loosen your grip a little."

Sam doesn't respond.

At the last possible second, Alex's car surges forward. It's not by much—barely half a car length—but it's enough. He crosses the finish line just ahead of the Ferrari, and the crowd erupts in cheers.

I feel my knees weaken with relief. "He did it." I say, half in disbelief. "He actually did it."

Miles lets out a long breath, tension draining from his face. "Yeah, he did."

But as we make our way down to the track to meet him, I can't shake the nagging feeling that something's off. Alex climbs out of his car, a victorious grin on his face, but his movements are stiff, his shoulders tense. It's like the weight of what he just risked hasn't fully hit him yet—or maybe it has, and he's just good at hiding it.

"Congrats, man!" Nate claps him on the back, grinning from ear to ear. "That was insane!"

Alex chuckles, but it doesn't reach his eyes. "Yeah, it was something, all right."

I step forward, hesitant. "Alex... why did you do this? What if you had lost or got hurt?"

He looks at me, and for a moment, I see something raw in his expression. "Because sometimes you have to prove something to yourself." he says quietly. "Even if it's stupid."

I want to ask him what he means, but before I can, Miles steps in, his tone light. "Well, you proved it, all right. Now let's get out of here before your car decides it's had enough excitement for one night."

Alex smirks, but there's a flicker of gratitude in his eyes. "Yeah, good idea."

As we walk back toward the party, I can't help but wonder what Alex is trying so hard to prove—and who he's trying to prove it to.

"I don't understand why people want to party till dawn." I say aloud as Miles and I walk toward his apartment, which is just a fifteen-minute walk from the party.

After the race, the four of them tried to convince me to join their *After New Year's Campout Party*—a night of tents, bonfires, and likely no sleep—but I wasn't up for it. The excitement lingered, but the chaos had worn me out.

I planned to take the subway, but Miles offered me his guest room since it was too late to travel. I hesitated, but then I remembered—I'd stayed at his place before while too drunk to think. At least this time, I was fully aware and in control.

Miles chuckles beside me. "Not everyone is built to crash after a night like this. Some people like to ride the high as long as they can."

"I guess," I mutter. "But I'm definitely not one of those people. Three hours of smiling and walking around were more than enough for me."

He shrugs. "Fair enough. I've never really been the party-all-night type either."

I glance at him suspiciously as he says, "What?" with a hesitant smirk.

"I don't believe that." I grin, narrowing my eyes.

"Well, this adult Miles isn't the party-all-night type, but teenage Miles? That's a different story." he defends himself with a grin.

"Okay." I mutter, rolling my eyes.

As Miles and I continue walking toward his apartment, the cool night air is a welcome relief after the chaos of the race and the party. We're talking in low voices, making small talk, when suddenly, the shrill sound of sirens pierces the quiet of the street. A few feet ahead, I notice flashing lights and the chaotic scene of a car accident on the Brooklyn streets.

A black BMW and another car are tangled together, their front ends crumpled from the collision. The streets, which had felt so lively moments ago, now feel eerily quiet except for the distant hum of the sirens and the murmurs of people gathering around. My heart skips a beat when I notice the details more clearly: in the unrecognisable car, a little girl, no older than three, is sitting in the backseat, her face streaked with tears. She's crying loudly, her tiny hands pressed against the window, her sobs echoing in the night air.

Without thinking, I stop in my tracks, my eyes fixed on her.

The woman driving the car is slumped forward, unconscious, blood oozing from a wound on her head. I can't see her face, but the sight makes my stomach tighten. In the BMW, a man is also unconscious, the airbag blown out in front of him. The scene feels surreal—a moment suspended in time, a stark contrast to the energy of the party just a few blocks away.

Within seconds, medics arrive, their sirens blaring as they rush to the scene. The crew springs into action, assessing the situation. A woman in a white medical coat hurries toward the car. She opens the back door and carefully lifts the little girl out, trying her best to calm her. But the girl only cries harder, her tiny body shaking in the woman's arms.

"Hey, sweetie, it's okay." the woman says softly. But the child doesn't stop crying, her sobs becoming louder and more frantic.

The woman looks back at the paramedics, trying to assess the situation, her expression a mix of concern and helplessness. The girl's wails fill the air as she reaches for the car, her hands outstretched. "Mama! Mama!" she cries, her voice breaking with desperation.

The woman in the white coat hesitates, her eyes flicking to the unconscious mother in the driver's seat. "We're going to take care of her, sweetie." the medic says gently, but the girl only cries louder, her tiny voice a heartbreaking sound in the chaos.

The medic gently tries to pull the girl away from the car, but the little girl fights against her. "Mama!" she cries, reaching her tiny hands desperately toward the wrecked car. The woman's grip tightens, but the girl squirms, her small hands still trying to break free.

"We need to go, sweetie." the woman says softly, but the girl only screams louder. "Mama!" She struggles, eyes wide with fear, her voice breaking.

The woman tries to calm her as they move away from the horrifying scene, but the girl won't stop crying and calling for her mother, still unconscious in the front seat. The woman looks back at the scene, helpless, as the child clings to her.

My chest tightens as I watch, the girl's pain pulling at something deep inside me. Her cries echo in my mind, a raw reminder of my own loss. I feel my heart break for her, for the helplessness in her eyes.

The scene around us muzzles as my heart hammers in my chest. The sound of the girl's cries, desperate and loud, seems to echo in my mind, twisting something deep within me. I try to focus on the present, but all I can think about is the image of the little girl, her hands outstretched toward the unconscious woman in the driver's seat.

The familiar sting of tears fills my eyes as the memories come rushing back—memories of my own parents, taken from me in a car accident four years ago, on my sixteenth birthday. I can almost feel the shock, the numbness, as though it were happening all over again. My parents—gone in an instant, just like that.

Since then, there has always been a reminder of what was taken from me, of what I'll never get back. And now, seeing this child—this tiny, helpless soul, clutching at the air for her mother—pulls me back into that dark place I've tried hard to crawl out of. The pain is all-consuming, and for a moment, I think I've stopped breathing.

I feel Miles's presence beside me, steady and grounding, but I can't seem to shake the weight of what I'm feeling. The girl's cries are like a trigger, unlocking everything I've buried deep down. Her small face, so full of pain and confusion, is like a mirror of my own helplessness, that same fear I felt when I was left all alone.

I turn away, my chest tightening, the lump in my throat almost unbearable. But the tears don't come, only a wave of bad, sad déjà vu. My mind races, caught between the present and the past, between this little girl's despair and my own loss.

I lost my chance. My parents are gone, and nothing will ever change that. But maybe, just maybe, this girl still has hers. Her mother might survive, might have a chance to hold her again, to reassure her that she's not alone.

I don't know them. I don't know who they are or where they come from. But I find myself silently praying for them—for that little girl who's far too young to lose someone so important.

"Are you okay?" Miles's voice seeps through my thoughts, cutting gently through the haze of sadness.

I glance at him, ready to lie, to say, *yes*, and move past the weight pressing down on me. But the word won't come. Instead, I hear myself say, "No."

"It's okay to not be okay." he says softly, his voice steady and understanding.

I nod slowly, my feet finding motion again as we continue walking. The weight of the scene we left behind clings to the air between us, thick and unspoken. Miles doesn't press me to say more, and I'm grateful. Sometimes silence says enough.

The sounds of the city—cars rushing by, distant conversations, the clinking of bottles being emptied—seem muffled now. Everything feels distant, as if I'm trapped in a bubble of thoughts I can't escape. I keep picturing that little girl, her hands pressing against the glass, her voice shaking as she called for her mother.

I don't know what makes me pause, but suddenly, I stop again, just a few feet from the entrance to Miles's apartment building. I can't move any further. My body feels heavy, like I'm carrying something I can't put down. Miles pauses beside me, his eyes searching mine.

He places a gentle hand on my shoulder, not speaking, just there. The warmth of his touch, the quiet understanding in his presence—it's enough to nudge me forward. I take a shaky breath and nod, taking the first step toward the door.

When we reach his apartment, the scent of his space greets me—a subtle mix of cedarwood and something faintly spicy. I step inside, the air warm and inviting, a stark contrast to the chill that still clings to my skin. Miles closes the door behind us, the soft *click* echoing in the silence.

"Do you want some water or something to eat?" he asks, his voice low, careful.

I shake my head, slipping off my shoes. "No, I'm fine. Really."

His brows knit together, but he doesn't push. Instead, he watches me for a moment, as though trying to decide whether to believe me. "If you need anything, just let me know, okay?"

"I will." I say softly.

He nods, his concern still evident, but he lets it go. "The guest room's ready, I'll just get a bottle of water."

I make my way to the guest room, the familiar coziness of it wrapping around me like a blanket. The soft glow of the bedside lamp casts a warm light on the space. Miles appears in the doorway a few moments later, leaning against the frame. "Mia?"

I glance up, meeting his gaze.

"You sure you're okay?" he asks again, handing me the water bottle, his tone soft but insistent.

I manage a small smile. "I'm okay, Miles. Really."

He hesitates but finally nods. "Night, Mia."

"Night." I whisper.

I close the door as he disappears down the hall, and sink onto the bed, the mattress giving way beneath me. I curl up under the covers, the weight in my chest still there but lighter now, as though his presence has helped lift it, even just a little.

As my head sinks into the pillow, the image of the little girl flashes in my mind again, but this time it doesn't feel as suffocating. I close my eyes and take a deep breath, letting sleep pull me under.

Miles

I crash onto my bed, the scene from earlier still replaying in my mind like a bad movie. The crumpled cars, the frantic cries of the little girl, and the lifeless figure slumped in the driver's seat—it's all too vivid. If it's haunting me this much, I can't begin to imagine what it must be doing to Mia.

I've asked her if she's okay, and she said yes. But I know she's not. It's in the way her eyes are betraying the spark she holds, the way she avoided looking at me for too long, and the heaviness in her footsteps as she walked to her room. She's hurting, and I wish there was something—anything—I could do to take that pain away.

But I know Mia. She doesn't want anyone hovering over her like a storm cloud, casting shadows where she's trying to find light. She's strong, fiercely independent, and carrying more weight on her shoulders than she lets on. That doesn't mean she's okay, though.

I run a hand through my hair, sighing deeply. The helplessness gnaws at me. I want to knock on her door, to sit with her and tell her it's okay to let it all out. But I also know that sometimes people just need space, and pushing her right now might only make things worse.

Instead, I grab my laptop and try to look through some documents, trying to distract myself. But it doesn't work. My thoughts keep circling back to Mia. To the way her voice sounded when she said "No" earlier—honest and vulnerable. I've never heard her like that before.

I set my laptop down and stare at the ceiling. I don't know what it is about Mia, but she makes me care in a way that feels different. Deeper. It's not just about wanting to make sure she's okay—it's about wanting to be the person she can lean on when she needs someone.

But tonight, she chose to retreat. And as much as it kills me to sit back and do nothing, I have to respect that.

I close my eyes, hoping sleep will come, but it doesn't. My thoughts stay with Mia, wondering if she's managing to rest, or if she's lying awake with her memories, fighting a battle she shouldn't have to fight alone.

I don't remember falling asleep. One minute, I'm staring at the ceiling, my mind buzzing with thoughts of Mia, and the next, I'm plunged into the depths of sleep without realizing it.

It doesn't last long.

A sharp, panicked voice pulls me from the fog of slumber.

"No! No, please!"

I bolt upright, my heart racing as I try to orient myself. The voice is muffled but distinct, cutting through the silence of the apartment.

It's Mia.

I'm out of bed in seconds, my bare feet hitting the cold floor as I rush to her room. The door is shut, but her cries are clear now—frantic, anguished.

"No! Don't go. Please!"

Then something in her language I can't understand.

I hesitate for a fraction of a second, my hand hovering over the doorknob. She might not want me barging in, but her cries leave no room for doubt—she needs someone.

I twist the knob and step inside. The room is dimly lit by the glow of the streetlights outside, casting faint streaks of light across her face. She's tangled in the sheets, her head tossing side to side, tears streaming down her cheeks.

"Mia." I say softly, keeping my voice low. "Mia, it's okay. You're dreaming."

She doesn't respond, still trapped in whatever nightmare has its claws in her.

I step closer, crouching beside the bed. "Mia." I say again, more firmly this time. "It's okay. You're safe. It's just a dream."

Her eyes snap open, wide and unfocused, her chest heaving as she gasps for air. For a moment, she looks right through me, as if she's still half caught in the dream.

"It's okay." I say gently, keeping my distance to avoid startling her. "You're here, Mia. You're safe."

She blinks a few times, her breathing still ragged, before her gaze lands on me. Recognition slowly dawns in her eyes, followed by a flood of embarrassment.

"Oh god!" she whispers, sitting up and burying her face in her hands. "I–I'm sorry. I didn't mean to wake you."

"You don't have to apologize." I say, taking a cautious step closer. "You were having a nightmare."

She shakes her head quickly, her hands still covering her face. "No. It's nothing. I'll be fine."

I don't press her, even though I know it's not nothing. Instead, I grab the bottle of water sitting on the nightstand and hold it out to her.

"Here." I say, twisting the cap. "Drink this."

She hesitates before taking it, her hands trembling slightly as she brings the glass to her lips.

The silence stretches between us, heavy but not uncomfortable. I sit down on the edge of the bed, and wait for her to speak.

Finally, she sets the bottle down, her voice barely above a whisper. "I keep having these dreams. They're always the same, but tonight... it felt too real. Too vivid."

She takes a shaky breath, her gaze fixed on the blanket bunched in her lap. "I keep telling myself I've moved past it, that I'm okay. But then something happens, and it all comes rushing back. Like it never really left."

"It's okay to not be past it." I say after a moment. "Sometimes things like this take time. And that's fine."

She gives me a small, tired smile, but it doesn't quite reach her eyes. "You sure you'll be okay?" I ask, my voice soft.

She nods, her gaze dropping to the blanket she's twisting in her hands. "Yeah. I just... need a minute."

I stand, giving her a little space. "If you need anything, I'm here." I say, pausing at the door.

"Thanks." she says again, her voice barely above a whisper.

I linger for a moment, debating whether to say more, but ultimately decide to give her the space she's asked for. As I close the door behind me, I can't help but feel a pang of helplessness.

Back in my room, I sit on the edge of my bed, running a hand through my hair. Sleep feels impossible now, knowing she's hurting just a few steps away. But I remind myself that sometimes all you can do is be there—and hope it's enough.

Sunlight filters through the blinds, casting faint lines on the floor. I'm sitting on the couch, my phone in my hand, unable to stop thinking about last night—the accident, the little girl crying, and how upset Mia was. She's still asleep, and her room is quiet. I don't want to wake her.

But I can't just sit here, doing nothing. I remember the name of the hospital from the medic's jacket and the ambulance parked at the scene. If there's even a chance I can help, I have to try.

I pull up the hospital's number and dial, my fingers steady despite the tension in my chest.

"Good morning. St. Jose Medical Center, how can I assist you?" a crisp voice answers.

"Hi!" I start, clearing my throat. "I'm calling about the patients from the accident on Montague Street last night. A woman and a man were brought in."

There's a pause on the other end. "I'm sorry, sir, but we can't release information about patients unless you're a family member."

I expected that, but it doesn't stop the frustration from bubbling up. "I understand," I say evenly, "but I'm just trying to make sure they're okay. Is there anyone I can speak to about their condition?"

"I'm afraid that's confidential." the employee replies firmly, but there's a hint of regret in their tone.

I take a deep breath, leaning forward as I try another angle. "Listen, my name is Miles Baudelaire."

I didn't want to pull that card. But I'm helpless.

There's a beat of silence. Then a sharp intake of breath. "Baudelaire?" the voice asks, noticeably startled.

"Yes." I say, my tone calm but purposeful. "My family has supported St. Jose Medical Center for years. I'm not asking for anything invasive, but if there's something I can do to help, I'd like to know."

The hesitation is palpable, the employee is clearly weighing their options. "I... I can't give you specifics." they finally say, their voice quieter now. "But... if this is truly about helping, I can tell you this much—the mother's condition is critical. She needs surgery, but..."

They trail off, and I can feel the tension hanging in the air between us.

"But what?" I press gently.

The employee sighs. "Without insurance coverage, it's unlikely she'll be able to afford the procedure. And without it... well, it's complicated."

That's all I need to hear. "How much is it?"

"I'm sorry, sir, I really can't—"

"How much?" I interrupt, my voice firmer now.

There's another pause, and then a reluctant answer. "Around thirty thousand dollars for the initial procedures. Additional care could raise the total."

"Fine." My response is immediate, without hesitation. "Send me the details for the payments. I'll cover it."

The employee stammers, clearly caught off guard. "Mr. Baudelaire, I... Are you sure?"

"Yes." I reply firmly. "No one should lose their life because they can't afford help. Make sure the surgery happens, and ensure her child is taken care of, too."

I can hear her fumbling for words before she finally manages, "Thank you, sir. I'll make all the arrangements right away."

Something stirs in me—an ache that won't let go. I can't stop here. "Actually," I add, my voice steady but urgent, "send me a list of all your patients needing surgery without insurance coverage. I'll cover their expenses too."

There's a stunned silence on the other end. "I... I'll need to speak to my supervisor, but I'll ensure everything is handled promptly." Her tone is a mix of awe and gratitude.

"Good."

As I end the call, a strange sense of relief washes over me. It's not a solution to everything—not even close. But it's something.

I'm about to get up and make coffee when I hear soft footsteps padding down the hall. Turning, I see Mia appear, her eyes heavy with sleep but softer than they were last night.

"Morning." she murmurs, her voice hoarse, like she's still shaking off the remnants of sleep.

"Morning!" I reply, setting my phone down. "How are you feeling?"

She hesitates, her lips curving into a faint, almost shy smile. "Better."

"Good." I nod, standing up. "Coffee?"

"Yeah." she says softly, tucking a strand of hair behind her ear.

In a few minutes, two steaming cups of coffee sit on the counter. Mia takes hers with a small, contented sip, and I watch the tension in her shoulders ease just a little.

Then it hits me—I almost forgot. "Excuse me for a second." I say abruptly, leaving the kitchen.

I head to my office, where I open a cupboard and pull out a small box, its edges neatly wrapped in matte silver paper. Returning to the kitchen, I place it on the counter in front of Mia praying this'll make her feel better.

"What's this?" she asks, eyebrows knitting together in surprise.

"Open it and find out." I say, unable to hide a small grin in hopes that this will take her mind of the hurtful things.

Her gaze flicks from the box to me. "Wait, this is for me?"

"Yeah." I reply casually, leaning against the counter.

"Why?" she asks, clearly caught off guard.

I shrug, keeping my tone light. "Consider it a New Year's gift."

Mia looks at the box again. "But I didn't get you anything." she says, her voice almost apologetic.

"You don't have to." I say with a chuckle. "Just open it."

Mia looks at the box for a moment, her fingers brushing against the edge of the paper. She hesitates, her gaze flickering up to me.

"Go on." I encourage, nodding toward it.

With a deep breath, she begins peeling away the wrapping, careful and deliberate, as though the contents might break under her touch. The silver paper falls away, revealing a plain cardboard box. Her brow furrows as she lifts the lid.

Her eyes widen, and her lips part slightly in disbelief. Slowly, she reaches in and pulls out one of the items—a pristine vintage Taylor Swift vinyl.

"Oh my god." she whispers, her fingers tracing the edge of the cover. She sets it down gently and pulls out two more. "These... these aren't manufactured anymore."

"No, they're not." I reply, unable to stop the grin spreading across my face.

Her smile widens in an instant, and then, as if a dam breaks, she bursts into laughter. It's light and melodic, filling the space between us like a melody I don't want to forget.

She shakes her head in disbelief. "So how many Swifties did you rob for this?"

I smirk, leaning against the counter. "I'm sorry, that information is classified."

Mia laughs again, shaking her head as she continues to sift through the vinyls. There must be at least twenty, each in perfect condition. She pauses and glances at me, her expression turning slightly sheepish. "Miles... I don't have a vinyl player. That vinyl Maverick gave me? It's just sitting on my shelf."

"I don't even remember about that." I say, feigning innocence.

Her eyes narrow playfully. "Sure, you don't. This is totally normal behaviour."

I shrug, still grinning. "And I know you don't have a vinyl player." I admit. "You never played it. You just stared at all the pictures in it."

She stares at me, her brows shooting up. "So what, is this some elaborate plan to make me buy one?"

I chuckle. "Or maybe, there's a vinyl player underneath all those vinyls."

Her smile fades as realization dawns. She reaches back into the box and pulls out a sleek, vintage-inspired vinyl player.

Her mouth falls open, and she looks up at me. "You didn't..."

"I did." I say simply.

Setting the vinyl player down carefully on the counter, she shakes her head. "You're unbelievable, you know that? Now I feel bad for not getting anything for you."

"Unbelievable in a good way, I hope." I reply, stepping closer, the distance between us shrinking.

Her smile softens, and her gaze lingers on me. "In a very good way." she says quietly.

The warmth in her eyes pulls me in, and I find myself tucking a strand of her hair behind her ear, my fingers brushing her cheek. Her breath hitches slightly, her coffee forgotten on the counter.

"You don't have to feel bad for not getting me anything." I say softly, my voice lower now. "Seeing you like this? Laughing, smiling—it's more than enough for me."

Mia looks up at me, her brown eyes shimmering with emotion. For a moment, it feels like the world falls away, leaving just the two of us.

"I don't deserve this." she whispers.

"You deserve everything." I reply, my thumb lightly grazing her jawline.

Her lips part, but no words come out. Instead, she tilts her head slightly, leaning into my touch. I can feel the warmth radiating from her, the subtle pull between us growing stronger.

"Miles..." she begins, but I don't let her finish.

I close the distance, my lips brushing hers in a tentative kiss. It's soft, unhurried, and when she kisses me back, it's like the final piece of a puzzle falling into place.

When we pull apart, her cheeks are flushed, her eyes bright. She lets out a nervous laugh. "So, is this how you always deliver New Year's gifts?"

"Only for you." I reply, grinning.

She shakes her head, her smile widening. "You're impossible."

"Impossible to resist, apparently." I tease, earning a light swat on my arm.

As she laughs again, I can't help but think that I'd do anything to keep that sound in my life, to keep this warmth between us.

CHAPTER 27

Mia

"When you said, *Let's spend Saturday evening together* I didn't think your Benz would be third wheeling too." I quip, crossing my arms.

"We *are* spending it together," Miles replies smoothly, a grin tugging at his lips. "While you learn to drive."

"I don't want to." I counter quickly.

"Last week, you said the complete opposite."

"I was kidding." I huff. "Learning to drive means sitting in the front seat. I can't get over that phobia—at least not yet."

He nods understandingly. "I know." he says patiently. "But think about it—you're not sitting shotgun. You're sitting behind the wheel. You're in control of the car."

I raise a brow, unconvinced. "Yeah, but I'm not in control of the other cars on the road, am I?"

He sighs, his tone softening. "Mia, you're learning to drive in an *empty parking lot*. No traffic, no pressure. You just have to learn the basics. No streets today or until you're ready, I promise."

I glance at him sceptically, the pit in my stomach widening. "Even if I learn, even if I manage to muster the courage to drive on an actual street someday... I don't even own a car, Miles. What's the point?"

"That's a pretty futuristic worry." he says with a chuckle.

I glare at him and declare, "I'm not driving."

"Yes. You are." He's not giving up. "I will be sitting right beside, guiding you through it all."

I don't speak. Because I don't know myself what to do.

"So... should we?" he asks, gesturing toward the black car parked in the lot. It sits there like it's smirking at me, daring me to take the wheel.

I glance around, taking in the empty parking lot. It's wide and open, with no cars or obstacles in sight, just trees in the distance. The weather feels as close to perfect as it can get in May—warm enough to skip a jacket but with a light breeze that keeps the air from feeling heavy. The late afternoon sun hangs low, casting golden light over everything, and the scent of fresh grass and blooming flowers lingers in the air.

"Alright." I say, letting out a deep breath. "Let's learn how to drive.'"

Miles grins triumphantly and opens the driver's side door for me. "First step, get comfortable. Adjust the seat and mirrors."

Sliding into the driver's seat feels surreal, weird, and scary. But there's something new here too—an unfamiliar excitement buried beneath my nerves. I glance at him nervously. "Okay, but if this ends with me driving into a tree, it's your fault." I blurt out.

Miles laughs. "Noted."

I adjust the seat and mirrors, fidgeting with the controls more than necessary. It's not about comfort—it's about control, and the more I try to find it, the more I feel it slip away. I feel like if my parents were watching me from wherever they are, they'd be happy to see me partially overcoming my phobia. They'd be proud. Although they're doubts, but they will always be there. I should probably be friends with them by now.

"Mia?" Miles's voice pulls me from my thoughts, soft and patient. "You good?"

I nod, blinking away the fears threatening to override my system. "Yeah, I'm fine."

"Alright," he continues, his voice calm and steady. "Press the brake and shift into drive. Don't worry, the car will move forward on its own. Just keep it steady."

I follow his instructions, my hands gripping the steering wheel so tightly that my knuckles turn white. The car inches forward, and I feel a strange mix of panic and excitement.

"Look at you." Miles says encouragingly. "You're driving, Mia!"

I can't help but smile. "This feels... kind of nice."

"Now try giving it a little gas." he says, nodding toward the pedal.

"Gas?" I echo nervously.

"Just a tiny bit. Trust me, you've got this."

Taking a deep breath, I press the gas pedal lightly, and the car picks up speed—just a little. The wheels glide over the asphalt, and for the first time, I feel a flicker of confidence.

"I'm doing it." I say, my voice filled with wonder.

"You are." Miles says, beaming. "Keep it steady. Stay straight. You're a natural."

I drive in a straight line, the empty lot stretching out ahead of me like a runway. The steering feels responsive under my hands, and for a moment, I forget my fears entirely.

"Let's try a slow turn." Miles suggests.

I nod, carefully turning the wheel. The car responds smoothly, and I manage a full circle without panicking. "Not bad, right?"

"Not bad at all." he agrees, his voice warm with pride.

We do a few more laps around the lot, and I start to relax. The sunlight dances on the windshield, and I feel like I might actually enjoy this.

But just as I'm settling into the rhythm, a brown blur darts into my path.

"Mia, brake!" Miles says, his voice sharp yet calm with urgency.

My mind blanks. My foot hovers over the pedal, but I hesitate, panic freezing me in place.

"Mia."

I finally slam the brake, and the car jerks to a stop. My heart pounds as I grip the wheel, staring out the windshield.

A small puppy stands a few feet ahead, its tail wagging as if nothing happened.

"Oh my God!" I breathe, unbuckling my seatbelt and stumbling out of the car. "Is it okay? Did I–"

Miles is already out, checking on the dog. "He's fine, Mia." he calls over his shoulder. "You didn't hit him. He's just scared."

The puppy tilts its head at us, then wags off toward the trees, completely unharmed.

I let out a shaky laugh, relief washing over me. "I thought I–" My voice trails off as a new sound reaches my ears—a soft wheezing noise.

Miles crouches beside the car, his expression shifting. "Uh-oh."

"What is it?" I ask, my stomach sinking.

He gestures toward the front tire, now visibly deflated. "You drove over something sharp. The tire's popped."

My jaw drops. "You're kidding."

"Nope." he says, pointing to the nail lodged in the rubber.

I groan, leaning against the car. "Great. First driving lesson, and I already ruined your car."

"You didn't ruin it." Miles says, standing up and brushing his hands on his jeans. "It's just a tire. Happens to everyone."

"But I–"

"Mia," he cuts in gently. "You did great. You stopped the car in time, and that's what matters. The rest is just... part of the adventure."

I shake my head, but his calm demeanor soothes my nerves. "No, this is a sign that I shouldn't be behind a wheel."

"Or," he says with a grin, "a sign you're brave enough to handle the unexpected."

I roll my eyes.

"Come on," he says, nudging me toward the car. "Let's call for a tow truck and grab some ice cream while we wait. I think you've earned it. We can continue this at some other time."

"I'm not continuing this." I retort.

"You'll change your mind." He says confidently.

"What makes you think that?" I question.

"I just know." He simply replies.

I glare at him, "You're too confident." I retort again.

He tucks a loose strand of hair behind my ear and leans down, his forehead resting against mine. "Mia, you did amazing today. I'm proud of you."

My breath catches as his lips brush mine in a kiss that's soft, lingering, and full of unspoken promises. The tension in my chest melts away, replaced by a warmth that only he seems to bring.

"Ice cream?" he whispers, his voice low and filled with affection.

I smile, my cheeks flushed. "Yeah. Ice cream sounds good."

He takes my hand, lacing his fingers with mine. "Then let's make it the best post-driving-lesson treat ever."

"If you say so."

"What are they doing here?" I ask again, my voice tinged with both curiosity and dread.

"They are your dummies." Miles says with a grin, pointing at Alex and Nate, who wave at me from their respective cars. "They'll be driving around as practice."

"No, I'm the dummy here." I reply, crossing my arms and glaring at him. My chest tightens at the thought of this new challenge. "I'm not ready, Miles. This is too much."

"Yes, you are ready." he says, his voice calm but firm, as if trying to convince both of us. "You've been practicing for a month now, and you're already a pro at parking lot driving. Now you just need to get used to having other cars around."

I hesitate, my hands clenching the hem of my jacket. The idea of navigating around moving vehicles sends a shiver down my spine. What if I mess up? What if I hit them? What if—

"Mia," Miles interrupts my spiraling thoughts, stepping closer. His voice softens, but his gaze remains steady. "You can do this. I'm right here with you."

I look at him, my resolve wavering under his reassuring gaze. Finally, I let out a resigned sigh. "Fine."

I slide into the driver's seat, my heart pounds in my chest. Miles hops into the front passenger seat, his presence both comforting and nerve-wracking. I grip the steering wheel tightly, my knuckles turning white. You've got this." Miles says, his voice steady. "Remember what we practiced—ease into the gas, check your mirrors, and take it slow."

Out of the corner of my eye, I see Alex and Nate start their engines, their cars humming to life. They're already circling the lot, keeping a safe distance but moving just enough to simulate real traffic.

"Here goes nothing." I mumble, releasing the brake and pressing gently on the gas pedal. The car inches forward, and my nerves spike as I see Alex's car in my rearview mirror.

"Relax, Mia." Miles says, placing a hand on my shoulder. "You're in control. Focus on your lane and ignore them."

Easier said than done. My hands feel clammy on the wheel, and I keep glancing at the mirrors to make sure I'm not about to hit anyone.

"You're doing great." Miles says after a few minutes, his tone encouraging. "Now, let's try a turn. Signal left." I flick the indicator, my stomach flipping as I approach the corner. Slowly, I turn the wheel, keeping an eye on Nate's car ahead of me. To my surprise, the car follows my command smoothly.

"You see? Perfect!" Miles exclaims.

I manage a small smile, the tension in my shoulders easing just a fraction.

"Alright, next challenge—merge into their circle." Miles says.

"What?!" My eyes widen in panic.

"Just merge in. You've got this." he assures me.

With a deep breath, I inch closer to the makeshift traffic, signaling to merge. Alex slows down slightly to let me in, and I slide into the flow of cars, my heart hammering.

"There you go! You're driving with other cars now." Miles says, his excitement infectious.

Minutes pass, and I find myself getting the hang of it. The fear that had gripped me begins to fade, replaced by a growing sense of accomplishment. "You're doing amazing." Miles says, smiling at me. "See? Told you; you were ready."

As we loop around the parking lot, I even dare to glance at Alex, who gives me a thumbs-up through his window. Nate honks playfully, and I laugh, the sound surprising even myself.

For the first time, I feel like I can actually do this.

CHAPTER 28

Miles

"They said it's my birthday party, but it looks like it's my..." I begin to say, but Alex cuts in, smirking, "Your ball. And your dad probably expects you to find your Cinderella—expect this Cinderella has got be rich since birth."

"Yeah, for an old French guy, he really waltz-ed into this Disney theme." Sam adds with a sly grin. "Pun intended."

I roll my eyes, glancing at the extravagant décor—the towering crystal chandeliers, gilded arches, and the orchestra playing softly in the corner. "Honestly, I wouldn't put it past him. He's always had a flair for theatrics. First, it was, *'You need a partner to handle the massive empire with you'* Now, it's, *'You need a queen to complete your kingdom'*. He just sprinkled some Disney on top, thinking I'd buy it."

"Are you going to buy it?" Alex questions, raising an eyebrow.

"Do I need to answer that?" I shoot him a glaring look.

"Nope. You don't have to... No." Alex stammers, his grin fading. "I was just joking, and I thought you'd catch on, but I think it's clear you're stressed... and missing her."

Of course, I'm missing her. I haven't seen Mia for exactly seventy days. We text every day, but we barely call because she's staying with her uncle in Mumbai, and since he doesn't know about us, we don't want to risk anything until she's out of college.

Mia left for India on the last week of June, after deciding she needed to spend time with her family during the summer holidays. She won't be back for another week. God, I miss her.

Just then, Nate storms beside me, leaning against the balcony overlooking the fake dreamy ballroom.

"There are so many girls down there that I don't think we've met before. What the heck is happening?" Nate asks.

"Nothing's happening. It's just Lucien Baudelaire playing yet another one of his games." I reply bluntly, sipping the scotch in my hand.

"Well, thank God Mia's not here to see that. I can only imagine how many girls will be *accidentally* slipping their arms in yours." Nate says, his tone teasing but with a touch of sympathy.

I let out a quiet bitter laugh, though my heart heavy with longing.

Only one more week.

One more week until I can see her again.

The thought would be enough to get me through the rest of the night. I think.

Then, I hear a familiar voice, soft but full of warmth.

"Oh, my little smiles, Happy Birthday!"

I turn around to see my Grandma standing there, her arms open wide. I don't even hesitate. I wrap her in a tight hug, my heart lightening just a little.

"Thank you, Gran." I say, my voice thick with emotion.

"Oh, you're welcome." She grins, pulling back to look at me. Her silver hair shines in the dim light of the ballroom, and there's a sparkle in her eyes that makes everything feel a little less overwhelming.

She turns to Nate with a warm smile. "Oh, Nate! How are you, dear?"

"I'm thriving. How are you, Grandma B?" Nate replies, returning the affection.

Grandma B is what Audrey started calling her when she was a toddler, and it stuck. Now, practically all my friends and Audrey's friends, and their friends; basically everyone calls her that too.

"I'm doing fabulous." she says enthusiastically, always radiating positivity.

Then she turns to Alex and Sam, exchanging pleasantries with them. The way she moves through the room with ease—charming everyone, yet always with a gentle, genuine spirit—reminds me of the people who matter. Not the ones chasing empty titles and status, but the ones who care about the small, real moments.

I take a deep breath, allowing myself a brief moment of peace in the whirlwind of my dad's expectations. At least I've got this moment, and at least I've got her.

"Miles, there you are. It's time to cut the cake." my mom says, approaching us.

"Yeah." I reply, handing my glass of scotch to Nate and following my mom and Grandma B down the stairs.

We reach the center of the room, where Dad is standing. A massive table with a towering cake is set up in front of him, surrounded by dignified guests and ladies. My dad, ever the master of attention, greets Grandma B first. I try not to focus on the way the grandiosity of it all feels like a suffocating performance, and my mom seizes the chance and mutters quietly to me, "Talked to any ladies tonight?"

"So you were in on it too." I question, my voice still a whisper of disbelief. "I thought it was just Dad scheming."

"Well, he did propose the idea, and I agreed." she replies calmly.

"Like how you're agreeing with every decision he's made about my dating life so far?" I bite back, my tone bitter.

"You don't have to be so angry about this, Miles. We're just trying to help you." she says, her voice soft. "Unless you're already dating someone?"

I freeze. My heart skips a beat as it feels like all the blood drains from my face. Should I tell her? She's my mom. I've trusted her with so much of my life. But what if this is a test? The way she has teamed up with Dad to find me a worthy and wealthy partner lately has me wondering whether she'll even consider love in this situation.

I pause, torn between the truth and the fear of shattering everything. How will she react if I tell her about Mia? The love of my life, the one who doesn't fit the mold of what my parents want me to have, but the one who I can't stop thinking about.

"No." that's my answer. Everything is perfect. The plan is going great—*Secret until* CEO. There's no need to slash a dagger through it. "No! But that doesn't mean you both should interrupt in my life." I add.

"Okay, we'll back off. I don't wanna fight on your birthday." She says, her tone placating.

I nod, relieved yet wary. She might back off, but Dad won't.

Just then, Dad glances around. "Where's Audrey?"

I scan the crowd but don't see her. She's not even with Nate. "I don't know."

"She probably went to the restroom or something." Dad says, gesturing for me to stand beside the cake.

The ceremony begins. The gold-sculpted knife feels heavier than it should as I cut the cake to the orchestral rendition of "Happy Birthday."

Half an hour. That's how long it takes to endure the handshakes, wishes, and polite chatter. It could've been longer if Nate hadn't swooped in to save me like a prince's left-hand man.

"Audrey's missing!" Nate says suddenly, panic lacing his voice. "She went to the restroom an hour ago and hasn't come back."

"She probably had a wardrobe malfunction or something." Sam suggests nonchalantly.

"Or maybe she went to pick up your birthday present." Audrey's voice chimes in as she appears from the crowd, looking perfectly composed.

Nate glares. "You could've said something."

"Since when do you pick out presents last minute?" This from Alex.

Audrey smirks. "Since the present arrived late."

I'm about to ask her to stop speaking in riddles when the air shifts.

And there she is.

My heart stumbles. Time seems to slow, the noise of the crowd fading into a low hum. She's wearing a stunning black gown, its elegant silhouette highlighting her every move. The tied shoulder straps add a delicate, feminine charm, and the playful hem detail draws attention without overdoing it. Her bold red lipstick draws the eye, a striking contrast to her warm, glowing skin. But it's her eyes—those elegant brown eyes, now a shade of honey under the soft light—that holds me captive.

But it's not the dress. Or the makeup. Or the eyes. It's her. She has a way to make my heart stop beating, make me forget how to breathe. Yet, she is also the one who keeps me alive, who fills my lungs with life, who makes everything feel possible again.

Her gaze meets mine, and my thoughts spiral. How does she manage to look so effortlessly beautiful? Like she stepped out of my dreams, straight into this room to remind me why I can't go a single moment without thinking of her.

God, I love her.

Wait—

What?

I Love her.

I love her.

Before I can process this sudden realization—

"I'm the late present." Mia says, her voice soft and teasing, but her smile is what undoes me even more. That smile—my anchor, my chaos, my everything.

And in that moment, it feels like she's the only person in the room.

I can't help it. The pull is magnetic, overwhelming. Before I know it, my feet are moving, drawn to her like she's gravity itself. My hand lifts, instinctive and yearning, reaching out to touch her—just a graze, a reassurance that she's real.

But before I can close the gap, she steps back slightly, her voice barely a whisper. "Public place."

The words stop me mid-motion, my hand frozen in the air. The reality of our situation crashes down like a tidal wave. She's right. We can't. Not here. Not with so many people watching, not with my father somewhere in this very room.

I hate it. I hate that I'm the reason for this secrecy, even though it was to protect us from my father's wrath. The weight of my decision, of my cowardice, sits heavy in my chest.

My eyes flicker to hers, catching the fleeting look of understanding and frustration in her gaze, and then I look around. Behind me, the hallway stretches out, quieter than the rest of the rented function manor and at the end of it, there's a door to a snug lounge room.

Without thinking, I lean closer to her, keeping my voice low but firm. "Follow me."

Her brows knit in confusion for a second, but then she nods. I turn and lead the way. As we weave through the crowd, I hear Sam say, "Yup, we are just ghosts. Ignore us."

We ignore her and move down to the hallway. My heart races with every step, anticipation and nerves tangling in my chest. I stop at the lounge door, pushing it open and holding it for her to enter.

As soon as the door clicks shut behind us, the world outside fades. The air between us is charged, thick with everything unsaid.

"I couldn't stand it." I say, my voice rough. "Standing there, pretending that you are just a friend."

Her expression softens, but there's a sadness in her eyes that cuts me deeper than words ever could.

"Miles..." she starts, but I shake my head.

"No." I interrupt, stepping closer. "I hate this. I hate that we have to hide. I hate that I'm too scared of him that this—" I motion between us—"this is real. That you're it for me, Mia."

Her breath hitches, and for a moment, she just looks at me, as if trying to decide what to say. Then she steps closer, her hand brushing against mine, grounding me.

"I know." she says softly. "And I hate it too. But it won't always be like this."

Her words are a balm to the ache in my chest, but they're not enough. Not when all I want to do is pull her into my arms and never let go. But even here, even now, I hesitate, because the walls feel too thin, and the world outside feels too close.

So instead, I take her hand, threading my fingers through hers. It's not enough, but for now, it'll have to be.

But then she looks up at me, her gaze so open and trusting, and I know I can't hold back anymore. Slowly, I lean in, giving her plenty of time to stop me. When she doesn't, I press my lips to hers.

The kiss is soft, tentative, but it holds everything I feel—the longing, the frustration, *the love*. Her lips are warm, and for a moment, everything else ceases to exist. It's just her and me, our breaths mingling, our hearts beating in sync.

When we pull apart, I don't let go of her hand. My eyes search hers, and before I can stop myself, the words spill out, soft and reverent.

"I love you."

I love her. I love her because she's unapologetically herself. She carries so much stress and lose, yet she faces every day with a smile, lifting up everyone who seems sad. There's a light in her that makes you feel like everything will be okay, even when it seems like it won't. And somehow, through all of her struggles, she never loses that spark—her light shines, and you can't help but be drawn to it.

Her eyes widen, her lips parting in surprise. For a moment, she's quiet, and my heart sinks. She doesn't feel the same. Of course, she doesn't. I've rushed this.

She blinks, her emotions unseen, and mutters, "Wow, this is a surprise."

Panic claws at my chest. "You don't have to say it back. I just—"

Before I can finish, she steps closer, cutting me off with her words.

"I love you too."

Her voice is steady, but there's a softness to it that makes my heart soar. Relief washes over me, so intense it nearly brings me to my knees. I pull her into a hug, holding her like she's the only thing tethering me to the earth.

"I mean it." she whispers against my chest, and I press a kiss to the top of her head.

"So do I."

She leans back slightly, her eyes twinkling. "I almost forgot—happy birthday, Miles."

"Thank you." I grin. "You didn't tell me you were coming."

"Then it wouldn't have been a surprise."

"Well, it's the best surprise ever." I say, my heart swelling with gratitude.

"I'm glad you liked it." Her smile grows, lighting up her face in a way that makes my chest ache. "You said you love me."

"I did." My voice softens as I brush a strand of hair from her face. "I love you, Mia. And I'll say it a thousand times if you want me to."

"I love you too." she replies, her smile so radiant it feels bigger than the whole Milky Way.

"This is the best birthday ever." I whisper, intertwining our fingers.

And for the first time in what feels like forever, everything feels right—until the door swings open, and panic floods through both of us.

We quickly pull apart, spinning toward the door, but relief sweeps over me when I see who's entering. It's just Sam.

"Your dad is looking for you." she informs me, her tone casual but her eyes sharp.

"I'll see you later." I tell Mia, stealing one last quick kiss before I leave.

She smiles, and for the first time tonight, I feel like I can breathe again.

Mia

Miles leaves, and Sam turns to me, raising a curious brow. "Where did you get the dress?" she asks.

"Audrey put me in it." I reply. "I thought it'd be uncomfortable, but it's actually really nice."

"Yeah, Audrey's closet is like a treasure chest of comfort and glam." Sam agrees with a grin.

She looks at me for a moment longer before asking, "Shall we go?"

"Yep." I say, nodding. "Wherever we're going."

Sam and I leave the quiet hallway, stepping back into the lively buzz of the ballroom. The air is warm, filled with the low hum of conversations and the gentle clinking of glasses. My fingers graze the soft fabric of my dress as we weave through the crowd. Sam keeps glancing back at me, her lips twitching into a sly smile.

"What?" I ask, narrowing my eyes at her.

"Nothing." She shrugs, but her grin gives her away.

"Sam, what?" I press.

"I just... am curious. You and Miles have gotten pretty close. So... I'm curious. Did you lose your virginity?" Sam asks carefully.

"God, no. Why are you so curious about my virginity?" I mutter.

"Because you've been dating for a long time now." Sam says like it's the most obvious thing in the world.

"So?" I retort.

"It's nothing. Forget about it." She says cryptically.

I glare at her a moment, debating whether to press further, but I let it slide as we make it to the opposite side of the ballroom, where another hallway stretches out. The lighting here is softer, warmer, casting everything in a golden glow. Sam leads the way confidently, her heels clicking against the polished floor.

"Where are we going?" I ask.

"Dining hall." she replies.

We take a left turn, and suddenly, the hallway opens into a massive dining hall. It's breathtaking—an intricate blend of Victorian elegance and modern sophistication. Crystal chandeliers hang from the high ceiling, their light reflecting off the polished mahogany table that stretches across the room. The walls are lined with tall windows draped in velvet curtains, and the air smells faintly of roses and expensive perfume.

This room is different from the main hall's theme but equally marvelous.

At the table, Alex is already seated, talking to a blonde man with striking dark grey eyes. A few other people are with them—faces I don't recognize, but their lively chatter and easy smiles make them seem approachable.

"Finally!" Alex exclaims, waving us over. "I thought you two got lost."

Sam rolls her eyes. "It's not a maze, Alex. We're just fashionably late."

We make our way to the table, and I slip into an empty chair beside Sam.

"Where's Nate?" Sam asks.

"Oh, he bailed on us for boyfriend duty." Alex replies.

"What do you mean?" I ask.

"He probably went to sit with the Baudelaires because he's Audrey's boyfriend." Sam explains.

"Yeah." Alex confirms with a sad nod.

He then leans close to my ear and whispers, "Why don't you go join them? You're his girlfriend."

I glare at him. "Do you want me to answer that?"

"God, calm down. Why is everyone angry at my jokes today? I'm just trying to be funny." Alex retorts.

"Because you're joking about delicate topics, dude." Sam interjects with a smirk.

Then, "Hey, what do you think of this one?" The blonde man asks Alex.

"Yeah, it's perfect." Alex answers. Then Alex turns to us, saying, "Shay, this is Sam and Mia. And girls this is Shay Hawkins."

"Hello, ladies." Shay greets us with a polite nod.

And then after a while the dinner is served.

"So, how was India?" Sam asks, looking at me with a curious smile.

"It was a good vacation, but I'll admit I kinda missed America." I reply, brushing a strand of hair behind my ear.

"I know, we have that effect." Sam quips, nudging me playfully.

"No, she didn't miss America; she missed America's sexiest man alive." Alex chimes in, leaning casually against the doorway leading to the dining hall where we'd just come from.

"Get over yourself." Sam retorts, rolling her eyes.

"Oh, Alex is sexy." a new voice suddenly says from beside Alex. An elderly woman, probably in her eighties or nineties, steps into view from the hallway. She's petite, with soft, silver hair tied in a neat bun, wearing a strip-patterned dress that speaks to a timeless elegance. Her presence commands attention, but it's warm rather than intimidating.

"Thank you, Grandma B." Alex says, his face lighting up with a big grin.

"She only said that to make you feel better." Sam fires back, folding her arms across her chest.

Then, Sam leans closer to me, her voice dropping to a whisper. "She's Miles's grandma."

I freeze, a jolt of recognition hitting me. *Grace Browning.* I'd seen her photos online, but in person, she carries an air of sophistication that makes my heart race. My mind starts to whirl with questions. Does she know? About Miles and me?

I glance around instinctively, wondering if Miles is nearby. As if reading my mind, he steps into view, walking up to his grandmother.

"I was searching for you, Grandma." he says warmly.

Grace raises an eyebrow, her smile full of playful mischief. "You weren't bringing me to meet your girlfriend, so I thought I'd take matters into my own hands."

My heart skips a beat. *Girlfriend?* She does know. My pulse quickens as I try to keep my expression composed, but the flush creeping into my cheeks betrays me.

Miles, meanwhile, turns visibly red, shifting awkwardly on his feet. "I was about to... but you ran off."

"Do I look like someone who can run after a heavy meal?" she teases, her tone light.

"I didn't mean it literally." Miles mutters, scratching the back of his neck.

An amused silence settles over the group, broken only by Grace Browning's pointed look. "Well then, at least introduce me now." she says, clearly enjoying herself.

Alex and Sam burst into laughter, their mirth contagious. Miles and I exchange a quick glance, both of us blushing but too flustered to stop it.

"I...I'm Mia." I manage, extending a hand toward Mrs. Browning.

Her grip is firm yet gentle as she shakes my hand. "I know, dear." she says warmly. "It's a pleasure to finally meet you. Miles has told me all about you."

My gaze darts to Miles, who's now blushing even harder. "So has he." I say with a faint smile, hoping to lighten the moment.

"Oh, so little Smiles here has been talking about me to his girlfriend. That's nice." she says, her words dripping with teasing affection.

"Little Smiles?" I repeat, the nickname catching me off guard. I glance at Miles, who looks as though he wishes the ground would swallow him whole.

"Did you have to call me that in front of everyone?" Miles grumbles. "You're embarrassing me."

"I'm not embarrassing you." Mrs. Browning says, feigning innocence.

"No, she's not. She's just exposing your secrets, *Little Smiles.*" Sam says, her voice brimming with mockery.

Alex and I stifle laughter as Miles groans, clearly regretting this entire interaction.

Before he can retort, the atmosphere shifts. Lucien Baudelaire steps into our conversation, and everything changes.

Alex immediately straightens up, no longer leaning against the wall. Sam's smirk vanishes as she folds her arms, suddenly serious. I clutch my phone tighter than I should, my palms clammy. Even Miles's usual relaxed demeanor gives way to a neutral, almost guarded expression.

The only person unaffected is Grace Browning, who greets Lucien Baudelaire with an air of ease that seems exclusive to her.

I'd thought Alex and Sam were exaggerating when they said Lucien Baudelaire could quieten a room with his mere presence. Now, standing here, I understand exactly what they meant.

"Oh, hello, everyone!" He says, his voice smooth and commanding. His gaze lands on Alex. "It's been a while, Alex."

Alex nods awkwardly.

Then he turns to me, his eyes sharp. "You must be Audrey's new friend."

He's talking to me. The words are directed at me.

Me!

My stomach flips. God, I wish I could disappear.

"Yes." I manage to utter, my voice barely steady.

"Mia, right? It's a pleasure to meet you." he says, extending a hand.

"It's a pleasure to meet you too." I reply, shaking his hand and praying my nerves don't show.

"I didn't mean to interrupt your gathering." he continues, turning to Mrs. Browning. "I just wanted to let you know that Seraphina is heading home. Would you like to join her?"

"Oh, yes. I'll be right there." she replies with her elegance.

Lucien nods. "Well, good evening, everyone. I hope you enjoy the rest of your night."

As soon as he's gone, we collectively exhale, releasing breaths we didn't realize we were holding.

"What was that?" I whisper to Sam.

"That's called the Lucien effect." she mutters back.

Mrs. Browning turns to me, her warm smile returning. "Mia, it was lovely to meet you. I hope I'll see you again soon."

"It was nice to finally meet you too, Mrs. Browning." I reply.

"Oh, call me Grandma B." she insists with a wink.

I nod, returning her smile.

"Bye, Alex, Sam—and Little Smiles." she teases one last time before leaving.

Once she's gone, Miles turns to Sam, "I swear, Sam, if you call me that nickname, I'll bury you six feet under." Miles threatens, glaring at her.

"Mia, handle your man. He's handing out threats like its candy." Sam quips, her grin as wide as the sky as she walks off.

Alex loses control of his laughter, nearly stumbling as he follows Sam, leaving me flushed as I yearn to get swallowed by the darkness.

As Miles leans in closer, his voice drops to a whisper. "Sorry about my grandma. She has a knack for... making an impression."

"She's wonderful." I say honestly, even though my heart is still pounding. "Though Sam has a knack to flush me."

"I didn't mind it. I would happily go with them calling me your man." he says.

"I'm gonna pretend I didn't hear that." I say, though I'm sure if my cheeks could physically turn red, they would.

Miles gives me a small, sheepish smile, chuckling a quiet laugh.

"You know," Miles begins, his voice low, "we could leave. Go to my place."

I blink, caught off guard. "But you're the birthday boy, are you allowed to leave."

"I am the Birthday boy." His tone soft. "I can leave whenever I want."

"Yeah, I'd like that." I whisper.

"Great. Let's go."

It's kinda nice that Miles wants to leave as much as I want to even though it's his party because I missed him. I missed his presence, his voice, his kisses. In fact, I'd jumped at the chance to book an earlier flight back to America just so I could be here for his birthday. But then I realise leaving won't be that easy.

"But wait wouldn't it be suspicious if we left together?" I ask, glancing around at the others. "I mean, our friends are all here, and you're the birthday boy. People would notice if we both disappeared especially your dad."

Miles groans, running a hand through his hair. "I hate that we're a secret."

"Only for some time." I say gently, placing a reassuring hand on his arm. I don't want to see him sad, especially not on his birthday.

His lips curve into a small, wistful smile before his eyes light up with a spark of mischief. "Okay, what if we leave with Alex? We'll walk out with him to the parking lot. Once we're in the car, no one's going to know who's with me."

I consider his plan for a moment before nodding. "That could work."

Miles grin, his mood lifting instantly. "Great. I'll go find Alex."

The plan unfolds seamlessly. After some casual goodbyes to Nate and Audrey, who are unwillingly preoccupied talking with Lucien Baudelaire, Miles and I follow Alex and Sam toward the parking lot. Sam has a mischievous glint in her eyes that says I know you are using us as a pawn to escape, but she doesn't say anything. Alex, as usual, is too busy yapping to notice much of anything.

Once we reach the parking lot, Alex and Sam head toward their car to leave for Colombia. Miles and I linger by his. When Alex looks back and waves, Miles gives a casual nod before opening the passenger door for me.

For a long time, I thought I'd never sit in the front seat again without feeling that crushing weight of fear. But as I slide in, there's nothing—no panic, no hesitation. Just a quiet realization that somehow, without even trying, Miles has made it easier. Sitting here doesn't feel like being trapped in the past anymore or scary. It just feels... normal.

I glance at him as he gets in and starts the car, my heart racing with a mix of excitement and something softer, something almost comforting. As we pull out of the lot, the tension melts away. The lights fuzz past us, and for the first time in weeks, it feels like the world consists only of the two of us.

"So, you really came back early just for my birthday?" Miles asks, glancing at me momentarily with a soft smile.

I shrug, feigning nonchalance even as my cheeks burn. "Maybe. I mean, it's not every day you turn twenty-four."

He laughs, the sound warm and infectious, filling the car with a comforting hum. "Thank you for coming. You made my night."

"Yeah, but it wasn't easy." I reply, turning to look at him. "I wasn't sure I'd make it—the flight kept getting delayed by an hour. I almost gave up."

"But you made it." Miles says simply, his eyes flicking toward me for a brief moment before returning to the road.

The silence that follows is filled only by the hum of the engine and the distant sound of the city. It's the kind of silence that feels safe, natural, like a pause in a melody.

After a moment, Miles speaks again, his tone quieter, more serious. "Mia, so... I'm set to be announced as CEO in a few months. Like, in December. There's going to be a party, and I want you to come."

I blink. "Wait—does that mean you'll finally become CEO?" I ask, not even trying to hide my excitement.

Miles glances at me again, his expression a mix of pride and something more subdued. "Um... unfortunately, no. Not right away. I'll officially take over in a year after that."

"Then why's the party so early?" I ask, genuinely curious.

"It's more of a transition thing." he explains, his tone even but with a hint of anticipation. "It's like a heads-up to everyone—employees, investors, clients—so they can adjust before it's official."

I nod, taking it all in. "Wow. That's... huge, Miles."

"Sorry." Miles suddenly says, his voice softer now, almost hesitant.

"Why?" I ask, turning to him, confused by the sudden shift in his tone.

"We'll have to wait another year." he says, his hands gripping the steering wheel just a little tighter.

I tilt my head, searching his face for meaning. When it clicks, I can't help but smile, wanting to ease the weight he seems to be carrying. "Miles, it's fine." I reply gently. "And honestly? This year hasn't been hard at all."

He exhales slowly, like he's been holding his breath, and glances at me. His eyes search mine, as if looking for reassurance in the depths of my gaze.

"You're sure?" he asks, his voice laced with a vulnerability he rarely shows. "I know this hasn't been the most conventional relationship. And sometimes, I feel like I'm asking too much of you—waiting, being patient. I just—"

"Miles," I interrupt softly, placing a hand on his arm. "You're not asking too much. I wouldn't be here if I didn't want to be. And as far as I'm concerned, this year's been...good. Better than I expected, even. I mean we didn't have to sprint and hide so that's a win. We just *were*—and that's more than enough for me."

His shoulders relax, a small, grateful smile tugging at the corners of his lips. "You always know what to say, don't you?"

"Not always," I tease lightly. "But when it comes to you, I seem to get it right more often than not."

He chuckles, the sound warm and genuine. "I don't deserve you, you know that?"

"Maybe not," I reply, a playful glint in my eyes. "But you're stuck with me anyway."

Miles laughs again, this time letting the sound linger in the air. It's a laugh filled with relief, gratitude, and something deeper—something that feels like hope. The city lights continue to blur past us, but the car feels like its own little universe, cocooned in a moment of understanding and quiet joy.

And just like that we reach his apartment, the cozy familiarity of the space wraps around me like a warm blanket. Miles drops his keys on the counter with a soft clink and turns to face me. There's a quiet, shy smile playing at the corners of his lips, a look I've come to adore.

"Thanks for making my birthday special." he says, his voice warm and sincere, the way it always is when he looks at me like this.

"I didn't do much."

"You're here." He steps closer, and his hand gently cups my cheek. "That's more than enough for me."

My breath catches in my throat, and for a moment, I forget how to speak. His touch is so tender, so sure, that it leaves me feeling like I'm floating. Before I can respond, he pulls me into a hug, his arms wrapping around me as if I'm the most important thing in the world.

My head rests against his chest, and I close my eyes, letting the warmth of his embrace wash over me. The rhythm of his heartbeat beneath my ear is steady and reassuring. In this moment, everything feels right, as though the world outside has faded away, leaving just the two of us, wrapped in this little bubble of warmth and affection.

"Happy birthday, Miles." I murmur, my voice soft, almost a whisper.

He pulls back slightly, just enough to meet my gaze. His eyes are full of emotion, his lips parted in a way that makes my heart race. "Best birthday ever." he says, his voice barely above a whisper.

I can see the sincerity in his eyes, and it fills me with a sense of peace and belonging.

"I'm glad you think that," I say, my voice softening. "But I do have a gift for you."

His expression softens even more, a small laugh escaping his lips. "You didn't have to." he says, his hand brushing against mine in a way that sends a jolt of electricity up my arm.

"I wanted to." I reach inside my purse that I dropped on the floor. My fingers find the small box, and for a moment, I hesitate, unsure if I'm truly ready to give him this. But when I look at him, I know. I know this is right.

I hand him the box with a shy smile. "Sorry, it's not wrapped." I mutter, feeling the weight of what I'm about to give him.

"That's fine." Miles takes the box from my hands with gentleness. He looks down at it, then back at me, his eyes filled with curiosity and something more.

His fingers trace the edges of the box before he lifts the lid, and I watch him closely as his eyes fall on the contents.

Inside, nestled on a bed of soft velvet, is the watch. It gleams softly in the dim light of the apartment—its gold case catching the light in a way that makes it almost looks alive. The cream-colored dial is simple yet refined, and the intricate sub-dials, the moon phase, the day-date windows—they all speak of timeless elegance. The leather strap is rich and brown, polished to perfection, giving the watch an air of sophistication.

"Miles," I whisper, my voice shaking slightly as I watch him take it all in. "This belonged to my dad. It was passed down to him from his father."

Miles looks up at me, his gaze soft but searching. "Mia, I... I don't know what to say."

"I know it's a lot," I continue, my voice barely a breath. "But it means something to me. It's more than just a watch—it's everything.

It's trust, it's safety, it's the pieces of me that I don't know how to share with anyone else."

The words hang between us, heavy with meaning, and I can see the realization settle in Miles's eyes. This is no ordinary gift. It's a piece of my father's legacy—a symbol of everything I've lost, everything I've held onto, and everything I'm giving to him.

"I want you to have it." I say softly, my heart racing. "Because I trust you, Miles. I believe in you. And maybe... maybe I've been holding onto something for so long, but I'm ready to let go. Ready to share what's mine with you."

Miles's hands tremble slightly as he holds the watch, the emotion in his eyes almost overwhelming. For a long moment, neither of us speaks. The weight of the gift, of everything I've just entrusted him with, hangs in the air.

Finally, Miles looks at me, his voice thick with emotion. "Mia, you have no idea what this means to me." He steps closer, his fingers reaching out to gently cup my face. "You're giving me more than I could ever ask for."

My breath catches in my throat. His touch is tender, but there's something else in it now—something deeper. His gaze flickers down to my lips, and I feel my pulse quicken.

"I don't know if I deserve this." he murmurs, his voice barely a whisper. "But I'll spend every day showing you how much it matters."

Before I can say anything in reply, his lips are on mine. The kiss is gentle at first, soft and slow, as if we're both trying to savour the moment. But as the seconds pass, the kiss deepens, becoming more urgent, more desperate. His hands move to my waist, pulling me closer, and I can feel the heat between us building with each passing second.

I respond without thinking, my hands sliding up his chest, feeling the warmth of his body through the fabric of his shirt. His lips are against mine, kissing me with a hunger that matches the need I feel stirring inside me.

"Mia," he whispers, his voice hoarse. "Are you sure?"

His words hit me like a wave, but there's no hesitation in my heart. "Yes." I murmur, my voice trembling with desire. "I'm sure."

And with that, we give in completely. The world outside disappears as we lose ourselves in each other, our connection growing stronger with every touch, every kiss. And as we move toward each other, I know that I'm giving him everything—my heart, my trust, my beliefs, and the love that will always remain, no matter what happens next.

I feel like a completely new version of myself. I don't hate it. I love it.

The air is crisp; carrying the lingering warmth of the night before, and the city outside is still cloaked in slumber. From where I sit, the Brooklyn skyline stretches endlessly beyond the grand piano, framed by towering windows that swallow the entire wall.

Miles's apartment reflects the quiet elegance of the morning. Floor-to-ceiling glass panes invite the city's glow inside, casting faint reflections across the sleek black grand piano that sits near them. Against the room's white and navy-blue theme, an orange couch— scattered with colourful throw pillows—adds a touch of warmth, grounding the space in a sense of comfort.

The world is quiet, save for the soft notes that spill from my fingertips—an absentminded melody that neither begins nor ends, but exists somewhere in between.

I don't even realize I'm playing, not really. My fingers graze the cool ivory keys, drifting across them like second nature, drawing out a tune I don't consciously recognize. Maybe it's something buried in my memory. Maybe it's something new, something born from this moment, from the way my heart feels light, yet full.

The sky shifts. The first blush of morning kisses the horizon. I watch it happen through the glass, lost in the way the city slowly stirs, stretching out of its deep slumber. I'm not sure how much time has passed when I feel movement beside me.

Miles settles onto the cushioned bench, the warmth of his presence brushing against me even before he speaks. He doesn't, not at first. He just watches, his gaze flickering between me and the way my fingers move effortlessly over the keys. The melody is quiet, thoughtful, weaving between us like an unspoken conversation.

His bare shoulder brushes against mine. His warmth anchoring me in place. For a moment, neither of us speak, letting the silence settle in, comfortable and intimate. Then, softly, he reaches out, his hand covering mine, stilling my movements.

I glance up at him. His expression is hidden, but his eyes—his eyes say everything.

"You play like you're dreaming." he murmurs, voice still laced with sleep.

I smile, tilting my head slightly. "Maybe I am."

He watches me for another beat before his lips curl into something soft, something rare. Then, without another word, he presses a single key—a deep, resonant note that vibrates through the air between us. Before I know it, I'm playing again, my fingers instinctively finding their place on the keys, a familiar melody taking shape.

And then, I start singing.

So, honey now
Take me into your loving arms
Kiss me under the light of a thousand stars...

The lyrics of *Thinking Out Loud* drift between us, and when I steal a glance at Miles, I find him watching me—completely lost. Lost in my voice, in my words, in *me*.

It makes me blush, but it also pushes me forward. The song shifts under my fingertips, evolving, morphing into something different, something unreleased, something entirely mine.

I begin to play a melody I wrote long ago, one that started on a guitar in a quiet room, one that has always belonged to him, even before I admitted it to myself.

Right before everything, everything
Right before I fell deep, fell deep
Right before, right before
I closed my eyes and dreamed...

I watch as realization dawns on his face. His expression shifts—curiosity melting into something deeper, something raw. Amusement flickers in his eyes, laced with admiration, respect.

His voice is quiet when he asks, "Did you write that?"

I nod.

His lips twitch into a grin. "Is it about me?"

I smirk, waiting just a beat. "Not everything is about you."

"Damn it!" he sighs dramatically.

I laugh, the final notes dissolving into the hush of morning as my fingers drift away. Before I can pull back, Miles entwines his fingers with mine, his touch deliberate, unhurried. The mischief in his gaze mellows into something quieter, something that lingers like a secret between us. His thumb skims over my skin in slow, featherlight strokes, sending warmth curling through me. And just like that, the moment settles—delicate, boundless, ours.

"It's beautiful." he says, voice sincere.

I swallow, warmth blooming in my chest. "Thank you."

His words mean everything to me.

I lean into him, resting my head against his shoulder as the sky outside shifts from deep blue to golden pink. His thumb brushes over my knuckles, absentminded but intimate.

And together, we watch the city wake.

Out there, the world stirs—relentless, demanding, alive. But in here, in this moment, it's just us.

CHAPTER 29

Chloe

"Honey, pass me that salad bowl." my mother says, pointing at the dish across the table.

I hand it to her.

The atmosphere is tense yet routine, as we sit around the dining table for dinner. My mind, however, is elsewhere, wrapped up in everything that's been happening.

"I have good news." my dad finally says, a smile tugging at his lips. "Caden will be out of rehab in two days."

"That's wonderful." I reply, trying to keep my voice steady, though my thoughts race.

Caden, my older brother, had gotten addicted to drugs a year ago, though no one outside the family knows. If they did, it would have shattered our family's reputation and the company's. So, Caden was quietly admitted to rehab, kept out of the public eye. Now that he's sober, he's coming back, and I should be relieved. But...

"I can finally start preparing to hand him the business." Dad adds.

What?

Hand him the business?

I don't know why I'm so surprised. Deep down, I'd sensed this was coming—subtle hints in Dad's comments over the last few weeks. Still, hearing it out loud stings in a way I wasn't prepared for.

"Why him?" I blurt out, struggling to keep my tone neutral.

"Because he was always supposed to get it." Dad answers as if it's the most obvious thing in the world.

"He's just getting out of rehab. That doesn't mean he won't relapse." I say, my voice trembling despite my efforts to stay calm. The anger bubbling inside me threatens to burst.

"He won't." my mother snaps, cutting me off. "He won't have his old friends around to drag him back into it. Now eat your dinner."

"But I've done everything I could for the company over the last year, and you're still thinking about him?" I shoot back, my words bitter. "I've worked hard, attended every meeting, came up with ideas to boost the business, and this is what I get?"

"And you ruined it all by saying no to Miles Baudelaire!" My dad's voice rises, sharp and accusing.

I open my mouth to respond in disbelief, but my mother silences me with an icy glare. "Go to your room. Now."

I can feel the hot sting of tears in my eyes, but I refuse to let them fall until I'm behind the closed door of my room. I slam it shut, my emotions unravelling as the tears begin to stream down my face.

I gave everything for this—my time, my energy, my ideas—and still, it's not enough. Why? Because I refused to play by their rules. Because I said no to Miles Baudelaire.

If only they knew why I denied him.

The world might have moved forward, but my parents remain stuck in the past, clinging to the outdated ideals of old-money business. And as a woman in this society—especially in this class—no matter how rich you are, you're still put down. Even if you're the daughter. Even if you've worked your ass off.

I've sacrificed parties, cut down on time with friends, and given everything to prove myself. And still, you eat shit. It's never a fair chance.

But I can't give up now. I've sacrificed too much to walk away.

"Thank you for coming." My voice is polite, composed, but there's an undercurrent of something sharper beneath it.

Miles sits across from me, his expression unreadable, but I can tell he's wary. We're back in the café where we met a year ago—the same place where I once told him my feelings were real, only to walk out when he didn't return them. But this time, I didn't call him here for closure because I'm simply over it. Instead I have a proposition.

I take a breath and cut straight to the point. "I'll be frank with you, Miles. I want to be next in line for CEO after my father. But he wants Caden to take over."

Miles leans back slightly, listening but not reacting. He already knows about Caden's stint in rehab—I'm sure of it. "Do you want to know why he won't choose me?" I ask, tilting my head.

He nods, probably assuming I just need someone to vent to. He shouldn't.

"Because I rejected you."

His entire demeanor shifts. He swallows, his jaw tightening as realization sinks in. For a moment, he says nothing, and then, finally, he asks, "What do you want me to do?"

I meet his gaze without hesitation. "I want us to make a deal."

A flicker of something crosses his face—curiosity, apprehension—but before I can elaborate, he stiffens.

"We'll get married—"

"No." The word is instant, firm.

I exhale, already anticipating his resistance. "Miles, just hear me out before you react."

His hands clench into restrained fists before he relaxes them with effort, gesturing for me to continue.

"We get married. You keep seeing Mia—just like you already are, in secret. And in return, we both get what we want. You secure your future as the head of your empire, and I get mine. When the time is right, we divorce. Simple, clean, mutually beneficial."

I let the words settle between us. This isn't about love. This is about power. And power requires sacrifice. And Miles isn't a man who walks away from a deal that benefits him.

Or at least, I think he isn't.

The silence between us stretches, thick and suffocating. I wait for him to see the logic in my offer, for reason to override whatever misplaced morality he's clinging to. But when he speaks, his voice is razor-sharp, cold, unwavering. "I said no."

I blink, caught off guard. "Miles—"

He leans in, voice lower, harsher, the weight of his words slicing through me. "We are *mates*, Chloe. Nothing more. Not even in a lie."

The sting is sharper than I expect, but I don't let it show. My lips curl into something resembling a smirk, though I feel anything but amused. "Don't be naïve. Power isn't given—it's taken. You and I both know that. This could be good for both of us."

His eyes darken. "No."

The scrape of his chair against the floor is abrupt, cutting through the air like a final verdict. He stands, grabs his coat, and looks at me one last time. "I'm not playing this game with you."

And then he walks away.

I don't call him back.

I don't try to stop him.

I just watch as he disappears through the door, a quiet rage simmering beneath my skin.

If he won't take the deal, I'll find another way.

CHAPTER 30
Mia

"Are you excited for today?" I ask, leaning against the kitchen counter, watching him move around with practiced ease.

"Very." Miles replies, sliding a steaming hot cup of coffee across the counter toward me. His voice carries that warm, effortless charm that always makes my heart flutter.

I take a small sip when he suddenly says, "I got you something."

I glance up in surprise, about to ask what he means, but before I can say a word, he's already disappearing into the living room. Moments later, he returns, holding a sleek designer Gucci box in his hands.

"What's that?" I ask, my eyes narrowing slightly as I eye the box with a mix of curiosity and anticipation.

"Open it." he says, his lips curving into a small, knowing smile that only heightens my intrigue.

My heart skips a beat as I take the box from him, my fingers brushing his for a brief moment. Lifting the lid, my breath catches.

Inside is a dress—no, *the* dress.

"Wow." I whisper, unfolding the fabric carefully, almost afraid I might ruin something so beautiful.

The gown shimmers in the soft morning light, made of green liquid-like sequins that seem to dance with every movement. Its sweetheart neckline is elegant yet daring, and the strappy backless design exudes sophistication and allure. It's perfect in every way.

"Do you like it?" His voice is gentle.

"Yeah." I reply dreamily, my fingers brushing against the fabric. It's soft, delicate, and impossibly luxurious.

"You can wear it at the party tonight." he says casually, though there's an unmistakable gleam in his eyes that makes my heart flutter even more.

"Okay." I murmur, a soft smile tugging at my lips.

He nods, his expression growing more serious. "I've decided to tell him about us after the announcement." his words are calm yet resolute.

The weight of what he just said hits me like a wave. My eyes widen, and before I can stop myself, I throw my arms around him in an impulsive hug.

"Really?" I gasp, burying my face against his chest.

Miles laughs softly, wrapping his arms around me and holding me close. "We won't have to be a secret anymore." he murmurs, pressing a gentle kiss to the top of my head.

I pull back just enough to look at him, my hands still resting on his chest. "But are you sure?" I ask, my voice laced with concern. "This is going to be a big deal, for both of us. For you especially."

His eyes meet mine, steady and unwavering. "I've never been more sure of anything." he says, brushing a strand of hair away from my face. "But the question is... are you ready? Because he's going to be angry."

The thought sends a shiver down my spine, but as I look into his eyes—so full of determination and love—I know the answer.

"Yeah," I say softly, my voice filled with certainty. "I'm ready."

He smiles, leaning down to press his forehead against mine. "No more hiding." he whispers, his breath warm against my skin.

"No more hiding." I repeat, my heart swelling with emotion.

For a moment, we just stand there, wrapped in each other's warmth, the weight of our decision sinking in. Tonight isn't just a party—it's the beginning of something new. Something real. Something worth fighting for.

And as I look up at him, the man who's given me his heart and trusted me with his secrets, I know that whatever happens next, we'll face it together.

"Will you hang out with Audrey and Sam till the announcement?" Miles asks, pulling the car into the driveway of their Mansion in Westbury, New York.

"Yeah. Don't worry."

His gaze lingers on me for a second as he softly says, "You look beautiful, Mia."

"Thanks." I murmur, blushing under his gaze.

"I'll find you after the announcement." He promises, kissing me on the lips.

"Somebody will see us." I whisper.

"I don't care." he replies, kissing me again.

Just then a sharp knock on the car window interrupts us.

It's Sam, grinning as she gestures me to come out.

"I'll see you later." I say, stealing one last kiss before stepping out of the car.

Sam loops her arm through mine as Miles drives off to park. Together, we walk up the elegant gravel pathway with stone edging.

I take in my surroundings. The estate is enormous, with beautifully manicured gardens, featuring vibrant flower beds, trimmed bushes of roses and... lilies, variety of lilies. As the sun sets, the white lilies at the estate take on a soft, radiant beauty that amplifies their elegance and purity, and the pink and orange lily hues deepen, making them look rich and velvety.

The exterior of the mansion matches the old European castles vibe with its elegant combination of medieval architectural styles. The mansion's façade appears bright and well-preserved, with stone walls and numerous large windows that add to its idyllic appearance.

This is my first time at Miles's family estate. I've been to his apartment, but never here. Though there's a reason for that—his Dad. He can't know about us. At least, not until tonight. I'm excited and nervous about that.

I just hope that when the time comes, his dad takes the news calmly.

Sam leads me toward the mansion's main doors, which surprises me since the party is supposed to be in the mansion's magnificent gardens.

"Why are we heading inside?" I ask.

"We have to find Audrey." Sam replies. "And you'll get to see the inside, too." She adds with a smirk.

"Okay!" I say, following her through the mansion's massive mahogany doors, which feature glass inlays and bronze accents.

Upon entering I am greeted by the mansion's grand double staircase which curves outwards gracefully, its ornate railings feature detailed floral or vine patterns, which perfectly aligns with the estate's grandeur. The polished marble steps shine under the soft light of chandeliers, and the rich wood platform at the bottom adds a touch of elegance, combining modern style with classic luxury.

As we reach the second floor, I pause to look down at the first floor below, where a formal drawing room comes into view. The room looks incredibly luxurious from here. I gaze around the mansion's palatial décor so dreamily like my eyes have never feasted extravagance before.

"Audrey's room's here." Sam says, pulling my eyes away from the mansion's opulent interior.

We walk into Audrey's room and find Nate lying on her bed. He greets us with a nod.

I'm surprised by Audrey's room—it's totally different from the rest of the mansion's theme. The wall behind her bed is painted a deep red colour, making it the focal point of the room. Her place feels like any teenage girl's, but with a little touch of sophistication. Glancing around at her room I can't help but wonder what Miles's room looks like? I wish I could find out.

I settle down on a light purple barrel chair.

Audrey emerges from the bathroom, and Alex barges into the room, swinging the door wide open.

"Breaking news, Caden Harrington was spotted here a few minutes ago—by me." Alex says.

"What? Wasn't he in rehab?" Nate looks surprised.

"Wait, he was in rehab. I thought the Harrington's said he was in Africa… feeding kangaroos or something." Sam adds.

"That was a cover story." Nate replies.

"Sam, kangaroos are native to Australia, not Africa." I correct her.

"Shut up, nerd." Sam retorts, rolling her eyes.

"Well, it's important to educate dumb people like you."

"Oooh… burn!" Alex exclaims.

At that moment, Miles appears in the doorway, beside Alex.

"What are you all doing here?" He asks, his brow arching slightly.

"And do you know Caden is here?" he adds as I stand up from the chair.

"We know." Audrey replies casually.

"And we were just leaving to join the party." Nate says, standing up.

"Okay then let's go." Miles urges.

We all begin filing out of the room, but as I reach the doorway, Miles gently pulls me aside.

"Where are we going?" I ask, glancing back at the others heading toward the stairs.

"I need to change my shirt." he says.

"Why?"

"It's itchy."

"How?"

"I don't know." he replies, opening a door.

"Is this your room?" I ask, stepping inside with him.

He nods, tossing his blazer onto the bed as he disappears into the closet. I take a moment to look around his room. It's completely different from Audrey's and doesn't match the mansion's ornate style either. The decor is neutral, with only subtle pops of colour, just like is apartment. The wall above the headboard is painted a deep navy blue, while photo frames of his family—vividly orange—are the only real bursts of colour, giving the room a subtle but much-needed vibrancy.

I draw open the curtains, flooding the space with soft light. "Who is Caden?" I call out.

"He's Chloe's older brother." Miles replies, emerging from the closet as he buttons a fresh shirt.

I nod slightly, turning to look out the window. The view of the estate's fences and gardens is stunning, and I don't want to take my eyes off it.

Just then, Miles wraps an arm around my waist, pulling me into him, and drops a soft kiss on my cheek, making my heart splutter.

Placing my hand over his, we stand together by the window, the world outside feeling distant as a gentle breeze brushes through the room. For a moment, it feels like it's just us—time frozen in a bubble of peace.

"Isn't your dad going to see us now?" I murmur.

"He's greeting guests in the garden, so no chance." Miles assures me.

"But what if he walks in here? Will you shove me into your closet?" I ask playfully.

Miles pretends to think. "Yeah, definitely."

I nudge him in the ribs, making him chuckle softly.

After a short pause, his tone turns serious. "I wouldn't have to hide you in the closet; I'd just have to tell him about us sooner."

Turning to face him, I say, "Honestly, I'm ready but I am scared for your dad's reaction when you tell him."

"He'd be pissed." Miles admits, brushing a strand of hair from my face, "But you don't need to worry about that. It'll be fine."

I nod, reassured by his steady confidence. Placing my hand on his chest, I say, "Um... we should go. Don't want the Man of the Hour missing from his party."

He kisses me softly on the lips, murmuring, "I don't want to leave."

"We have to." I insist, though the warmth of his closeness makes me hesitate for a moment before gently nudging him toward the door.

He unlocks the door, and we start to leave when I notice something missing. I turn back and glance at his bed, spotting it instantly.

"What happened?" Miles asks from behind me.

I grab his blazer, forgotten on the bed. "You forgot your blazer." I say, stepping closer.

Before he can take it, I hold it up and slide it onto his arms, helping him wear it quickly.

"Thanks." he says with a grateful smile.

Miles and I go separate ways as soon as we step into the gardens. He heads toward a group of his business associates, while I head over to join Sam and Audrey.

"Nate and Miles gifting you dresses for this lame party almost makes me feel like I should get a boyfriend too." Sam grumbles, folding her arms.

"Maybe you should." I suggest.

"I said *almost*. Don't get ahead of yourself." Sam says, rolling her eyes.

I smirk at her response. Sam would rather jump off a cliff than get a boyfriend. I remember asking her once why she wasn't interested in dating, and she gave me a trademark Sam reply. *"They're nothing but a waste of time."* she had said. *"You have to tell them where you are all the time. Then you waste the rest of your time wondering where they are. Don't want that. Don't need that."*

Classic Sam.

"Forget about boyfriends, and tell me why is this party soo lame? Where's the dance floor, and the pop music?" Sam complains.

"Because it's a business party, Sam." Audrey explains patiently, as though this should be obvious.

"I *know* that, but what's wrong with actual fun songs? What the hell are these musicians even playing?" Sam retorts.

"They're playing classical music." I reply.

Sam's eyes widen in mock horror. "Let's request something fun, then!" she says, grabbing my arm and dragging me toward the musicians.

She leans in and whispers to the cellist, "Could you play *Physical* by Dua Lipa?" The cellist looks at her, clearly baffled and annoyed. I pull Sam away before she gets hit by the cellist cello for inappropriate song requests.

"They're not a DJ. They're not here to play your song requests." I explain, calmly.

"I know that, but I figured, why not give it a shot?" Sam shrugs, completely unapologetic.

Normally, Sam isn't this ridiculous, but she got her period today, and it's making her extremely cranky, so I guess anything's possible right now.

Shaking my head, I drag Sam back to our table, make her sit down, and hand her a glass of water. Audrey, meanwhile, is deep in conversation with a group of girls at a nearby table, leaving me to manage Sam's antics all on my own.

I'd be lying if I said I didn't agree with Sam, though. This party is kind of boring. Maybe it's because I can't spend time with Miles since his parents might see us—or maybe it's just the party. My eyes wander around the garden, trying to find something interesting to focus on.

That's when I spot someone familiar in the crowd of men dressed in tuxedos and women in satin, sparkly gowns. She's dressed like a marvellous queen—Grandma B.

She walks toward our table slowly but gracefully. I meet her halfway and accompany her to the table. She sits down with her warm smile and says to Sam and me, "Mia, it's good to see you again. You both look beautiful."

"Thank you!" we both say together.

"You look lovely yourself." I add warmly.

She smiles broadly, the wrinkles on her face becoming more visible, which somehow makes her look even more radiant.

"Oh, would you bring me the gourmet sliders from that waiter?" Grandma B says in her sweet voice, pointing toward a waiter carrying a tray of snacks.

"Sure." I reply, getting up from my chair and catching up with the waiter. I return to our table a couple of minutes later with the fancy snack.

"Thank you!" Grandma B beams with gratitude.

I smile back warmly.

Sam and I join Grandma B, sharing the food as the soft hum of classical music drifts through the air. Right at the moment, Alex joins us; stealing the last bite left from Sam's hand, just as she's about to eat it, which makes her angry.

She grunts, hitting Alex on the shoulder, making him squeal, "Ouch!"

"What's wrong with her?" he mouths.

"Periods." I mouth back.

He shakes his head in understanding, his expressions saying '*Ah that makes sense*'.

"Alex, did you bring a date with you?" Grandma B asks.

"Ah, no! Today I came solo." Alex replies. "I did impress a few ladies here, but they got too clingy. It was like being attacked by piranhas."

"Alex, are you ever going to stick with one person?" I probe.

"Mmhm! No, he's gonna die alone." Sam answers for him, shaking her head.

"So are you." Alex retorts.

"No I'll find someone just to despise you, but sometime later, though. No rush." Sam replies, leaning back in her seat.

Well. At least Sam has hopes to find the one to get ahead of Alex. Good for her. On the other hand, I'm not so sure about Alex. He's a completely different story. He goes through girls like shows on Netflix—he enjoys them for a while, then moves on to the next without a second thought.

Meanwhile, I've already cast Miles as the leading man in the movie of my life.

In that instant, Audrey returns from the nearby table and sits on the chair beside me, muttering, "I just saw Chloe."

Alex perks up. "Where?"

Audrey points toward the far end of the party area, where bushes of white lilies mark the boundary.

We all turn to look, spotting Chloe deep in conversation with Lucien Baudelaire. We're all watching them that I almost don't notice Nate appearing beside Grandma B. "Grandma B, Mrs. Baudelaire has asked for you." Nate informs her politely, his tone steady and respectful. "You too, Aud."

"Yes, of course." Grandma B murmurs softly. She takes Nate's offered hand as he helps her rise, leading her toward where she's been summoned. Audrey follows closely, heading to join her family at the announcement area.

Nate returns back five minutes later, and takes a seat at the table. "The announcement will commence in a few minutes."

As we all face the direction where we spotted Chloe earlier, everyone's faces lit up with excitement over the upcoming announcement, I can't help but feel a little scared.

Don't get me wrong—I'm proud of him and happy for this moment—but I'm also terrified of what comes next: Miles telling his dad about us and the brutal reaction that might follow. And do you know what my biggest fear is? That his dad might force us to break up. But I'm ready. I have to be.

I bite my lip, willing myself to focus on the present instead of spiralling into *what-ifs*. Everything will go smoothly, I tell myself. It has to.

"Welcome everyone!" Lucien Baudelaire's commanding voice booms through the microphone.

I snap back to reality, shifting my attention to where the Baudelaire family is now gathered. Miles stands beside his father, his posture confident. Audrey, Grandma B, and Seraphina Baudelaire flank them, all poised and radiant under the glow of the garden lights. The Harrington's are nearby, their presence adding to the prestige of the moment.

Lucien continues, his tone brimming with pride. "I think you all are aware why we are gathered here tonight." He places a hand on Miles's shoulder, his smile warm but commanding. "My son, Miles," he says, pausing to build suspense, "has proven himself ready to take over Baudelaire & Browning Global Enterprises."

The applause begins immediately, but I can't help noticing the gravity of Lucien's words. For him to step down after twenty-two years—after building Baudelaire Global Enterprise from the ground up through sheer effort and sacrifice—is monumental. Everyone in this room knows how rare it is for him to entrust anyone with the legacy he's worked so hard to create.

A ripple of applause fills the garden as Lucien steps back, letting Seraphina take the microphone.

"In two weeks, Miles will officially assume the position of CEO." Seraphina Baudelaire announces, her voice clear and elegant. The applause grows louder, and I join in, clapping along with the rest of the crowd.

"For the first year, he'll be in a transitional phase as you all know." she continues, her smile as polished as her words. The applause swells again, and I glance at Miles. His gaze briefly scans the room before landing on me. Our eyes meet, and his expression softens for just a moment, a silent reassurance passing between us.

My heart swells with pride for him—he's worked so hard for this moment—but the knot in my stomach tightens all the same. This is his world, one build on wealth and power, one I'm not entirely sure I belong in. I just hope, for both our sakes, that I'm wrong.

Lucien's voice cuts through the applause, his next words sending a chill down my spine. "I have one more piece of good news." He pauses, his smile broadening. "My son will be engaged to Chloe Harrington in two months."

Time spins too fast.

Too Fast.

And shatters.

The applause continues, louder now, echoing in my ears like a cruel taunt.

My son will be engaged to Chloe Harrington in two months.

The words play on repeat in my mind, each echo hitting harder than the last.

I glance around, catching snippets of murmured congratulations. Someone at a nearby table says, "They'll make a perfect pair." and it feels like a dagger to my chest.

My gaze darts to Sam, Nate, and Alex. Their stunned faces mirror my own disbelief, but it offers no solace. A tear escapes before I can stop it, and I quickly wipe it away, hoping no one notices.

My eyes search for Miles, desperate for a logical explanation to this happenstance. But instead, I find Chloe standing beside him, her family flanking her. She's dressed in a black satin gown, bright-eyed, smiling like she's conquered the moon.

I turn my focus back to Miles, searching his face for some sign of truth. He smiles, but it doesn't reach his eyes, because it's a fake smile, isn't it?

It *has* to be fake.

It's fake.

His eyes land on mine, but before I can decipher his expression, people begin rising from their seats, moving to congratulate the supposed happy couple. Nate is the first to recover. He pushes back his chair and gets to his feet. "I'll find out what the hell is happening." he says, striding toward the crowd with purpose.

Sam and Alex both turn to me. "Are you okay?" Sam asks, her voice soft but laced with concern.

I open my mouth to answer, but the words won't come. Because no—I'm not alright. I don't know what's happening, or why Miles isn't coming to me, why he isn't explaining any of this. My eyes dart back to the announcement area, but this time, I don't see Miles or Chloe anywhere.

My heart sinks like a stone. "No. I'm not alright." I whisper, my voice shaky. "Sam. I want to go."

Sam nods without hesitation. "Let's go." she says, her tone firm.

She glances at Alex, whispering, "Keep me updated." Then the two of us slip out of the gardens, Sam gently placing her hand on my arm for comfort. Once in her car, as she pulls out of the driveway of the Baudelaire Mansion, I finally ask, my voice still unsteady but firm, "Did you know? Did any of you know?"

Sam shakes her head, worry etched into her features. "No, M. None of us knew. This is news to all of us."

I slowly turn away, rolling down the window. The cool night air brushes against my face, but it doesn't soothe me. Instead, it feels like a harsh reminder of the truth I can't escape: nothing in life is ever meant to last, at least not for me.

I glance down at my phone. No messages. No missed calls.

No Miles.

Instead my eyes zero in on the time.

10:48 PM

One hour and twelve minutes until my birthday.

My fucking birthday.

Because every bad thing has to happen on my birthday.

Because I'm not meant to be happy.

Not now.

Not Ever.

CHAPTER 31

Miles

"Welcome everyone." My dad begins.

His voice commands attention, smoothly transitioning from pleasantries to a more serious tone as he makes the announcement. The guests clap, and I smile. Then, he hands the microphone to Mom. She says a few words, then passes it back to Dad.

"I have one more piece of good news." He says, his voice filled with calculated kind of excitement. "My son will be engaged to Chloe Harrington."

My world stops.

Every sound around me fades into the background, leaving only the thunderous pounding of my heart in my ears.

I glance at him, anger and confusion etched across my face. He looks back at me with a mocking smirk and leans in close, his voice a low murmur in my ear. "Did you think I wouldn't know about that girl? Now wipe that frown off your face and smile."

I force a smile, masking the rage and pain boiling inside me, because everyone's watching. My eyes dart across the sea of faces, searching desperately for Mia, but Chloe steps in front of me, blocking my view. Her presence feels like a fuel to an already blazing fire.

I scan the seats again, my eyes finally landing on Mia. Her face is pale, her expression stony and confused, as though she's searching for answers. But before I can do anything, the guests rise from their seats and start moving toward us, offering congratulations for something I wasn't even a part of.

I try to break away, to reach Mia and explain that I had no idea this was happening, but my dad's grip on my arm stops me.

My anger simmers dangerously close to boiling over. I want to scream at him, but I can't. My hands are tied, bound by expectation and circumstance.

Devon approaches, his handshake firm, his smile wide. "Congratulations!" he says cheerfully. Then he winks at me. "You didn't tell me anything man. Sneaky guy."

I nod, forcing another fake smile.

I glance at Chloe, lowering my voice. "Did you know?"

"Yes." she replies simply, her tone almost dismissive.

I want to ask her why, but another guest intercepts, offering yet another round of congratulations.

When my dad becomes distracted in a conversation with Mr. Dawson, I seize the opportunity. Grabbing Chloe's wrist, I pull her behind one of the towering lily bushes, away from the prying eyes and endless handshakes.

"Why didn't you tell me?" I demand, my voice low but sharp.

"I wanted it to be a surprise." she replies, her lips curling into a smirk.

"You wanted an engagement with *me* to be a surprise." My voice rises by an octave. "Have you lost it?" Now I've lost control of my tone.

"I had to do what I had to do. You didn't leave me with any choice."

Her response stings, but it's her expression that cuts deeper. The Chloe I thought I knew wasn't this person standing in front of me now. This Chloe imposes selfishness, her demeanor cold and ruthless.

"So you told him about us." I voice my suspicion, my voice tight with anger.

Her smirk widens.

"Why? Because I didn't take up your offer." My tone rises, the frustration evident.

"Listen, Miles..." she starts, but Nate's voice interrupts us.

"What the fuck was that?" he snaps as he approaches. His expression mirrors my own, equal parts disbelief and fury.

I turn to him quickly. "Where's Mia?" The panic in my voice rising.

"She's at the table. She looks like she just saw the end of the world." Nate replies grimly.

I break away, my strides long and purposeful as I head toward her table. Hope tugs at my skin as I silently pray that Mia didn't believe anything that just went down. But on my way my dad intercepts me, blocking my path.

"Where do you think you're going?" he asks, his tone icy.

"To pick up the pieces of your mess." I snap, my voice venomous.

Hearing my reply, Nate steps back slightly, shaking his head as though trying to ward off the brewing storm between me and my dad. He doesn't say anything, but his expression speaks volumes: a silent warning, a plea to hold my tongue before I provoke the beast any further. But it's too late. The damage is already done.

"My mess." My dad shrugs, his smugness only deepening. "Do you really think she's worth all this? That girl—she's a nobody."

"She's *not* a nobody!" I growl, my voice rising. "And stop calling her that girl. Her name is Mia."

"And you'll stop these seeing her." he retorts coldly.

"I won't." I say, my voice defiant. "Because I love her. And what would you know about love. You never loved mom or anyone. Not even your own children. Everything is always business for you."

The words feel like a declaration of war.

My father's smirk vanishes, replaced by something colder, sharper. "Then let me make this clear: if you call off the engagement, you'll never make CEO. I'll cut you—and Audrey—from the

Baudelaire name. Then go fend for yourself. I'll destroy that girl too. Whatever life she has now, she won't have that too. I will shatter every shard of dignity she has. You know I mean it."

My dad's words hang in the air like a noose tightening around my neck. "*You will never make CEO. I'll cut you and Audrey from the Baudelaire name. Then go fend for yourself. I'll destroy that girl too. Whatever life she has now, she won't have that too. I will shatter every shard of dignity she has.*"

The weight of his threat is crushing, a reminder that one wrong move could despair everything—not just for me, but for Audrey and Mia too. Shoving past him, I don't even spare another glance. My only focus is getting to Mia.

When I reach the table, she's nowhere to be seen. Instead, I find Alex and Audrey in conversation.

"Miles and I had no idea." I hear Audrey say to Alex, her voice strained.

"Where is she?" I demand, my urgency growing.

"Sam took her back to the dorm." Alex answers, his tone calm but firm.

Audrey looks at me, worry flickering in her eyes, but I don't have the time to comfort her. I am already on my way.

Behind me, Nate's voice calls out. "Wait!"

I ignore him, my focus entirely on reaching Mia. But Nate catches up, sliding into the passenger seat just as I unlock the car.

"I'm coming too." he says, his voice leaving no room for argument.

"Nate, this isn't…"

"I'm coming. After hearing that delightful conversation with your dad, I don't want you to do something stupid." he says, his jaw set.

I don't argue. The engine roars to life, and I peel out of the driveway.

"This is exactly what I was afraid of." Nate mutters after a moment, almost to himself.

I grip the wheel tighter, my knuckles white, my foot pressing harder on the gas. I don't respond. Words are meaningless right now. All that matters is getting to Mia.

After a long stretch of silence, Nate finally breaks it. "What are you going to do?"

What am I going to do? I don't know. If I break off the engagement, the fallout will be like a ripple turning into a tidal wave, sweeping Mia and even Audrey into its destruction. If I stay, the weight of my betrayal will suffocate the one person who matters to me the most. I have to find a middle ground soon.

"I don't know." I answer through clenched teeth. "But I need her to know that I didn't betray her."

Minutes later, I pull up in front of Mia's dorm building, not bothering to check if the car is parked properly. I leap out, slamming the door shut behind me, and head for the stairs, taking them two at a time. Nate follows close behind, matching my urgency.

When I reach her dorm, I knock—harder than I probably should—but I don't care. A few moments later, the door swings open, revealing Sam.

I storm past her without waiting for an invitation, heading straight for Mia's room. Behind me, Sam yells, "Are you serious, Miles? Engagement?"

I ignore her, but Nate doesn't. "Miles didn't know either." he says quickly.

"What?!" Sam's voice rises with disbelief. "He didn't know about his own engagement?"

I don't stick around to hear more. Reaching Mia's door, I push it open without hesitation and step inside

Mia is sitting on her bed, staring at the floor, her left leg jittering restlessly, indicating that she is nervous and scared which hurts me too. Her soft brown eyes lack the usual glimmer of joy and hope, clouded by unspoken pain. It takes her a second to notice me, but before she can react, Sam storms in behind me.

"She doesn't want to talk to you." she snaps, her tone as sharp as a whip.

"It's okay, Sam." Mia says quietly. Her tone is steady, but I can hear the hurt buried beneath it.

Sam hesitates, glaring at me before sighing and leaving the room. I close the door behind her, locking it, shutting both her and Nate out.

I cross the room and kneel in front of Mia, my hand resting gently on her thigh to still her jittering leg. "I didn't know." I say, my voice barely above a whisper.

"I figured." she replies, her tone distant.

"So… did you tell your dad about us?" she asks after a moment, her eyes searching mine.

I exhale heavily, feeling the weight of the truth. "He already knew. Chloe told him."

Her body stiffens at the mention of Chloe, but I explain. "I swear, Mia, I didn't know they'd do this. I don't understand why my dad thought announcing a fucking engagement would solve anything—or destroy us."

Mia's gaze sharpens, a flicker of hope breaking through the pain. "So, you called it off, right?"

I falter, my silence answering her question.

Her face crumples slightly, disbelief washing over her. "You didn't." she whispers.

"M, it's not like that." I say quickly, reaching for her hands.

She pulls back. "Don't, Miles."

"Please, just listen." I beg, taking her hands in mine again, my voice trembling with desperation. "The engagement—it's not real, not to me. It's just something to keep my dad off my back until I take over. While everything is happening, the engagement, we'll still be together. It'll just have to stay… a secret again. For a while longer."

I don't tell her about my dad's threats to destroy her life if we stay public. She doesn't need to carry that weight. We can do this—stay together secretly for a year. We've done it before; we can do it again, this time more carefully. It will be *our* secret.

Only *ours*.

"M, after this phase, no more hiding." I plea. "Once I take over, I'll fix everything. I'll make it right. I promise."

Her eyes glisten, the faintest trace of a tear forming. "Do you know what comes after an engagement, Miles? A wedding."

"I'll avoid it." I insist.

"You can't avoid a wedding for a year." she counters, her voice breaking slightly.

"I'll find a way. I'll figure it out. I'll..."

"Miles." Her voice cuts through my rambling, calm yet filled with finality.

I stop, my chest heaving as I search her face for something—anything—that tells me she believes me.

She shakes her head slowly, a single tear sliding down her cheek. "This is the end."

"No." My voice cracks as I try to say it firmly. "Don't say that. Please, no."

"I've had the last half hour to think about it, about what might come next, and I don't think I can do it. I can't." Her voice trembles as she shakes her head. "I can't be your... mistress, hidden behind a black veil, while you get engaged under white lights—while Chloe plans a wedding, books a venue, goes dress shopping. I can't. I can't be part of an illicit affair. That's not who I am."

Her words feel like a twist of knife in my chest, stealing the air from my lungs.

"Mia, please. I'll fix this. I swear I'll fix this."

"Miles, I'm only here for six more months anyway, after that my visa will expire and I'll fly back home. Now we'll have to face that fact. I'm not here forever." She whispers. "And something's are destined to be momentary even when it's hard to let go."

"I'll renew the visa. This doesn't have to be momentary." I say.

She shakes her head, her voice soft but unyielding. "Right person, wrong time does exist."

My head drops, and I bite back the sob threatening to escape as my shoulders tremble.

"Hey." She whispers gently, her voice tugging at the strings holding me together. "Look at me."

I force myself to meet her gaze, every part of me trying not to shatter as she continues, "Maybe in the future, we'll cross paths again. Maybe then we could happen. But now's not our time."

She sniffs, wiping at the tears staining her cheeks. "Sometimes, we have to let go. We have to let go to the secret of us."

"I don't want to let go. You are my breath, Mia. I will lose it."

"People learn to breathe again." She says, that's all she says. "We both have to move on."

I open my mouth to speak, but no words come out. A broken sob escapes instead, and I lower my head, clutching her hands as if letting go would mean losing her forever.

The silence stretches, broken only by the uneven rhythm of our breathing. My phone rings, but I ignore it, unwilling to release her hands. She gently pulls away, and the absence of her warmth feels like a gaping hole in my chest.

My phone pings loudly. "Pick it up." Mia says softly.

I pull the phone from my pocket, my fingers trembling. A text from Audrey flashes on the screen: *Mom is searching for you.*

Slowly, I rise, my body feeling like lead. My eyes linger on her, searching for any sign she might change her mind. "Mia..." I whisper, my voice fragile, but she meets my gaze and says, "Bye, Miles."

The words hit me like a final blow.

I cross the room, each step heavier than the last. The silence between us is deafening, filled with all the things we'll never get to say, all the moments we'll never have.

At the door, I glance back one last time. She tries to offer that soft smile—the one that, at other times, could melt my world and make me fall in love with her all over again. But this time, it's weak and painful, twisting something deep inside me. I can't bring myself to say goodbye—I'm too afraid it will make this real.

The door creaks open, and as it closes behind me, it feels like I've left a part of myself in that room with her.

Sam and Nate are waiting in the living room, their faces etched with concern. The air feels heavy, like something sacred has died.

I pass them silently, opening the main door and stepping into the corridor. The hallway stretches before me, endless and hollow. At the end, I glance back, half-hoping, half-dreading that Mia will come after me. But the door remains closed, the silence louder than any words.

Descending the stairs, the weight of her absence hits me, sharp and immediate. By the time I reach the building's exit, the secret of us has already become a memory—a bittersweet fragment of something beautiful that slipped through my fingers.

Nearing my car, I toss the keys to Nate. "You go back to the party."

He catches them. "Where are you going?"

"Back to my apartment."

"I'll drop you off." he says, concern thick in his voice.

I shake my head, my voice barely above a whisper. "Just go, Nate."

As Nate climbs in my car, I turn in the other direction, heading for the nearest subway station. The air is cold, the night eerily quiet apart from the occasional rumble of a passing vehicle. I keep my hands shoved into my pockets, my head low.

At the station, I realize I don't have my MetroCard. I sigh, irritated with myself, and buy a new one before stepping onto the platform. The familiar faint smell of grease and metal fills the air, mixing with the distant hum of an approaching train.

When the train arrives, I step into the near-empty car, sinking into a seat, the doors sliding shut as the train lurches forward.

I close my eyes, hoping the rhythmic clatter of the train will soothe the ache in my chest, but it only makes it worse. Memories flood back, vivid and relentless.

I remember showing her how to navigate the subway, how her brow furrowed as she tried to make sense of the maze of lines and numbers on the map. Her fingers brushing against mine as I handed her the MetroCard, my voice steady as I explained the process. I watched her swipe through the turnstile for the first time, a small smile spreading across her face when she got it right.

I remember the moment the train doors closed, the two of us sitting side by side. The way she relaxed. It felt like something I could have done forever—just sitting next to her, hearing her talk, being a reason for her smile.

That damn smile.

The train screeches to a halt at my stop in Brooklyn, snapping me from the weight of the bittersweet memories. I force myself to stand, my legs heavy, and make my way out of the station. The walk to my apartment feels like a dream—disjointed and surreal.

When I finally push open the door to my place, the emptiness swallows me whole. The quiet is oppressive, pressing down on me like a weight I can't escape.

Just as I drop my keys onto the counter, my phone buzzes in my pocket. I pull it out, glancing at the screen. It's my dad.

My chest tightens, anger flaring to life beneath the grief. *Of course, it's him.* The reason for all of this. The reason Mia and I had to part ways. The reason my life is unravelling.

The phone keeps buzzing, his name flashing like a taunt.

I snap.

With a sharp motion, I hurl the phone across the room. It crashes against the wall, shattering on impact. The sound echoes in the silence, startling me into stillness.

For a moment, I just stand there, staring at the broken pieces of my phone scattered across the floor. My hands are trembling, my chest heaving.

But the anger doesn't help. It doesn't fix anything. If anything, it makes the ache sharper, the emptiness deeper.

I sink onto the couch, my head in my hands, the weight of everything finally crushing me. The room feels colder, darker, and no amount of shattered glass or broken calls will bring her back.

"Miles. Miles."

The voice pulls me from a restless sleep, soft yet persistent. My eyes flutter open, and the familiar warmth of my mom's face comes into view. She's standing above me, her expression a mix of concern and tenderness, her hand lightly shaking my shoulder.

I groan, sitting up on the couch, my body heavy as if weighed down by everything from the night before. The shattered remnants of my phone screen on the floor catch my eye, a painful reminder of just how much I lost in a single night.

"Mom." I mumble, my voice hoarse.

Her brows furrow as she sits down beside me, brushing the hair off my forehead like she used to when I was a kid. "Miles, you've had me worried sick. You didn't answer any of our calls." She pauses, her voice softening. "I'm sorry for what happened with... with *Mia*."

"How do you know?" I ask, suddenly terrified.

Her words hit me harder than I expect, and I turn to her, my throat tightening. "How do you know?"

"Audrey told me." she says quietly.

I shake my head. "Great. Everyone knows."

"Why didn't you tell me before that you were dating her?" she asks gently.

"I don't know." I admit, leaning back against the couch. "Maybe I thought you'd side with Dad."

Her face falls, and she looks away for a moment before meeting my gaze again. "Miles, I've never been on his side when it comes to forcing decisions on you."

I stay silent, unsure how to respond.

"Did you know about the engagement?" I ask finally, my voice sharp with bitterness. "Please tell me you didn't."

Her expression shifts, a mix of guilt and sadness. "Yes." she admits, "but I thought you knew too. Your dad told me the day before that you wanted to marry Chloe and that you'd asked for it to be announced."

My jaw tightens, my fists clenching. "And you believed him?"

"I didn't." she says quickly. "It sounded so unlike you, but...I didn't think he'd lie about something like that."

"Well, he did." I snap, the anger boiling over. "He lied, and lied, and now I've lost her."

Her expression softens further, her eyes glistening. "Miles, I'm furious at him too. You know I am."

"Then can't you change his mind?" I say, my voice breaking.

Her shoulders slump as she shakes her head. "I really wish I could." she says softly.

"It's not like I didn't try." she continues after a pause. "I did, last night, when I found out about everything, but he wouldn't budge. You know how stubborn he can be."

The hopelessness in her voice mirrors the ache in my chest, and for a moment, we just sit there in silence.

"I don't know what to do, but I can't just let her go." I admit finally, my voice barely above a whisper.

She places a hand on mine, squeezing gently. "You'll figure it out, Miles. You always do. And whatever you decide, I'm here for you."

Her words offer a small flicker of comfort, but it's fleeting, drowned out by the weight of everything that's happened.

I hesitate, the memory cutting deep. But I tell her anyway. "I told her we could date in secret again. That after a year, when I'm CEO, I'd leave Chloe."

My mom winces, then gives me a look of exasperated affection. "Oh Miles, that's so French."

For a second, I stare at her, confused. Her words feel out of place—almost funny—but instead of softening the moment, they only make it worse. "What's that supposed to mean?" I mutter, dragging a hand down my face.

She raises an eyebrow, a hint of humour flickering in her eyes despite the heaviness of the conversation. "You know exactly what I mean. Affairs, secrets, promises that may or may not be kept... It's all so *dramatic*. Your French side is showing, my dear."

I blink at her, unsure whether to laugh or cry. "I'm serious."

"So am I." she says, her tone softening. "You're asking someone to gamble their heart on a promise you can't guarantee. It's unfair to her... and to you."

The truth in her words stings. Instead of replying, I sink deeper into the couch, wishing I could vanish into the cushions.

"Miles." she says softly, coaxing me to look at her again. "Some people come into our lives for a reason, to teach us something we'll carry forever. It hurts, but instead of mourning their loss, focus on the lesson they leave behind."

A lesson?

What was the lesson?

To never be in love again? That letting your heart be free and open to someone is wrong? If so, fine. Lesson learned. Never again.

Never!

"I know you're hurt." my mom says gently. "And I know facing you're dad feels unbearable right now, but we still need to leave for France in a few hours."

"You should take a shower." she continues, "I'll finish packing your bag."

Wordlessly, I push myself off the couch, my body aching from the hurt and weight of everything I can't fix. My legs feel leaden, every step an effort. A cold shower. Maybe it'll numb the ache. Maybe not. Or maybe it'll drown out the screaming in my head.

Maybe I'll slip.

Maybe my skull will crack against the bathroom tiles.

Maybe I'll wake up in a hospital, machines beeping, skin stitched, soul quieter.

And my memories wiped clean.

Maybe I won't remember this godforsaken ache in my chest.

Maybe I won't remember her.

Maybe I'll forget the way her smile felt like sunlight. The way her voice softened every cruel corner of me.

Maybe I'll forget.

Forget that once upon a time, I met a girl.

And she had me falling.

But in the end, what I thought was the soft cradle of lilies, was a mirage.

Because—

I landed in hell.

I step into the shower. Cold water spills down my bare skin, and for a second, I feel nothing. Then it hits me like a stone brutally aimed to puncture my lungs—

Today is Mia's birthday.

It's her birthday.

A tear escapes before I can control it, lost in the cascades of water.

And all I can do is stand here—

Wishing.

Praying.

That maybe I do get hurt.

CHAPTER 32

Mia

Professor Kessler seems to be teaching a very interesting topic judging by the expressions on the students' faces but I'm not paying any attention, I can't. I really can't.

It's been three days since everything happened, and all I'm thinking about is whether breaking up with Miles was the right decision or not because I'm hurting and so is he. I mean, it logically was right, but emotionally it feels like the worst thing I've ever done.

I always saw heartbreaks in movies, read about it in books, and wondered if it really hurts that bad. Now I'm experiencing it, and the answer is yes. When my parents died, I thought nothing, no feeling, could be as devastating as this, but losing Miles hurts equally as bad as that. Yet again I've lost a piece of me. And it really hurts.

Maybe it hurts because it's the ache of not being able to love them the way you used to. Maybe because you never imagined waking up one day and not finding them beside you. Maybe because you can't be there when they're at their lowest. Can't hold their hand through the dark. Can't laugh together like you used to. Can't dream of a future that's already slipping away. All you can do is visit back memory lane, which just leaves a hallow trail of what could have been.

And thinking about this and doubting about my decision is not really helping me but I can't stop it. My mind made the decision of letting him go for the sake of both our lives but my heart is not yet ready to accept that.

I shift uncomfortably in my seat, nausea creeping in like a tide. My stomach twists and my chest tightens. Sam did say I shouldn't attend any lectures today, but I didn't want to fall behind. Maybe I should've listened to her.

Raising my hand, I mumble some excuse and quickly leave the classroom. I speed-walk through the cold, sterile walls of the hallway to the restroom. I storm into one of the stalls and puke. Flushing the toilet, I close the lid and sit down. That's when it hits me. I was supposed to get my period five days ago, and it still hasn't come. My cycles have always been regular. This is unusual. And now I'm throwing up, even though I haven't eaten anything questionable. I don't think stress from the breakup is making me sick.

There's only one explanation that makes sense.

I really hope it's not that.

I leave the restroom, my mind racing, and almost crash into Maverick.

"There you are. I was looking for you." he says.

"Why?" I ask, trying to keep my voice steady.

"You left your bag in class." He says, handing it to me.

"Oh! Thanks." I say, pasting a small smile when all I want to do this cry.

"But what are you doing here? The lecture's not over, is it?" I ask, trying to sound casual.

"No, it's not. But when you left, you looked stressed, so I thought I'd check on you." he says, his voice soft with concern.

"That's really kind of you, but I'm fine. Just needed to use the restroom." I reply quickly.

"Are you sure?" he presses.

"I'm fine, Maverick." I snap, the words sharper than I intended. We both freeze for a moment, caught off guard. "I'm sorry." I say, my voice softer. "I'm just having a rough day."

"Its fine." he says, his tone understanding.

"I've got to go." I mumble after a long pause, excusing myself.

Later, I sit in my dorm room's bathroom, staring down at the results of four pregnancy tests. Each one shows two red lines. I run a shaky hand through my hair, trying to hold back tears, but one escapes, quickly followed by more. What am I going to do? I don't even know how to feel—happy, scared, sad?

How am I going to tell him?

How am I gonna tell him after breaking up with him?

I take a few minutes to let myself cry, the weight of the situation crashing over me, then I stand up. I walk out of the bathroom, pick up my phone from the couch, and call Miles with shaky hand. My entire body goes rigid as the phone rings and rings until it goes to his voicemail. I try again, but the same happens. I let out a frustrated sigh, feeling anxious and helpless.

I wash my face, fix my getup, grab my bag and head out to the subway station. I take the train to Brooklyn and walk to his apartment which is close. I knock on his door. No answer. I pull out the spare key he gave me and let myself in, but he's not here.

Then, I remember what Miles said to me a few days ago.

"I'll have to fly to France with my dad the day after the announcement."

I collapse on the couch, the overwhelming weight of it all consuming means I cry myself to sleep there.

When I wake up, the apartment is consumed by darkness, my surrounding as quiet as the land of the dead. It takes me a minute to remember what had happened and where I was. I check my phone—no reply or call-back from Miles. I decide to stay the night here. It's already seven, and the next direct train back won't be until nine. I don't want to travel that late.

I text Sam to inform her I won't be back till morning.

I make myself a sandwich, eat it, and go to sleep in the guest bedroom because it feels weird to sleep in Miles room without him.

I wake up at seven, groggy but resolute. The weight of last night lingers, pressing into my skin like a fading bruise.

The kitchen is silent except for the soft gurgle of the kettle. I brew myself a cup of tea, its warmth seeping into my palms, but it does nothing to settle the unease gnawing at my chest. I reach for my phone, dialling Miles again.

Voicemail.

I exhale sharply, then try again. And again.

Ten calls. Ten times sent straight to voicemail.

Maybe he's avoiding me because he's angry. Maybe he's hurt. Maybe he just needs time. But my patience is thinning with every passing second. Waiting a whole week for Miles to break this news will wreck me—leave me pacing, overthinking, suffocating under the weight of the unknown. I refuse to let that happen.

My fingers tremble as I compose the message.

Mia: *I'm pregnant.*

I finish drinking the tea in silence, glancing at my phone time to time for Miles's reply or call. But when I'm in middle of washing the cup, my phone pings, I quickly see who the text is from and almost drop the cup when I see it's from Miles. I wipe my hands on the kitchen towel and open the text.

The message leaves me cold.

Miles: *I don't want anything to do with it.*

I reread the text in disbelief. This doesn't sound like him. This can't be him.

Mia: *Not a great time to joke Miles.*

My message sends, my heat clinging to the hope that he is teasing, a twisted attempt at humour, but the response is immediate, shattering.

Miles: *I'm not joking. We're not compatible, and you know it. That's why you ended things. Don't try to use this pregnancy to get back together.*

Miles: *We are over.*

I try to call him again but he declines it and then a text from him comes.

Miles: *Don't call me. We Are Over.*

I can't breathe it's like the air is sucked out of the room. My chest tightens as a sob breaks its way out. Tears stream down, unchecked, mixing with the snot that clogs my nose. My body shakes as though the apartment's air conditioning has rusted. I'm down bad, like he has stripped away my clothes and nothing is left. Like I've woken in nothing but blood.

I stagger to the couch, forcing myself to breath slowly. The grief begins to morph into anger, the tears drying from the heat of my rage. My mind swirls with questions—questions that will never be answered.

What is wrong with him? How could he do this? How could he back out like this?

Was I just a passing fling? A game or maybe a bet?

This always happens to me, the people I start to trust abandon me. My parents left, albeit due to an unexpected accident, they still left me. My relatives who always pretended to be nice to me turned cruel when it came to raising me after my parent's death, and now Miles. I loved him, I told him I loved him and so did he, but he saw forever so he smashed it up.

I love you.

We are not compatible.

I place a hand on my belly, a quiet reminder that I'm not alone. A new life stirs within me—a fragile, yet unyielding responsibility. I know I lose my grip and don't think rationally when I'm pissed but this decision isn't born out of rage. This decision is for me and for my child because I cannot stay in the same city where Miles walks, where his shadow lingers in every breath of air I take.

You might think this is the coward's way out and maybe it is, but sometimes the strongest people crumble and crawl into hiding—not because they are scared but because they are picking up the pieces of their shattered heart, stitching their deep scars in the shadows, so they won't be toppled over again. They are not cowards; they are the real fighters, battling something bigger than the world: themselves—their darkest, most vulnerable selves.

The Plane is set to land at the airport in less than fifteen minutes, and with every second that ticks by, my nerves coil tighter, like a spring threatening to snap. I stare blankly out the window, watching the clouds blur into a pale grey as we descend, but all I can see are the memories playing behind my eyes.

I mentally flip through the chapters of my journey in America. Sixteen months. Sixteen beautiful, heartbreaking, chaotic months. These last few days—hell. But even hell couldn't erase the moments that made me feel alive. Sam's late-night rants, Audrey's bold easy-going attitude, Nate's kindness, Alex's laughter, and... *Miles*.

God, *Miles*.

He gave me everything I never knew I needed—my first kiss, first date, he fucking helped me get over my front seat phobia by teaching me how to drive. But he betrayed me in ways that shattered the girl I used to be. But I loved him.

Still do.

And no matter how hard I try, I can't erase him. He should've stayed. He should've fought. This unborn child isn't just mine—it's his too. And yet, he found a way to slip out, leaving me holding all the weight.

The Miles I knew would never leave someone marooned, let alone me. But I guess people change. Or maybe they never were who we thought they were.

How did I let this happen though? I went to America to find myself, to grow. And now I'm returning home as a disaster. Would my parents hate me for this? Or worse... would they pity me? I must've made them restless in heaven.

I was supposed to be the one who had it all figured out. Smart. Cautious. But now I'm a mess. I'm scared. How can I even *think* about raising a child when I don't know how to fix myself?

How do I tell Uncle Rohan?

The plane touches down, and the jolt sends a silent tear spilling down my cheeks. I wipe it away quickly as the pilot announces the landing. No one notices. No one ever does.

I walk out of terminal 2, my steps heavy, and then I see her—Nidhi. Waving like nothing's changed, like I'm still the girl who left months ago. Without a word, I throw myself into her arms, and she hugs me like she's been waiting a lifetime. Her embrace is the first warmth I've felt in days like she's been waiting a lifetime.

She grabs my suitcase as we walk to her car in silence. As soon as we are inside the car, I let my guard down and collapse into her shoulder, tears streaming down my cheeks. She holds me, gently stroking my hairs, murmuring soft words of comfort, and I finally let it all out—the grief, the guilt, the fear.

When no tears are left, she drives me to Uncle Rohan's apartment. It's six in the morning, and I know Uncle Rohan's probably still asleep. He knows I'm back, he knows I have something important to talk to him, but he doesn't know that important talk would paint a different picture of me in his eyes.

As we step out of the car, I take a moment to look around. The society looks exactly the same as it did when I left. The gentle morning breeze brushes past me, the first rays of sunlight peek through the trees, and birds are chirping softly in the background. For most people, it might feel like a fresh start, a new beginning. But for me, it feels like I'm about to shatter that calm—like my presence here is going to disturb the peace, especially for Uncle Rohan.

We take the elevator to the sixth floor, and my breath grows shallow. When I ring the bell, my fingers tremble. Within seconds, Uncle Rohan opens the door, sleep still lingering in his eyes, but he looks excited to see me after so long.

I pretend I'm happy too for a brief moment.

And then Nidhi and I enter the apartment, and I begin. I start to tell him everything, my voice cracking as I try to explain what can never fully be explained. He listens in silence. No interruptions. But I can see it—the way his expressions darken, the way his jaws clenches, the way his eyes flicker with something between shock and disbelief.

When I finish, he stands abruptly. Pacing. Breathing heavily. His silence is louder than a thousand screams. Nidhi and I exchange a nervous glance. She reaches for my hand, grounding me, but even she can't hide the dread in her eyes.

"Uncle," I say, my voice shaking. "I'm sorry. I know I'm a big disappointment."

"Yes. You are a disappointment." He stops pacing, but his tone is controlled. "This is not you. I never expected this from you. I mean this is something I thought Nidhi would do. But..."

Nidhi clears her throat.

"I take absolutely no offence." She mutters flatly.

Uncle Rohan ignores her.

"I'm sorry." I whisper, the words catching in my throat. "I really am."

He exhales slowly. "I know you are. I also know you regret it. And that's already punishment enough. No scolding, no yelling will turn back time to fix everything."

A pause. A breath. Then he says, softer than I expected. "But everything will be okay. I'm here."

And just like that, something in me breaks again—only this time, it's the tension. The fear. The isolation. I stand and wrap my arms around him, burying my face in his shoulders. No tears now. I've cried them all. "I'm sorry."

"It's okay." He murmurs.

Nidhi snorts. "Well, speaking of punishable offences... what are we going to do about Miles? Because I vote we kill the douchebag. I'm ready to take all the blame and go to prison."

I shake my head. "Let's just forget about him."

They both fall silent, exchanging a look. They nod.

But I know we won't really forget.

Some ghosts never leave.

The way Uncle Rohan reacted has left me stunned. I expected anger, judgment—maybe even being kicked out—but instead, he has met me with calm understanding. It's more than I could've hoped for.

But right now, I'm down bad. I'm sitting in the balcony, staring at the sky, begging it to come and pick me up. The texts, Miles' recent behaviour—it didn't sound like him, and that's what has me tangled. He made me feel like I was the chosen one, but now I'm back where I came from. And now, I feel so alone in my own home.

And amidst my hate for him right now, I still love him. But I can't have him because he has basically thrown me away.

The door creaks open, and Nidhi steps onto the balcony, sinking into the chair beside me. She doesn't say anything at first, just tilts her head back, staring at the night sky like I am.

"You okay?" she finally asks.

"No." I whisper. "Too many emotions. Too many feelings."

"That's called heartbreak." she says softly.

"Well, I hate it." My voice wavers. "I hate it because I still love him. And to top it off—I'm pregnant. A permanent reminder of him."

Nidhi doesn't flinch. She just nods, absorbing my words. "Either way, that's not something you'd ever forget." Her voice is calm, steady. "Maybe the baby will heal you in a way you don't expect."

She's trying. She's really trying. But nothing will help, not really. Not unless the person who caused the pain comes back—and he's not coming back.

The next words slip out before I can stop them. "I'm not ready, Ni. I'm not ready to be a mom."

She turns to me, her face expressionless at first, but then I see it— the understanding, the concern. She's surprised, maybe, but not judgmental. And when I expect her to tell me I'm wrong, she doesn't. Instead, she says, "It's okay. You're young, and maybe stupid," *I am stupid.* "but you aren't alone. No one's going to judge you for what you decide."

I stare at her concerned yet understanding face, and unintentionally shake my head, my chest tight, my eyes stinging. I will never forget this part of me. But I can't keep it.

And fuck it if I was in love.

Fuck it.

Time to wave that ship goodbye.

22 Months Later…

CHAPTER 33

Mia

"How much time left?" I ask, my legs jittering from anxiety.

"30 minutes." Leo says.

Nine months ago, in January, I returned to America with nothing but determination. I walked into one of the most prestigious record labels in the country—Moonlit Records—with my guitar slung over my shoulder and a mission in my heart. By some twist of fate, I arrived at their main office at the exact same time as Blake Carter, the founder.

She was kind enough to give me three minutes of her time to make an impression—just the length of an elevator ride. I poured my heart into those three minutes, playing her one of the most heart-wrenching songs I'd written about *him*. It was hard, playing that song, but it got her attention. And now, here I am.

Last month, we released the first single off of my debut album, called *Love Blackout* and later the second single *Ended*. Both of these singles hit the billboard top 200 in two weeks which led me to announce my debut album which is releasing right now at midnight, in thirty minutes as Leo Rivers—my producer, said.

We've worked our hearts and souls to compose and make this album possible in the eight months' time frame; I hope it's worth it. I hope coming back to a place where my heart shattered into millions of pieces worth it.

Not all the songs are about him, though. And not all of them screech about betrayal. It was necessary to add a sprinkle of happiness to the album or a wave of calmness to it so I don't come off as a complete psychopath. I couldn't let my temper dominate the narrative of my first big project.

That's why I included *Fantasy*—the song I wrote the night of our first date. This song reminds me of our first kiss, so I wasn't going to put it on the album, but at the end of the day, it's a good track (according to Leo). This track was a moment of innocence, untouched by the heartbreak that would follow.

This album isn't just a story of heartbreak; it's a tapestry of all the emotions that have made me who I am. Love, loss, hope, and resilience.

"How'd the date go?" Leo asks, breaking my thoughts.

"We are friends." I say slowly. "Your cousin is sweet but I'm just not ready to date yet."

"Good for you." Leo says, his eyes flickering to the phone in his hand. "Although the paps don't think that."

He shows me a photo of me and Myron Balise leaving a restaurant in New York City two days ago. The headline blares: *Quarterback Myron Balise and New Rising Music Sensation Mia Malhotra Make Waves on their NYC Dinner Date.*

I frown, running my fingers through my hair. "You know, I wasn't expecting any paparazzi. But then again, I was on a date with the most famous quarterback in America. It's pretty self-explanatory."

Leo chuckles, his eyes glinting. "How were all the camera flashes?"

"Like a tornado." I mutter, shaking my head. "Thank God the car was only five seconds away. Otherwise, I might've gone blind."

It was overwhelming being the center of attention, but I've accepted this reality. I've changed. Everything I've been through has shaped me into someone bolder, more independent, more responsible. The spotlight doesn't seem to scare me anymore.

"I was surprised, though. Some of them were shouting my name—'Mia, look here!'" I shake my head, remembering the chaos. "I thought they were only there for Myron's photos. But it was... strange. I felt a mix of pride and annoyance. It's like I'm not just a background character anymore. I'm part of the headline."

"You're more famous than you think." Leo says, his gaze thoughtful.

"Huh... More known, maybe." I reply, offering a small smile. "We'll talk about 'famous' later."

That's when my apartment's door swings open.

Yes, *my* apartment—small, rented, but mine. Two bedrooms, a kitchen, a bathroom, and a living room. Cozy, not too modern, but comfortable.

Nidhi walks in, a bag of Chipotle in her hand.

"Thank God Chipotle was still open this late." She announces.

"They always are." Leo remarks, pulling out the containers.

I take a bite of my burrito, scrolling through Instagram on my phone. That's when I stumble across a post from Audrey. A pang shoots through my chest, unexpected, sharp.

I never wanted to cut any ties with them, but when I flew back to India, any contact with America felt unsafe. It was too destructive, threatening my already weakened soul. So I wiped everything—email, number, deleted my any social presence as much as possible.

"I don't know why the algorithm keeps suggesting me their Instagram accounts." I mutter, almost to myself. "I don't even follow them."

"Maybe because you used to follow them when you were in college." Leo suggests.

"Nah. I had an inactive insta handle back then."

"But didn't Sam and Audrey post photos with you?" Nidhi says. "Maybe the algorithm saw your face and was like, Hey, that girl and that girl are connected."

"Could be." I shrug, but the thought unsettles me.

"Do you think Miles has listened to the singles?" Leo asks quietly, his tone more careful now.

I glance at him, my throat tightening. He knows everything. When we first started working on this album, my lyrics were raw—unhinged. Leo questioned it, and I blurted everything out. He's like a big brother to me now. Eight months of being cooped in a studio together will create that bond.

"I honestly don't know." I reply, staring down at the burrito in my hands, my stomach churning. "I even doubt he remembers me."

"No." says Nidhi, her voice firm. "He remembers you. Remember the call?"

The call.

Six months ago, Nidhi got a call from an unknown number. Turned out to be Miles. According to Nidhi, he called to apologize, but she told him to fuck off—with a *sweet*, sweet threat.

And I think Nidhi did the right thing.

But it still lingers, doesn't it?

How much sad did Miles think I had? Did he really think he could just waltz back into my life just to tear it down again? No! I reached my limit of sorrow and the remnants carried me here, to this album, to this stage. To prove that I'm not someone you can just throw away when the fun ends.

Leo says, "Guys, only five minutes left."

"Yay!" Nidhi exclaims, pulling a bottle from behind the couch.

"What's that?" I raise an eyebrow.

"Celebratory champagne." she replies.

"You know I don't drink."

She grins. "You don't, but Leo and I do."

"Since when do you drink?"

"I've only had it once. Just once. It's fine."

"I'm not responsible for what happens next, Ni."

"I know." she says, already pouring glasses for herself and Leo.

As the clock ticks down, I stare at the screen. My heart pounds. This is it. Everything I've worked for—every sleepless night, every tear, every note, every fleeting smile—has led to this moment.

Three.

Two.

One.

CHAPTER 34
Miles

The tires screech against the road as I speed toward Columbia. The moment our private jet landed, my mind was already here, racing through every scenario that would bring me face-to-face with her again. It's five in the evening. She has to be in her dorm.

I take the stairs two at a time, my chest tightening with every step. By the time I reach the third floor, my pulse is a drumbeat in my ears. I knock, almost desperate, and the door swings open to reveal Sam.

Her usual smirk is missing, replaced by something unfamiliar—pity.

"Where's Mia?" I demand, stepping past her.

"She's gone." Sam says, her voice barely above a whisper.

"Gone where?" I ask, a sharp edge creeping into my tone.

"India."

The word lands like a sucker punch to my gut. "When is she coming back?"

Sam hesitates. Her eyes soften in a way that twists the knife deeper. "Miles, I don't think she's coming back."

That memory plays on a loop as I stare at the massive billboard outside my office window now. Mia's face is front and centre, framed by the kind of high contrast, dramatic lighting that perfectly matches the expression she's wearing—Rage, her eyes seeking for revenge.

Her debut album cover.

Released a month ago.

Illicit Rage.

The image is hauntingly beautiful. Her face is tilted slightly downward, her dark eyes gazing intensely right at the camera, as though she's looking into a memory she'd rather burn to ashes. Her hands frame her face, partially covering it, with elegant rings adding a touch of sophistication and drama. The wet, textured hair and bold makeup, particularly the dark lips, accentuate the edgy and unapologetic mood of the composition.

The black-and-white tone enhances the contrast, giving the image a raw, timeless quality while emphasizing the shadows and textures. The long sleeves, paired with the deathly vulnerability of the pose, evoke a mix of strength and emotion, making it feel both intimate and powerful.

Her name, her angry yet painful eyes, her defiant and unfiltered expressions—they stare back at me through the glass as if mocking me.

This is what you lost.

I never imagined seeing her like this, larger than life, literally. I also never imagined losing her like I did.

When I flew back from France, the first thing I did was go to her dorm. I had hope then. It wasn't much, but it was enough to keep me moving. Enough to make me believe that if I could just see her, I could fix it. I could fix *us*. I could convince her to hold on.

But life had other plans. Plans that ripped her from me before I could make things right.

I was a cold mess without her. France was supposed to be a CEO-defining moment, but all I could think about was Mia. The meetings, the proposals, the applause—it all felt meaningless. I wasn't fully there.

I kept replaying her absence, like a cruel joke. Every silence screamed her name. Every laugh in the crowd sounded like hers, until I realized it wasn't and felt that hollow ache all over again.

And now? Now, she's everywhere. On billboards, in headlines, on the radio. The world gets to have her while I don't. And this album—her songs—are daggers.

I've tried to understand the lyrics, tried to piece together the story she's telling, but it feels like she's talking about a different version of us. The name of the album hints at something completely else than what happened—a rebellious fury born out of suppressed anger.

In the song *Marooned* she sings about being left stranded in her time of need. I don't get it. I was trying to fix things, wasn't I? She's the one who broke up with me. But somehow, I'm not angry at her for making herself the victim and expressing it in a dangerous and bold way. I'm... confused. Was she trying to tell me something I missed? A cry for help I didn't hear? Because it feels like something bigger than our breakup happened while I was in France. Something I never saw coming. And now I don't have a way to understand it because I can't get to her.

Her sudden disappearance to India, cutting off all ties, didn't feel like her. I tried to contact her, but it was like she had wiped out her existence. No phone number, no email, nothing. Few months after I officially took over the entire company, I tracked down her best friend's number. That call still haunts me.

Seven months ago...

The line crackled as the voice on the other end picked up. "Hello?"

"Hi, is this Nidhi Desai?" *I asked, my voice shaking.* "It's Miles. I... I need to talk to Mia."

There was a pause, then a sharp laugh that wasn't friendly. "You've got some nerve."

"Please, I just need..."

"No." *she cut me off. Her voice turned icy.* "Listen to me carefully douchebag. If you ever—EVER—try to contact Mia again, I'll personally make sure you regret it. Do you understand? Because I have no problem flying to New York, knocking on your fancy office door, and..." *she paused, her tone razor-sharp,* "... slitting that throat of yours and just... let's just say you'll wish you'd never called."

I froze. The line went dead before I could respond.

I glance at the wedding ring on my finger, thinking about how Mia was spotted on a date with Myron Blaise almost two months ago. Thinking about how Mia has moved on while I'm still stuck in the loop of what could have been with her. Time moved forward. I got engaged, married, Chloe took over her father's empire, and her brother went back to rehab, I officially got the CEO position while my dad retired. Life moved on. But here I am, living in the past.

"I don't understand what she's so angry about. I mean, she's the one who left." Audrey says, standing next to me, staring at the billboard. She's been pissed at Mia since the album's singles released, unable to make sense of the lyrics. She also thinks Mia is playing the victim, but she's really angry while I'm just... lost.

"She's a completely new person." Audrey mutters.

I don't respond. My eyes are fixed on Mia's gaze in the photograph, those uncompromising, dangerously captivating eyes that hold secrets I can't decode. Secrets that, maybe, I'll never understand.

That's what's so terrifyingly interesting about people—everybody wants a happy ending, but not everyone gets one. And some, like me, are left trying to piece together what went wrong when the story ends without a goodbye.

"I don't even think the album's that good." Audrey adds.

"Well, it did break a few records." Alex chimes in. "Leo Rivers produced it, after all. And if you listen to the songs as a stranger, they're... kind of incredible."

Illicit Rage did break countless records in its first week: the biggest streaming month for a debut album by a new artist. And most Spotify global streams in a single month for a pop album, making Mia an official popstar.

"Whatever. Let's go, Miles." Audrey says, nudging me. "We need to pack for the festival."

The festival.

It's all anyone has talked about for months. *Capital FM* and *iHeartRadio's* collaboration, *The WorldBeat Soundlympic Fest*, has become the pinnacle of global music events—a monumental celebration of artistry, culture, and unity. A festival that doesn't just bring the biggest names in music to one stage but it's a chance for the music industry to create a historic moment that will echo years to come, like an Olympic torch passed every four years.

This is only the second time the festival is being held. The phenomenal event four years ago took place in London's Wembley Stadium, a ground-breaking three-night spectacle that made headlines around the world. Critics hailed it as "The greatest musical gathering of the decade." and fans were left with memories they'd remember for a lifetime.

And now, it's America's turn. Michigan Stadium has been chosen as the venue for this year's edition.

"Four years ago, Wembley set the bar. Now, it's our turn to raise it." one of the festival organizers had declared during the press conference. The challenge was clear: outdo the spectacle of London.

The buzz only grew when the performers were announced. Every genre is represented—pop, rock, R&B, hip-hop, country, and even classical fusion.

"Three nights, one stage, the world's heartbeat." reads the tagline plastered across every screen and banner, perfectly encapsulating the festival's essence.

I wasn't planning to go to this music festival, but thanks to Nate bailing, Audrey and Alex roped me in.

"*Come on, man. Ed Sheeran's performing.*" Alex says.

"*And if you're worried about Mia being there, she won't.*" Audrey adds. "*They finalize the performers a year ago.*"

Mia being there wouldn't be a curse though—it'd be a blessing at a second chance with her.

At least, that's what I thought months ago. But now? She's dating Myron Blaise, and Audrey's probably right—Mia won't be there.

Probably.

"Oh my god. I'm so excited!" Audrey exclaims, practically sprinting towards the VIP check-in point.

We get our tickets scanned and walk into Michigan Stadium. The stage immediately catches my eye. It juts out boldly into the stadium, its sleek, futuristic design impossible to miss.

A long runway stretches deep into the crowd, ending in a massive, star-shaped platform. Every inch of the stage is panelled with what looks like LED screens—floor to edge—glowing faintly beneath the overhead lights.

Audrey and Sam immediately start snapping photos and filming reels, capturing every moment for their Instagram pages. Alex jumps in, striking a few poses, while I'm relegated to the role of cameraman, snapping endless pictures for them until the concert finally begins.

The opening artist is Sabrina Carpenter, kicking things off with her song *Nonsense*. Even though it came out nearly seven years ago, the crowd dances like it's a brand-new hit. Four more global artists take the stage after her, filling the next hour and half with high-energy performances.

Then, Ed Sheeran steps onto the stage. Ed Sheeran is my favourite artist—the only one I really listen to. Seeing him perform *Thinking Out Loud* live should've been incredible. But instead of feeling the magic like everyone else, I feel hollow. It was Mia and my song. While others are singing along or sharing kisses during the final notes, my stomach twists. It's not the music or the moment—it's me and my broken heart.

As he exits the stage, the stadium goes pitch black. A hush falls over the crowd. Suddenly, the massive screen flickers to life, showing a glass falling and shattering into tiny pieces. The sound of breaking echoes through the stadium, followed by an image of petals slowly drifting down—white petals to be exact. The atmosphere shifts, and a wave of anticipation ripples through the audience.

The screen blinks out again, leaving the crowd in suspenseful silence. Then, a heavy, pulsing bassline begins—deep, relentless, and electrifying. Spotlights flash erratically, illuminating the stage in bursts of white and red, creating a chaotic and dramatic ambiance. On the screen, bold red letters appear: Illicit Rage.

The crowd erupts into wild cheers as the spotlight shines on a single figure emerging from the shadows at the back of the stage. My breath catches in my throat. It's her. It's Mia.

Her silhouette is unmistakable. The spotlights lands on her, and her outfit becomes visible on the big screen. She's wearing a bodysuit designed with sparkling red sequins, creating a bold and striking look. It has long sleeves, a deep V-neckline, and a high cut, highlighting her sharp, fierce stage presence.

She has paired the bodysuit with black thigh-high boots, which adds to the edgy and powerful aesthetic. Her hair is styled in loose waves and perfectly styled *bangs*.

The heavy beat of the song drops, and Mia's voice cuts through the noise, sharp and commanding.

The stage comes alive around her, the screens displaying fragmented visuals of stormy skies, neon-lit cityscapes, and glowing bursts of red and white. Dancers surround her, their movements bold and sharp, perfectly complementing the song's raw energy. The choreography is fierce, unapologetically powerful, matching the rebellious tone of the lyrics.

Audrey grabs my arm, her voice barely audible over the noise. "This is insane! Miles are you okay?"

I nod, but the truth is, I'm anything but. Because while everyone else sees a rising star on that stage, all I see is the girl I lost. And tonight, under the glaring stadium lights, it feels like she's slipping even further away. Audrey was right—she's changed. Not in a bad way, though. She's bolder, stronger, someone who has moved on and has no intentions of looking back. Her style has changed so has her demur, making her fierce and perilous.

"Should we go? We should go." Audrey says, her voice laced with concern.

"No." I reply firmly.

That's when Mia moves toward our side of the stage.

Only then do I realize just how close our seats really are to the stage.

Just as I convince myself she won't notice me in the crowd, the big screen flashes a burst of white light for a brief moment, illuminating our section. Her eyes lock with mine. She falters for the briefest second, her performance face slipping, but she quickly recovers and moves back to the center of the stage. The song ends.

The thunderous beat drops, Mia stands center stage, head tilted back, arms raised in victory. The crowd explodes in cheers and applause, the energy of the performance leaving them breathless. Slowly, Mia lowers her arms, her chest rising and falling as she catches her breath. A sly, confident smile plays on her lips as she steps closer to the microphone.

"Welcome to the Illicit Rage set of the WorldBeat Soundlympic Fest!" she announces, her voice clear and vibrant.

The crowd roars again, swaying their lit wristbands in the air.

"I've waited so long to bring this album to life, and tonight, you're getting the first glimpse." she says, her smile widening. "I just walked around the stage and saw you singing, screaming the lyrics, which means so much to me." she continues, her face lighting up. "Seeing this energy is absolutely unreal."

The crowd cheers wildly, jumping and clapping. Mia beams, but her eyes never stray toward our section again. She's perfected the art of looking everywhere but here, and it feels like a deliberate choice.

She adjusts the strap of a gleaming black guitar as it's handed to her. "Let's keep this energy going." she says, her fingers brushing over the strings as she transitions seamlessly into *Fantasy*. The crowd's cheers swell again, and the night carries on with the same electrifying momentum.

As she starts singing the song, my ears somehow hear a girl say to her friend, "This song must be about Myron."

For some reason, those words hit me like a slap. I know exactly who this song is about—*me*—but the whole world thinks it's inspired by that football player. I try to push the thought away, but it lingers, echoing in the back of my mind.

The song ends, and the dancers flood the stage again as the intro to another song begins to play, and I find myself staring at the stage, at Mia, with intense focus. Sam, Alex, and Audrey watch me closely, their concerned expressions clear. They're probably waiting for me to break out in hives.

The song ends, and the dancers, vocalists, the band, and Mia take a bow. "Thank you so much, everyone!" she calls out, before exiting the stage.

I stare at the now vacant spot where Mia just stood, my thoughts a jungle of chaotic mess. Every time I think I've sorted through my feelings, it's like another branch grows back, leaving a void I can't seem to fill by myself.

"Guys, I'm going to take an Uber back to the hotel. You all enjoy the show." I say loudly, watching as the stadium goes dark and silent once again after Mia's performance.

"Hey, no. We'll come with you." Alex insists.

"No. You have fun." I reply, trying to brush it off.

"I don't think anyone's having fun right now, Miles." Sam says.

"We're all still in shock. And besides, there's only an hour left before the concert ends." Audrey adds.

"Fine." I say, my voice low.

The stage lights up again, signaling the start of a new artist's performance, but none of us are focused on that. We push through the thick crowd of excited fans, making our way toward the exit.

It takes almost fifteen minutes to find my car in the sea of parked vehicles, and nearly an hour to escape Michigan's late-night traffic on our way to the hotel.

The drive is awkwardly silent, the hum of the engine the only sound filling the space between us. No one speaks. Normally, I would've welcomed the peace, but tonight it feels suffocating, giving my mind free reign to wander back to Mia.

"How are you feeling?" Nidhi asks as I step out of the back entrance of the stage and rush straight towards my dressing room.

"Anxious." I reply, my legs shaking as I sit down on the couch.

"You're always anxious. Tell me something else."

I hesitate. "No, actually. I saw Miles in the crowd."

The second the spotlight hit me, my nerves shot through the roof. But as I started singing and the crowd began to sing along, I felt a wave of confidence. For a moment, I let myself relax. Until I saw *him*.

"Are you sure it was Miles? It's pretty dark out there in the stands." Her tone shifts to serious.

"No, it was him. I'm sure of it."

Since the festival first started, I've only *dreamed* of attending it because of the incredible ticket prizes. But just minutes before I performed on its stage, everything felt surreal. The sound of the fans cheering felt so sweet and enchanting, but then I saw Miles. It didn't make me appreciate the crowd's energy any less—it just startled me, I guess.

I don't think he was here on purpose, though. He couldn't have known I was performing since I was one of the secret acts. There are three secret performers, announced for each consecutive night, and I was the one for tonight.

I know what you're thinking: Always the *fucking* secret.

Although I didn't mind this one.

"Hey, forget about him, okay? Now he's not the only one with power. You are too. So we don't give a fuck about him." Nidhi says, comforting me.

I rest my head on her shoulder, a yawn slipping out. "Should we go back to the hotel?" she asks gently.

"I kinda want to." I admit guiltily. "But weren't we going to watch the rest of the show from the tent?"

"Oh, we can do that tomorrow. Either way, I miss that munchkin."

"Me too."

"You change into comfy clothes. I'll let the coordinator know we're leaving and call the driver."

"What would I do without you?" I yawn again, smiling.

"Die." she replies flatly.

I chuckle, getting up to change. I slip into a warm grey hoodie and sweatpants, then sit in front of the vanity mirror to wipe off my makeup, but I'll need a long shower at the hotel.

Nidhi returns a few minutes later. "All set. Let's go."

Grabbing our bags, we head out. I spot the dancers, vocalists, and band members who performed with me tonight—people I've rehearsed with for weeks. I make my way over to them.

"Thank you so much, guys." I say, pulling them into a group hug.

After saying goodbye to my colleagues, Nidhi and I hop into the car, fighting through Michigan's late-night traffic on our way back to the hotel.

CHAPTER 35

Miles

Arriving at the hotel's parking lot, I pull into a spot and park. We don't waste any time—no one even suggests roaming around the hotel. We all head straight for the elevator. As it ascends to floor fifteen, the quiet between us feels thick, unspoken. Sam digs through her bag, her fingers brushing against the soft yellow fabric of her purse, clearly searching for the keycards to room no. 15F and 15G.

"Sam, you should've given the keys to me." Says Audrey flatly.

"Oh, they're not lost. They're here somewhere in my purse, don't worry." Sam replies with a dismissive chuckle, still rifling through it.

I lean against the brown wood-panelled wall of the corridor, prepared to call the manager in five minutes for spare keycards. My tired eyes linger on the soft glow of the hallway lights, casting long shadows, the air heavy with a mix of luxury and quiet.

In that moment, the elevator dings, and as the doors slide open, I hear a familiar voice—soft and gentle. My heart jolts as my eyes land on the woman standing just a few feet away in the elevator.

For a split second, I forget to breathe. She's there, just twenty steps away, but it's like the world has stopped spinning. Her presence, as commanding as ever, fills the long space between us. I take in her black, wavy hair and bangs, the familiar curve of her jawline, the way she holds herself with quiet strength. But what truly catches me off guard is the small bundle in her arms. My heart stutters in my chest.

The baby, barely old enough to speak, stretches his tiny hands toward the elevator buttons, his little fingers brushing them, clearly curious. But Mia gently pulls him back, her voice soft yet firm. "No."

The baby, in his sweet, fragile voice, looks up at Mia and whispers, "Mumma."

The word is so small, yet it consumes me like an avalanche. It's soft, full of innocence, but its weight is unbearable. *Mumma*. It lingers in the air, echoing in the hollow space between us, sinking deep into my chest.

And then, it happens.

A searing pain splits through me, unavoidable and merciless, as if every beat of my heart is tearing it apart from within. My breath catches, sharp and jagged, and my ribs feel like they're caving under the pressure. The ground beneath me seems to shift, pulling me into a void where everything I thought I knew is no longer true.

Mumma. He called her mumma.

Mia's his mom.

The realization is a dagger, twisting cruelly, carving out a hollow in the very center of me. My legs refuse to move, rooted to the spot as if burdened by the weight of my anguish. I want to run, to scream, to make sense of the chaos disintegrating inside me, but I'm paralyzed.

The ache spreads, unfurling like vines wrapping around my chest, tightening until I can't breathe. My vision blurs as the elevator door slides shut, separating me from her, from the life I thought we had.

And all I can do is stand there, drowning in the silence, with that single, innocent word—*Mumma*—echoing over and over, shredding what's left of my heart.

Then, Alex says, "Was that Mia?" in a shocked tone, snapping me out of my thoughts as my heart lurches, adrenalin firing through my veins.

In two strides, I'm at the elevator, jabbing the call button repeatedly like it'll force the doors open faster. The small screen above flashes 17—a cruel taunt.

Without thinking, I turn on my heel and bolt for the stairwell.

My footsteps echo in the narrow space as I take the stairs three at a time, my patience thinning with every step. My mind races faster than my body, a taint of questions and emotions tangled together, all leading to one thing: Mia.

When I burst onto the 17th floor, the hallway stretches out in front of me, eerily quiet. I glance around, searching desperately for any sign of her—of the baby—but there's nothing. No black waves of hair. No soft coo of a child. Just empty silence mocking me.

An intrusive thought creeps in, uninvited: *Maybe I should knock on every door.*

I exhale sharply, frustrated with myself. Why did I rush up here? What did I think I'd find? *Why did I want to see Mia so badly?*

My mind whispers lies I shouldn't believe—*You still have a chance.* But I know the truth. I don't.

I'm married. She's with Myron. And that baby... that baby might be his.

It pierces my chest like an arrow aimed for the heart. I swallow hard, but it doesn't stop the silent tear that spills down my cheek. It slides slowly, deliberately, as if the universe itself has decided to remind me, *You're too late.*

Mia has moved on. And in her arms, she held the proof.

The elevator behind me dings again. I don't turn, not until I feel a soft hand on my shoulder. I glance beside me to find Audrey, her features silent, "Are you okay?"

Am I okay? The question slashes me, sharp and cruel.

For so long—since Mia broke up with me, since she vanished without explanation, since I spent days, weeks, months, almost two years trying and failing to reach her—I held it together. I swallowed the tears. I buried the questions. I convinced myself I'd moved on.

But standing here, it all erodes.

Because now, for the first time, the truth is undeniable. Whether I accept it or not—

I've lost her. My world. My queen.

And I have nothing left.

I lost it all for an empire that doesn't provide me any solace.

Just pain.

"No." I finally reply, a feeble attempt at keeping my voice steady but it comes out teary.

Audrey's hand remains on my shoulder, a grounding presence in the storm raging inside me. Her touch is light but steady, a silent offering of comfort. I don't turn to face her immediately. I can't. My eyes remain fixed on the far end of the hallway, as if Mia might magically reappear, as if this isn't already over.

"Miles," Audrey's voice is soft, laced with understanding. She steps closer, her expression carefully neutral, but I see the worry in her eyes. "Talk to me. Please."

My throat tightens, and I shake my head, willing the lump to disappear. Words feel impossible, tangled and buried beneath the scar in my chest. But Audrey doesn't move away. She doesn't let me retreat into the silence.

"I..." My voice cracks, and I hate how vulnerable I sound. I take a shaky breath, forcing myself to meet her gaze. Her presence is steady, patient, waiting for me to continue.

"It's her." I finally manage, my voice barely above a whisper. "She was right there. Audrey, she was right there. And that baby..." My voice falters, breaking under the weight of the word.

Audrey's eyes soften further, her hand gently squeezing my shoulder. "I know." she says simply, as if those two words can somehow ease the storm inside me. But they don't. Nothing can.

"She's moved on." I choke out, the words tasting bitter on my tongue. "And I... I don't even know why it hurts so much. I should be over this. I'm married, Audrey. I have a life. I shouldn't..."

I trail off, unable to finish the sentence. The weight of my emotions is too much, and before I can stop myself, I sink to the floor, my back against the cold wall. My hands rake through my hair, pulling slightly, as if the physical sensation can drown out the turmoil in my mind.

Audrey kneels in front of me, her voice calm but firm. "Miles, stop. Stop tearing yourself apart over this."

I look up at her, my vision blurred by unshed tears. "How can I not? She's... she was everything, Audrey. And now she has a child. A life that I... that I'll never be part of."

Audrey doesn't reply right away. Instead, she sits beside me, her shoulder brushing against mine. The silence stretches between us, not heavy this time, but comforting in its own way. Finally, she speaks.

"You're allowed to feel this way, Miles. You're human. Seeing someone you loved so deeply... it's not something you just move on from."

I close my eyes, leaning my head back against the wall as a shuddering breath escapes me. "I've lost her." I whisper. My voice trembles as I continue, "I had hope, but now... now I've lost her."

Audrey's expression softens even further, her eyes brimming with quiet empathy. She steps closer, placing a warm, grounding hand over mine. Her touch is gentle, yet firm—like an anchor in a storm.

"You didn't lose her, Miles," she says softly, her voice steady but kind. "You're just... realizing that life took you both in different directions. And that's okay. It's painful, but it's okay."

"It doesn't feel okay." I murmur, my voice barely audible.

"It never does at first." she replies, her tone gentle, unwavering. "But you'll get through this. You always do. And you're not alone. We're here for you, Miles. Even if it feels like your world is falling apart, you're not alone."

Her words chip away at the despair surrounding me, creating a small crack in the wall I've built around my pain. I glance at her, searching for something—anything—to hold onto, and I find it in her eyes. Her gaze is steady, unwavering, filled with a kindness I don't feel I deserve.

But it's too much.

The weight of it all crashes down on me, and before I can stop it, my vision blurs, and the first tear spills down my cheek. Then another. And another. My chest heaves, the sobs breaking free from the depths of my soul, unrelenting.

Audrey doesn't say a word. She doesn't offer platitudes or tell me to stop. Instead, she moves closer and wraps her arms around me, holding me as I fall apart.

And in that moment, as the tears pour and my pain spills out in waves, I let her.

CHAPTER 36

Mia

The hotel—Michigan Boulevard, is well-known for its elite celebrity stays, expensive taste in cuisine, and—oddly enough—its signature fragrance. As we pull into the VIP parking lot, I spot Madeline, Neel's temporary babysitter, waiting for us.

"He wanted to see the fishes in the pond, so I brought him down ten minutes ago." she says, gently handing Neel to me. "And I saw your text, so I thought I'd meet you here."

Nidhi lands a kiss on his bright pink cheeks. "Hi, munchkin. I missed you."

Neel's face brightens, wiggling with excitement at seeing us after long seven hours.

"Thanks, Madeline." I say warmly.

"You're welcome. Call me if you ever need a babysitter while you're in Michigan." she replies with a professional smile.

"I will. Thanks."

"Bye-bye, little guy!" she coos at Neel before leaving.

We head toward the elevator, the three of us.

I know what you're thinking—

The day I went to the doctor, planning to end the pregnancy, I couldn't go through with it. It wasn't that I didn't have doubts—God knows I did. Could I be a good mother? What would I tell him about his father? How could I raise a child with no job, no stability? But in that moment, I knew one thing: I was human, not heartless. I couldn't end a soul's life just because I doubted mine.

People say, *if you're scared of parenting, don't have kids–you'll ruin their life.* Maybe they're right. But I also knew I had Uncle Rohan, my best friend, and at least enough courage to try–to love again.

And somehow, things worked out. The moment I saw Neel for the first time in the pale, white hospital, a jolt of lightning surged through me, filling me with power I didn't know I had. It gave me the guts to fight for his bright future.

You know the expression *'Fall or Fly'*? Well, after recovery, I chose fly–literally. Uncle Rohan and Neel and I flew to the U.S., helped me settle into a tiny apartment, find a babysitter, and rebuild. It wasn't easy, but I landed the risk-worthy deal with Moonlit Records.

And now, here I am–not quite at the top of the food chain, but damn sure on my way up.

We step inside the elevator, and before I can press floor 18, Neel wiggles in my arms, his small hand reaching for the buttons. "You want to do it?" I smile, pointing to the right number. He pushes it carefully with his little finger–then, with a cheeky grin, presses 15 and 17 as well.

"I guess we have a few stops before reaching our room." Nidhi giggles, shaking her head with a fond look.

"Tell me about it." I say, laughing softly as Neel claps his hands, his grin wide and triumphant.

The elevator jolts to a stop at 15–our first unnecessary pause, thanks to my little troublemaker. Neel wiggles again, leaning slightly toward the buttons, but this time, I gently hold him back. He chuckles, clearly aware of his naughtiness.

I press the button to close the doors, but just as they begin to shut, Nidhi looks up from her phone. "I think I just saw a pale-faced Miles right before the door closed."

"What?" I say sharply, my heartbeat spiking at the mention of him.

Miles.

Here.

In the same hotel as us.

"Hey, don't panic. It was probably someone else. And besides, if it *was* him, he would've sprinted inside the elevator by now, begging for forgiveness for his stupid mistakes." she says lightly, attempting to reassure me.

I exhale, slowly shaking my head, though my heart still races like a runaway train. Nidhi's probably right—it couldn't have been him. And maybe the person I thought I saw during the performance wasn't Miles either. Maybe it was all just a mistake.

But even as the elevator's hum of movement resumes, I can't shake the uneasy feeling in my chest. My mind replays the split second Nidhi mentioned his name, and something deep inside me stirs, unsettled.

Because what if it *was* him?

CHAPTER 37

Miles

Last night was a rollercoaster of emotions. I don't know what I'd have done if Audrey wasn't there. She held me while I cried like a toddler who injured its knee—only, in this case, I wounded my heart. A knee injury can be mended, but my heart? It's beyond repair. There's nothing physically wrong with it. It isn't bleeding, there's no visible hole in it, and yet it hurts in a way I can't explain—a deep, permanent scar. A tattoo I didn't approve of.

And now, my mind feels like it's going to implode, consumed by questions I can't answer. Mia is a mom now. *How?* When did this happen? That child looked at least a year old. Did she and Myron date long before that New York outing? Was she already with him when we were together? Or did this happen after?

I've replayed every moment, every conversation we ever had, trying to find the cracks I missed. Was I blind? Was I just a phase for her? All these questions are clawing at me, demanding answers I can't get. Even though Mia and I are breathing the same air, standing on the same ground, it feels like there's a chasm between us. So close, yet so far.

That's why I came for a run this morning. I thought maybe it would clear my head, help me focus. But it's useless. The more I try to outrun these thoughts, the more they latch onto me, dragging me down. I should head back to New York. Getting swamped in work might be the distraction I need. I have that catch-up meeting with Mr. Kline to prepare for anyway.

The garden I'm running through is beautiful. It should be soothing—the trees lining the pavement, the gentle sway of leaves in the cool breeze—but it isn't. Not when I am left lost in a world I no longer recognise. I take a turn along the path, jogging a few steps, and then I stop.

My heart slams into my ribcage.

She's here.

Not miles away. Not a continent away. She's right here.

She's walking toward my way, her head down, focused on her phone. My body freezes, every muscle locking in place as if the universe is mocking me. I should look away, turn around, do anything but stand here like a fool. But I can't. I'm cemented to the spot, every part of me drawn to her like a magnet. She looks up.

Our eyes meet, and for a moment, the world tilts.

She stops walking, and I swear, time stops too. Her face is carved from stone, and it drives me insane. Is she shocked to see me? Is she mad? Sad? Or... guilty?

Does she feel guilty for leaving me without an explanation? For not telling me what I was doing wrong? For not giving me enough time to fix it? For not giving me a second chance—a chance I begged for?

The questions resurface, louder this time, suffocating me. My chest tightens, and I know I can't hold it in any longer. I have to ask. I have to know. I have to know if I was all she was with when we were together.

My lips part, the words forming on my tongue. But then, as if fate has decided to screw me over again, someone interrupts.

"Are you Mia Malhotra?"

The voice belongs to a girl who seems to be in her early twenties, bright-eyed and brimming with excitement. Mia hesitates, her expression shifting ever so slightly, before she replies, "Yeah."

The girl squeals, practically bouncing on her toes. "Oh my God! I heard the album. It's everything."

"Thank you." Mia says, her tone polite, but there's a flicker of something else in her eyes—something guarded.

"Can I get a photo?" the girl asks eagerly.

Mia nods, agreeing.

The girl fumbles to take out her phone but then notices me standing there, frozen in place. Her gaze shifts, and she walks toward me, clutching her phone like a lifeline.

"Sir, um... would you mind taking a photo of us?" she asks politely, holding out the phone.

I don't say a word. I just take the phone from her outstretched hands, my fingers curling around it. My movements are mechanical as I step back and lift the device, framing the shot.

The girl beams beside Mia, glowing with excitement. Mia smiles too, but it's not the smile I remember. It's not soft neither is it fake—it's professional. Polished. Trained.

I snap the photo, hand the phone back, and the girl gushes her thanks before walking away, practically radiating joy.

And then it's just us again.

The silence between us returns, heavier than before. It presses down on my chest like a weight I can't shake.

Mia shifts her stance, as if she's about to say something, her lips parting slightly. But before the words can escape her, my phone buzzes loudly in my pocket, shattering the moment.

I grit my teeth, anger and frustration bubbling under my skin. Of course. Of course fate couldn't let me have this one moment. This one chance.

With a sharp exhale, I reach into my pocket for the ringing phone. The sound cuts through the stillness, pulling me away from the moment. By the time I glance up, she's already turned around, her pace quickening, slipping further from my reach.

"Mia—" her name catches in my throat, but it's too late. She's already slipping away, like sand through my fingers, disappearing into the distance.

My hand instinctively reaches out, but it's futile. She's already gone, her form becoming a fade, and I'm left standing there, watching her slip further away.

The questions burn in my chest, unanswered, a silent storm raging within me. It's as if everything I wanted to say, everything I needed to understand, just woved away with her.

I linger, my hand suspended in the emptiness, grasping for a moment that has already slipped through my fingers. Silence settles over me like a heavy shroud, thick and unrelenting, pressing into my lungs until I can barely breathe. The ache of unanswered questions churns within me, a restless tide crashing against the fragile walls of my mind. But before the weight of it can pull me under, a vibration shatters the stillness—the phone in my hand trembling again like an echo of something lost.

I glance down at the screen, seeing Nate's name flash across it. The timing is cruel. A sharp exhale slips past my lips as I answer, my frustration bleeding through the words.

"This better be urgent, Nate." My voice is tight, ragged.

There's a pause, followed by Nate's voice, far too upbeat for the chaos running through my veins.

"Woah! I don't know what has you all hyped up, but I do think this is urgent, man." Nate's tone is laced with something I can't quite place—something like excitement, or maybe concern.

"What is it?"

I can hear the rustling of the phone as Nate shifts, clearly trying to gather his words. "Alright, here it is. I was talking to Myron Blaise—yeah, that guy—just a minute ago. And guess what? He's not dating Mia."

I freeze, every muscle in my body locking up. I can feel my heart stutter in my chest. "What?"

"Yeah. He says they're just friends. They only met about a couple of months ago, man. That's it. No romantic connection. I know you were thinking that the baby... well, you know could be his but..." Nate's words come out quickly, almost too quickly, like he's afraid of what I might do with them.

The silence that follows is suffocating. I'm anchored to the spot, my mind spinning as the pieces of this puzzle start to shift in impossible directions.

Mia and Myron... just friends.

Couple of months ago.

This... This is a twist I never saw coming. It wasn't Myron. The baby isn't his.

I open my mouth to respond, but no words come out. A thousand thoughts crash into my mind, all at once. I feel like I've been holding my breath for years, and now it's finally time to exhale. But it's not relief I feel—its confusion. It's uncertainty.

If the baby isn't Myron's... then whose is it? Is it even really hers? But he called her *mamma*.

The realization hits me hard, like a punch to the gut. My mind starts racing. Could it be... mine? Could she—could Mia—have been carrying my child all this time? How long has she been hiding this from me? And why?

I clench my fist, my phone slipping slightly in my grip as I try to process what Nate just said. My heart beats louder, faster, until I feel like I'm drowning in the sound of it.

"Miles?" Nate's voice breaks through my fog. "You good, man?"

I swallow hard, forcing myself to breathe, trying to steady my thoughts. I shouldn't be asking these questions now, not with so much still unclear. But I can't stop myself. I need answers.

"Yeah, I'm fine." I say through gritted teeth, though I know I'm anything but. "Thanks for letting me know."

I hang up, my mind reeling, my pulse racing in my ears. The silence in the air feels suffocating. My hand grips the phone tightly, the weight of the truth—or what I think might be the truth—crushing me.

She's kept it from me. Mia has kept so much from me.

And now, there's a chance—just a chance—that I might be the father of that child.

It's a thought I can't shake, a fear I can't push away. Every ounce of anger, regret, and longing swirls inside me like a storm, threatening to tear me apart. What happened? How did we get here? Why didn't she tell me?

I feel like I'm losing control of everything, the ground slipping out from under me.

The pressure of the phone in my hand feels like ballast, but I can't stand the stillness anymore. I need to move. I need to do something. My mind races with the realization that the baby might be mine, and everything I thought I knew about Mia has just been shattered.

I shove the phone back into my pocket, my fingers shaking as I take a step forward. I can't sit still. I can't breathe. I have to find her.

My legs move before I even consciously decide. I start jogging, then running, the steady rhythm of my feet hitting the ground pushing away the thoughts swirling in my mind. My chest burns, but I don't care. I need to get to her. I need to know the truth.

Every step feels like I'm closing the gap, but at the same time, it's as if she's slipping further away. I don't even know where I'm going, only that I have to get to her, to hear her voice, to see her face, to get the answers.

As I sprint down the sidewalk, I catch a glimpse of someone walking toward me. Alex.

"Miles, slow down, man!" Alex's voice cuts through the pounding of my heart, his brow furrowed in confusion. "What the hell is going on with you?"

I don't stop. I can't. My breath is ragged, my pulse is loud in my ears. I just keep running, ignoring the sharp sting in my chest.

"Hey, Miles!" Alex calls again, this time taking a few long strides to catch up with me. He reaches for my arm, grabbing it with a firm grip. "What's up, man? You're acting like you're running from a stray dog. Talk to me."

I stop, but only for a second. I look at Alex, my frustration spilling out, words tumbling from my mouth before I can stop them.

"I need to find Mia." I tell him, my voice strained. "I don't even know where to start, but I have to talk to her."

Alex's eyes narrow, concern flooding his expression. "Mia? Why? What's going on?"

I don't have the words to explain. It's too complicated. Too much. All I know is that I need to see her. I need answers to why. I need to know.

"The baby might me mine, Alex." I admit, my voice low, almost like a confession. "And I can't sit here not knowing. I need to know the truth."

Alex stands there for a beat, the confusion in his eyes slowly turning into understanding. But it doesn't stop the urgency in my chest, the gnawing, suffocating feeling that I might lose her forever if I don't act now.

"Alright, alright." Alex says, holding up his hands. "Holy shit!"

"Holy shit!" he repeats again.

"Yeah, I know." I say. "Now, I've gotta go."

"Wait. I get it. But man, slow down. Let's figure this out first, okay? We can't just go running off all wild." Alex says.

"Figure what out. I need to find her." I shoot.

"That only. Let's not illogically run everywhere. Let's look into places." He suggests. He's right. I'm so fucked up right now that I can't think straight.

"Okay." I say, trying to calm myself.

Alex and I set out, scanning the area systematically. My mind is a whirlwind, but Alex's calm demeanor keeps me grounded. I suggest we check the tennis courts nearby.

"I doubt she'd be there." he murmurs.

"Doesn't hurt to try." I reply.

We walk towards the courts, the tension between us thick. Alex glances at me. "What are you going to say to her?"

I hesitate, unsure. "I don't know." And I really don't. All I know is that the child could be mine. If that's true, why did Mia hide it? Why did she run away? We broke up, yes, but she could've told me. Everything I thought I knew about that time of my life—almost two years ago—feels like a blurry, fractured line.

As we near the courts, the faint rhythmic *thwack* of tennis rackets meeting balls catches my attention. My pulse quickens. Could it be her?

We step through the gate. The sound grows louder, reverberating in the air. And then I see her.

Mia and Nidhi are on opposite sides of the net, their movements fluid and purposeful. A pop song plays faintly from a nearby speaker, but I barely register it. My focus narrows entirely on Mia.

She notices us first. Her racket falters, and the ball clatters onto the court. She lightly stumbles back, her eyes widening. Nidhi, noticing Mia's change in demeanor, follows her gaze. Her racket slips from her hands and hits the ground. I hear her mutter something under her breath, likely a curse, before she strides across the net to Mia's side.

Mia's eyes lock with mine, and her expression sharpens. She's angry. But why? Why is she angry? I should be the one angry. I'm the one desperate for answers. The air shifts, and so does the music. Taylor Swift's voice filters through the speakers.

Alex leans in and whispers, "It's 'imgonnagetyouback.' Sometimes music has a sick sense of humor."

I exhale, glancing at him sharply before stepping forward to confront Mia, but before I can speak, a tennis ball hurtles through the air. I stare at her, stunned. She's furious. And different. So different. I pick up the racket Nidhi dropped and instinctively hit the next ball she serves my way.

Before long, we're locked in an aggressive rally, hitting the ball harder than necessary. The cycle seems unbreakable.

I shout trying to break the aggressive play, "Why did you leave?"

Mia slows, the question breaking through her anger. She stammers but then replies firmly, "Why are you asking questions you already know the answers to?"

"I don't," I shoot back, dropping the racket. It thuds against the court. "And I have so many questions." My voice is quieter now as I step closer to the net.

Mia stays silent. The world around us feels muted. "Why didn't you tell me?" I ask.

"Tell you what?" she fires back, also stepping closer to the net.

"The baby you were holding last night in the elevator," I say, my voice steady despite the storm inside me. "Is he my son?" my voice cracks.

She smirks, though sadly, her eyes no longer angry but full of pain. For the first time since I saw her on stage and in the elevator, I see the old Mia again—the one I fell in love with. Still love. And I wonder if this Mia will let me in again. Trust me again. Because the one who returned after two years is stronger and more mysterious. All I feel right now is the overwhelming urge to hold her and ask her to let me in, to bridge the chasm between us. Yet, the net feels like an unbreakable barrier, keeping us apart.

"I don't know if you've lost your memory or what," she says quietly. "But you should check your call history and the texts I sent you." She glances at Nidhi, then back at me. "If you haven't deleted them."

Then she turns and walks away, leaving the court. I shout after her, "What do you mean? Which texts?" But she doesn't stop.

Before I can follow her, Nidhi has filled my vision. "I warned you, didn't I? Yet you acted like an asshole."

Before I can process her words, a sharp punch connects with my nose. My hand instinctively goes to my face as I hear a tiny crack.

"Shit!" Alex mutters, rushing toward me.

"I threatened to kill, but I punched instead. Be grateful." Nidhi says coldly before walking away.

"Are you okay?" Alex asks, inspecting my nose. "Dude, you're bleeding. We need to get you an ice pack, or a doctor."

But I'm not listening.

I can barely breathe through my nose, the blood clogging it, the pain sharp and persistent.

What did Mia mean by checking my texts?

I never received any messages from her after the breakup. My phone had been shattered to pieces that night, but I'd gotten a replacement when I arrived in France.

Could something have gone wrong then?

Ignoring Alex's protests, I start sprinting toward the hotel. "Miles, you're heading straight towards death!" Alex calls after me. Then he curses and follows.

I enter the lobby, wiping the blood from my nose with a handkerchief. Near the elevators, I spot Mia and Nidhi waiting.

Alex tries to hand me a handful of ice cubes from a complimentary champagne bucket. "At least hold this to your nose." he pleads.

I toss the bloodied handkerchief into the trash and shout, "Mia, wait. Please."

They both turn.

Mia's gaze drops to my nose, her expression shifting to concern. "What happened?"

Before I can answer, Alex bursts out, "Your insane best friend punched him."

"Nidhi!" Mia turns to her, a mix of disbelief and exasperation on her face.

Nidhi shrugs, turning to Alex as if she were discussing the weather. "Not as insane as when you supported *your* best friend saying, 'I don't want anything to do with it.'"

"He never said whatever that is." Alex defends me, pointing his finger at Nidhi, who death-stares him.

But I ignore them and focus on Mia. "I never received any calls or texts from you after the breakup. I swear."

Mia takes a deep breath, her lips pressing into a thin line.

Two minutes pass.

"Stay here." she says firmly to Nidhi before walking to the elevator and pressing the button.

As the doors open, she steps inside and turns to face me, her posture rigid but her look wrapped with mystery. "You have until Floor 22." she says flatly.

"I'll take it." I enter the elevator in two strides.

The doors close, and the world narrows to just us. The air feels thick with our proximity, with everything unsaid, with everything I need to know before time runs out. I calm myself to think through. "When did you find out about the pregnancy?" I ask, keeping my voice as steady as I can manage.

She doesn't look at me. Her gaze is fixed on the panel of buttons. "Three days after we broke up." she says quietly, her voice barely above a whisper as if recalling that day.

Floor 1.

Her words hang heavy in the air, and I struggle to process them. Before I can speak, she asks, "Did you really not know?" There's pure disbelief in her voice.

"If I had…" My voice falters before I regain control. "If I had, things would be a lot different today." The weight of what I didn't know—what I might have lost—feels suffocating.

Floor 2.

Her expression tightens, her frustration palpable. "How could you not know?" she presses, her words sharper now. "You didn't pick up my calls, but you replied to my texts, Miles. You knew."

"No!" I say, shaking my head, "I didn't."

Floor 3.

I close my eyes briefly, the memories of that night rushing back like a flood. The night we broke up. I remember walking into my lifeless apartment, the silence echoing louder than my thoughts. I was so consumed by anger, by heartbreak, that I hurled my phone across the room. It hit the wall with a sickening crack, the display shattering into pieces—much like my composure and my heart.

Floor 4.

"That night, I smashed my phone." I admit, my voice heavy with the weight of regret.

I glance at her, searching for any hint of understanding, but her face remains impassive.

"When we got to France, I replaced it." I tell her.

Floor 5.

Melanin handled everything. She reactivated it, checked the contacts, and made sure it was good to go. I trusted her—I didn't think to look myself. I was too busy throwing myself into work, trying to forget. Meetings, pitches, introductions—it was all a brief diversion. And when I was in the conference room, Melanin had my phone. It was always with her. Always.

Floor 6.

I pause, the realization settling in. "I never saw your calls, Mia. I never saw your texts. Not because I ignored them—because I never knew they existed."

"It is your phone, how could you not…" Mia begins.

Floor 7.

"Melanin had my phone the whole time." I mutter with regret.

Mia crosses her arms in realization, her lips parting slightly as if to respond, but she stops. Finally, she says, "I'm sorry she did that. But you're telling me that for almost two years, you didn't once think to look? To reach out? One call to my friend and then you gave up."

She looks so hurt.

Floor 8.

"I did look." I plead, stepping closer. "Every day, I stared at your number, calling, texting. But there was nothing, Mia. Nothing. You shut me out completely. And I thought you'd moved on. That I was a chapter you wanted to close and not look back on."

Floor 9.

Her lips press into a thin line, and she finally looks at me. "I tried, Miles. I tried to tell you. Over and over again. I called, I texted,

I poured my heart out, and it's not like there was no response... there was. It was very hurtful. That made me leave because I lost the only balance I had. Because I lost the one person I thought cared about me. The one person who used to see me. And that killed me. So I hid. Okay. I shut everyone out."

Floor 10.

I stare at her, my heart pounding. "I never sent those messages. I would never say those things to you. I've always cared. I swear on everything, Mia, I didn't know. And if I'd known—Mia, if I'd known..." I swallow the lump in my throat. "I would've been there. I would've never left."

Floor 11.

The words hang heavy between us, thick with the pain we've both carried for far too long.

Floor 12.

Floor 13.

"No." Mia's voice is soft but firm, and it cuts through me like a knife. "It wouldn't have changed anything."

"That's not true." I can feel the ache in my chest, the heat of my frustration rising. "That's not true. If I'd known—"

Floor 14.

"It's true." she interrupts, her voice steady but filled with a deep sorrow. "Even if you'd known what you know now then, nothing would've changed. Not really."

"That is not true." My voice rises, desperation making it crack. My eyes sting with tears I'm trying so hard to keep in check, but Mia continues.

Floor 15.

"Would you have told your dad? Would you have said, 'Dad, this is... this is my girlfriend, and she's pregnant. You're going to have to fucking deal with it'? Would you have said that?" She swallows, her eyes glistening with unshed tears. "I don't know. But you made your choice, Miles. You always chose your status, your empire over me. That's the truth."

Floor 16.

The words hit me like a blow to the chest. Is this how Mia felt? I made her feel this way. I never meant to. I never wanted her to feel like that. But I did. And now I can't seem to take it back. "Mia, I never thought you'd feel like that." My voice cracks with the weight of everything unspoken. "I'm sorry. I swear, I never meant for you to feel like that. But you're my everything. You always have been."

Floor 17.

She looks at me, her expression cold. "Keep believing that." she says quietly, her voice laced with something I can't quite grasp.

I feel the elevator rise, but my world sinks. This morning, I thought I'd lost her completely. Then, I got the news—the best and the worst of my life. I might have a son, but that I might have lost moments as a dad. But then I felt hope again. There's a chance. A chance to fix everything with Mia, to prove that I can be the man she deserves.

"Let me fix this." I say quietly, my voice shaking. "I'll prove to you that I can be better. That I can be there for you—and for him."

Floor 18.

Her breath hitches, her eyes widening slightly at the mention of *him*. But she quickly schools her features, her voice quiet but firm. "Miles, there's a wedding ring on your finger." Her words hit like a punch to the gut. "You're married, and I'm... different now. We're different. There's no chance left. We had our time."

"But you said it before," I beg, "Right person, wrong time."

"Unfortunately," her voice soft but final, "the timing is still wrong. And maybe the person too."

Floor 19.

There it is.

My humanity gone.

I don't know how to blink, how to breathe, how to move, how to feel.

I don't know anything.

Floor 20.

She pauses for a long moment, her gaze flickering with something fragile.

Floor 21.

"You know I almost wish we'd never met."

I find myself asking. "Why almost?" my heart drowning.

"Because then I wouldn't have what I have now." she replies, her voice thick with something unspoken. "It's a hard truth I had to accept."

Floor 22.

The elevator chimes softly as it comes to a stop on the 22nd floor. I let out a sharp breath, my heart pounding against my ribs. The doors slides open, but to me, it feels agonizingly swift—time itself refusing to be on my side. Fate isn't either. Mia moves to step out, only to falter, hesitation freezing her mid-motion.

"Miles," she says, her voice laced with an uneasy edge. "Sorry about your nose... on Nidhi's behalf."

She steps out, and I almost let her go. But I can't. Not like this. "Wait." I say, stepping forward.

I glance up at the corporate sign by the door: *Daycare.* She must be here to pick up our son. *Our Son.* The thought stops me cold. Before she can say anything, I find myself speaking, the words rushing out before I can stop them.

"What do I have to do to get you back? To get him back?"

Her eyes meet mine, and for a moment, there's a flicker of something, a mask of hidden thoughts. She takes a breath, her words cutting through the space between us. "Miles, have you ever wondered if I want to come back?"

And just like that, the lilies in my heart fall to the floor, their petals scattering like all the love I thought I still have for her and still do. Her gaze softens when she sees the hurt on my face, and she continues, "But... I believe you when you say you didn't abandon me on purpose. So, I won't stop you from meeting him. But not right now. We both have a lot to think about."

The weight of her words crashes over me, but I manage to find my voice again, barely. "You're here to pick him up." I murmur, a statement more than a question.

She nods, silent for a moment. As she turns, I call out, "What..." the words catching in my throat. "What's his name?"

There's a brief hesitation before she glances over her shoulder, and in a voice that almost breaks me, she whispers, "Neel. His name is Neel."

The name hits me like a wave—heavy, sweet, and unbearable all at once. It settles into my chest like a lifeline.

And just like that, she disappears through the daycare doors without a glance back. I step into the elevator, the weight of my new identity pressing down on me—a father who still hasn't gotten a chance at fatherhood. Thoughts of all the moments I've lost with my son—*Neel*, flood my mind. His first steps, his first word, his birth. I missed everything. I haven't even met him. I don't even know what he knows about me. The frustration simmers as I stand there, so close to him yet bound by Mia's request to wait. I know I have to respect her boundaries, but it tears me apart.

The cracks in my resolve deepen with each passing second, the loss clawing at my chest. And then, the anger surges—white-hot and undeniable—because this all happened because of Melanin.

She knew.

She hid it.

And she's going to pay for that.

CHAPTER 38

Miles

"Melanin, in my office. Now!" I command, the anger thick in my voice.

I arrived in New York right after my conversation with Mia. A conversation that cracked open the doors to painful truths I couldn't have imagined. Two years. Two years of missed moments with my son—moments I'll never get back—all because of Melanin. I can feel the anger bubbling inside me. She's lucky I'm not firing her in front of everyone but I can't hold it back any longer.

I march towards my office, with Melanin trailing behind me, startled and confused. Her face is like a mirror I don't even want to look at, but I can't tear my eyes away from it.

Once inside, I don't bother with pleasantries. I walk straight behind my desk, my hands gripping the edge, trying to keep myself from snapping. The words come out sharp, cutting through the heavy silence that hangs between us. "How dare you hide Mia's pregnancy?"

The question lingers in the air, hanging like an accusation, and my voice cracks from the pressure. The steadiness I once had is gone, drowned in a flood of hurt and betrayal.

Melanin stiffens, and I can see her panic rising. Her forehead is slick with sweat, and her hands tremble ever so slightly. She's scared, I can see it. I wait for her to speak, and when she does, her words come out in a rush, as though she's trying to explain herself all at once.

"I noticed all the missed calls," she says quickly, her words tripping over each other, "and I thought I'd tell you about them after you came out of the meeting, but then I saw the text, and I immediately came to your meeting room. But before I could get inside, Mr. Baudelaire came in my way. He asked me what was the matter, and I told him. I'm sorry. I'm so sorry."

Her voice falters, and she adds, "He... he told me not to tell you. He said it wasn't my place to get involved and that I should stay out of it. I didn't want to, but I was afraid of what would happen if I didn't listen. I'm sorry."

She's speaking so fast, her guilt palpable. But as I listen, something shifts inside me. It's not Melanin. It was never Melanin. It was my dad.

My chest tightens, the weight of betrayal heavier than I ever thought possible. My dad—the man who was supposed to support me, guide me, had hidden the truth from me. To tell me to break up with my girlfriend is one thing, but to hide the fact that she was pregnant with my child? That's an unforgivable low.

I take a sharp breath, my mind racing with everything I've learned. My heart feels like it's being squeezed in a vice.

"You didn't do this." I murmur, more to myself than to her, my voice barely above a whisper. "It was him... my dad."

Melanin stands there in stunned silence, her wide eyes locked onto mine, but I can see the understanding flicker across her face.

Just then, she speaks again, and her voice trembles with fear. "I am fired, aren't I? I'll pack my things."

I shake my head, the weight of everything still crushing me. "No, Melanin, you are not fired." The words sound foreign on my tongue, but they come out with surprising clarity. "And... I'm sorry. I shouldn't have snapped at you. It's just... a lot."

She blinks, confusion flickering in her eyes before she responds. "No, I'm sorry. I should've never told him. It was *your* deeply intimate matter, and I exposed it. I should've told you. I've felt guilty about that day... since then, and always will."

Her voice cracks on the last part, and for a split second, I almost feel bad for her. But that guilt is nothing compared to the weight of what my dad did.

I take a deep breath, trying to steady myself. "I accept your apology, but it was more his fault than yours. You didn't know any better. It's him I'm angry with, not you."

Her shoulders relax slightly, but she doesn't look entirely relieved. She's been living with this guilt for far too long.

"Now, get back to work." I tell her, my voice firm but not unkind.

She nods quickly, grateful for the reprieve. She turns and leaves the room, her footsteps growing distant, but they don't give me the peace I need.

I crash into my chair, the anger still ruling inside me, but now there's something else—an aching void of helplessness. I want to run to the mansion, to confront my dad, to expose his failure as a father to my mom. I'm sure she has no idea about any of this, and the thought of her living in the dark, oblivious to his manipulation, drives me crazy.

But as much as I want to face him, there's something I have to do first. Something that makes me free to get Mia back. And Neel. I haven't lost hope. I know Mia is my person and she knows it to. Right now she is just hurt. So I need to make things right with them, to somehow bridge the gap that's been forced between us by all these lies.

I can't focus on my dad yet. Not until I fix this.

An hour passes in tense silence before the sharp sound of heels on the floor disrupts my thoughts.

"You requested my presence, *husband.*" Chloe says, her voice laced with mock sweetness as she steps into my office.

"I won't be for long, Chloe." I say bluntly. "Have a seat." She raises an eyebrow but sits gracefully. I slide a file across the desk toward her.

She flips it open and scans the contents. When she looks up, her expressions are cryptic. "I thought all the fake business dinners and pretending to be a happy couple were turning into something real." she says with a smirk.

"You shouldn't have." I reply coldly. "We don't even live on the same street."

She grabs a pen from the holder and signs the divorce papers with a flourish. "All done, *ex*-husband." she says, sliding the file back to me.

"I kinda expected this when she released the album." Chloe says, standing. "Great album, by the way. Tell Mia that."

"Goodbye, Chloe." I say, my patience wearing thin.

She smirks when her gaze lands on the small trash can beside my desk. With deliberate precision, she slides the wedding ring she bought herself off her finger and tosses it into the can with a soft clink.

"I see you've already thrown your out." she says, her eyes flicking briefly to my bare ring finger. Her smirk deepens as she adds, "Pleasure doing business with you."

I glance at the trash can, the discarded symbol of what we once pretended to have, and then meet her gaze. "You can go. Chloe." My tone devoid of any emotion.

She starts to leave but stops near at the door. "Are you back together, though?"

"None of your business." I reply flatly. "Wasn't two years ago either."

She smirks. "I'm going to guess no. But good for Mia. Sooner or later, she'd have realized you'd always prioritize this company and that seat over her." She gestures to my chair. "We're birds of a feather, you and I. We'd do anything, play any game, to climb to the top. We would've made a great marriage. But you loved a popstar."

She turns to leave again, but I stop her with one final statement, my voice heavy with anguish. "And I never thought you'd be so heartless as to prioritize your throne over a dad's right to hold his son, to hear his first laugh, to watch his first steps—all the moments I'll never get back."

Chloe freezes, her back to me. Slowly, she turns, her expression uncharacteristically soft. "I didn't know. I didn't know she was..."

Her usual confidence seems to drain away, leaving her standing there, vulnerable and exposed. It's a side of Chloe I've not seen for so long, and for a fleeting moment, I'm not sure how to respond. The silence between us stretches, heavy with unspoken truths.

"I've done a lot of things in the name of ambition," she continues, her voice trembling slightly, "but if I had known, I would've never..." She trails off, unable to finish the sentence, as though the weight of what she's implying is too much to bear.

I study her carefully, searching her face for any sign of deceit, but all I see is regret. "It doesn't change anything." I say quietly, my tone empty of the anger that had fueled me moments ago. "Your priorities were clear, Chloe, from the start. And now I have to clean up the mess left in the wake of everyone else's choices. Even mine."

Her lips press into a thin line as she processes my words. For the first time in all the years I've known her, she seems at a loss for a response. She nods stiffly, as though accepting a truth she can't argue with.

"Goodbye, Chloe." I say, my voice steady but final.

This time, she doesn't turn back or smirk or throw out one of her signature quips. She walks out of my office quietly, her heels clicking against the floor like a metronome of finished business.

As the door closes behind her, I lean back in my chair, the tension in my chest unrelenting. The confrontation didn't offer the closure I'd hoped for. If anything, it's left more questions—about my father, about all the choices that led to this moment.

I glance at the divorce papers on my desk, a symbol of one chapter ending. But the real story—the one that matters—is just beginning. And this time, I'm determined to write it on my terms, starting with Mia and Neel. No more lies, no more missed moments. It's time to make things right. But one last task to attend.

I storm into the mansion, my footsteps heavy on the marble floors as I make my way up the grand staircase. Each step feels like it's echoing the storm raging inside me. My thoughts are so loud I can barely hear my own breath.

I reach my dad's office, my hand already gripping the door handle, only to find it empty. I don't stop. I march across the expansive hallway, the faint smell of leather and cologne lingering in the air. His bedroom door is cracked open, and I don't hesitate before pushing it open. There he is, packing a suitcase like nothing's wrong. Like everything's just another day in his perfect world.

"Do you even feel guilty?" I ask, my voice steadier than I thought it would be, even as my fists clench at my sides.

He doesn't flinch. Doesn't even look up from what he's doing. "I'm gonna need more than that, Miles." His voice is calm, too calm, as if we're discussing some trivial matter.

I take a step forward, eyes burning with a mix of anger and disbelief. "I think you know what I'm talking about." I don't wait for him to speak.

He finally looks up, his eyes sharp, calculating as if examining what's in my head. "You met her in Michigan, didn't you?"

I don't answer. Instead, the question I've been carrying for so long burns through me. "Why did you do it?" The question feels stupid even as I ask it, because I already know his answer. But I need to hear him say it. I need him to admit it.

He sighs, his fingers still moving methodically over the clothes he's folding. "To protect your status. You were going to get married to someone else. How would that have looked for you—and for the company?" His words are plain, detached, like he's reading from a script. But even though I expect it, it still hits me like a punch to the gut.

I watch as he continues his task, folding another shirt with an almost practiced indifference, and my anger spikes. "That's it. That's all you're gonna say?" My voice cracks, the words trembling with frustration and pain. I know he won't care, I know he won't even apologize, but I can't hold it in anymore. "You're not even gonna apologize?"

His face hardens, but his tone remains eerily calm. "Well, I thought she'd drop the child. I mean, she didn't really seem the single mother type. But for your satisfaction...I'm sorry." He delivers the words with such a cold, rehearsed tone that it feels like he's mocking me.

Before I can say anything further, the door to the room swings open wider, and my mom steps in, her eyes wide, her body stiff with tension. She's heard the rise in my voice, and I can see the panic flashing in her gaze.

"What is going on?" She asks, her voice edged with concern.

I can barely bring myself to look at her. I want to scream, to tell her everything, but the words catch in my throat. I swallow hard before I force myself to speak. "Your husband... deleted all my messages and missed calls from Mia, which were about..." My voice breaks, a lump forming in my throat, "that said she was pregnant."

The room falls silent, the tension so thick it feels like the air itself is pressing down on us. I glance at my dad's face, but there's nothing there. No remorse. No guilt. He's still sitting there, his hands poised over his suitcase as though this is just another day.

My mom's face turns pale, her eyes darting between the two of us. Her breath catches, and I can see the shock settling in, but there's something else there too. A flicker of realization.

"Pregnant?" Her voice is shaky, barely above a whisper.

"Yes."

Then I turn to him, my anger out of control from his plain and unregretful expressions. "And you have the audacity to sit here, packing your bags, pretending like everything's fine while I'm left in the dark about my own son."

I hear my father's breath hitch as he slowly stands up, his expression finally changing, but not with guilt—just cold calculation. "This is not the time or place for this," he says stiffly, as though the situation doesn't warrant any emotional response. "I've got things to do."

"What do you mean, things to do?" I ask frustrated.

"Sera and I are going on a cruise for the week." he states flatly, like it's no big deal. Like it's something normal, something expected.

The words land like a heavy weight in my chest, and a surge of betrayal floods through me. How could he just... leave? How could he act like none of this matters? My heart aches, the depth of his indifference sinking in. I look over at my mom, who stands motionless, her mouth slightly open, but no words escape. She's frozen, and it's as if she's seeing him for the first time—really seeing him.

"I am not going anywhere." my mom finally speaks, her voice low, but firm.

My father's eyes narrow at her. "Sera—"

"When you announced his engagement without even informing him, I let it go." mom says, her voice thick with barely contained anger. "I shouldn't have, but I did. But this... this is too much. I'm at a loss for words. I'm done with you. Done defending your actions. You are not the Lucien I met." The tremor in her voice betrays her, and for a moment, I think I see the walls she's built around herself begin to crack.

"Sera—" he tries again, his voice tinged with a coldness I don't recognize.

"I really don't want to hear what you have to say." Mom's voice is steady—final. There's no hesitation, no room for argument. She stands taller than I've ever seen her, her shoulders squared, her chin lifted in quiet defiance. Her eyes are locked onto him, unwavering, unshaken.

The room is thick with tension, suffocating in its silence. The weight of everything—the lies, the betrayal—presses down on my chest. My dad doesn't speak. He doesn't plead. He simply watches, his expression veiled. But there's something in his eyes, a flicker of something I can't quite name. It's not regret. It's not guilt. It's just... nothing.

And then, just like that, my father, the man who should now at least attempt at an apology, turns his back and walks away. The door clicks shut behind him, sealing him out of our lives.

A breath shudders out of me. I should feel relief. I should feel something. Instead, all I feel is the vast emptiness his departure leaves behind.

My mom turns to me, her fierce resolve crumbling as she cups my face in her hands. Her warmth, her presence—it's the only solid thing in this moment. "I'm so sorry." she whispers, and it's the kind of apology that carries years of pain.

"Mom, it's not your fault." I murmur, shaking my head.

But her gaze shifts, narrowing as she notices the faint redness on my still-healing nose. Her fingers brush over it gently. "What is this?" she asks, her voice laced with concern.

"Nothing." I respond too quickly, but before she can push further, I wrap my arms around her, burying myself in her embrace.

For now, I let her warmth dissolve the ache, even if it's only temporary.

CHAPTER 39

Mia

The car cruises down a quiet Kansas City street, the late evening casting golden hues over the glass buildings and bustling sidewalks. The soft hum of the engine fills the space between us, mingling with the distant echoes of city life. I glance out the window, watching as neon signs flicker to life against the fading light. Somewhere in the distance, the faint sound of a saxophone plays, carried on the breeze from a street performer's corner.

Neel sits on my lap, his tiny hands clutching one of his favourite toys—a miniature black car he insists on bringing everywhere. His soft weight grounds me, his presence a soothing balm to the nervous energy simmering beneath my skin. He traces circles on my arm absentmindedly, his head resting against my chest.

"So, just to clarify," Nidhi begins, breaking the silence, her tone dripping with mock seriousness. "You *know* Nate is going to be there, and if Nate is there, Miles *might* be there too. And yet, here we are, still heading straight toward the lion's den?"

I roll my eyes. "Yes, Nidhi. Myron's a good friend, and he invited us. Plus, it was Nate's first League match—he deserves a congratulations from a girl who's not spoken to him for two years."

Nidhi twists in her seat to face me fully, her eyes narrowing like a detective uncovering a juicy clue. "So, Miles is definitely gonna be there. And yet you're completely unbothered by that fact? Interesting."

I sigh, resting my elbow against the window and leaning my head on my hand. "I'm not bothered. *Why* are you so bothered?"

"I'm not bothered; I'm concerned. There's a difference." she says, her tone firm but kind.

Her words settle uneasily in the air. I don't respond immediately, keeping my focus on the waver of trees and streetlights outside. It's been two weeks since my conversation with Miles in the elevator, and somehow, he's been in my head more now than he ever was before.

I thought the two years I spent living with the belief that he had abandoned me—abandoned *us*—would make me hate him. And it did, for a long time. But the truth I learned that day has undone all of that. Knowing he had no clue, that his own people betrayed him, makes me feel... sad.

It was hard—still is hard—to raise Neel. Even with Uncle Rohan, Nidhi, and so many great people in my life, it's been an uphill battle. But I was there for all of Neel's firsts. I got to hold him through every milestone, every tear, every laugh. Miles? He didn't even know he was a dad.

"I just worry for you, Mia." Nidhi continues, her voice softer now. "You used to avoid situations like this at all costs. But now it feels like you're running straight toward the trouble."

Her words pull me back to the present. I glance down at Neel, his little fingers still drawing invisible pictures on my skin, and something inside me loosens.

"He's not a trouble." I say quietly, my eyes fixed on the streaks of light outside the window. "When Miles told me he was the one on the darkside, I wanted to cry. I wanted to crumble, Nidhi. But I couldn't let myself be vulnerable in front of him, so I got angry instead. He didn't deserve that." My voice falters, dipping to a whisper. "I kind of want him to meet Neel."

Nidhi shifts in her seat, her gaze softening. For a moment, she just watches me, her concern giving way to something gentler. Then, leaning closer as if sharing a secret, she lowers her voice. "Why do I have a feeling you're also here to give him another chance to explain? You still miss him, don't you?"

I don't answer. My silence is enough.

The car falls into a heavy silence for a moment. Nidhi's sharp features soften, her usual witty retorts nowhere to be found. She reaches and squeezes my hand gently.

"Mia, today's going to be a rollercoaster of emotions for you." she says, her voice quieter now, almost reverent. "I'll be praying for you—and Neel."

Neel, still gazing out the window at the city wrapping around, turns his head at the sound of his name. His eyes flick between us. "wath." he asks in that adorably curious tone only a child can pull off.

Nidhi chuckles and pats his knee. "Nothing, munchkin. Just grown-up talk."

Neel furrows his brow for a moment before shrugging it off and returning to the window.

The car slows as we approach the towering skyscraper at the heart of Kansas City. Its gleaming glass façade reflects the bustling city lights, a beacon of understated elegance in the night sky. At street level, a small crowd of paparazzi lingers near the entrance, their cameras flashing sporadically as they await the next big name to step out. But our car bypasses them entirely, turning smoothly into a private driveway that leads to the building's secured parking lot.

The hum of the city fades as the car glides to a stop inside the pristine underground garage. The soft glow of overhead lights highlights the sleek cars parked in neat rows. A suited bodyguard is already waiting for us, his broad frame imposing but his demeanor calm. He steps forward to open my door, nodding respectfully as he greets me.

"Ms. Malhotra." he says in a low, professional tone.

"Hello." I reply, shifting Neel in my arms as I step out. Nidhi follows close behind, casting a glance at the security cameras discreetly lining the ceiling.

"Well, this is subtle." Nidhi mutters with a smirk, eyeing the private setup as the bodyguard gestures toward a sleek elevator tucked into the far corner.

I force a laugh, trying to ignore the knot of nerves tightening in my stomach. My palms are clammy against the soft fabric of my dress, and I swipe them discreetly against my side before adjusting my hold on Neel.

Before we reach the elevator, Nidhi grabs my arm, her expression uncharacteristically serious. "Listen to me, Mia," she says firmly, her voice low. "No matter what happens in there, you've got this." she says, her grin equal parts reassuring and mischievous. "And if Miles says anything dumb, I've got a killer speech and a killer knife prepared."

I can't help but laugh at her dramatics, the sound easing some of the tension curling inside me. "Of course you do."

As we step into the elevator, The bodyguard presses a button for the designated party floor. The soft whir of the elevator fills the silence as we ascend. Neel wriggles slightly in my arms, his excitement bubbling over as he stares at the illuminated numbers above the doors. I glance down at him, and his wide-eyed excitement reminds me why I'm here.

For him.

So he can meet his father. If Miles is even here.

The elevator dings, and the doors glide open, revealing a brightly lit foyer. Just a few feet ahead, another grand door stands tall, separating us from the vibrant energy beyond. As we step through, the atmosphere shifts instantly. The party is lively with lavish atmosphere of the party. The buzz of conversation and clinking glasses fills the air. I scan the room, spotting familiar faces—people I've met since I returned to America. I first crossed paths with them at a party I attended with Leo when the NFL launched the DreadLock Falcons.

Back then, Nate hadn't been recruited yet. The team had been expecting someone else, but at the last minute, that player pulled out, and Nate was brought in as a last-minute replacement. He was directly announced as a player at the first game two days ago. So that was a surprise to me too, though I couldn't attend the game.

Thank God I couldn't.

We step further into the party, exchanging smiles and casual greetings with a few recognizable faces. The lively hum of conversation fills the air, blending with the soft strains of background music. Myron and the other football players come into view, their boisterous laughter carrying above the crowd.

"Hey, winners." I call out, weaving through the crowd toward them.

"Hi, Mia." Myron greets warmly, his grin as broad as ever.

The others chime in with their greetings, and Neel, ever the charmer, responds with a delighted coo. His innocent joy draws laughter and cooing tones from the group. It's a relief to be surrounded by friends who aren't tethered to my past, their energy light and uplifting.

Yet, the knot of unease in my stomach tightens. My eyes flicker over the room, scanning for the one face I'm both eager and dreading to see. Nate hasn't made an appearance yet, but I know he's here. I can feel it, an unspoken certainty that he's somewhere nearby. And if Nate is here, Miles might be too. The thought is both thrilling and terrifying.

As the group's conversation shifts to celebrating their victory, I catch sight of Leo near the bar. His DreadLock Falcon's jersey, black hairs streaked in blonde highlights and confident demeanor makes him stand out in this room.

"Nidhi, can you watch Neel for a bit?" I ask, glancing at Neel who is now in Myron's arms.

"Got it." she replies.

Shaking my head to her response, I make my way toward Leo. He looks up as I approach, surprise lighting his face.

"Well, well," he says, turning to lean casually against the bar. "Didn't think you'd actually show up."

"Here I am." I reply, slipping onto the stool beside him.

Leo smirks. "Don't worry, I can take a hint and change the subject." He raises his glass in mock solemnity. "Good news: the album's still blowing up. There's even talk it might be nominated for VMA's."

My eyes widen. "Really?"

"Mmhm." he hums, his tone teasing. "You're officially a big deal, Malhotra."

The weight of his words settles over me, a mix of pride and disbelief. It's a far cry from where I started, back when I thought music would be my only outlet. I never imagined I'd find myself here—surrounded by people who believe in me.

"So," Leo begins to say, tilting his head but I interrupt his speech, my eyes catching on something—or someone unforgettable, "Hold that thought." I mutter to him before walking towards that person.

The lively chatter and flicker of pop lights at the party fade into the background as I make my way toward the little girl who's standing on her tiptoes, trying to reach a tray of chocolates on the table. Her tiny fingers stretch out but fall just short of her goal. I step closer, a soft smile tugging at my lips.

"Need a little help?" I ask gently.

The girl startles slightly at my voice, looking up at me with wide green eyes. Her cheeks turn a rosy pink, and she nods shyly. Without hesitation, I reach for the chocolates and hand them to her.

"There you go." I say, kneeling to her level. "What's your name?"

The girl clutches the chocolates to her chest, her gaze darting between me and the tray as if unsure how to respond. Finally, she whispers, "Lily."

And just like that the air is knocked out of my chest.

Her name, paired with her face, hits me like a wave. My heart clenches as a tear wells up in my eye, unbidden, as a memory surfaces.

New Year's Day, nearly three years ago—a girl's tear-streaked face, her cries piercing through the chaos of the accident. Sirens. Blood. Chaos. Rush. I've never forgotten that day, never forgotten her.

I swallow the lump in my throat, forcing a steady breath. "Hi, Lily." My voice trembles slightly as I ask, "Do you know where your mom is?"

Before she can answer, a woman's voice cuts in. "Was she troubling you?"

I rise quickly, turning to see a woman with kind eyes and a concerned smile.

"Oh no," I reply, shaking my head. "She just wanted some chocolates."

The woman crouches slightly, brushing a stray curl from Lily's face. "Is that why you ran over here, Lily?" she asks sweetly.

Lily blushes even more and hides behind her the woman's leg, peeking out timidly.

The words tumble out of me before I can stop them. "Are you her mother?"

The woman straightens, meeting my gaze with a warm smile. "Yes, I am. Why do you ask?"

I can't help the grin that spreads across my face. Relief and happiness floods my chest as I realize Lily's mother—this woman—survived. She pulled through. "It's just…" I hesitate, shaking my head slightly.

Recognition dawns on her face. "Wait—you're Mia Malhotra. The singer."

I laugh softly. "That's me."

She smiles wider. "Great album and that performance at the festival? Incredible."

I flush at the compliment, feeling a mixture of pride and gratitude. "Thank you."

"We were both there." the woman says, glancing down at Lily, who's now clutching her leg.

"Weren't we, Lily?" she adds with a chuckle.

Lily buries her face in her mother's dress, her muffled voice betraying her shyness. The woman strokes her hair fondly. "She's a bit shy."

"I can see that." I reply, my voice light.

The woman extends her hand. "Sorry, where are my manners? I'm Sarah Letterman. Pleasure to meet you."

I shake her hand warmly. "Nice to meet you, Sarah."

As the handshake lingers, I know I can't let this moment pass. I need to ask. Even if it reopens old wounds, I need to know. I take a deep breath. "Sarah, I know this is personal, but... were you in a car accident three years ago?"

Sarah's smile falters, her expression clouding with something bittersweet. She nods slowly. "Yes." she says softly. "How do you know?"

I hesitate. The memory of that day presses against my chest. "I was there." I admit, my voice barely above a whisper. "I saw your daughter. I could never forget her face. She was crying, calling for you. It... it broke my heart." I swallow hard. "I lost my parents in a car accident, and seeing her like that—it stayed with me. I worried about her. About you. But I'm so glad she didn't lose you."

Sarah's eyes glisten as she places a hand over her heart. "I'm glad she didn't lose me too. And I'm so sorry about your parents, Mia."

I smile through the tears threatening to fall. "yeah"

Sarah sighs, a sad yet contemplative look crossing her face. "That day... it changed everything for me. It's actually why I decided to come to this party. I'm a party planner, and back then, I used to organize kids' birthday parties. But after the accident, I had to rebuild everything. And now my life is so much better, and bigger because of a stranger."

She pauses, her gaze distant. "The person who saved my life—the one who paid for all my surgeries and covered the medical expenses for everyone else in that hospital—his name is on the guest list tonight. After the accident, the nurse told me that he was the first person to call the hospital, asking about my condition. But he never came to see us, so we never got the chance to thank him. Maybe that's why he never showed up—because he didn't want the gratitude.

She exhales softly. "That's why I'm here tonight. Normally, I never attend the events I plan—I leave that to my employees. But this time... I had to come."

My breath catches in my throat. "Who is it?" I ask, my voice barely steady.

Sarah looks at me, her expression resolute. "Miles Baudelaire, if you've heard of him."

The name lands like a soft, inevitable blow.

Of course it was him.

And that's why I loved him.

Still love him.

Everyone has a dark side—some more powerful than others. And Miles? He was one of them. He wanted recognition as much as he wanted love. But that wasn't a bad thing. Because he cared. He *always* cared.

And now, standing here, I understand that more than ever. Fame is intoxicating, addictive—a sweet poison disguised as a dream. I've seen it first-hand. And maybe, deep down, I never truly blamed him for wanting more. Because no matter how much he chased success, he never really let go of what mattered.

"Yeah!" I finally say, my voice softer. "I've heard of him. What a kind man."

Sarah nods. "Yeah, but I haven't seen him around yet."

I don't know why I say it, but the words slip out anyway. "I'm sure he'll come."

Maybe because I *want* to see him. Because I need to tell him I'm sorry for what I said in the elevator—that I didn't mean most of it.

Miles grew up swimming in wealth, but money doesn't dictate the kind of person you are. And he didn't just throw money at the problem—he *cared*. Enough to make sure strangers survived.

I did say hurtful things to him that day, out of two years' worth of anger. But I don't think he's the wrong person.

I *do* want to let him in.

I still love him. I don't think I ever stopped—it was just buried under layers of resentment. And yes, what I said about him caring for the Empire was true. But I don't believe he'd sacrifice time with his son for it. I don't he ever would.

I believe in that.

But still... I can't shake the feeling that our timing is still wrong.

Miles should be in Neel's life. I have no doubt he'll be a good dad.

But *us*?

I just don't know yet.

"I'll see you around, Sarah." I say with a smile at Lily.

"Yeah." She mutters.

The minutes tick by like hours as the party swirls around me, a dapple of laughter and music that ebbs and flows like a tide. Neel is back in my arms now, his tiny body resting against mine as he clutches his favourite black toy car. His chubby fingers tap against the plastic, a rhythm only he understands, while his lips form half-words and gibberish phrases that occasionally make me smile despite myself.

Leo has drifted away, caught up in a lively discussion with someone. Across the room, Nidhi is leaning against the edge of the bar, her body angled toward a strikingly handsome man. Her expression is playful, her laughter cascading in waves that seem to catch his attention entirely.

I try to focus on Neel, his warm, tiny frame a comfort against the unease curling in my stomach. But my gaze keeps wandering, scanning the room as the golden lights drapes a look of sophistication over the room. The crowd shifts and sways, faces moving in and out of view like waves crashing against the shore. Laughter bubbles up from every corner, filling the room with an almost tangible energy.

I catch sight of Myron in a circle of teammates, their arms slung over one another as they recount some post-game story, punctuated by raucous cheers. There's no sign of Nate, though, and no sign of the face I'm both dreading and yearning to see.

Neel shifts in my arms, his little hands tugging at the neckline of my dress. "Mamma." he babbles, his eyes wide with excitement as he points at nothing in particular.

"What is it, sweetheart?" I ask softly, following his gaze, but there's nothing there. Just more people, more noise, more memories threatening to surface.

"Ma," Neel insists, his voice louder this time, though the words are still unintelligible. He starts bouncing slightly, his energy infectious even as my heart weighs heavy with anticipation.

"Okay, okay, settle down, munchkin." I murmur, pressing a kiss to his temple. His giggles melt me, but the knot in my stomach refuses to loosen.

And then it happens.

A voice, familiar and yet distant, like a forgotten memory suddenly remembered, cuts through the noise.

"You must be Neel."

The words hit me before I even turn around, the voice unmistakable, its tone laced with both nostalgia and a weight I can't quite place. My heart stops, and for a moment, the room seems to tilt.

I swivel slowly, clutching Neel a little tighter as if he might somehow shield me from what's coming next. And there he is.

Nate Dawson.

His tall frame is almost unchanged, though his shoulders seem broader, his presence more commanding than I remember. His familiar face—equal parts kind and mischievous—looks down at Neel with a soft, almost reverent expression.

I open my mouth to speak, but no words come out. It's as if the air has been sucked from the room, leaving me standing in the eye of a storm which would lead to the earthquake.

"Hi, Mia. It's been a long time." Nate says gently, his voice carrying more weight than it should. His gaze drops briefly to Neel, who is staring up at him with wide, curious eyes, his toy car forgotten in his hand.

Neel, as if sensing the importance of the moment, tilts his head and babbles something indecipherable, his tiny voice breaking the silence that stretches between us.

Nate chuckles softly.

"I think he's trying to say hello," I manage to say.

Nate crouches slightly, smiling. "Oh, hi, Neel."

I swallow, forcing steadiness into my voice. "I won't lie—I was searching for you. Congratulations on the win"

His gaze flickers to mine, something unspoken flashing through his expression. "Thank you. And I was searching for you at the game. I heard Blaise invited you."

I shift slightly. "I had some work."

"Of course you did." His lips quirk up in a knowing smile. "You're a very busy woman now."

I arch a brow, smirking. "You should be grateful you're speaking to me without an appointment."

He chuckles, shaking his head, but his attention drifts back to Neel. There's a pause, a beat where something settles in the air, heavy and inevitable. I know what he's thinking before he even says it.

"His eyes are blue." Nate murmurs, almost to himself. "Just like Miles."

A tightness forms in my chest, but I nod. "I know. They made forgetting Miles a little complicated."

Nate exhales, his gaze lingering on Neel, then shifting back to me. "Yeah... I can see that."

"I know you both talked," Nate says after a moment, his voice quieter now. "And since then, he's been devastated."

I sigh. "When did you switch from footballer to attorney?"

"Since I care about my friend." His reply is firm, unwavering. "It wasn't his fault. He never meant to hurt anyone."

"I know," I admit.

His tone softens, almost pleading. "Then would you give him one last chance? I know it's not my place, but... I've never seen him like this. I spent two years angry at you for his misery, but now I know it wasn't either of your fault. It'll take time, but—just one chance."

I exhale slowly. "Your friend is a married man." The words come out quieter than I expect the weight of the realization settling heavily in my heart.

Nate smirks. "No. He's a recently divorced, very available man."

Really.

I glance at Neel, who is thankfully too busy opening and closing the tiny doors of his toy car to notice the conversation. But I don't respond.

Before the silence stretches too long, Nidhi suddenly appears, her voice cutting through the moment. "I saw a dance floor in that section," she says, gesturing excitedly. "I thought I'd take Neel with me."

Then she notices I already have company. Her brows knit together in recognition. "Oh, hi! Wait... you were on the football team, right?"

Nate nods. "Yeah."

I glance at him before adding, "He's also Miles's best friend."

Nidhi's eyes widen slightly before she leans toward me and whispers, "Is he the museum one?"

I nod.

"Okay, do you want me to chase him away?"

"No." I whisper back.

She nods, turning back to Nate. "I went to your dinosaur museum in New York. Total disappointment."

At the word dinosaurs, Neel perks up excitedly in my arms.

Nidhi sighs dramatically. "Yeah, we were both disappointed. They weren't moving."

Nate chuckles, his expression teetering between amusement and disbelief, like he's debating whether to correct her or let it slide.

To save Nidhi from embarrassing herself further, I explain, "They visited Dawson's Prehistoric Park last month in New York. And they expected the big ones to walk, not just the tiny models."

"Oh," Nate says, nodding. "Well, I don't really follow that stuff, that's my brother's department, but I do know they're working on models that—"

Nidhi cuts him off with a wave of her hand. "I don't need the science lesson. Just let me know when they actually start walking."

Nate chuckles, shaking his head. "Will do."

While they talk, my gaze flits around the room, a strange unease settling in. If Nate is here... then where is Miles?

The thought lingers, but I push it aside. I glance at Nidhi. "You should take Neel to the dance floor."

She shrugs. "Okay."

I shift Neel into her arms, and she grins at him. "We're gonna go dance, little man."

Neel claps his hands. "Yay!"

A small smile tugs at my lips as they head toward the dance floor, disappearing into the party.

I turn to Nate and say, "I'm pretty sure Miles set you up for all this, but of all the things I said to him," I swallow, "I never said I stopped loving him. I was just angry. Rage is a very complicated thing. And if you blab what I just *said*, you will find yourself in the hands of my best friend. She will not be friendly."

Nate exhales with relief. "I won't blab, and it was Alex who set me up to talk. My plan was to lock you both in a room."

"FYI wouldn't have worked." I say. "So where is he?"

Nate coughs. "I actually don't know."

Then Myron motions toward Nate. "Finally here, man. The boys are waiting, let's go."

"I'll be right there." Nate says.

Then he turns to me. "So, the chance?"

"Depends on how Miles delivers his speech, wingman." I say.

"I have hopes." He grins before leaving.

I mean it when I say I'm going to give Miles a chance. I mean it with every pulse in my body, every breath that dares to hope. Because never in my life have I seen someone care the way he does—not just with words, but with actions. Paying for surgeries out of his own pocket instead of tossing a donation into the void? That's not obligation. That's heart.

Maybe I shouldn't care about the timing anymore. Maybe I never should have. Fuck timing. It was never really on my side.

I weave through the party, my gaze scanning the room. This time, I'm not just moving aimlessly—I'm searching for him. But somehow, I end up right back where I started, near the abandoned bar.

And that's when I see it.

The glint of a familiar watch catches my eye, and my heart stutters. I shift my gaze, following the flicker of metal, and there he is.

Sitting on a barstool beside Audrey, effortlessly composed. He's dressed in all black—a sleek turtleneck under a dark blazer—pulling off the look of the CEO that he is.

And on his wrist, like it was made for him, sits my father's watch. The one I gave him with my trust.

Something inside me melts.

Because in that moment, it all comes rushing back—the reason I gave it to him in the first place. Miles had been so kind, so genuine. Sweet and charming in ways that had nothing to do with words and everything to do with the way he looked at me, the way he made me feel.

And despite everything I've said, everything I've thought over the past two years... I know he loved me.

He still does.

My breath catches as my gaze lifts from the watch to his face.

Miles is already looking at me.

Before I can process it, he abruptly stands up, the stool scraping against the floor. Almost instinctively, Audrey stands too, as if pulled by the shift in energy. The movement is so sudden, so synchronized, that for a second, I just stand there, frozen.

It's him.

The man who once held my heart so effortlessly. The man I convinced myself I had to let go of. But now, standing before me, he looks tired. Like he gave up on life. And I hate to see that.

I notice the faint smudges under his eyes. The tension in his shoulders. I can feel him holding his breath.

My gaze drifts to the sharp slope of his nose—it looks like my best friend's punch has healed.

Thank God.

But he still looks... loving, caring.

The same young man I met four years ago.

Before I can stop myself, the words slip out.

"You're still wearing the watch."

Miles doesn't hesitate. His voice is steady, deliberate. "Why would I stop wearing something that at least gave me a sense of being close to you?"

His words hit me like a tidal wave, but instead of sinking I'm finally swimming.

Audrey clears her throat, shifting uncomfortably. "I should—uh—go find Nate." she says, though it's obvious she just wants to give us space. She spares Miles a quick glance before disappearing into the crowd, leaving the two of us standing there.

Miles takes a step closer.

The warmth of his presence is immediate, familiar. It doesn't matter how much time has passed, how many mistakes were made—he's still Miles, and my heart is still traitorous enough to recognize that before my mind does.

"You knew I'd still wear it." he says, softer now.

I shake my head. "I didn't. I thought it'd be at a landfill somewhere."

He's about to say something but I interrupt, "And I hate it that I thought of that."

Now, he doesn't know what to say, he's wondering if I still hate him or I've cooled down. So I speak, "Do you remember that girl we saw at the accident? Her name is Lily."

He smiles, which seems like relief as he replies, "Yeah, I know. I just met her."

"If you would've told me what you did for her mother at the hospital sooner," I murmur, "I might've warmed up."

His brows lift slightly in amusement. "That was all I needed to do?"

"Not technically," I say, tilting my head, "but I would've unblocked you."

Miles actually laughs, a quiet, genuine sound. And for the first time since I came back, I see it—that smile. The one I used to trace with my fingers, the one that used to make me feel like everything in the world was okay.

And damn it, I missed it.

But just as quickly as it appears, it fades. His face turns serious again, his expression coded. Then, he says something I don't expect.

"If you want, without a second thought, I will resign as CEO."

My stomach clenches.

"Don't," I whisper, and suddenly, I feel like the worst person in the world. "I don't want that, Miles. And I'm sorry I even said it."

His jaw tightens. "No, that's true. I should have quit instead of pushing you."

I shake my head. "You're not a quitter, Miles."

And then, before I can stop myself, I step forward and kiss him.

It's not planned. It's not thought out. It's impulsive. It's just pure, raw emotion—a collision of everything misunderstood, everything lost, everything we still are.

Miles doesn't hesitate. His hands come up, one sliding around my waist, the other cupping my cheek as he kisses me back like he's afraid I'll disappear if he doesn't hold me tight enough. Like he's been waiting for this moment as much as I have.

And maybe he has.

The world blurs. The music, the chatter, the clinking of glasses—it all fades into the background, leaving only us.

When we finally break apart, his forehead rests against mine, his breath uneven. His grip on me doesn't loosen.

"I missed you." he admits, voice rough.

My fingers tighten on the fabric of his blazer. "I missed you too."

And for the first time in two years, I let myself believe that maybe—just maybe—this time, love doesn't have to lose.

"He's Neel's father." a familiar voice exclaims.

Miles and I instantly straighten, turning toward the sound. And just like that, we find ourselves being stared down by Alex, whose grin is practically splitting his face in half. Myron stands beside him, looking utterly stunned, while Nate remains neutral—though I catch the faintest smirk playing at his lips. Leo, ever the composed one, just folds his arms across his chest.

The room is almost empty, blissfully unaware of the moment Miles and I just shared. Most of the part is busy mingling in the bigger room next door. But these guys? They are very much paying attention.

My throat goes dry. "Yeah."

Myron is still staring at us, blinking rapidly before his head snaps toward Nate. "Wait. You knew? You knew your best friend was dating Mia, then why the fuck you asked if *I* was dating her?"

Nate doesn't even bother answering, just shrugs like it's old news.

Leo unfolds his arms and drapes it over Myron's shoulder, steering him away. "Family drama, bro. Family drama."

Alex, meanwhile, is cracking up. "This is a masterpiece. One second, there's punching and shouting, and the next, there's kissing. You guys should get an award for this." He winks. "I'm gonna find Sam and Audrey and give 'em the good news."

I groan. "Alex—"

Too late. He's gone, leaving a trail of chaos in his wake.

I barely have time to recover before Nate smirks at Miles. "So, when's the wedding?"

Miles doesn't even blink. "At your funeral."

Nate clutches his chest dramatically. "Ouch! Cold, man. Real cold."

Then his gaze shifts behind me, and his smirk grows. "Today's your lucky day Dad."

Miles frowns. "What?"

And then I hear Nidhi's voice. "Oh, hi."

I turn—and there she is. Nidhi stands with Neel, her expression slightly hesitant, like she's testing the waters. "I'm sensing... Zen?" She glances at me for confirmation.

A slow smile curves on my lips.

She exhales in relief. "Thank God. 'Cause I left my knife on the dance floor."

"wat?" Neel chirps, looking utterly fascinated.

Miles grips my hand tightly, and I feel the tremor in his fingers. His sapphire blue eyes lock onto Neel, wide and impenetrable, and I know—know—his heart is racing. There's awe there, excitement, nervousness. He's seeing his son.

I squeeze his hand.

Neel frowns slightly at the tension in the air, and Nidhi, sensing it too, mutters something to him before shifting him into my arms. Then, without warning, Nate grabs Nidhi's hand and drags her away, muttering, "Let's talk about walking dinosaurs."

I barely register it.

Miles is still looking at Neel.

And Neel is looking at him.

The music is suddenly too loud, the lights seem to penetrate an intimate important moment. Any second now, someone might barge in and disturb something this delicate.

I lean in. "Should we go out to the foyer?"

Miles blinks, snapping out of the trance he was in. "Yeah."

I glance around. Sure enough, Nate and Nidhi are standing nearby, pretending to have a conversation but obviously eavesdropping. I roll my eyes and ignore them.

Instead, I adjust Neel in my arms and lead Miles toward the entrance, past the pulsing neon glow of the party. As we step into the quieter, golden-lit foyer, the change is immediate. The partyer's muffled sound hums from the inside, but it's just white noise.

Neel wiggles slightly, his big sapphire eyes flicking between me and Miles, as if sensing something important is about to happen.

And then, in this quiet moment, standing in the bright golden light, I realize—

It's time.

The air is cooler here, laced with the crisp scent of night, carrying the distant silence of the city. The warm glow of chandeliers pools across the marble floor, casting elongated shadows that stretch toward the grand entrance.

I take a deep breath, steadying myself.

Miles stands beside me, unmoving, eyes locked onto Neel like he's afraid to even blink, as if this is a dream that might slip away if he does. His grip on my hand is tight—tighter than before—his fingers trembling ever so slightly against mine.

And Neel... Neel is watching him too. Observant, curious. His eyes flicker between us, his tiny brows furrowing in the way they do when he's thinking really hard about something.

I set him onto the floor and crouch down to his level, tucking a loose strand of hair behind his ear. "Neel," I murmur, brushing my fingers against his soft cheek. "You remember how I told you your dad was far away? Somewhere very, very cold?"

Neel nods slowly, his little hands clutching the fabric of my dress. "Cool land." he whispers, his voice small but firm.

I exhale a shaky breath, my heart pounding. "Yeah, well he's not far anymore." I reach for Miles' hand and bring it forward, just enough for Neel to see. "He's here. This is your dad."

Neel's eyes widen, his gaze snapping up to Miles, who swallows hard.

A second passes.

Then another.

Another.

And then—

Neel's lips part slightly, and a soft gasp escapes him. His little chest rises and falls as realization dawns, as the pieces click into place in that sharp, ever-curious mind of his. "wat." he whispers, wonder lacing his voice.

Miles inhales sharply, and I swear I see his eyes glisten under the golden light. He drops to his knees, the tension in his body unravelling as he reaches a hesitant hand forward. "I—" His voice cracks. He clears his throat. "Hi, buddy."

Neel stares at him for a heartbeat longer.

Then, without hesitation, he steps forward.

Straight into Miles' waiting arms.

Miles lets out a broken breath as he catches him, his hands cradling Neel like something fragile, something precious, something he never wants to let go of. His fingers tremble as they weave through Neel's soft hair, as they press against his tiny back, holding him close, anchoring himself in this moment.

And Neel, ever the observant, quickly adjusting child, melts into him. He buries his face into Miles' chest, his tiny arms trying and failing to reach around his neck. His small body relaxes completely, as if this is where he's always meant to be.

I press a hand to my mouth, overwhelmed, watching the scene unfold like something out of a dream.

Miles buries his face into Neel's shoulder, his breath uneven, his hold unshakable. He doesn't speak—he doesn't need to. Every fiber of his being is poured into this embrace, this one, singular moment.

Neel shifts slightly in his arms, tilting his head back just enough to peek up at Miles. His cheeks are flushed, a soft pink blooming across his fair skin. And then—oh—he ducks his head down again, shyly tucking his face into Miles' shoulder.

Miles lets out a quiet, shaky laugh, his lips pressing against Neel's temple.

The happiest man alive.

And for the first time in what feels like forever—Miles looks complete.

We three look complete.

CHAPTER 40

Miles

I can't believe I'm hugging my son. I just can't, but it's true. His small frame is wrapped securely in my arms, fitting perfectly against me, as if he was always meant to be there. I close my eyes, pressing my cheek against his soft hair, breathing in the faint scent of warmth and innocence. His tiny hands clutch my shirt, holding on as if he's afraid I might disappear, but I'm not going anywhere. Not now. Not ever.

A lump rises in my throat, but I swallow it down, choosing instead to hold him tighter, to cherish this moment that I never thought I'd have. His heartbeat flutters against my chest—small, steady, real. And for the first time in a long time, I feel whole.

I lift Neel in my arms, his delicate eyes locking onto mine. "His eyes are blue." I whisper to Mia, my voice thick with awe.

"I know." she says softly, her hand finding my shoulder, grounding me. Her touch is warm, reassuring.

Neel looks back and forth between us, his tiny face curious and wide-eyed. I feel my heart swell, an overwhelming wave of love crashing through me. I glance at Mia, then back at Neel. "I love you guys." I say, my voice cracking.

I turn to Mia, sliding my free arm around her shoulders, pulling her closer. "I love you." I whisper, my forehead resting against hers.

A tear slips down her cheek as she smiles. "I love you too."

In this moment, with Neel cradled in my arms and Mia by my side, everything feels complete. I hold them both tighter, vowing silently to protect this happiness, to never let go.

Before I can let the feeling fully settle, the sound of hurried footsteps echoes through the foyer, followed by an unmistakable thud.

"Ow—Sam!" Audrey's exasperated voice rings out.

"Move. Talk to her." Sam huffs, stumbling slightly before catching herself.

Neel shifts his head at the sudden commotion, his big, curious eyes darting toward the newcomers. I shift him in my arms with careful grace, securing him against me as he watches Sam and Audrey with open fascination.

And just like that, both of them freeze, their playful bickering momentarily forgotten.

Audrey claps a hand over her mouth, while Sam's eyes go ridiculously wide. "Oh. My. God," she whispers dramatically, staring at Neel like he's the most precious thing she's ever seen.

Neel stares right back, equally entranced.

I let out a quiet breath, amusement curling at the edges of my lips. *Our son is meeting so many new people today.*

But just as the moment lingers, Sam suddenly seems to snap out of it. She nudges Audrey sharply and mutters under her breath, "Talk to her."

Mia steps forward just then, her voice cautious yet hopeful. "Hi, Sam and Aud."

Both of them straighten, their faces smoothing into something unreadable. "Hiii!" they respond neutrally, their voices slightly too even.

Then, without missing a beat, Sam gestures toward Audrey and bluntly announces, "She feels guilty for judging you for the past two years."

Mia's breath catches. Her eyes flicker with something raw—sadness, understanding, relief—all at once. She takes a small step toward them, her voice softer now.

"I should've told you guys."

Audrey finally meets Mia's gaze, regret pooling in her eyes, and for the first time in a long time, the space between them doesn't feel so impossible to cross.

"You didn't owe us any explanation." Her voice full of understanding.

A breath of relief shudders through Mia before she steps forward and wraps Audrey in a hug. Audrey tightens the embrace like she's making up for lost time, and Sam joins in without hesitation.

"I missed you both." Mia whispers.

"We missed you too." Sam and Audrey chorus.

And in that moment, I feel it—fate, by my side again, as if it had always been guiding us toward this. As if it wanted us to be mended in the hard way.

Neel, watching the embrace with wonder, suddenly extends his tiny arms forward, wanting to join. And we do.

Then I feel two more bodies press into the circle—Nate and Alex.

"There's no hug without me." Alex slurs.

"Just don't squish my son." I warn, and everyone laughs.

Happiness rings through the air, bright and free, like a family long lost but finally found again.

I hear Mia turn to Nidhi, her voice full of quiet invitation. "Come."

Another arm wraps around us, linking the final piece together like a mirrorball catching the light.

We have all been broken once. We have all struggled, stumbled, and fought battles no one else could see. We have carried the weight of eclipsed departures, stood at the shorelines of what-ifs, and tried to outrun the ghosts of our past. We have known exile, felt the sting of being left behind, and learned that time doesn't always heal the way we wish it would. But somehow, despite it all, we found our way back. And, here we are—standing, together.

There are so many versions of us. But right now, only one stands—the one built from forgiveness, love, and the quiet understanding that some things are meant to slip away while others find their way home, drawn by invisible twines we never quite saw but always felt.

We are not echoes of the past, nor the fleeting ache of something that almost was. We are here, together. And maybe that's what matters most—that after all the storms, all the lost summers and winters, all the splintered variations of ourselves, this is the one that remains: shimmering, beautiful one. The one built from the embrace of hearts, dance of gathered familiar souls, and the unshakable bond of friendship. The one that glows, bright and untouchable, in the presence of happiness, of home, where love is not something to long for—it's something that stays.

NEW YORK TIMES

Breaking News: Mia Malhotra—the new rising popstar, who has stolen the hearts of countless people with her beautiful voice and lyricism is apparently dating Miles Baudelaire—the CEO of the billion dollar Global Baudelaire & Browning Enterprises.

And the sources have also confirmed that they have a two year old son. Shocking!

Epilogue

Neel coos softly in my arms, his small fingers gripping the sleek body of his black toy car. His eyes light up as he presses the switch at the bottom, making the headlights glow with a soft, steady light. I watch him, my heart swelling with a tenderness that's hard to put into words. I love it. I love him.

He squirms restlessly in my arms, his tiny body vibrating with excitement. It doesn't take me long to realize why. Mia's uncle and Nidhi have just entered the tent. Neel's wide, eager eyes land on them, and a delighted squeal escapes him.

Though Mia's uncle only arrived in America two days ago, he chose to stay at a hotel instead of with us, and I can only guess why. Maybe he needed time. Maybe he wasn't ready to accept all of this—me, me back in Mia's life, me in Neel's life, me everywhere.

A heavy silence hangs in the air, thick with the weight of thoughts we're too cautious to voice.

Then, as always, Nidhi steps in, cutting through the tension with her characteristic lightness.

"I love awkward silence." she says with a dramatic flair, crossing her arms, a teasing smirk tugging at her lips.

I sigh, unable to suppress the faintest smile. Of course, she does.

Mia's uncle finally clears his throat, his voice measured yet firm. "I'm Rohan Kirloskar, as you know. You can call me Mr. Kirloskar."

"Okay." I mutter, nodding.

Then he adds, his gaze steady and intense, "But I'm glad you are not a bad person, Miles. I had some heavier words instead of bad, but... Neel is here."

I meet his gaze, understanding the weight of his words. The unspoken warning. The cautious approval.

"Okay. Thank you." I reply, my voice calm but sincere.

Just then, as if on cue, Neel leans forward in my arms, gesturing to be put down. I lower him gently onto the ground, watching as he roams around the VIP tent, exploring his little world with innocent curiosity.

After a few minutes, the arena lights dim, signaling the beginning of the show. I know Neel's ears are sensitive to the high decibels of the crowd as he's only two, so I pull out a pair of noise-cancelling headphones specially used for concerts and carefully place them over his little ears.

He looks up at me, his brow furrowed in confusion. "Why, Dad?"

It's been a year now since he first called me that, and every time he does, my heart seems to expand, holding the weight of all the love I've ever known. Every time, it feels like my heart forgets to contract, like it's smiling in a way words can't capture.

"To protect your ears." I reply softly, my hand resting on his tiny head, my voice steady but filled with a quiet, overwhelming love.

As the arena lights up again and fades back, the excitement in the crowd heightens, a wave of anticipation filling the air. I adjust Neel's headphones one last time, making sure they're snug over his little ears. His gaze sweeps the arena, his curiosity piqued by the energy around him.

The crowd's buzz fades into silence as the stage lights blaze to life, casting a single spotlight on the center. The roar of the audience erupts in unison, and the sound feels like it shakes the very ground beneath us.

Mia steps onto the stage, bathed in the brilliant lights, her presence commanding every eye in the arena. The crowd cheers, their voices blending into a single powerful chorus. I take a deep breath, my chest swelling with pride, knowing she's right where she's meant to be.

I hold Neel a little tighter, my heart expanding with something I can't quite put into words. There, under the spotlight, she looks unstoppable—powerful and radiant. She's in her element, her dream unfolding before the world, and I'm just... grateful. Grateful to be here, to witness this moment, to know that she made it.

Neel's no longer focused on the stage but on me—his little hands gripping at my shirt as if he's trying to say something, "Mumma?"

I smile softly, squeezing him gently, my voice a quiet whisper, "Yeah, buddy."

And as the music fills the arena, I realize, in that deep, unshakable part of me, that no matter how far Mia goes, no matter how many stages she steps on, I'll always be right here—standing by her side, holding our son, witnessing the beauty of her journey. I feel the weight of it, the unspoken promise that this love, this support, will never fade.

Mia's voice soars, and for the first time in a long time, I understand what it means to truly belong—right here, with her, with Neel, with this family we've built together. And as the music wraps around us, I know that no matter what, this is home.

The End.

Acknowledgement

First and foremost, I want to express my deepest gratitude to my amazing friends, Vaibhavi Bankar and Sonam Zope. You both were the first to hear the idea of Illicit Affair, and from that moment on, you listened to me blabber about the plot endlessly. Thank you for being my sounding board, for your unwavering support, and for tolerating my obsession with this story. I couldn't have asked for better friends to share this journey with.

A special thank you to Sanavi Jagtap, the best critic I could ask for. Your keen eye to detail, insightful feedback, and constant encouragement helped me refine this book. You always knew exactly where the mistakes were, and I'm forever grateful for that.

A big thank you to my cat, Taffy, who faithfully sat beside me during countless hours of writing, patiently blinking at me to calm down as I banged my head over the plot. You're truly the purrfect writing companion.

To everyone who picked up this book and gave it a shot—thank you from the bottom of my heart. As this is my first project, knowing that you chose to spend your time reading Illicit Affair means more to me than words can express. Whether you loved it, found flaws in it, or simply turned the pages out of curiosity, I appreciate you. Stories exist because of readers like you, and your support—big or small—fuels my passion for writing. I hope this book brought you even a fraction of the emotions I poured into it.

Last but certainly not least, to my parents—thank you for your endless love, support, and belief in me. Your constant encouragement made this journey possible, and I am beyond thankful for everything. From the very beginning, you nurtured my love for stories and always reminded me that I could achieve anything I set my heart to. I hope I've made you proud.

Next Stop—*Illicit Desire.*

www.ingramcontent.com/pod-product-compliance
Lightning Source LLC
LaVergne TN
LVHW091702070526
838199LV00050B/2259